FATAL CROSSING

LONE THEILS

Translated from the Danish by Charlotte Barslund

A

Arcadia Books Ltd
139 Highlever Road
London W10 6PH

www.arcadiabooks.co.uk

First published in Great Britain 2017
Originally published as *Pigerne fra Englandsbåden* by Lindhardt og Ringhof 2015
Copyright © Lone Theils 2015
English translation © Charlotte Barslund 2017

ISBN 978-1-911350-03-3

Typeset in Garamond by MacGuru Ltd
Printed and bound by TJ International, Padstow PL28 8RW

ARCADIA BOOKS DISTRIBUTORS ARE AS FOLLOWS:

in the UK and elsewhere in Europe:
BookSource
50 Cambuslang Road
Cambuslang
Glasgow G32 8NB

in the USA and Canada:
Dufour Editions
PO Box 7
Chester Springs
PA, 19425

in Australia/New Zealand:
NewSouth Books
University of New South Wales
Sydney NSW 2052

FATAL CROSSING

1

The balding man looked like any other middle-aged, African school-teacher. He wore light grey cords and a freshly ironed shirt. Calmly and methodically he poured Earl Grey tea into floral china cups. Nora caught a faint hint of almond oil and detergent as he leaned over the small, battered table with the tiled top and politely added milk to her tea. He dropped two lumps of sugar into his own cup and stirred it once. Then he started his account of executions, rapes, mutilations and murders.

The stories swirled around Nora's head, one atrocity overtaking the next. Schoolchildren witnessing the gang rape of their teacher before they themselves were hacked to death with machetes. Massacres of villagers that went on until the murderers were too tired to lift their arms and so they locked up the survivors with the corpses until the next day when the killing resumed. The man, who for his own security could only be referred to as 'Mr Benn', resumed his monotonous narrative.

Nora clutched her cup. The urge to throw hot tea into the face of the impassive man was overwhelming. To get a reaction, detect a hint of humanity in his expressionless face. Emotion. Regret.

And yet she controlled herself. Because that's how Nora Sand, foreign correspondent for the Danish weekly magazine *Globalt,* operates: she listens, she gathers information, and she writes. She's a pro.

'I have one final question,' she said in a neutral voice.

He gave her a look that had left humanity behind a long time ago.

'Yes?'

'Why? Why did you do it?'

He gave a light shrug. 'Why not? It's what they deserved. They were nothing but cockroaches. All we did was clean out the kitchen.'

Nora shuddered. She fumbled with a button on her Dictaphone. Then she switched it off and got up, a little too abruptly.

Pete, who had been sitting in the corner, rose too, swapped lenses on his camera and got to work.

Shadowy photographs of the man who now called himself Mr Benn. Blurred pictures of his face. Close-ups of his dark hands. And although Mr Benn's hands were clean and his nails well manicured, Nora thought she could still see traces of blood.

They were the images of a man who had kept his liberty because he had chosen to inform on those higher up the chain of command. His evidence had enabled him to pass through the British asylum system and today he enjoyed a peaceful life in a southern English coastal town where the most exciting thing that ever happened was the annual fete. Nora wanted to throw up.

Pete appeared outside. Nora dug out the car keys and tossed them to him. He caught them in mid-air.

'You drive. I'm knackered,' she said, getting into the passenger side of his battered Ford Mondeo.

He raised his eyebrows. 'Tough?'

He was a man of few words, but when he did speak what he said was weighty and uttered in an unmistakable Australian accent.

Nora had a lot she wanted to get off her chest, but the words stuck in her throat.

'There are limits to how much –'

Pete quietly stowed his equipment in the boot, got in and started the car. Instead of following the road that would take them back on to the motorway to London, he chose the coastal route.

Nora said nothing. They had worked together ever since she first came to London five years ago as a rookie journalist. After countless assignments and trips ranging from Africa to East European countries, they could practically read each other's minds.

The sun cast its last rays of pale daylight across the landscape, as they reached the small fishing village of Brine and parked behind a pub.

Nora shivered and pulled up her jacket collar around her ears.

They strolled down to the beach where the grey sea merged with the mother-of-pearl sky. The wind nipped at their cheeks, and half an hour later Nora could feel the poison slowly leaving her system. Or rather, it was encapsulated, reduced to a manageable size and stored in a dark place inside her on a shelf with stories of similar contents and calibre.

'Come on, let's head back into the village. They do great fish – I've been here once before with Caroline,' Pete said.

As always a touch of sadness crept into his voice when he mentioned the love of his life, who had long since gone back to Melbourne and married a surgeon.

They strolled up narrow lanes that felt eerily abandoned during the working week before the onslaught of the tourist season.

'Hey, hang on.'

Nora had stopped outside a shop very different from the pastel-coloured motley of pottery shops and delis selling smoked fish that usually drew in the tourists. The paint on the front was peeling and the windows were filthy, but Nora could make out something behind the window pane: a scuffed, tan leather suitcase, the perfect addition to her collection at home.

She tried the door, which, much to her surprise, opened.

A smell of mould and dust wafted towards her from a room crammed full with so much stuff that the walls looked close to collapsing. Leather-bound books were stacked in tall piles along one wall, and against the other walls bookcases were laden down with crystal glasses and mismatched china.

The few gaps between the bookcases were taken up with paintings of varying quality. Nora surmised that ships were a favourite subject.

In a backroom a scratchy Glenn Miller record had just about finished being 'In the Mood'. Behind the counter a man with a huge red beard was humming along to it while polishing a brass candlestick.

'Welcome,' he said with a smile.

Nora smiled back and had a quick look around the shop. She was briefly tempted by a scallop-shaped, silver plate butter dish, but her attention returned to the suitcase she had seen in the window.

'May I have a closer look at that, please?' she asked, pointing to it.

The man wiggled his way out from behind the counter. He was big, but moved with remarkable agility as he zigzagged between shabby second-hand furniture and tired-looking house clearance stock

He removed a tin box and a stack of LPs and eased out the suitcase from under the goods displayed in the window.

'It came in only last week. Excellent condition,' he said.

Nora reached out her hand to touch. Real leather. Dark brown, scratched. Just the right shabby appeal.

'So, how much were you thinking?' she said casually.

The man grunted and narrowed his eyes. 'How about fifty pounds?'

Nora pulled a face. 'I was thinking more like twenty.'

'It's real leather,' he countered.

Nora tried the lock. It didn't open. She frowned. 'Is it jammed?'

The man shrugged. 'It's nothing that a hairpin and a bit of dexterity wouldn't fix,' he then said.

'Yes, but there could be anything inside that suitcase. And it might be mouldy.'

The man took it from her and shook it. It made a low thud.

'Hmm. Could be paper. Listen, if you agree to forty quid, you'll get the contents for free. Sold as seen. Who knows? You might find a winning lottery ticket. Chance of a lifetime!'

Three minutes later Nora emerged, thirty pounds poorer, but holding the suitcase.

'You're incorrigible,' Pete said, rolling his eyes.

'I know, I know. But you have to agree it'll be perfect for that spot under the coffee table next to the cabin trunk.'

Pete shook his head and dragged her onwards up the hill.

They ate freshly fried plaice with mushy peas and hand cut chips. When they were finally back in the car and Pete had put The Eagles on the CD player and programmed the satnav to 'home', Nora had recovered enough to start composing the article about the school-teacher from Rwanda in her mind.

When Pete dropped her off outside her flat in Belsize Park, she was bone tired and only just managed to drag herself through the door, clean her teeth and collapse into bed.

2

The sound of Big Ben echoed through her flat. It was the special ringtone on her mobile she had assigned to her boss, Oscar Krebs. Among his staff he was known as the Crayfish because of his knack for spotting weaknesses in a story and snipping away at it with his claws until it fell apart, or the journalist came back with more convincing research. Or so he said. Others at the magazine claimed the name matched the colour of his face when he was stressed.

Nora respected his obsession with double- and sometimes triple-checking every story before it was published in *Globalt*. However, she was thoroughly fed up with the Crayfish's chronic inability to grasp the concept of Greenwich Mean Time. Forgetting she was one hour behind him in Copenhagen was bad enough. Insisting she was one hour ahead was even worse. Having tried repeatedly to explain it to him, Nora had come to accept that there are certain things in this world you'll never teach your boss.

'You've been up for hours, I imagine,' the Crayfish said, sounding bright-eyed and bushy-tailed.

Nora squinted at the alarm clock on her bedside table. It was six thirty a.m. British time. She swung her legs over the edge of the bed.

'Hmm.'

'Excellent. When can you deliver Rwanda? We've scheduled you for page seven, and we go to print early this afternoon.'

She muttered something about two o'clock Danish time, rang off and staggered into the flat's only decent room which she had turned into a living room/study/library/kitchenette. Still half asleep she observed her usual morning ritual – she turned on her laptop, then the TV to BBC News 24, switched on the kettle – and plodded towards the tiny bathroom.

And that was where her routine was brought to an abrupt halt when suddenly she found herself sprawled on the hall floor, having tripped over the suitcase she had dumped there late last night. The lock had sprung open and a pile of Polaroids had spilled out of the gaping suitcase. Nora sat up on the floor and opened the suitcase fully.

She picked up the Polaroids and flicked through them. All were of young girls, teenagers. Lone girls standing up against walls, inside and out, in a pose with few variations. They all looked straight into the camera lens.

Some flirted openly with the camera, a smile on their lips. Others looked shy and awkward. Judging by their hair and clothes, Nora took the pictures to range from sometime in the 1980s, based on the MC Hammer trousers, hair gel and oversized sweatshirts, up until the 1990s, where there was one picture of a girl wearing a T-shirt with U2 on it.

The collection must be that of an amateur photographer; this much she had learned from working alongside Pete. It wasn't a professional portfolio, rather a quirky little insight into a provincial photographer's tentative attempt to master the difficult art of photography. A man who was fascinated by young women, but who had clearly never learned anything about choosing a subject or lighting, and didn't possess an ounce of artistic flair. She shrugged and was about to close the suitcase when her eyes were drawn to an image that stood out from the rest.

Two girls in the same picture. A smiling blonde, slightly chubby, but pretty. Next to her a petite, dark-haired girl scowled at the photographer. It must have been summer; they were wearing shorts and standing against a white background. She dated the faded 'Feed the World' T-shirt to one or two years after the Live Aid concert in 1985.

But it wasn't the T-shirt that had caught her attention. It was the sign with the big red arrow behind the two girls and the caption, in Danish, that read: *Car Deck 2*.

She put the Polaroid to one side and went to the loo, cleaned her teeth and splashed water on her face. Made herself a cup of strong Nescafé, adjusted the colour with milk, sat down in front of the computer and turned on the Dictaphone.

Mr Benn's emotionless voice filled the room, and in the hours that followed there was nothing but him and his horrors in Nora's life. Her fingers flew across the keyboard.

Nora had submitted her article and while she waited for feedback, she made a half-hearted attempt at tidying up the piles of paper on her desk. She checked the fridge and wondered if she had the energy for a trip to Whole Foods in Kensington. She could spend hours at their three floors stocked with exquisite foods and would always come home with an empty purse and her arms laden with Italian goat cheese, spelt crackers, organic blackcurrants or cheesecake from the bakery. But she could feel that today wasn't one of those days.

Something about the picture from the car deck kept troubling her; it evoked the sadness you feel when looking at old photographs of soldiers, grinning young men who thought they were immortal, but today exist only as letters carved on a mossy war memorial in Normandy.

She tried to shake off the sense of tragedy. By now the two girls had probably been married and divorced several times over, and forgotten all about a ferry crossing made decades ago.

Yet Nora picked up the Polaroid of the two girls once more. One dark, the other fair. The gaze of the blonde girl was hard, as if challenging whoever had been behind the lens: What the hell do you want? The dark one looked shy. Her head was tilted and her gaze turned downwards, as if she dared only peer up indirectly at the spectator.

She turned over the picture. Nothing on the back.

The hiss of her entryphone interrupted her thoughts.

'Yes?' she answered tentatively.

'Good afternoon – this is the police. Someone has reported a domestic disturbance,' she heard in Danish spoken with a broad north Jutland accent.

Argh! It had completely slipped her mind that she was meant to be having lunch with Andreas today.

The two of them had been friends since Sixth Form, but at their leavers' ball Andreas had too much to drink and declared her his undying love. When Nora had felt unable to reciprocate his feelings and asked if they could just stay friends, he had avoided her from that moment on.

Soon afterwards Nora had gone Interrailing, then travelled to England for her gap year, and Andreas was accepted by the Police Academy. Since graduating he had worked his way up the ranks and was now with Violent Crimes. Nora had kept an eye on him from afar and now time appeared to have healed his wounded pride. He had found her on Facebook and sent her a message saying he would be in London for a couple of weeks as he was taking part in a Scotland Yard course on terror cells.

Nora checked her diary, which had ended up under an old copy of the *Guardian*, a WHO report on child poverty and an article about immigration torn from *The Economist*.

Quite right. It read: Lunch, Andreas 1.30 p.m.

'So what's it to be?' he said through the intercom.

She buzzed him in. 'Come upstairs. I'll be ready in a sec.'

The square shoulders and the corn-yellow hair over brown eyes were Andreas, just as she remembered him. And yet she could see that the years had left their mark on his face. He had grown up.

He opened his arms without a word and she disappeared into his enormous embrace.

'Still as lovely as a mermaid,' he said with that crooked smile of his.

Nora rolled her eyes.

'At least you haven't grown a walrus moustache like a cartoon copper. That would have been more than I could handle.'

She flung out her hand and invited him into her flat, which

seemed even more microscopic with a towering, muscular police-man inside it.

'I've been working since I got up this morning. I need a quick shower before we go anywhere. Would you like some coffee while you wait?'

'Really? I thought you were taking me to lunch in your Kung Fu dressing gown. You've grown rather dull in your old age, haven't you?' Andreas grinned and had a good look around her flat.

Nora pretended to be affronted, pointed to the kettle and tossed her head.

'Water. Coffee. Milk in the fridge. I'll be in the bathroom.'

She let the warm water cascade over her body while she wondered where to take Andreas. There was the organic Honey Bee Café around the corner, or they could go to the tapas bar by the tube station. She dismissed the idea. Too exotic for the North Jute he still was. She decided on the little Turkish place behind the supermarket.

She dried her hair and quickly put on a nearly clean white T-shirt, a pair of black jeans and sandals. A line around her blue-green eyes and a dab of lip gloss later she was pretty much ready to have lunch in style.

When she returned to the living room, Andreas was sitting pensively with a mug of coffee in one hand and the Polaroid of the two girls in the other.

'Is this a story you're working on?'

Nora shook her head.

'I bought an old suitcase yesterday and that picture was one of a bundle caught behind the lining,' she explained, gesturing towards the suitcase still lying in the hall. 'I don't know what it is, but something about that photo bugs me. And I'm annoyed that I can't place it. It feels as if I ought to know,' she said.

Andreas narrowed his eyes. 'It looks like one of the girls is wearing a bracelet. Do you have a magnifying glass?'

Nora rummaged around some drawers and found one under a pile of safety pins, coloured chalk and old chargers she had never got round to throwing out.

She took the Polaroid from Andreas. He was right; on the wrist of one of the girls she could make out a bracelet with individual letters on single beads. It was out of focus, but Nora thought she could read an 'L' … and possibly an 'E' or an 'I'.

Lene? Line? Lisette? Lea? None of those names brought her any closer to finding out what it was about the picture that intrigued her. Was there something familiar about the ferry where the picture had been taken?

Andreas interrupted her train of thought. 'I don't know about you, but I haven't had any breakfast yet, so how about it? Am I going to get something to eat today or what?'

Soon they were seated in Abdul's and Andreas had impressed Nora by ordering from the menu like a regular customer. *Köfte, cacik* and *pide*, and he even said *Tesekkür* to Abdul, who had put on his best smile in honour of the occasion.

Nora raised her eyebrows.

'What?' Andreas said archly. 'Or maybe you don't think Aalborg Airport has international departures?'

'I'm sorry. Only I remember you as more of a meat and two veg kind of guy. I had to nag you for hours to get you to try lasagne,' she said with a rather sheepish smile.

'People change,' he said with a light shrug.

Abdul fetched a jug of ice water and Nora's thoughts started circling the picture of the two girls once more.

'Something about that photo keeps bothering me. It's as if I ought to know the girls,' she began.

Andreas nodded. 'Same here.'

'OK. Two girls. One of them has a name starting with L. Or maybe she had a boyfriend whose name began with an L. On a ferry? Lise on the ferry? Line? Lis …?'

And suddenly, just as Abdul placed a red plastic basket of warm Turkish bread on the table, the penny dropped.

'Lisbeth!' she said, slapping her forehead. 'Christ Almighty, Andreas! It's Lisbeth. L for Lisbeth. Don't you remember the case? The girls from the England ferry?'

It was one of those cases that sometimes featured in documentaries. Last Easter when she went back to Denmark and had lunch with Trine in her holiday cottage, Nora had caught the end of a programme which declared – yet again – that what had happened to Lisbeth and the other girl, whose name Nora couldn't remember, was still a mystery.

Andreas nodded, tore off a chunk of bread and popped it into his mouth. 'Yes. I remember that.'

Nora racked her brains to recall the case. 'Something about them going missing from that ferry. And how they were never seen again.'

Andreas shrugged. 'It's an old case. My guess is they ended up at the bottom of the sea. And they'll never be found. Come to think of it, my Uncle Svend works with one of the guys who investigated the original case.'

Their food arrived, and they fell silent while they filled their plates. When they had been eating for some time, Nora could no longer restrain herself.

'Please would you call your uncle? I have to know right now.'

Andreas leaned back and watched her through half-closed eyes.

'You don't think it can wait until we've finished our lunch?'

'Please? I'll get the coffee,' she tempted him.

Andreas let out a small sigh and found his mobile.

Nora caught Abdul's eye and signalled 'coffee' while Andreas rang his uncle.

The coffee arrived in a small copper jug with tiny glasses and two pieces of Turkish Delight neatly arranged on a white paper doily.

Nora poured coffee for Andreas and herself, while he spoke to his uncle. She sipped the strong coffee and added a lump of sugar to take the edge off the extreme bitterness.

Andreas rounded off the call. 'All right then, give my love to Annika.'

He took his time, drank some coffee, pulled a face and added sugar.

Nora looked daggers at him. 'Right. Out with it.'

'You were spot on. My uncle works with Karl Stark, who was a young sergeant in Esbjerg back when the girls disappeared. He has never been able to let the case go.'

'So what happened?'

'My uncle could only remember a few things: the two girls lived in a care home for troubled kids near Ringkøbing. Eight of the kids and three adults were on a three-day trip to London. But on the ferry Lisbeth and Lulu disappeared. Vanished into thin air. Or deep water, if you like. Never to be seen again. Lisbeth's black backpack was found on the sun deck, and that's the only clue.'

'Ah, that was it. Her name was Lulu, the other one,' Nora interjected.

'A TV programme investigated the case last year, so I'm guessing that was the documentary you caught the end of,' Andreas ventured.

Nora thought for a moment.

'Hmm. Does your uncle still live in Esbjerg?'

'No, he met the love of his life, Annika, and they've moved to Dragør. He works for the Copenhagen Homicide Unit now, as does Karl Stark. Do you want me to ask my uncle for his number?'

Nora nodded. 'Yes, please.'

Without being asked Abdul brought more coffee. And winked at Nora when she sent him a puzzled look.

'It's a special day, Miss Nora. Lovely to see you without your mobile, and not here just to get a takeaway to eat at your desk,' he grinned.

Andreas shook his head and smiled. 'Some things never change. Or maybe they do?' he said.

And so began the inevitable conversation. About who was doing what. What had happened to Ole, Klaus and Red Rita; who had married, who was at home with the kids or wedded to their career.

'And how about you?' Nora asked lightly when Andreas had

accounted for divorces, civil service careers and one twin birth among their former classmates.

She had checked his Facebook profile the moment he had contacted her, obviously, but information was sparse. He hadn't listed his status as married or single. All she had been able to deduce from the groups he belonged to was that he continued to compete in triathlons, hadn't lost his enthusiasm for Monty Python and was still a Chelsea supporter.

'Yes, what about me?' Andreas echoed.

At that moment her mobile rang. It was the Crayfish.

'Hey, you. Not a bad article. But I want you to rewrite some sections. I think it might be possible to identify him from the geographical information, so disguise it. And shorten the third paragraph. He's repeating himself. I'm just sending it back to you now. Your deadline is in thirty minutes. Bye.'

He had rung off before she had time to reply.

Nora fished out a twenty-pound note from her purse and placed it on the table.

'Sorry. Work,' she explained.

Andreas's face was inscrutable.

Nora tried to placate him. 'How long are you in town?'

She was rewarded with one of his crooked smiles. 'Off you go. And let's keep in touch by email.'

3

Nora woke up to a short trumpet fanfare announcing that the budget airline was congratulating itself on arriving yet again on time at Copenhagen Airport.

It was one of those red-eye flights, which meant she had to wake up before four a.m. to get to Stansted Airport, and she had gone straight back to sleep before the plane had even taxied down the runway.

The book she had been planning on reading – an ambitious tome about oil conflicts in Africa – lay unopened on her lap, and she stuffed it back into her handbag before she got up and headed for the arrivals hall.

There he was in all his glory, waving a Starbucks paper cup, as if she wouldn't have spotted his dark green suit immediately. She knew no one else who wore a waistcoat. Especially not in June. Most of his beaming face was covered by a grey beard. Christian Sand was a prominent historian specialising in sixteenth-century Denmark and had named his daughter after the famous princess Leonora Christine.

'Dad. There really was no need for you to pick me up.'

'Always a pleasure. Anyway, I had some time on my hands before going to that conference in Stockholm next week. I'm working on a new theory about Leonora Christine and her husband's flight from imprisonment in Hammershus Castle,' he explained in an animated voice as he grabbed Nora's suitcase.

They drove home to Bagsværd in the small, pea-green Fiat Punto that had ferried her father around for over a decade. The car had originally belonged to her mother, but after she left them, her father had kept it as a token of almost twenty years of largely happy marriage.

The house had an unmistakable smell of dad. Dusty books, pipe smoke, leather, and rye bread cold-proving in a big clay bowl in the utility room. He made them coffee in a cafetière in the kitchen, while Nora dumped her suitcase in her old bedroom on the first floor. Her stripped-pine bed was where it always had been; even her old *Tintin* posters were still on the walls. It was always possible that something might one day prompt Christian Sand to take an interest in interior design and update the house, but Nora couldn't currently imagine what it might be.

She unpacked her party dress with the spots and put it on a hanger to give it time to straighten out before tomorrow evening.

'The party starts at five. We'll stop by Aunt Ellen's first to give her and Uncle Jens a lift to the hotel,' her father explained. 'David isn't going. He's at the allotment. He can't cope with all those people,' he added with a small sigh.

It came as no surprise to her. Her highly intelligent older brother had never been officially diagnosed as autistic, but going by what Nora had read, that was pretty much what he was.

His job as an actuary with a leading insurance company made full use of his mathematics talent and also allowed him to work from home most of the time, and thus avoid contact with those baffling and frustrating human beings that peopled the world.

On a good day he was a bit introverted and shy. On bad ones he was out of reach. You dealt with David on his own terms, or not at all.

'Never mind, I'm sure it'll be a great party, Dad. Got your speech ready?'

Her father nodded.

Nora had been looking forward to seeing her favourite aunt, who lived in Kalundborg, and had made sure to take time off to go to her seventieth birthday party.

'All right then, if you must, but make sure you pop into the office, seeing as you're in Copenhagen anyway,' the Crayfish had ordered her.

And she intended to do just that before having a late lunch with Louise at Danmarks Radio's Ørestad complex.

She took the S-train from Bagsværd Station, got off at Nørreport and walked the rest of the way to *Globalt's* editorial offices which occupied two floors in a building with an antiquarian bookshop on the ground floor.

'Heeey, Miss Sand,' Anette in reception called out brightly.

In a long line of journalists, editors-in-chief, photographers, proofreaders and researchers worn out by working for a magazine as ambitious as *Globalt*, Anette was possibly the only constant presence at the office.

She had been there since *Globalt* published its first issue, and had assumed the role of mother hen for journalists and editors. She organised their dental appointments, sent flowers to their wives when they worked late and listened to major and minor grievances without ever repeating them to anyone else.

The Crayfish wasn't the first editor to suggest adding her name to the colophon. Without her, he claimed, the magazine quite simply wouldn't go out each week.

Nora produced a box of Liquorice Allsorts bought at the airport from her bag and placed it on the counter.

Anette wagged a finger at her. 'Bad girl! You know very well they're not good for me,' she said with ill-disguised delight.

The box quickly disappeared into the top drawer where it would remain until the next emergency that required a spoonful of sugar.

'The Crayfish is in the meeting room, they've just finished their one o'clock meeting. He's in a good mood today,' she added.

The meeting room was hidden behind a kitchenette and could only be reached by navigating filing cabinets and piles of bound newspaper collections, whose raison d'être no one could remember.

'Ah, our foreign correspondent, if I'm not mistaken,' the Crayfish said with a smile and popped a piece of nicotine gum into his mouth.

It was a standing joke at the office that the Crayfish might have quit smoking two years ago, but since then he munched his way through a packet of nicotine gum a day. In the run-up to a deadline, it wasn't uncommon to see him chuck three pieces into his mouth at once.

A collection of empty mugs had been left on the conference table. One was a pretentious Penguin mug with a Virginia Woolf quote that belonged to the cultural editor Viola Ponte. A mug the sports editor would nick every day, so Viola Ponte was forced to use a chipped Brøndby FC mug no one would own up to bringing into the building.

The noticeboard behind the Crayfish was covered in A4 sheets, draft magazine pages at varying stages of completion. Some already featured text and photographs. Others were glaringly empty with only a few keywords scribbled in haste.

'Right, so tell me: What's keeping you busy these days?' the Crayfish said, leaning back in his chair and interlacing his fingers behind his neck.

'Well, I have a few ideas. Pete and I have talked about spending some time in Africa gathering stories. For example, we could –'

'Sure, but we've just run the Rwanda story. Don't you have something more … local?' the Crayfish sounded impatient.

'The Middle East?' she ventured tentatively.

'Hmm …' the Crayfish sounded unconvinced.

Nora took a deep breath.

'OK. I have something that might turn into a story. I don't know if it has legs yet. Do you remember two girls going missing on the ferry to England?'

The Crayfish shook his head as if trying to retrieve a snippet of information from a brain used to processing the finer points of American foreign policy from the *New York Times* and the intricacies of the Frankfurt Stock Exchange.

'Er. Not really.'

'Like I said, I don't know if it has legs. But I've come across a picture that might be linked to the case. It was huge at the time. Two teenage girls went missing from the ferry from Esbjerg to Harwich in the 1980s.'

'Hmm. Isn't that a bit … historical? It sounds more suited to a woman's weekly, in my opinion. Just before the crosswords,' the Crayfish said.

At that moment Anette entered with a stack of documents.

'For signature. And preferably a bit quicker than the last time,' she admonished him and turned on her heel.

'Anette, you're a very ordinary sort of person,' the Crayfish intoned pompously.

Anette rolled her eyes.

'Do you remember a story about two girls going missing from a ferry … in – now when was it, Sand?'

Before Nora had time to answer, Anette burst out: 'You bet I do! I was a teenager when it happened and I would read anything about it I could get my hands on. It was years before I dared to go on a ferry again.'

'Really? So you would like to read more?'

'Yes!' Anette declared firmly and marched back to reception where the telephone had started ringing.

'I see.'

The Crayfish stared out of the window for a while.

Nora cleared her throat discreetly.

'OK, Sand. Let's give it a go. It's a bit outside our remit. But why not. Two weeks. And you're not relieved of your usual duties while you're busy solving mysteries. Understand?'

'Yes. Thank you. However, I can't promise you that –' she began, before the Crayfish's mobile started beeping like a pacemaker in his shirt pocket. He took it out and frowned as he looked at the screen.

'Hmm. A Russian number. I have to take this,' he said with a wave, indicating her audience was over.

She did a tour of the office. Most staff had already left for their summer break, but in the picture section she found Magnus absorbed in editing photographs from his most recent trip to Afghanistan.

War photography didn't usually appeal to her, but Magnus already had three international awards under his belt despite being only twenty-five years old, and he had surpassed himself yet again. He had caught in frozen moments the fear in their eyes, the dust, the despair, the boredom and the rush of victory.

He turned around when he sensed her looking over his shoulder.

'Hi, Nora,' he said casually before turning his attention back to the screen.

'Magnus, what's the situation with our photo archive – is it accessible to us journalists?'

'Of course it is. Just search the database. What are you looking for?'

'A story from the mid-1980s.'

'Then it won't be in our archive, sweet pea. As you know *Globalt* didn't see the light of day until 1998.'

After a pause, which he used to adjust the colour contrast in a desert landscape, he said, 'But you could always try ServiceMedia. They've collated most of the press photos ever issued by Danish media. You can use my password, if you keep quiet about it.'

'Thank you,' she said, sitting down at the nearest computer.

First she googled 'disappearance England ferry' and quickly found several articles about how Lulu Brandt and Lisbeth Mogensen had vanished without a trace.

By clicking back and forth she found out more about the story in the national newspapers, *Ekstra Bladet* and *BT*, as well as a large feature in a local newspaper, *Ringkøbing Amts Dagblad*, in which the journalist had stressed that the care home where the girls lived – a place called Vestergården – was only fifteen kilometres from the town of Ringkøbing. She printed out the pages so she could read them later.

She then made a note of the date of their disappearance – 4 August 1985 – and logged on to ServiceMedia's homepage and searched using Magnus's password, which turned out to be Hendrix78. She didn't ask, but he explained it himself.

'My dog,' he said with a grin, pointing to a picture of a drooling boxer hanging above his desk.

There were eight pictures from the case. *Ringkøbing Amts Dagblad* had three. The first showed Vestergården, the second a broadly grinning man with a full beard described as Kurt Damtoft, warden of Vestergården, and she had a vague feeling that she had seen the third picture before. The two girls on it were part of a group of smiling teenagers standing in the port of Esbjerg, waiting to go on the trip of a lifetime. Lisbeth appeared to squint against the sun, and next to a gigantic ghetto blaster a dark-haired Lulu was smiling shyly at the camera.

She clicked on to *Ekstra Bladet* and *BT*. Both featured pictures from the court case against Kurt Damtoft and two of his colleagues. 'Grievous neglect!' *Ekstra Bladet* raged. Both newspapers had reprinted the pictures of the two girls at the port with the ferry in the background.

'The last picture of the girls alive,' read one of the captions accompanying an article, which went as far as concluding that 'the two beauties from Jutland were murdered at sea'.

Nora rummaged around her handbag and found her diary where she was keeping the Polaroid of the two girls. She pulled it out and studied it again.

The picture in *Ekstra Bladet* clearly wasn't the final picture taken of the girls while they were still alive. Someone had photographed Lisbeth and Lulu on board the ferry while they were apart from the other teenagers from Vestergården. The question now was who, and why no one had given it to the press when the investigation into the missing girls was at its peak. And what was it doing in a suitcase from Brine.

In return for a cup of coffee, Magnus agreed to scan her picture into the computer. She emailed it to herself, and got him to print out some paper copies. Then she printed out a couple of the group pictures and stuffed everything into her bag before she left to catch the train to Ørestaden.

4

She had met Louise when they both sat the entrance exam to the School of Journalism. Something about the petite girl with the crewcut and the dangling earrings had piqued Nora's interest during the break. When they started talking, it soon became clear that they shared the same dry sense of humour, and that Louise had forgotten to bring food or money for a whole day of tests.

After a few detours via alternative, underground magazines, Louise had surprised everyone by landing a job with DR, the Danish state broadcasting corporation, where today she was a feared and respected producer on the news desk. Sources notorious for refusing to appear on TV could somehow never say no to Louise. She was a woman who made things happen.

Nora got off the train, walked up to the main reception and signed in. Three minutes later a beaming Louise came rushing down the stairs with a stack of papers under her arm.

'Hello, gorgeous! Great to see you,' she said, checking her wristwatch in the same movement.

'I have twenty-five minutes. I'm waiting for a call from Bertil Brask's people,' she said, referring to the latest discredited CEO to run a company into the ground.

'He's willing to go on TV?' Nora was astonished.

'They're considering it, and that's good enough for me,' Louise said, sounding optimistic.

They went to the canteen.

'How is Tobias?' Nora asked when they had sat down with their lunch.

Louise pulled a face. 'He's already planning his confirmation next year. I don't know how that happened. One moment I had a sweet, cuddly boy with dimples, now there's a surly teenager with white iPod earplugs permanently attached to him, moping around the house. That is, when he bothers to come home at all.'

At seventeen Louise had got pregnant by a bass player in a British band. She never saw the bass player again, but nine months after the group's triumphant farewell concert in Denmark, Tobias arrived. Somehow Louise had managed her studies and a baby while living on a grant, without any help from her disapproving parents.

They talked about men. About their bosses and about how a seemingly endless series of cuts had led to redundancies among several of their former colleagues, in print media as well as radio and television. When Louise finished her water and made to get up, Nora remembered the Polaroid in her bag.

'I wonder if you could help me. I want to view a programme that was broadcast last year. An episode of *Unsolved*.'

Louise got up, took her tray and carried it to the stand.

'No problem. The archive owes me a favour. I'll call them now.' She pulled out her mobile and made an appointment for her.

'Just ask for Susanne,' she said to Nora.

Her phone rang in the middle of their farewell hug.

'Yes. Speaking,' Louise said in her business voice. She waved to Nora and mouthed 'Bertil Brask'.

Nora followed the signs and eventually found the archive, which was run by a smiling, slightly chubby, grey-haired woman in a canary yellow shirt, who was sitting behind a counter.

'Are you Susanne?'

The woman nodded. 'And you were sent by my friend Louise? How can I help you?'

Nora explained what she was looking for, and Susanne entered the information into her computer.

The answer appeared less than ten seconds after she hit 'enter'.

'Here we are. *Unsolved*. Repeated on the fifth of April last year,' she said, writing down a long number on a piece of paper.

'Wait here,' Susanne ordered before getting up from her office chair, walking past Nora and through a door that required her to run the ID card dangling from a string around her neck through a card reader.

Nora sat down and studied the modern design of the room, which looked as if all evidence of humanity had been systematically erased. Everything was sharp angles and glass partitions.

She jumped when the door opened and Susanne reappeared holding a large, grey cassette.

'Here you are. You can't take it with you, but you can watch it in there,' she said, pointing to a door with a sign that read *Meeting Room 2*.

Nora took the tape, entered the room, turned on the video player and sat at the empty conference table.

Unsolved's red logo rolled across the screen to the sound of the ominous signature tune that had introduced the programme for the last ten years.

The host, Jens Blindkilde, appeared wearing a trench coat in front of what must surely be Esbjerg Ferry Terminal. As always, his face assumed a grave expression.

'Tonight we investigate a case that has haunted Danish and British police for years. The case of two young women who vanished without a trace on a ferry going from Denmark to England. The case of the girls from the England ferry,' he said in a portentous voice.

Nora rummaged around her bag and found a pen and a notepad with some blank pages. Half an hour later the credits rolled across the screen, and Nora reviewed her notes.

Lulu and Lisbeth had last been seen about half an hour after the ferry departed from Esbjerg. A female passenger, whom Blindkilde and his researchers had managed to track down, believed she had seen them in the company of a man, but couldn't after all these years remember whether he was dark or blond, tall or short. Despite the presenter using the term 'sensational' three times during the programme to describe the witness, Nora was unconvinced. It looked like a dead end. They had tracked down Lulu's biological father, but he had declined to take part. He hadn't seen his daughter since she was taken into care at the age of ten.

In a written statement he had said that 'not a day goes by when I don't think about what could have happened to my sweet little Lulu'.

There was a short extract of an interview with a man called Karl Stark, who after serving as a police officer in Esbjerg, went on to become a detective inspector in Copenhagen. A few short minutes which showed a tortured, grey-haired man who didn't seem to have much to add.

In one shot he looked straight at the camera. 'Those girls deserve justice. Somebody out there must know what happened to them,' he appealed.

Nora pressed to eject the tape, popped it back in the cassette case, went out to Susanne and returned it to her with thanks.

She walked outside into the sunshine, took her mobile from her pocket, searched www.krak.dk for a telephone number and called Andreas's uncle, Svend Jansson, who lived in nearby Dragør. He remembered her well and would be happy to ask Karl Stark if he had time to discuss the case with her. Two minutes after she had rung off, she received a text message with an address in Dragør and an invitation to morning coffee the following day.

There was a loaf of freshly baked rye bread in the kitchen when she got up the next morning. She carved off a chunk, added some cheese and went out on the terrace to catch the early light.

Her father was absorbed by a column in *Weekendavisen*, but grunted amicably under the parasol when he noticed her.

'Please may I borrow the car today?' she said with her mouth full of rye bread.

'Yes. As long as you're back in time for us to drive to Kalundborg,' he replied and continued without further introduction: 'How is your mother?'

'Fine, I think. Last time I spoke to her she was on her way to a mosaic course in Tuscany. Patrick is still nagging her to move to Devon. But she's staying in London,' Nora said.

'Is that right? Then again, what on earth would she do with herself down there?' Her father wondered out loud.

'There's no risk of that happening. She needs to live within walking distance of the British Library, the British Museum and her beloved papers. Otherwise she'll start climbing the walls,' Nora said. 'The question is, can Patrick stick it long term.'

'Well, she just happens to be the country's foremost Cromwell expert. In my opinion, he's the one who has to up sticks and move. Devon!' he snorted.

Nora went to shower and left him to his newspaper. The truth was she loathed talking about Patrick and the past because it ripped open old wounds that were better left to heal. She hated reliving the day she had come back early from her morning swim with Andreas and found her mother on the drive with a small, purple, wheeled suitcase, waiting for a taxi.

'Mum, where are you going? Have you been crying?'

Without answering her question, her mother had said: 'Nora – why are you back so soon?'

Before Nora had time to say anything else, the taxi arrived. And Elizabeth was gone.

Nora had walked slowly inside the house. To the remains of a man she called dad. A man who had just lost the love of his life and would never understand how it had happened.

What had happened was an apple grower by the name of Patrick from Devon, and Nora had refused to exchange a single word with him or her mother for the next five years.

She shook off the thought while she dried her hair.

Half an hour later she was ready to go to Dragør.

She drove around the old fishing village for a while before she found the small yellow house on Skippervænget.

A shirtless Jansson was sitting in the front garden drinking cold water from a thick-bottomed glass. It was clear that he had just finished cutting the lawn. On the table in front of him were a small, turquoise Thermos flask, two coffee cups and a copy of *Søndag* open on the crossword pages. There was a pair of red women's spectacles on top of the magazine.

He looked up quizzically when she stopped outside the white picket fence.

'Nora?'

She nodded.

'Come in,' he said as he sized her up. 'Yes, I do remember you. You used to go swimming with Andreas, didn't you?'

Nora confirmed it, and Svend Jansson went inside to fetch extra coffee cups for Nora and Karl Stark. When he reappeared, he nodded in the direction of the magazine and the spectacles.

'Annika has just popped next door. Something about a new fish recipe she wants to try this evening,' he explained. 'But I don't suppose that's why you're here. Karl's coming in a minute. He doesn't have all that much time. I believe he's off to watch his grandchild play volleyball.'

'I saw him on *Unsolved*.'

'Yes. He thought that we owed it to the girls to keep looking, I guess. What if there was someone out there who could remember something after all these years? A tiny detail that could give us a break into what really happened,' he said sadly, and shook his head.

At that moment the garden gate opened and the grey-haired man Nora had seen on the TV strode towards the garden table.

His gaze was as firm as his handshake.

'Nora Sand,' he said, glancing quickly at his wristwatch. 'I have less than twenty minutes to spare, and I'm doing this as a favour to Svend.'

Nora appreciated his frankness.

'OK. Then let's get started. I saw you on *Unsolved*. Did you get any leads from it?'

Karl Stark shook his head.

'I spent the whole evening manning the phone lines that people were invited to call. We received fourteen calls. All pranksters or false confessions. A man from Greve believed he had seen Lisbeth alive and well at his local fitness centre, where she taught spinning every Wednesday evening. A medium from Herning swore that Lulu's earthly remains were near water. Which, all things being equal, shouldn't really surprise anyone.'

'What do you think happened?' Nora asked.

Karl Stark took his time before replying. Poured coffee, added a spoonful of sugar and stirred.

'I genuinely don't know. I've pondered it for years. It was one of my first cases after coming to Esbjerg. I've lost count of the number of times I've reviewed the file, asking myself what more we could have done, what we failed to check. People don't just vanish into thin air. Could they have jumped overboard in a suicide pact? I don't believe it,' he said and then he lowered his voice.

'The press were never told this, but we found a cutting in the backpack Lisbeth left behind. It was from a teen magazine and was about how to become a model in London. Why would she jump overboard, if she had dreams for her future?'

He raked his fingers through his hair, and shook his head.

'I'm an old fool. When I moved to Copenhagen, I brought a copy of the file with me. The first few years I took it out whenever I had time. I would stare at it, look for non-existent links until I nearly went mad. It's like when the dentist has drilled a tooth. The tongue keeps probing it. But now … when the TV programme produced no new leads, I think I just gave up. Nor did we have grieving relatives calling us to ask about the investigation. It's so many years ago and there are always new cases to investigate.'

Nora took out the printouts from *Ekstra Bladet* and placed them on the table.

'Is it correct that this is the last picture of the girls?'

Karl Stark looked at her, then down at the article with the picture of the group from Vestergården waiting to embark. He nodded.

'There are no others in the file, nor have any witnesses come to you with any pictures?'

He shook his head briefly.

Nora produced her diary from her bag, took out the Polaroid and placed it on top of the headlines.

'I'm hoping you could tell me about this,' she said.

Karl Stark snatched the Polaroid and narrowed his eyes to study it more closely. Seconds later he dropped it as if he had been burned.

'Christ Almighty, girl! Where's that picture from? I've never seen it before.'

He tore a page out of Annika's magazine and folded it around the photograph.

'Who has touched it?'

'Eh. Me … Andreas. No one else, I think. Not since I found it, certainly,' Nora said.

Stark took a deep breath. 'This is the first new evidence we've received since shelving the investigation,' he said. 'Tell me right now how you got that picture. I want to know everything.'

Nora helped herself to coffee and told him the story of the small fishing village of Brine and the suitcase filled with Polaroids of young women.

While she spoke, Svend Jansson went inside and came back with a pair of tweezers and a white envelope into which he eased the picture. Afterwards he handed the envelope to his old colleague.

'I hope you don't mind if I keep this,' Karl Stark said, but he wasn't asking for permission.

'We'll see if Forensics can come up with anything. I doubt it, but at least it'll give them something to do,' he quipped. 'I'll chase it up myself. There may be nothing to it. But I have to know,' he added gravely.

'Hiiii …' a bright, female voice called out.

Annika came walking up the garden path, her arms laden with fresh rhubarb.

'Look what Flemming gave us!' she exclaimed happily before turning to the guests. 'Did he offer you coffee?'

Karl Stark nodded, emptied his cup and shook hands with Nora and Annika before disappearing down the garden path on his way to the volleyball game.

Nora stayed another half an hour and wasn't allowed to leave until she had accepted a jar of home-made strawberry jam.

Back in the car she rang her brother on impulse. It rang four times before going to voicemail, which invited her to leave a message.

'Hi, it's sis. I'm in town.' Nothing more was needed. If he wanted to meet up, he would get in touch.

She reversed the car out of the drive and drove back to Bagsværd.

The birthday party exceeded all expectation. Aunt Ellen could liven up any occasion with her floral dresses and her belly laughter, and her gregariousness was only heightened when surrounded by her beloved family and friends. There had been toasts, songs and a long walk by the sea in the evening sunset.

The next morning Nora had the rare pleasure of a phone call from David and she drove to the allotments on Amager with fresh crusty rolls and one of those cinnamon Danish pastries she knew he couldn't resist.

They spent a couple of hours together, and David seemed to be in a good mood as he showed her around his collection of peonies – one of his few interests to rival his passion for algorithms. Not once did he ask her about her life in London.

Nevertheless, she told him. About Andreas, who was in London, and how the week before last she had been out driving with Pete and how the 'photo mobile', as they had christened Pete's Ford Mondeo, had nearly conked out on the motorway. Nora smiled fondly when remembering the photographer's impressive arsenal of Aussie swear words. Rather than laugh at the comic tale about a panicking Pete, David declared gravely that it was very important to always check the engine oil before embarking on a long drive.

'I think he's learned his lesson,' Nora assured her brother before driving back to Bagsværd.

Her father wasn't at home, so Nora wolfed down a quick sandwich before packing her things and catching the train to the airport.

5

An hour later, Nora was checking the departure board in the transit area. It was still too early to go to the gate. She pottered around the bookshop and scanned the bestseller lists without getting her hopes up. There was no point in buying anything in English; books were much cheaper in London, but every now and then she felt the need to sink her teeth into a good Danish novel.

She wasn't tempted by any of the fiction though, and carried on past the travel literature to a small, non-fiction section with books on the quickest way to succeed in business, and how the Soviets endured the siege of Leningrad. In the crime section, however, she found a blood-curdling bestseller promising accounts of the most macabre British murders in recent history, called *Murders of the Century*.

The notorious British child killer Yvonne Loft stared maliciously from the cover with a smile on her lips, as if the ten young lives she had been convicted of taking were nothing but a cruel joke understood only by her and her accomplice lover.

Nora picked up the book on impulse and flicked through to a central section of black-and-white photographs. To illustrate the Yvonne Loft case further, the author had found a picture of the murdering lovers eating ice cream while holding hands and grinning from ear to ear. The caption made Nora want to throw up.

'Yvonne Loft and Harry George enjoy a day out in Brighton. The picture is believed to have been taken a few hours before the couple abducted and killed seven-year-old Timothy Kent.'

Was it possible to eat ice cream while planning to kill a child, Nora wondered? It wasn't the cruelty itself that was the most horrifying. It was the imperceptible way it wormed its way into normality, into everyday life, thus teaching us that we can never feel safe. That a friendly face can hide the most profound evil.

The smiling couple in love, licking strawberry ice cream from a cone while planning to rape and strangle someone's son. The friendly schoolteacher from a village in Rwanda going berserk with a machete in a rush of blood. The nice husband in a suit who drowns his wife in the bath to get his hands on her life insurance. Nora shuddered and was about to put the book back when her gaze fell on the opposite page where a picture in the bottom left-hand corner jumped out at her.

The small picture made the hairs at the back of her neck stand up.

Resolutely she stuck the book under her arm, marched up to the counter and paid for it, before making her way to the gate.

As soon as she had found her seat on the plane, she returned to the picture and studied it in more detail.

A young woman with her hair piled up on her head was staring silently into the camera. She was standing with her hands by her sides in front of a white wall. Nora didn't remember seeing the face before, but it could easily have been one of the Polaroids from the suitcase.

The caption wasn't particularly informative. 'Nineteen-year-old Jean Eastman, the discovery of whose body led police to the apprehension of William Hickley.'

Nora found the chapter about William Hickley – or Bill Hix as he insisted on being called.

The book was riddled with clichés: William Hickley had suffered a deprived and loveless childhood with a domineering mother. He had never known his father. The boy had had major problems making friends at school pretty much from day one, and had instead turned to photography, which became his all-consuming hobby.

He was living with his mother when at the age of thirty-two he was undone by something as trivial as a flat tyre. He had pulled over on a main road to change the tyre one Friday afternoon in October 1992. A friendly rural police officer had stopped to offer his assistance. Before William Hickley had time to decline his help, the kind-hearted police officer had already opened the boot in search of a jack and the spare tyre.

What PC Ross Carr saw that day left such mental scars that he never returned to active service, but retired with a nervous breakdown and sleep problems two years earlier than planned.

Jean Eastman had been a local beauty, who worked at a florist's in Dorchester, but there was nothing beautiful about her as she lay curled up, naked and cold, on a piece of dark green tarpaulin. Where her eyes had once sparkled, there were now two gaping holes and in her open mouth PC Carr saw a darkness that would haunt him for the rest of his life. Her tongue had been cut out.

William Hickley fled on foot while the officer threw up on the verge. But after being on the run for one week following a national manhunt, he was eventually spotted by an ornithologist near a holiday cottage in the Lake District.

The cottage was surrounded and when Hickley realised that he was outnumbered, he gave himself up. The investigation led police to Hickley's mother's house and down to the locked basement, which was her son's domain. Vanessa Hickley fought tooth and nail against the police investigation and continued to insist to this day that her son was the victim of a miscarriage of justice.

In the basement, which had been turned into a darkroom, police found a rental agreement for a warehouse outside Dorchester. The address was three kilometres from the location where Hickley had had the puncture. In the dilapidated building police found three wrecked cars, five women's handbags, a set of scalpels, eight bras, two sofas and a locked cupboard. When they broke into the cupboard, they found driving licences and other personal papers belonging to five women who had all been reported missing, including nineteen-year-old Jean Eastman.

At the bottom of the cupboard police also found an envelope containing twenty-three pictures of women, all in the same pose: standing against a wall with their gaze aimed straight at the camera. But it wasn't that which shook the team of investigators or caused the biggest headlines. It was the macabre discovery of fifteen tongues, neatly preserved in vinegar in a glass jar and placed at the bottom of the cupboard, which the press named the 'Cabinet of Horrors'.

Detective Inspector James McCormey's hope of a simple confession and a guilty plea was dashed during his first attempt at interrogating William Hickley.

It soon became clear that Hickley intended to plead insanity in order to avoid a prison sentence. He claimed that God had told him to kill and eat Jean Eastman.

'Why did you cut out their tongues?'

'God told me to eat their words. Their empty, girly chatter. Stuff them right into my mouth with love,' William Hickley explained in all seriousness.

James McCormey tried repeatedly to appeal to William Hickley and his alter ego, Bill Hix, to end the uncertainty and suffering of the families of the missing women. And to identify the fifteen tongues.

He was met with only gibberish or silence. William Hickley was sent for psychiatric evaluation.

A panel of five experts agreed by a majority of one that Hickley was capable of understanding the extent and consequences of his crimes, and he was thus declared fit to stand trial.

Dorchester police managed to identify nine girls from the twenty-three photographs that Hickley had left behind. The remaining pictures were released to the UK media. Five women contacted them. Two hadn't even known that William Hickley had photographed them. The other three told similar stories of a young, dark-haired man who had promised them modelling work.

Mary Johnson, aged sixteen, said she had been approached while waiting for her father outside the National Gallery in London. When her father came out and she turned to introduce him to the photographer, the young man had vanished into thin air. She didn't see him again until police asked her to pick him out from eight photographs of men who matched his description. She pointed to William Hickley without a moment's hesitation.

James McCormey and his team worked themselves ragged trying to find the earthly remains of the fifteen women with no tongues. They excavated Vanessa Hickley's garden from top to bottom. An operation whose only results were the bones from a long dead dog, which was categorised as a Collie, and a claim from Mrs Hickley for police harassment.

Next forensic technicians concentrated on the ground around the warehouse. Slowly and methodically they worked away from the building in concentric circles. A cheer went up when a technician found evidence that the earth four hundred metres from the warehouse had been disturbed within the last year. Experts carefully worked their way through thin layers of soil only to reveal the remains of bones, which turned out to be those of cows.

The Crown Prosecution Service decided to concentrate on the one case where there was enough evidence to secure a conviction rather than compromise future trials. William Hickley was duly convicted of the murder of Jean Eastman and was given a whole life tariff. He was transferred to Wolf Hall Prison where he remains to this day, the author stated, adding that four British Home Secretaries so far had refused to allow Hickley to appear in front of the parole board.

However, for James McCormey the investigation wasn't over. Every year without fail he would visit William Hickley in an attempt to make him give up the location of the remaining fifteen bodies. For the first two years Hickley sat behind armoured glass, picked up the phone and listened to McCormey with a contemptuous smile. He never said a word, but let McCormey plead desperately while staring him down.

The third year he indicated that he had found God and was willing to atone for his sins.

'The families need peace of mind,' he confided in McCormey with feigned piety while drawing a map of Underwood, a forest some thirty minutes' drive from his childhood home in Dorchester.

McCormey had to twist several arms and call in more than a few favours before being allocated resources to examine the area.

Even so the Crown Prosecution Service tried to talk him out of it by appealing to his common sense: Hickley was already behind bars and there were plenty of new and unsolved murders to occupy police and forensic examiners without them having to dig up the past.

'Why are you really doing this? The man is in prison. For life.'

'The truth. We owe it to all the families who live without knowing what has happened to their loved ones,' was McCormey's answer.

'At the time this book went to print,' the author wrote, 'no bodies have been found in Underwood.'

The plane started circling Stansted, and Nora yawned to relieve the pressure in her ears.

She checked the copyright page of the paperback. It was the fifth edition. Much could have happened since it was first published. She wondered what McCormey would say about the case today.

Had Lisbeth and Lulu been the victims of William Hickley, the man who called himself Bill Hix? Nora was tempted to dismiss the theory as more than a tad absurd. After all, Dorchester was a long way from Harwich, and no one knew if the two girls had even made it to the UK. On the other hand, the year was about right. As was the photograph, except it featured two women rather than just one. But it could have been taken by another disturbed person, a copycat.

Nora reviewed various scenarios in her head while she queued at passport control, a line that seemed to grow longer each time she entered the country.

While she waited for her suitcase to appear on the conveyor belt, she turned on her mobile and called Pete.

'Airport emergency,' was all she said.

It was their code to activate a longstanding agreement to provide company and dinner for whoever arrived alone at a London airport. Being a single traveller was fine most of the time, but some days it was just too depressing to weave in and out between kissing couples, overjoyed families and taxi drivers with signs that never displayed your own name, in the certain knowledge that there was no one to pick you up, and you were going home to an empty flat. Their airport emergency agreement postponed the inevitable and made it slightly more bearable.

'Daaaarling!' Pete exclaimed in what was supposed to be his domestic goddess voice. 'I've been waiting for your call for ages. I'm sitting here with a family-sized portion of chilli, all on my ownsome. And me, who can't tolerate all those beans.'

'I'll be there in ninety minutes,' she promised and rang off.

She grabbed one of the few remaining copies of *The Sunday Times* at the newsagent and discarded the boring sections on Home, Sport and Driving before taking the news sections with her to the coach and letting herself be transported back into town.

Pete served his chilli with cold Corona, home-made guacamole and a lengthy speech about why they ought to go to Ghana soon to investigate. A couple of hours later Nora called a cab, which took her the last stretch home to Belsize Park.

She picked up her post in the hallway and turned on her laptop, which warmed up while she changed out of her travelling clothes. Pete's chilli was still burning her throat, so she found a bottle of water in the fridge and drank it in big gulps.

She checked her inbox. Two emails from the Crayfish. She barely had the energy, but knew from past experience that she might as well open them now or she would just be tossing and turning in her bed, and ultimately get up to read them anyway.

The first was short and imperative: *Call!*

She checked her watch. It had to be a quarter past one in Denmark, and she had a hunch that the Crayfish's poor sense of time zones didn't include an appreciation that the phenomenon worked both ways.

She clicked to open the next one.

Planning meeting tomorrow. What's happening with that ferry story?

'Take a chill pill,' she said out loud. Typical Crayfish to think that hey presto she could magic up the world's best scoop over the weekend.

A thought, which had been nagging her ever since the plane, suddenly resurfaced.

She rummaged round the bottom of a chest of drawers and eventually found what she was looking for: a pair of grey woollen gloves. She had taken on board Svend Jansson's words about not leaving fingerprints.

Then she pulled the suitcase from Brine out from under the coffee table and opened it.

At first she removed the envelope with the remaining Polaroids. She intended to take a closer look at them later. Then she adjusted her desk lamp so it would act as a spotlight while she examined the scuffed leather suitcase.

She felt along the lining and discovered a hole in the stitching that might explain how the photographs had come to be sold along with the suitcase. She carefully checked the rest of it. There was nothing else of significance. A few specks of tobacco, a red button and a receipt dated 1983 for petrol from a BP station.

Disappointed, she turned the suitcase upside down to shake out more secrets. And that was when she spotted it. On one side of the suitcase a name had been written with a silver pen in a thin, quivering hand.

Bill Hix

'Bloody hell!' she burst out.

For a while she sat staring alternately at the suitcase and out of the window, where refuse collectors had started the night shift and were scrambling around with recycling bins.

Then she sat down in front of her laptop and wrote an email to the Crayfish.

6

The Crayfish rang the moment he checked his emails that morning.

'You just keep working on that story. Two missing girls and a suitcase that used to belong to a British serial killer. Sounds like a scoop to me. When can you have something ready?' he asked before Nora had even had time to say her name.

Rumour had it the Crayfish was such a workaholic that he couldn't stop himself from opening his laptop at breakfast, where his long-suffering wife and two children had to compete for his attention with the *New York Times*, *Frankfurter Allgemeine* and *Financial Times* websites before the first cup of coffee. And, of course, his emails. And his breakfast.

Nora could hear crunching and she presumed that the Crayfish's jaws were busy churning their way through a bowl of cornflakes.

'It won't be this week,' she quickly interjected when the Crayfish paused to swallow his coffee.

'Humph. Why not?' He sounded almost offended.

'Because things take longer over here,' Nora explained for the umpteenth time.

The problem with editors back home was that they were used to working for important media. In Denmark, magazines and newspapers were taken so seriously that even government ministers, as a rule, would make the effort to return calls when a journalist asked for a comment.

In London, *Globalt* was just a small fish, maybe only a daphnia, in a very large pond. Few people had heard of the magazine and if Nora ever tried to set up an interview at ministerial level, the intern to the assistant to the press secretary would laugh right in her face. That is, if she even made it that far up the system.

Many people thought she was German. Or Dutch, which wasn't necessarily an advantage or even made much difference. In British politics, however, there was the national press and then there was everyone else. With the possible exception of American heavyweights such as *Time* and the *New York Times*, whose correspondents seemed to have better access than most.

By now Nora had learned to navigate her way around, find alternative sources and contacts that could help. But it still took her longer than if she could simply pick up her phone and get the information with one call.

'Give me a couple of weeks. Preferably three,' she begged him.

The Crayfish growled and complained, but gave in eventually in return for her squeezing a background feature on the crisis in British diplomacy into her schedule.

'And Bo Helmersen wants to know what's happening with the obituary of the prime minister. One day we'll be needing it, only then you'll be away reporting from Timbuktu,' he joshed her.

'All right. I'll have a look at it,' Nora promised.

'What's your next move?' the Crayfish wanted to know.

Nora pondered it.

'At some stage I think I'll need to contact Bill Hix, as he calls himself. Confront him with the Polaroids. Find out if he knows anything about what happened to Lulu and Lisbeth. But it could take weeks to get permission to visit him in prison. That is, if he even agrees to see me in the first place,' she warned him.

In the background she could hear the clatter of coffee cups, and a girl's voice calling out to her father that she would be late for school if they didn't leave now.

'Oh well, you'll work something out,' he said in his distracted voice. 'Send me an email when you have more. And listen … I've been thinking, we'd better contact the police about that suitcase. We're going to play this one by the book,' he said and rang off before Nora had time to respond.

She took a quick bath and with a towel wrapped around her long, dark hair, she went hunting for some clean clothes. She wished that she, like most of her male colleagues, had a sweet and kind person living at the same address. Someone who made sure everything at home ran like clockwork. That there was always milk in the fridge, clean and freshly ironed shirts in the wardrobe and that the TV licence was paid on time.

Nora scowled at her bulging laundry basket before she found an only slightly crumpled floral summer dress behind a pile of sweaters in her wardrobe, and stepped into her beloved Clarks sandals.

She packed the laptop into her bag, stuffed *Murders of the Century* into the front pocket, along with her notebook, a few pens and her mobile.

Then she slammed the door behind her and walked five minutes to the nearest Starbucks. There were days when it was simply too deathly dull to work from home. Days when she felt the need for life around her – people coming and going, the hissing and slurping of coffee machines. Yummy mummies sheltering from the summer rain, schoolkids in uniforms competing to text the fastest, and business people trying to give the impression they were in a busy and successful office while shouting into their mobiles to drown out the smooth jazz from the café's speakers.

She ordered a grande latte in a paper cup, found a leather armchair, and placed the laptop on the small circular table. Then she opened a new document and titled it: *The Girls from the England Ferry.*

X

First there were the English clues and then there were those from Denmark.

She found her notes from the TV programme and reread them. She wondered why no one from Vestergården had been willing to be interviewed by DR.

Nora connected to the café's Wi-Fi and entered the name into a search engine. Vestergården was the name of a nursery school outside of Slagelse, a retirement home in Kerteminde, and a family farm by Henne Strand. Google knew of no children's home by that name.

Well, that would've been too easy.

She found the homepage of Ringkøbing-Skjern Council, clicked until she found Social Services and wrote down their telephone number.

A search on www.krak.dk showed there were four people registered in Denmark by the name K. Damtoft. None of them lived in Ringkøbing or even nearby.

If she were to tell this story properly, she needed a better understanding of the girls. Discover where Lulu and Lisbeth had come from. Right now they were simply abstract stereotypes. What were their dreams? Why had they ended up at Vestergården, a place where damaged and difficult youngsters were sent when all other efforts had failed? When they were what social workers liked to call 'beyond educational reach'.

If she were to have any hope of getting her readers to care about the fate of the two girls after all these years, she had to show them who they were.

She was well aware that even a tenuous link to a British serial killer would sell the story, but merely adding information about the bloodthirsty Brit without proving the link wouldn't work.

Her coffee was getting cold. Even so, she took a sip and looked up the homepage of a budget airline. She would have to go back to Denmark once more.

But first she had to track down a man.

She called Scotland Yard, having learned from experience to avoid the press office, which served mainly as a kind of Bermuda Triangle where enquiries from journalists disappeared under mysterious circumstances, never to be seen or heard again. Frankly, they might as well record a message telling you that if the information you were looking for wasn't on their homepage, you should give up now.

Instead Nora asked to be put through to Detective Inspector James McCormey.

She heard the receptionist look up the name on her computer.

'He no longer works here. May I ask which investigation this relates to?'

'Do you know where he is now?' Nora asked her instead.

A new pause.

'My colleague thinks he might be in Folkestone or somewhere else along the south coast. Unless he's retired. Can someone else help you?'

Nora mumbled a thank you and rang off.

Half an hour and seven police stations later she struck gold in Dover.

'He's out on a job. He'll be back after two o'clock. Can I take a message?' the officer said.

Nora dutifully stated her name and telephone number before the inevitable question: 'May I ask what this is about?'

'A very old case,' she replied, and hung up.

When it got to three thirty and he still hadn't called, she rang back.

'He's just on his way in. Please try again in twenty minutes,' promised the same male voice which had taken her original message.

Half an hour later she finally got through to McCormey. He sounded out of breath and irritable.

'Yes. What is it?' he snapped.

'Good afternoon. My name is Nora Sand. I'm a journalist with the Danish magazine, *Globalt*, and –'

He cut her off immediately: 'I'm not speaking to the press about this case. We have confirmed there are seven fatalities and five casualties have been admitted to hospital. All further communication is to go through our press office. There's already a press release on the internet. Goodbye.'

'Yes, but I'm not calling about –' Nora had time to say before she realised that he had already hung up.

She pressed recall. It went straight to voicemail. She rang off without leaving a message, but changed her mind and rang back.

'DI McCormey,' she said in her best upper-class English to the voicemail. 'I'm not calling to talk about your current investigation. I'm calling because I believe I have information relating to a case from the 1980s. It concerns William Hickley, also known as Bill Hix.'

She left her number and repeated her name.

If that didn't make him call back, nothing would. According to *Murders of the Century* William Hickley had been McCormey's biggest case ever; a case that had ended up defining his career, for better or for worse.

Nora packed up her laptop and jumped on a bus to Hampstead. She was queuing at the French bakery for a loaf of sourdough bread when her iPhone buzzed in her handbag.

'McCormey here,' said a weary voice, and carried on more tartly: 'Let me guess. You've drawn a map of where the girls are buried in Underwood. An area where nothing has been found despite twenty years of searching. A remote corner that was simply overlooked by hundreds of volunteers and professionals. Or perhaps you have a confession from a brand-new source proving it wasn't William Hickley who killed the girls?'

'No. I don't.'

'Well, in any case, please do send me an email about your undoubtedly fascinating revelations. You'll find a link if you go on to our website at –'

'I think I've found his suitcase.'

There was silence down the other end. McCormey cleared his throat.

'What did you say your name was?'

Nora introduced herself again.

'OK, Miss Sand. That's a new one. And how did you come into possession of a suitcase belonging to a man who was locked up in the last millennium?'

Nora briefly explained how and where she had found and bought the suitcase, and how she had later discovered Bill Hix's name on its side.

'With all due respect, Miss Sand. I know what you journalists are like, you love a good story. God help us. But seriously, any mentally disturbed person could have written "Hix" on the side of that suitcase. It was probably never even in William Hickley's possession. We did ransack his home,' McCormey pointed out.

'No, I understand that,' Nora said. 'It's just that the suitcase contained photographs. Pictures of young women.'

Down the other end McCormey went quiet again. She could hear the rustling of paper in the background.

'I can meet with you tomorrow morning at eleven thirty. Make sure you're on time. I'll give you thirty minutes to convince me. Bring the suitcase.'

'Thank you,' Nora said. 'I'll see you tomorrow.'

She bought her sourdough, nipped into the greengrocers for watermelon and fresh peas, and then called Pete on impulse.

'Fancy coming over tonight, darling?'

Pete heaved a melodramatic sigh. 'How long have we known each other?'

'Eh … five years, something like that,' Nora ventured.

'And to your knowledge during that time have I ever – and I repeat, ever – not watched live football matches on the telly when we're in London?'

Nora slapped her forehead. Of course. 'When does it start?'

'Kick-off is at eight o'clock.'

'Then come round for an early supper. I'll cook risotto. Bring your camera and you won't have to wash up.'

'And you'll let me leave in time for the pub? Promise?'

'Scouts honour,' she assured him.

'Were you ever even a Girl Scout?'

'Call yourself an Australian? You should be into rugby and cricket, not football.'

'See ya later, Sheila,' he said in his broadest Crocodile Dundee accent and rang off.

Using the Anglepoise lamp as a spotlight, Nora made Pete take pictures of the suitcase from every imaginable angle. Afterwards she placed the Polaroids on the table, one after the other, so that he could photograph them as well.

She had a hunch that McCormey would want to keep them when he – like her – became convinced that they had once belonged to a serial killer.

7

She reached Platform 30 at Charing Cross Station seconds before a whistle signalled the doors were closing. The Northern Line service had been as irregular as it was most mornings, and the tube train, which was supposed to have gone via Charing Cross, had suddenly changed destination to Bank, so she had to jump out and change at Euston. It had cost her at least ten precious minutes.

She had still had five minutes before departure when she reached Charing Cross, and there would have been ample time to buy newspapers and a cup of coffee, if it hadn't been for a tourist in the queue, who didn't know how to speak coffee.

'So does that mean that a grande is the biggest coffee, or is that the venti? And is it possible to get an Americano with milk?' the man wanted to know while the line of morning-weary Londoners lengthened behind him.

Nora tried to stay calm as she waited with *The Times* and the *Guardian* tucked under her arm and the correct money in her hand. When her turn finally came, it was two minutes before departure and she had to sprint to the train, balancing the macchiato, newspapers and the bin liner into which she, for want of anything better, had put the suitcase.

She flopped on to her seat, opened the *Guardian* and realised immediately why McCormey had sounded exceptionally stressed the day before: 'New Chinese tragedy in Dover,' the paper announced over a picture of something that looked like a refrigerated lorry from the Netherlands.

She quickly scanned the story. It was just as familiar as it was sad. A group of Chinese people had tried to reach the promised land of Great Britain by hiding behind tomatoes in a refrigerated lorry. Something had gone terribly wrong. Either the driver had been unaware of his cargo, or he had forgotten to stop and give his stowaways some fresh air. When heat-seeking equipment revealed their presence on the ferry, it was too late for more than half the group that had dreamt of a better life.

Seven had died from a lack of oxygen and five, who were suffering from frostbite and shock, had been admitted to hospital for observation. The police had no comments as to how close they were to catching the human traffickers behind the tragedy.

The Times had relegated the story to page three; however, it carried an incandescent editorial about how France's wishy-washy immigration policy had created a problem that the French were dumping on Great Britain in their typically underhand manner.

'Until we show our so-called friends in Europe that we are not the rubbish bin for the continent, we have to rely on border police, border police and more border police,' the paper thundered.

Such views irritated her, and she reminded herself yet again that it was a bad idea to read editorials in the morning. She sipped her coffee and stared out at the soft, green hills rolling past. It looked like yet another warm summer's day. Just like yesterday, when seven people died from cold and a lack of oxygen.

Dover police were housed in a surprisingly well-maintained, redbrick building in the centre of Dover. Nora turned up at reception, showed her press card and was asked to wait.

She sat on a hard wooden chair while she looked around the room. A *Crimestoppers* poster with a freephone number dominated the noticeboard. Next to it was a picture of a broken little girl lying on the tarmac with blood trickling out of her mouth. 'Don't drink and drive' it said in red letters above her. Below was a photocopy of what appeared to be a leaflet from the Home Office. 'Know your rights' it said in every known language from Chinese to Russian.

A uniformed female police officer with red hair entered the room and looked around for Nora.

'Detective Inspector McCormey is ready to see you now,' she said in a formal tone of voice and led Nora through a corridor, up some stairs and down a passage. At the end she knocked carefully on the closed door.

'Yes?' they heard.

They entered. McCormey was sitting behind his desk. Three staff sat in front of him. Two of them clearly police officers plus a third man whom Nora took to be a newly recruited press officer. His hair was too long and his suit a tad too well fitting for him to belong to the forces of law and order.

'Miss Sand. We're just finishing. Has someone offered you tea?' McCormey asked.

The redhead disappeared and returned soon afterwards with two mugs filled to the brim with milky tea.

The three staff rose to their feet.

'Briefing at twelve noon at the Port Office,' one of them said, and clicked his pen.

'Twelve noon,' McCormey repeated and closed the door behind them.

Nora quickly sized him up and compared him to the man from the Bill Hix case. The years had left their marks. His hair had gone grey and he had gained a little weight, but his gaze was just as intense and he looked like someone who kept in respectable shape and took care of his health.

As if to confirm Nora's thoughts, he pulled open a drawer and took out a shiny green Granny Smith apple.

'Please excuse me. I always get hungry this time in the morning,' he said, and sank his teeth into the apple.

He seemed more approachable in person than he had on the telephone.

'OK, Miss Sand. You're here about Hickley. You have my full attention … And twenty-five minutes,' he said, glancing at his wristwatch.

Without further ado Nora handed him the bin bag with the suitcase. He placed it on the table.

'One suitcase – as promised.'

He examined it closely.

'More specifically a suitcase with the name Bill Hix on the side,' he stated with forced neutrality and shrugged his shoulders. 'As I said to you yesterday, it could belong to anyone.'

Nora produced the envelope with the Polaroids from her bag and handed them to McCormey. He opened a drawer in his desk, rummaged around and found a pair of thin, white latex gloves, which he put on before he opened the envelope.

He looked at Nora. 'I presume that you've touched the pictures,' he said with a hint of reproach in his voice.

Nora nodded. 'I didn't know they might be evidence. In fact, they fell out of the suitcase, so I had to pick them up,' she explained.

'Hmm. Before you leave, tell reception you need fingerprinting,' he said, and took out the pictures.

Nora had counted them last night. There were twelve in total, and James McCormey arranged them in a calm and measured way as if he were a croupier in a casino dealing cards for blackjack. Three ruler-straight rows of four pictures in each.

He took his time scrutinising every single photograph, every single face, before his gaze moved on to the next. Finally he looked up and shook his head sadly.

'Unfortunately, Miss Sand, I don't recognise a single one of these girls. I'm sure you're an honest person, and that's why I'll be honest with you: that investigation haunted me from the moment I was assigned to it. I had fifteen tongues and no bodies. If you knew how many weekends, how many hours and months I've spent walking through Underwood with and without sniffer dogs. How many missing persons files I've reviewed, and how many grieving parents

I have visited. Then you would also know how much of my life this case has consumed. Even when the case was officially closed and Hickley went to prison, and everyone congratulated me and patted me on the shoulder, I couldn't let it go. When there were no more man hours left in the budget, I investigated it in my own time,' McCormey said.

Nora could see a vein throb in his forehead, but the Detective Inspector pulled himself together with a deep breath and changed his voice to a softer pitch.

'I'll even be honest enough, Miss Sand, to admit to you that the case nearly cost me my marriage, and that I would probably still be working on it, if a farsighted boss hadn't forced me to transfer to London, and later here to Dover. Now I try to catch human traffickers rather than killers. Although sometimes the two are the same.'

McCormey remembered the half-eaten apple in his hand and tossed it into the bin under his desk as if he had lost his appetite merely by talking about the case.

'My point is, I understand completely why you would think the pictures were connected to the Hickley investigation. They're the same type of photos. But I'm telling you right now that if any of those girls had even the most tenuous connection to that case, even the very faintest link, I would have remembered. Sometimes I have nightmares about all the young girls who never made it home. Your suitcase probably belongs to some joker with a penchant for the macabre. It wouldn't surprise me if these girls are all alive and well somewhere out there.'

Nora produced from her bag a copy of the picture of Lisbeth and Lulu, which Magnus had scanned for her at *Globalt*. 'How about these two? Have you seen them in connection with the case?'

McCormey narrowed his eyes as he studied the picture. Then he shook his head.

'They came from Denmark, they disappeared on the ferry to Harwich, and they've never been found. Do you remember the case?'

McCormey shook his head again. 'No, I'm afraid not. They weren't on our radar during the Hickley investigation, this much I can tell you. Besides, there are two of them in the picture, so it falls outside his normal pattern.'

'Could it be a copycat?' Nora said, returning the picture to her bag.

'I doubt it has any significance. All those girls couldn't just vanish into thin air without somebody noticing,' he said.

Nora kept her mouth shut to encourage him to continue.

'OK,' he said with a deep sigh, gathered up the twelve pictures, returned them to the envelope and pulled off his gloves with a snap. 'I'll get someone to look into the whereabouts of these girls, if only to confirm that they're safe and sound. The Hickley case is closed, the man is in prison, and I don't have the resources to reopen the investigation. Certainly not on a Dover budget. But I know a man in London who might want to take a look at it. His name is Jeff Spencer, but don't call him. He never takes calls from reporters. He'll call you if he has any questions, understand?'

There was a knock on the door, and the red-haired police officer popped round her head.

'Mrs Amijehan is here. This time with her interpreter,' she announced, while Nora gathered up her things and got up from the chair.

'One final question?'

McCormey looked at her with an impatient gaze.

'What was the name of Hickley's lawyer?'

His smile bordered on the sarcastic. 'Ah. That's easy because it's the most bizarre name I've ever heard in court: his name was Christian Cross. I remember thinking he ought to be a priest with that name.'

They shook hands, and she thanked him for his time.

'Thanks for the suitcase, Miss Sand. Call me in a week's time, but don't expect miracles. This is an old case.'

Mrs Amijehan was already on her way, wearing a colourful

lime green sari, a subdued-looking interpreter on her arm, when McCormey called out after Nora.

'Don't forget to get fingerprinted!'

8

The next morning Nora rang Cross Law Associates. They were easy to find on the internet, and Nora noted that the firm's offices were less than a stone's throw from Bow Street Magistrates Court. She asked for Christian Cross and was put through to a secretary whose well-modulated voice reminded her of a 1950s film star.

The secretary apologised sincerely, as if it were a loss to her personally that Mr Cross was currently in court, and not expected back until late afternoon.

'Would you be interested in speaking to young Mr Cross instead?'

'Eh?'

'Mr Christopher Cross. If it's a criminal case, I can assure you that Mr Christopher is just as successful as his father,' the secretary said.

'Actually, I would prefer to see Mr Christian.'

'Very well. He can see you tomorrow morning at eleven thirty here at his office. Bring the relevant papers.'

Nora was aware that it might be pushing it to let the secretary think she was a potential client, but she comforted herself by saying she hadn't said anything that wasn't true, and if she had introduced herself as a reporter interested in Bill Hix, she would probably have been offered an appointment the next working day in a month of Sundays that happened to coincide with a blue moon. That is, never.

She rang off and on the spur of the moment looked up the homepage of Brine Tourist Office, found the shopping section and clicked through ice cream parlours, antique dealers and potteries. It came as no surprise to her that the dilapidated shop where she had bought the suitcase didn't feature among those recommended by the Tourist Office as to how to spend your money in Brine.

She had forgotten the name of the shop, but remembered that it had been a few doors up from a mint-green and pink teashop with a large daisy above the door.

Google Street View had passed by it, and she recognised its grey, peeling-paint shopfront, not far from what turned out to be the Daisy Dairy Café. She searched the address, but as far as she could see there were no telephone numbers or names associated with the mysterious bric-a-brac shop in Seaview Street. Instead, she found the number for the Daisy Dairy Café, and rang it.

'Hello, this is café,' someone said in a heavy Russian accent.

Nora explained that she was looking for a phone number for the second-hand shop two doors further along.

'No telephone. No telephone,' said the woman on the other end.

'Please could I get you to leave them a message?' Nora asked hopefully.

'Mr Smithfield, he only come here sometimes,' the woman explained impatiently.

Eventually the woman agreed to note down Nora's mobile number and pop it through the letterbox.

It was worth a try. However, she couldn't guarantee that the woman would do what she had promised.

Afterwards Nora searched Directory Enquiries' website for any Smithfields in Brine to see if there might be a home address with a number. No results. 'Would you like to search for something else?' the computer asked.

Nora closed the laptop.

The next morning she got up a little earlier than usual, and took her time ironing one of her two remaining clean white shirts, while she listened to the news and as often before, considered hiring a cleaner.

As she looked at the pile of laundry and the film of smog on the windows, which was unavoidable when your windows faced London's traffic, the thought was tempting. But something stopped her from responding to one of the many notes stuffed through the letterbox by Polish or Hungarian women hoping to earn money for a better life.

She loathed spending her precious spare time on domestic duties, but hated even more the thought of letting a stranger into her territory and paying them for doing what she didn't want to do herself.

She carefully hung the shirt on a hanger, found her faithful navy blue jacket and skirt suit at the far end of her wardrobe and placed it on her bed. She had acquired it because in the UK there were many situations where your life was made a little easier if you donned a uniform.

She smiled at the memory of the day she had bought it in the summer sales at Harvey Nichols. Louise had come to London for some retail therapy, and when Nora stepped out of the changing rooms wearing the suit, Louise had bent double from laughter.

'Oh, excuse me, Miss, please would you point out the emergency exits again and demonstrate how to put on your lifejacket?' she had spluttered.

Nora had caught sight of her own reflection in the big mirror and conceded that Louise had a point. All she needed was pink lipstick and her hair up in a bun and she would be the perfect flight attendant. She couldn't help smiling at herself.

'Welcome to Nora Air. We hope you'll have a pleasant journey. In a moment we'll come through the cabin with an offer of a good thrashing.'

Ever since then the suit had been known as the 'Nora Air outfit' and today its job was to convince Christian Cross that a journalist was in fact the next innocent little lamb he should save from the clutches of the brutal English legal system.

X

The front office smelled of furniture polish and flowers. A woman, the owner Nora presumed of the film star voice from the telephone, was sitting behind a computer with a mug whose oval wedding portrait celebrated that the royal couple, Camilla Parker-Bowles and Prince Charles, were finally able to live happily ever after.

'Welcome, Miss Sand,' she said with an obliging smile. 'Please take a seat, Mr Cross will be ready for you in a few minutes.'

Nora made herself comfortable on the Chesterfield. On the low table in front of her three newspapers looked as if they had just been ironed by an invisible butler.

She was lost in an *Economist* editorial about the faltering economy of Congo when she heard noises behind the heavy oak door that she presumed led to Mr Cross's office.

The door opened and a man in his mid-thirties appeared wearing a suit fitting him so perfectly, he might as well have been holding a sign saying Savile Row.

Nora peered up from the magazine. The man's hair was blond and his eyes light grey; more than anything, he looked like a lawyer in a commercial, the type used to sell exclusive chocolate, car insurance, or Armani suits.

He acknowledged her presence and nodded briefly, before he turned around and addressed the open office door. 'Goodbye, father. I'll see you for lunch in the club on Thursday.'

'Mr Cross will see you now,' the secretary said, and got up.

Christian Cross was sitting behind a desk Nora estimated to be the size of her bathroom. The green, deep-pile carpet in the office absorbed all sound like a piece of kitchen towel soaks up a glass of spilled milk.

The walls were covered with leather panels and paintings depicting an earlier age where foxhunting was not only legal, but also the preferred hobby of many affluent rural Brits. The painter had lingered on the pack of foxhounds and men in Pink coats with hunting horns, and on the horses that would eventually carry their riders to a fox which, after hours of being chased, would collapse from exhaustion and be torn to pieces by the dogs.

'Do you hunt, Miss Sand?'

The voice was deep and melodic, as male voices can be after years of marinating in vintage brandy and Havana cigars. The emerging pot belly, which not even the exquisitely tailored suit could hide, bore evidence that several good dinners had preceded the cigars.

Nora shook her head. 'My work rarely allows me time to get out into the country,' she said in a neutral tone.

'What a shame. I have a small place in Wiltshire. It makes London bearable,' Christian Cross said amicably.

Nora concluded that the lawyer's view and her own of what constituted a small place probably diverged.

Pleasantries out of the way, Christian Cross picked up a fountain pen from the desk and leaned back in his chair. 'I gather it's a matter of urgency. How can I be of service?'

Nora took a deep breath and jumped right into it. 'William Hickley.'

It was as if windscreen wipers swept across Christian Cross's face. The amicable smile disappeared and was instantly replaced by a frosty expression.

'I can't deny that I was – and still am – William Hickley's solicitor. That's a matter of public record. But I have nothing further to add,' the lawyer said, sounding slightly put out. 'But seeing that you're here, and have already wasted both your time and mine, I would be interested to know why you want to ask about a client who is obviously protected by attorney-client privilege?' he added.

'I represent *Globalt*, a Danish magazine, and I'm hoping that you can set up a meeting between your client and me,' Nora said frankly.

Honesty is usually the best course. At least when you already have one foot in the door.

When Christian Cross chuckled, the laughter came right from his belly with a deep bass.

'You could have saved yourself the journey,' he said, while he shook his head at her absurd suggestion.

'I can't categorically deny your request on behalf of my client. I'll pass it on, of course. But this much I can tell you: a few years ago the *Sun* offered William Hickley fifty thousand pounds to tell his story. He turned them down point-blank. He was so offended he even refused to meet with the journalist to negotiate the amount upwards. But perhaps your Danish editor has deeper pockets than the *Sun*,' he said with more than a hint of irony in his voice.

Nora thought how the Crayfish squirmed on the rare occasions he was asked to sign a receipt for more than a hundred and fifty pounds.

'You can tell your client we don't pay. But I have information about his two Danish girls.'

'I beg your pardon – what Danish girls?'

Nora shrugged. 'I'm sorry. That's confidential information I couldn't possibly share with anyone expect William Hickley,' she said in exactly the same pompous tone of voice that the lawyer had just used himself.

Obvious irritation flitted across Christian Cross's face. 'Very well. I'll make sure that your message is passed on to Mr Hickley,' he said, tight-lipped. 'But don't forget that I was present throughout his trial. No Danish girls were involved in the case. None. They were all British,' he pointed out and stood up abruptly from behind his desk.

He was shorter than she had expected, Nora saw as she handed him her business card. Christian Cross glanced at it briefly.

'And now, Miss Sand, we should not take up any more of each other's time,' he said firmly, and walked towards the door.

'When do you think I can expect to hear from you?' Nora asked politely.

'It so happens that we're in the process of preparing a new hearing regarding a release on parole or at least a transfer to a different prison. If the British authorities won't budge, it might be a breach of his human rights. And then we have a case. Would your magazine be interested in covering that story?' he asked, before answering his own question a second later. 'Oh, you wouldn't? I hadn't expected you to, either. I'm meeting Mr Hickley next week. Until then I would prefer not to have to deal with any more bizarre attempts to muddy the waters. You'll be contacted in due course, but if I were you, I would lower my expectations quite considerably and start looking for another story. Have a good day,' he said, and flung open the door.

'Mrs Metcalfe, please would you get me Sir Howard on the phone?' he said. Her audience was over.

Shortly afterwards she was back in the street. She took out her mobile. It was almost lunchtime and the Cross office was within walking distance of Scotland Yard. Andreas didn't answer his mobile, but she left a message and three minutes later, he called her back.

9

His lunch break started in twenty minutes; Nora secured provisions from the nearest Pret A Manger – chicken sandwiches, apple juice and fruit salad – and took up position right underneath Scotland Yard's triangular sign.

Andreas emerged from the revolving door wearing a dark grey suit, talking to a colleague. Seeing him look so mature and professional made her warm to him. Like a stranger she would like to get to know better. He glanced around and smiled broadly when he spotted her.

They walked to St James's Park and found a grassy spot in the shade under an old oak tree. Nora cursed her skirt as she tried folding her legs to find a delicate compromise between comfort and decency. When she had finally wriggled into place, they attacked the food.

'Caught any terrorists yet?' she said in between mouthfuls.

Andreas hesitated while his gaze lingered on a couple of teenagers across from them. They looked as if they intended to test how far two people could actually go in a public place without being arrested for indecency. Quite a long way it would appear, Nora noted to herself.

'Hello? Am I disturbing anything?'

Andreas looked at her with an expression in his eyes she couldn't define.

'I can't discuss my work.'

'You're kidding me?'

'No. If I tell you, I'm afraid I'm going to have to kill you,' he declared with a poker face.

She slapped his shoulder, but couldn't help grinning. 'You idiot. And here was I thinking I might invite you to the seaside this weekend.'

Andreas raised his eyebrows. 'Really?'

'So, it's partly work. I need to check something in a coastal village called Brine. But I thought we might turn it into a trip. That is, if you still like swimming in the sea?'

The invitation had poured out of her without her thinking it through.

As teenagers, they had gone swimming nearly every morning. In the sea during the summer, in the swimming pool in the winter. But after Andreas's embarrassing declaration of love, they had avoided each other for more than a decade. Nora shrugged. It was a long time ago, it no longer mattered.

She gazed across the lake and noticed the many au pairs, who had congregated with buggies in the sunshine, along with tourists and office workers on their breaks.

'Is this about the girls from the England ferry?' he asked after a long pause.

Nora nodded.

'OK. I was supposed to go to Liverpool this weekend with a friend to watch a football match, but he called off. So, I'm game,' he said.

Nora's thoughts ran wild, and in her mind's eye she suddenly saw Andreas sitting on the edge of a four-poster bed in a darkened room with closed curtains in a hotel in Brine. She imagined his face as she reached out her hands to unbutton his white shirt. One button at a time.

As if he could read her thoughts, he turned his head and looked into her eyes for longer than was polite.

Then guitar riff from 'Smoke on the Water' ripped the air apart. The sound was coming from Andreas's jacket pocket and he fumbled awkwardly as he pulled out his mobile.

'Yes?' he said in a low voice.

Nora tried to control herself. What was she thinking? Andreas was Andreas, and there was absolutely no reason to change a formula that had worked for her for years.

After a few 'hmms' and a single 'right' Andreas ended his

conversation with 'Listen, now is not a good time. I'll call you tonight.'

Afterwards he refused to look her in the eye. Nora sipped her juice and feigned indifference as she studied a group of Japanese tourists whose meeting point, despite the sunshine, was a large, yellow brolly.

'That was Birgitte. My girlfriend. She also works for the police,' Andreas said after a lengthy pause.

Nora put on her best Botox smile. One of those where the intention is definitely there, but the muscles are frozen.

'Lovely. I'd like to meet her. Will she be coming to London?'

'I don't think so,' he said dismissively, scrunched up the sandwich packet and checked his watch. 'I'd better head back.'

Nora nodded and rose to her feet without too much protest from the uncooperative suit.

'Do you still have access to police databases at home?'

Andreas nodded.

'Please would you check what happened to Kurt Damtoft from Vestergården? I can't find him anywhere.'

'I'll look into it. See you Saturday.'

'Yep. I'll rent a car and pick you up,' Nora said in her most casual voice, and waved goodbye to him before making her way to the tube.

She kicked herself mentally all the way home. What the hell did she think she was doing? When she entered the flat, she nearly choked from the stuffy heat and the tight suit. She tore off her clothes and turned on the cold tap in the bathroom.

Five merciless minutes under a cold shower and a Coke Light straight from the fridge later, the world began to look more normal. She put on a pair of shorts and a moth-eaten T-shirt with a black-and-white picture of The Cure and a caption proclaiming that 'Boys Don't Cry', then sat down resolutely in front of her laptop and pulled out her notebook.

It was about time she wrote that obituary, but when she happened to come across an article on a Brussels top summit, she had a flashback to a school trip where she and Andreas had played truant and sneaked away from a Danish EU politician's never-ending lecture on the budgetary powers of the European Parliament, and had found a bar in the African quarter of the Belgian capital.

She rewound her memory to the small room with the hypnotic bongo drum rhythm and clear rum served in shot glasses with cane sugar and lime. Had they come close to having a moment that night? But then they had bumped into a group of drunken Brits who insisted on dragging them across the road to an Irish pub and their intimacy dissolved into partying, chaos and Guinness.

Had he wanted them to be more than friends even then?

Suddenly Nora knew what would help. She clicked on Skype, saw to her delight that Trine was online and called her old school friend.

Trine had turned her boundless capacity for empathy into a career and trained as a psychotherapist. Since publishing a couple of popular books on relationships, she had become something of an expert and one of those familiar faces TV journalists invite into their studios for softer stories. Trine always turned up with a red pout and thick, yellow plaits. That was her USP and it worked. Everyone remembered the relationship therapist with the Heidi plaits and the Marilyn Monroe lips, and Trine raked it in giving lectures and holding weekend workshops for broken-hearted Danes.

But to Nora she was still the chubby teenager who once threw up in her father's front garden on her way to a party before collapsing on top of her brand new glasses.

'Hello, gorgeous. Long time no see,' Trine said, turning on her webcam.

Nora could see that Trine was sitting on the terrace outside her holiday cottage near Rørvig. At the edge of the screen she could make out a glass of white wine.

'I'm just putting the finishing touches to my latest bestseller: *The Ins and Outs of Jealousy*. I've promised my publisher I'll deliver next week. I've dispatched Johannes and the kids to my mother-in-law in Sweden,' Trine explained, and lit a cigarette.

Nora shook her head. 'And you're still smoking?'

Trine giggled guiltily. 'Only on social occasions, as you can see. And this is a social occasion, isn't it? Is the smoke bothering you?' she said, deliberately blowing smoke straight at the screen.

Nora feigned a coughing fit.

'So, my friend. Found yourself an English gentleman yet? Please say you're calling to invite me to your wedding at a Scottish castle with kilts, bagpipes and the Loch Ness monster. I'm desperate for a break.'

Nora could feel herself blushing. 'Eh. No, I wouldn't say that,' she said.

'Right, then, what is it? Something's up. You know I can always tell,' Trine declared with expert confidence and sipped her wine.

Three seconds later, Nora was looking at a strange pattern of droplets across the screen. Trine had spluttered her wine everywhere at the utterance of a single word: Andreas.

'Are we talking about Andreas-Andreas? I mean, our Andreas? Andreas T. Jansson?' she asked when she had fetched some kitchen towel and dried the screen.

'Yes,' Nora sighed before launching into an account of how he had unexpectedly announced his arrival on Facebook, and later turned up in London. About St James's Park. About PC Perfect, as Nora had already decided to nickname Birgitte.

Trine shook her head when Nora finally paused for breath.

'Nora Sand. You have the world's worst timing!' she concluded. 'Didn't you know that man *pined* for you – and I use the word pined advisedly – from the moment he first met you?'

'No. Not really.'

'No, you didn't because you were blind! While you were messing about with that Salomon who played the saxophone, Andreas suffered in silence. He was so hard hit that everyone could see it. Everyone except you.'

'His name was Samuel and he played the clarinet,' Nora interjected meekly.

'Whatever.' Once she was in full flow, Trine was unstoppable.

'But why didn't anyone tell me?' Nora protested.

Trine counted her fingers. 'One: because it was obvious, it would be like telling you the sky is blue. Two: because it was Andreas's business if he wanted you to know. Three: hmm. There is no three.'

Nora rolled her eyes.

'You were the class soap opera. We even had bets on the outcome. I, for one, know that Markus lost a hundred kroner when Andreas finally plucked up the courage to tell you at Hanne's party, and you turned him down.'

Nora winced at the thought. Trine continued castigating her.

'And now – now of all times – you've finally noticed Andreas. Do you want to know what that's all about?'

Nora had a hunch that she didn't, but Trine was now in full psychoanalysis mood.

'You're attracted to unavailable men. And it wouldn't be the first time. Remember when we went Interrailing and you lusted after that blond Swede on Mykonos for a week? When he finally asked you out, you lost all interest. I think you have a built-in reluctance to commit. Otherwise you would have been paired off long ago. The only reason Andreas suddenly interests you, is because he's no longer available. That's your pattern,' Trine declared.

'But what if I was feeling this way before I even knew about Birgitte?' Nora objected.

'You probably sensed it subconsciously,' Trine opined. Nora nodded pensively.

'So it's just a fixation?'

'Yes. Sleep on it. It'll be gone tomorrow. Have a glass of wine. Who knows, it might even pass in thirty minutes,' Denmark's favourite couples' therapist promised her.

They said goodbye as always with a promise that it was about time to meet up, either in London, at Trine's holiday cottage or in Copenhagen.

Nora followed doctor's orders and found some leftover white wine in her fridge. It smelled sour, but after a few gulps, it didn't taste too bad. She stared down into the street, wondering if she should go food shopping, when a faint ping from her computer announced a new email.

It was from him.

Something fluttered inside her chest.

The email didn't contain ardent declarations of love. Just a short and direct message.

'Kurt Damtoft's last known address is with his daughter Liselotte Bruun, who lives in Søndervig. He has a criminal record, but has served his time,' Andreas wrote, before concluding his email with a functional: 'See you Saturday.'

See you? Was that really the best he could do? No love? No hugs? Just see you.

Nora shook her head as if hoping she could shake off thoughts of Andreas, and chanted a mantra, which had served her well in the past: *Get a grip*.

The man has a girlfriend. He's taken. Forbidden fruit.

Saturday was four days away. Four days and a trip to Denmark during which she had to get over him.

10

She regretted not calling in advance as she drove the rental car up in front of the glum, yellow brick bungalow on the outskirts of Søndervig.

It had been raining pretty much the whole time since she landed at Karup Airport in central Jutland, and it wasn't until she turned into Fjordvejen that the water masses retreated, only to lie across the sky like a leaden threat of more to come.

The front garden was covered in coarse yellow grass, and by the front door there was a blue ceramic pot with a withered plant that might once have been a widow's-thrill.

The house looked as if no one had lived there for months. Nora walked up to the door and pressed the doorbell without getting her hopes up.

Shortly afterwards the door was opened by a gangly boy of about thirteen. He was wearing an Iron Maiden T-shirt and tight, black stretch jeans that highlighted his stork legs.

He said nothing. Just stared quizzically at her.

'Erm. I'm looking for Liselotte Bruun. Does she live here?' Nora said.

He looked her up and down. 'Are you from the council?' he wanted to know.

Nora shook her head.

'She's in her studio,' he said at length and made to close the door.

Nora had time to jam the door with her foot. 'And where's that?'

He stared at her as if she had just announced that she didn't know where Ringkøbing was, or that the North Sea was wet.

'Liselotte's Pottery Studio. In the high street. There's just the one,' he said with a roll of his eyes.

She found it straight away. The white painted building lay slightly recessed from the road connecting the high street to the holiday homes area, but the big sign was impossible to miss. The shop was filled with blue glazed pots similar to the one by the front door, lidded casserole dishes and jugs with *Søndervig* written in black. A handwritten sign in the window announced that they spoke German in the tourist season.

An old-fashioned bell rang when Nora opened the door.

She could hear noise coming from the back room, and soon afterwards a tired-looking, red-haired woman in her mid-forties appeared. She wiped her clay-stained hands on a dark blue apron.

'Yes?'

Nora was about to say something when the door opened again and a German couple entered the shop. Instead she went over to a stand with postcards of the traditional images that are sold across Denmark every summer: heather hearts, dunes, sunsets and lyme grass.

The woman served the couple in perfect German, and then turned to Nora: 'So, have you made up your mind yet?'

'I'm not here to buy anything. I'm looking for Kurt Damtoft. Do you know where he is?'

The woman's eyes narrowed, the expression around her mouth grew bitter and her body slumped.

'Well, good luck with that. Does he owe you money, too? Funny, you look too smart to lend money to a guy like him.' Her voice had hardened.

Nora shook her head. 'No. It's about an old story. I'm a reporter and I'm investigating what really happened to the girls from the England ferry,' she explained.

The woman seemed to deliberate for a moment, then she held out her hand. 'I'm Liselotte. You'd better come round to the back. There's coffee.'

Nora followed her into a room with a low ceiling and dominated by a large kiln. A wet lump of clay was sitting on a turntable, and there was a kettle and a couple of home-made mugs on a narrow Formica table by the room's only window.

Liselotte filled the kettle from a tap by the kiln, turned it on and found a crumpled packet of Marlboro Light in her pocket.

'I've only got instant,' she said.

'Never drink anything else,' Nora grinned.

Liselotte took a seat by the turntable, while Nora poured water into both mugs and sat down on a stool by the table.

Liselotte shaped the clay, the cigarette dangling from the corner of her mouth. A few quick turns later, she cut a jug from the turntable with a piece of wire and placed it on the shelf to dry next to eight other identical jugs.

Then she sat down on a battered olive-green office chair, the back of which creaked every time she moved.

'My dad. My dad. Well, what's there to say,' she said, taking a deep drag on her cigarette.

'He's an alcoholic. That's no secret, I guess. Steals anything that isn't nailed down to get money to buy booze. He no longer lives with us. We couldn't take any more, Malte and me.'

She heaved a sigh.

'The boy couldn't keep seeing his grandad going to the dogs like that. Towards the end we had to lock everything up. The telly. The stereo. Malte's PlayStation. He stole everything,' she said.

Nora looked at her. 'That must have been hard.'

'Worst thing is, it was that case that tipped him over the edge. Before that he used to like a strong beer from time to time, sure. But after those two girls went missing and he was charged with negligence because he had had a couple of elephant beers on the ferry, it was as if he gave up completely. He started drinking every single day.'

Liselotte blew on her coffee then sipped it. 'My mum pissed off soon afterwards. We haven't seen her since she met a bus driver and moved to Germany.'

Nora guided her back to the story. 'Do you remember anything from back then – anything about the girls?'

Liselotte laughed with derision. 'What do you think? We lived at Vestergården in a flat that came with the job, and my dad insisted on treating every single one of those losers as if they were family. At least once a week they would come round for dinner. The only one who ever thought it was a great idea was my dad,' she snorted.

'I was the same age as Lisbeth and Lulu, and I was supposed to have gone with them to London. But my mum said no. She didn't want me mixing with people like that more than I had to.'

'What were the girls like?' Nora asked.

'Lulu was as meek as a lamb. I believe that her mum had been drinking heavily while she was pregnant, so Lulu was a bit dim. Don't get me wrong, she wasn't retarded, but she wasn't the sharpest knife in the drawer, either. I remember one of the boys made her think you could get a tan from sitting in front of the test card on the telly, so she did that for a couple of nights wearing only her knickers, until my dad found out.'

'Now Lisbeth, on the other hand. Lisbeth was a bitch. Cold, calculating and terrifying. If she found out you had a weakness, then she would chip, chip, chip away at it until you felt like shit.'

Liselotte touched her red hair subconsciously. 'Now for me it was my red hair, of course. But for some of the bigger boys it wasn't just their appearance. She had picked up some information about their home life and she knew how to press all the right buttons. There was one guy, Erik, whose mum was a junkie and a hooker. And then there was Oluf's dad, who was a paedophile and in prison. She never let them forget it. And she was so devious that the grown-ups rarely found out. A whispered comment here and there, a sly glance. She was actually quite good-looking, but she was just as rotten on the inside as she was pretty on the outside. I don't think my dad ever really realised how bad things were with her.'

The forgotten cigarette in the ashtray had turned to ashes. Liselotte stubbed it out and lit a fresh one.

'I only went to my dad about her once. I had got a boyfriend by then, his name was Jens. I'd met him in the youth club and I really fancied him; I had invited him home for the first time. That night I had my first kiss,' she said with an embittered expression around her mouth.

'Lisbeth must have seen him turn up on his Puch Maxi, and waited for him to leave. I don't know what she said to him, but he never came back. I was distraught. Later she told me gleefully how she had dragged him into the bushes in the back garden, and that they had done it in full view of my bedroom while I was sitting behind the blinds dreaming about him and doodling in my diary. We were only fifteen. Jens, of course, denied everything, but he wouldn't look me in the eye, and I knew that Lisbeth was telling the truth. I tried to speak to my dad about it, but he just said that's love when you're young, and that we would probably work it out amongst ourselves. But Lisbeth wasn't in love with Jens. She just wanted to ruin it for me. Have something that was mine.'

'What happened to Jens?' Nora was keen to know.

'Not a lot. And Lisbeth dropped him like a hot brick. She let him know he was immature and that their fling in the back garden had been a mistake. Now he's married with two kids. Works for Vestas.'

'Do you know anything about Lisbeth's or Lulu's families?'

Liselotte shook her head. 'No details. I know that Lulu's dad lives somewhere in Copenhagen. Lisbeth's parents died when she was little, I believe. My dad might remember something. But then you'd better catch him before he gets too wasted,' she said, checking her watch. 'The Lamp opens in half an hour. That's your best bet. I think he lives in one of the holiday cottages with a woman called Jytte, but I don't know exactly where. Sometimes it's best not to know too much.' She smiled grimly.

'Do you know what happened to the others who went on the trip?'

Liselotte shook her head again. 'Nah. It all happened so fast once Social Services closed Vestergården. I mean, I know that one teacher died from cancer a few years later – and I think the other one moved to Australia. And I guess the kids were sent to other institutions. But

God only knows where they are now. In jail, I'd guess, most of them. They were heading that way.'

Nora drank the rest of her coffee. It had grown cold and bitter. 'Thanks for the brew,' she said and made to get up.

'Is this going in the paper?' Liselotte wanted to know.

'Well,' Nora hesitated. 'If I use it in an article, I promise to call you first and check the quotes. Is that all right?'

Liselotte nodded silently, returned to the turntable and chucked a lump of clay on to it.

'You don't mind seeing yourself out, do you?'

X

Nora treated herself to a quick trip to the North Sea before she went to the pub. She weaved her way through clusters of tourists, ice cream parlours and seaside shops hawking everything from plastic shovels to sarongs and water pistols. Once she had climbed the dunes, she felt serenity kick in.

You never knew just how much you missed the North Sea until you stood right in front of it, feeling infinitely small.

Along the English coast the Brits had their piers with fruit machines, bright lights and stalls selling candyfloss. Beaches where you could have a ten-minute donkey ride, and where children were so boisterous their parents were forced to scream and shout. Beaches where people dumped tons of rubbish every single day, and where it seemed only natural to munch your way through takeaway food and inflict your passion for techno on everybody else.

A Danish beach would be regarded as busy if you could make out one other person in the distance. Nora slipped off her sandals, carried them in her hands, and felt the icing-sugar sand between her toes.

So Lisbeth was no angel. Might she have been killed by someone she knew? Had she crossed the line once too often? Had she been a bitch to the wrong person? Was it possible that Bill Hix had absolutely nothing to do with her disappearance? But then what was her picture doing in his suitcase? And where did Lulu fit into all of this?

Nora turned around and wandered back to the town.

X

The pub's official name was The Lantern, but to the locals the maritime overtones were pretentious nonsense cooked up for tourists; in the local dialect it was only ever known as 'The Lamp'.

A stale smell enveloped her the moment she opened the door. The room was dark, but behind the counter a middle-aged man was wringing out a dishcloth under the hot tap. He nodded to her before he started wiping the counter slowly and methodically. In the background, the popular 1970s musician John Mogensen expressed his musical opinion on living at number nine, Lonely Street.

Nora perched on one of the battered bar stools and ordered apple juice. The bartender nodded, found her a bottle of Rynkeby in the fridge, and opened it.

'Ice?'

'Yes, please.'

'I'm guessing you're not from around here,' he said as he put a glass filled to the brim with ice cubes on the counter.

'You can tell that simply because I ordered apple juice?' Nora said in disbelief.

'No. But trust me, none of the locals would waste twenty kroner on apple juice when you can buy two litres for the same money in Aldi in Hvide Sande,' he explained. 'Not that it's any of my business. But most people come here to drink,' he said, gesturing towards the beer kegs.

'I'm looking for Kurt Damtoft,' she explained.

The bartender grunted. 'Have you been talking to Liselotte?'

Nora nodded.

'She's a good kid. It's a real shame that –'

The door was flung open with a crash. A slightly overweight woman in leopard leggings and a black, tight-fitting, low-cut top marched in. Her hair had been bleached, but her roots were showing, and the hoops dangling from her ears were big enough for a parrot to perch in each of them, without the wearer noticing.

'Bugger me, I'm thirsty, Sjønne. A pint and a chaser, please,' she demanded.

Sjønne was ahead of her. He had already lined up the pint and was busy pouring Nordsøolie into a shot glass. Glancing at Nora, he kept the bottle in mid-air.

'So, how about it, Jytte, do you want me to pour Kurt's at the same time?'

'Yes, go on. He'll be here in a minute.'

Nora could see that Kurt wasn't particularly drunk when he arrived, but also that he was hell-bent on remedying that situation as quickly as possible. It was essential to catch him now.

'Are you Kurt Damtoft?' she asked with no introduction.

He peered up at her suspiciously. 'Who's asking?'

'My name is Nora Sand. I'm writing about the girls from the England ferry.'

'Bugger off. That old story. I don't want to talk about it.'

'Fair enough,' Nora said, turning to the bartender. 'I think Kurt would like another beer and a chaser. I'm buying.'

Kurt scowled for a moment. 'And Jytte,' he then said.

'And Jytte,' Nora agreed.

The woman in Kurt Damtoft's life took her drinks and went to play on one of the fruit machines. He let out a deep and heartfelt sigh before he knocked back his Nordsøolie in one smooth movement, and looked across to Nora.

'So, what do you want to know?'

One and a half hours and four rounds later, Kurt Damtoft reminded Nora more than anything of a tangled-up cassette tape. Some of the things he said made sense, while others sounded like incoherent muttering and meaningless noise.

Nora looked down at her notepad. She had listed the names of the other six youngsters who had been on the fatal journey.

Bjarke Helgaard
Oluf Mikkelsen
Erik Hostrup
Sonny Nielsen
Jeanette Viola Tobis
Anni Olsen

Below she had written 'Viborg? Mikkelsgården?' It was the name of the town and the care home Kurt Damtoft believed most of the young people would have been transferred to when Vestergården was closed.

'To be honest with you, I couldn't bear to be part of closing it down. Watching my life's work crumble in front of my eyes. In the end, I just walked away from it all – it got too much for me. Do you understand?' he said in one of his more lucid moments.

Nora tried keeping him anchored in reality, but it was a losing battle. She realised now why Kurt Damtoft had never featured in the TV documentary about the girls.

'Do you remember anything about Lisbeth's or Lulu's families? Where they were from?'

Kurt Damtoft turned to her and stared at her with glassy eyes.

'My girls aren't dead. They've just gone out for a while,' he rambled. 'Why would you think that?'

'Because they sent me a postcard … I think,' he slurred.

'Is that right? Do you still have it?' Nora asked, unable to hide her scepticism.

'I got bugger all left of anything,' Kurt Damtoft said, turning towards the fruit machine. 'Jytte! I want go home now!' he shouted over the music.

Nora took her leave politely, settled her not-inconsiderable bar bill and asked for a receipt, knowing full well that the chances of the Crayfish reimbursing her were minimal.

'What happened to Vestergården?' she asked the bartender while he sorted out her change.

He shrugged. 'The place has been vacant for years. A few years ago there was talk of turning it into a kind of conference and holiday centre. Then the financial crisis happened. I don't even know who owns it these days. The council, I guess.'

'Where exactly is it?'

He wiped the counter again as if it was the most important job of the day. Took his time before he replied.

'Lyngvej. Third road on your left when you drive towards Ringkøbing. It's some way into the plantation.'

Nora thanked him and left him a shiny twenty kroner coin by way of a tip.

X

As she got into the car, Big Ben chimed from the bottom of her handbag.

'Yes, boss?'

'How do you always know it's me?' the Crayfish wanted to know.

'Modern technology has come a long way in recent years,' she said enigmatically.

'Hmm. Am I getting my money's worth out of you?'

Nora outlined her efforts so far.

'What happened to the English lead? Anything from Hickley's lawyer?'

'Not yet. He isn't meeting with his client until later this week.'

'What about Hickley's old mother – is she still alive?'

'Good point, I don't know.'

'Hmm. Call Emily in Research. She might be able to get you something on the other kids from Vestergården.'

Nora said goodbye and did as she was told.

Emily had started as an intern in the dawn of time, but had found working for *Globalt* infinitely more attractive than a job at a public library and had become a full-time employee after finishing her librarianship training. In addition to running the electronic newspaper archive, she researched everything from Swedish prostitution legislation to the number of nursery places in Roskilde council to the average wage in Indonesia – or any other bizarre question journalists might happen to ask.

'Helgaard, maybe. Hostrup, possibly. Tobis, probably. Nielsen, Mikkelsen and Olsen – forget it. Their surnames are too common,' she said. 'I'll call when I have something. Remind me of your mobile number, will you?'

Nora gave it to her, and headed for Ringkøbing.

She found Lyngvej easily. A narrow cart road led to a pine plantation, and the tall grass between the cart tracks revealed that this place no longer had daily or even weekly visitors.

The road bent and she pulled up in front of the house that had once been Vestergården. A main building that must have been the original farmhouse, and two typical 1970s concrete extensions, painted dark red in a failed attempt to match them to the main house. Two sacks of cement were lying in the yard. One had a hole in a corner and a little had spilled out. Abandoned scaffolding lay next to it.

Nora stopped her car and got out. In the silence that ensued she could hear the engine click as it cooled and a bird's furious squawk in the forest. The smell of resin, sea and heather lingered in the air. She held up her mobile to take some pictures and walked closer to the house. The greasy, salty air had obscured the windows. This was where Lisbeth and Lulu and the other teenagers had left one August day all those years ago. Full of dreams and hopes, and excited about their trip to London. A trip that would change the lives of all the broken souls who had ended up at Vestergården.

The flat where Kurt had lived with his family was in the main building. And the two extensions must have housed the boys and girls, respectively. Nora wandered around the main building and headed for a hill to get a better view of Vestergården.

The grass in the back garden was so tall that you would need a scythe if you were ever to turn it into a lawn again. Nora turned and looked back at the house; the window panes stared silently back at her. As she turned she sensed rather than saw it. A slight movement out of the corner of her eye. A glimpse of something darker than the rest of the window. She shook her head and dismissed the thought. But the next moment the darkness returned. There was someone inside the house. Was it inhabited after all? Nora looked around.

There was no sign of anyone. No cars, no bicycles. If someone had come here, it must have been on foot. She walked back, carefully approaching the house. Was that a face she had seen? Hidden behind the dark windows?

When she came closer, she could see she was looking through a kitchen window. She pushed her face right up to the glass and cupped her hands to shield against the sunlight. The kitchen sink was covered with clear plastic and on the kitchen table there was a plastic bucket with something that looked like dried paint. A coffee mug with a teaspoon sticking out of it was sitting next to it, and near the mug there was a large, rust-coloured splodge that looked like a handprint. There was another handprint on the once-white tiles on the wall by the sink. Was it blood? Nora narrowed her eyes and peered further into the kitchen. She tried wiping away the salty film with one hand, but succeeded only in smearing it across the glass.

She jumped when the crash of a door slamming rent the silence. Where had it come from? She started running to the other side of the house, but tripped and fell in the tall grass. When she got back on her feet, she heard the roar of a car engine. She raced back to the yard. The garage door had been opened and she just had time to see the back of a black 4x4 as it cornered the bend in the road. Her hands were shaking as she retrieved the car keys from her pocket and jumped into her car, but when she reached the main road, there was no sign of the black car anywhere in the flat landscape. It appeared to have vanished into thin air.

Nora tried to shake off the incident and looked up directions to Viborg on her mobile.

X

Her mobile rang an hour later. Nora pulled over and took Emily's call.

'Tobis died from a drug overdose five years ago. Her body was found by a tourist at Copenhagen Central Railway Station.'

Nora pulled the list out of her handbag and crossed her out.

'Helgaard, Bjarke. Now I can't guarantee it's the same guy, but his name pops up in connection with several biker gang cases. He's the spokesman for a Chapter on Nørrebro. A beefcake on steroids, judging by the pictures. Hostrup. Now that was interesting. There's a Hostrup Gallery in Copenhagen. The owner is listed as E. Hostrup. Then there's a teacher from Kolding, also called E. Hostrup. And someone called E. Hostrup lives in Hedehusene, but currently is in prison for watching child porn on the internet.'

Bingo, Nora thought.

Now only Anni Olsen, Sonny Nielsen and Oluf Mikkelsen remained. Perhaps they would know more about them at Mikkelsgården.

'Ah, yes about that. Mikkelsgården is still an institution for young people. The warden is called Jette Kvist. She's able to meet with you tomorrow morning at ten, but warns you in advance that she can't or won't discuss individual cases. No matter how ancient they are. I'll text you the address,' Emily said in her usual staccato style.

Nora managed one question before Emily hung up. 'Please would you check something else for me?'

'Yes. What is it?'

'Vestergården. Lyngvej with a Ringkøbing postcode. Who owns it – any information from the Land Registry office?'

'Give me five minutes.'

Nora took the chance to stretch her legs while she waited. She managed barely four minutes of exercise.

'The local council owns it. Again. They bought it back for next to nothing from a construction company two years ago. That company had bought it from the council for almost twice that amount only the previous year. Clever council. The construction company, however, went bankrupt.'

'And would you happen to know the name of the construction company?'

'Funny, I had a hunch you were going to ask. It was called Feriehuset ApS. A private limited company now dissolved. However, directors included gallery owner Erik Hostrup. I mention it merely because I came across his name earlier.'

'Emily, remind me why you're not a journalist?'

'Oh, it's too dull,' she said and rang off.

Nora checked her rear-view mirror before rejoining the motorway, but slammed on the brakes when she spotted the black 4x4 again. It was driving steadily towards the layby where she was parked. And then it carried on.

She craned her neck trying to see the driver, but the windows were tinted and the registration plate covered in mud. She could just about make out the outline of the letter K and the number seven.

Not even Emily could work her magic with so little information. That is, if it even was the same car.

11

The name Mikkelsgården conjured up an image of the sort of thatched farm that ought to feature in a 1950s Danish family film starring a very young Ghita Nørby. The reality was more like the film set for 1970s East German social realism. As she turned into the drive, she saw grey, badly maintained concrete that had started to crumble, and tiny windows that gave the building a menacing look.

'All visitors must report to reception without exception,' a bright yellow sign announced, the only source of colour in the grey landscape.

Nora checked her watch and strangled a yawn. It was five minutes to ten. She had had a rotten night's sleep at a hotel. She cursed the hotel tradition of tucking sheets and blankets in so tightly under the mattress that you either had to tear everything apart or accept sleeping like a butterfly skewered on a pin in a display cabinet.

She had fallen asleep during the late DR2 News and woken up around three in the morning with pins and needles in her legs from the stranglehold of the sheet. Once she had got out of bed in order to make it more comfortable, she found it practically impossible to get back to sleep.

She couldn't remember the origins of the fairy tale where a man is told he can have all the riches in the world, but the only condition is he mustn't think about a tiger. An impossible task, of course. When you put all your effort into *not* thinking about a tiger, you have already failed.

That was the way it was with Andreas now. The only thing she didn't want to think about was him. And the only subject her thoughts kept churning over was him. She tried talking herself to sleep. Listing every state in the US alphabetically, wondering about meeting Bill Hix, phrasing the questions she would ask him in his cell if he ever agreed to see her. But when she wasn't thinking about Andreas, she was obsessing about PC Perfect.

It wasn't until five o'clock in the morning that she had finally nodded off, dreaming restless dreams about big, blond Valkyries chasing after her with police truncheons. It had taken thirty painful seconds under the cold shower to bring her partly back to life.

She found a liquorice lozenge in her jacket pocket, locked the car and rang the reception bell.

Shortly afterwards she was ushered into Jette Kvist's office behind the second glass door in a long corridor covered with dark green institutional linoleum.

A framed poster for Tunø Jazz Festival hung above the desk, and below it sat a petite woman with horn-rimmed glasses and a long, dark plait down her back, munching a cheese sandwich.

'Nora Sand?' she said, struggling to finish chewing. 'Please excuse me, but I get up at six in the morning, so I'm always starving at this hour. Tea? I only have green tea. Will that do?'

Nora asked for a glass of water and was given it quickly and cold from the tap.

'You're here about the children from Vestergården?'

Nora nodded.

'I want to help you as much as I can. But we need to agree right now that none of what I say in this office ends up in *Globalt*.'

'I'll never quote you without permission,' Nora promised, hoping that would suffice.

Jette Kvist carefully wiped her fingers on a piece of kitchen towel, opened a desk drawer and produced a buff-coloured file.

'Five of them came here. Erik, Oluf, Sonny and Bjarke joined the boys' wing. Jeannette was two weeks away from turning eighteen when it happened, so she was allowed to go to Copenhagen on her own. But we also got Anni. Remember, she was only fourteen years old at the time.'

Jette Kvist looked up from the file. 'Now this is where it gets more complicated as to what I can tell you. Client confidentiality.'

'Does anyone here remember what happened when the children arrived? Were they upset? Were they keeping secrets? Did they ever mention Lulu or Lisbeth?' Nora pressed her.

Jette Kvist shook her head sadly. 'It's so many years ago now. Any staff who were here then have either retired or changed jobs. All I have to refer to are notes taken at the time.'

Again she looked at the file. 'There are some notes here, but I have to say they're of a highly personal nature. It's not information I have the right to pass on. But if it's any consolation, there's nothing which has any connection to that case, in my opinion,' she said.

At that moment her mobile buzzed on her desk. Jette Kvist reached out for it and checked the display. 'I have to take this call. It's my child's nursery.'

She took the phone, got up and went outside and into the corridor. Just before she closed the door, Nora heard the surprise in her voice: 'A fever? That doesn't make any sense. He was absolutely fine this morning.'

As soon as a small click from the door announced that Jette Kvist had gone, Nora leaned forwards in her chair. She had been able to read upside down since she was seven. It was a game she and David had played on long car journeys across Europe with their parents to visit historical sites.

'Bjarke Helgaard. Referral to psychologist. Sexually deviant behaviour.'

The door opened again, and Nora stretched out in her chair to cover her sudden movement.

Jette Kvist seemed flustered and grabbed a light-coloured summer jacket from a peg behind the door. 'I need to go get my son,' she explained.

'Just one more thing. Do you know what happened to any of the children – where did they end up? I think I've worked out what happened to Erik, Jeanette and Bjarke. But do you know anything about Sonny, Oluf or Anni – where would I find them today?'

'Try the canteen.'

'Eh, pardon?'

There was a hint of a smile at the corner of Jette Kvist's mouth. 'Yes. Try the canteen. Anni turns up for work in the kitchen every morning around nine. She should be there now.'

She herded Nora out of her office and carefully locked the door behind her.

'The canteen is that way,' she said, pointing to the end of the corridor.

The smell of minced beef wafted towards Nora and reminded her that she had skipped breakfast. A chubby woman in a chef's jacket that had once been white was busy pouring the contents of an over-sized tin of tomatoes into a giant saucepan. Nora took her to be in her forties, but she had not taken good care of herself. Tufts of grey hair peeked out under the blue plastic cap, her nails were bitten to the quick, and she had bags under her eyes.

Nora looked about her. The kitchen was clean and tidy. The decay was restricted to Anni herself. Possibly.

'Are you Anni?' Nora asked.

The woman nodded.

'Do you have a minute?'

'I don't mind talking, but I haven't got time to sit down. Lunch is in ninety minutes,' she said, bending down to one of the ovens and pulling out a banana tray cake.

The sweet, spicy aroma was irresistible. 'Please may I have a piece,' Nora said hopefully.

'You can put five kroner into that,' Anni said, pointing to a piggy-bank shaped like a pink flamingo.

Nora perched on a stool while Anni cut her a slice of cake, placed it on a white napkin and set it down on the table next to her.

Then she went to the sink, tipped a few kilos of carrots out of a bag and started peeling them efficiently and methodically next to Nora.

'Who are you and what do you want?' she said in voice which more than implied that the answer was of little interest to her.

Nora introduced herself and explained that she was taking a closer look at the Lulu and Lisbeth case. Before she had even finished the first sentence, she could see that the subject made Anni very uncomfortable. Her pale cheeks flushed, and the movements of the peeler grew increasingly irate.

Finally she turned to Nora. 'Why can't you people understand that I just want to be left alone?' she hissed.

Nora looked at her quizzically.

'They were here from the telly last year. I didn't want to talk about it then – and I still don't. So get it into your thick skulls.'

'I'm not from the telly,' Nora said in her most reassuring voice. 'But I would still like to know what you have to say. And, if you prefer, it can stay just between the two of us. I'm only trying to understand what happened back then.'

By now Anni had red patches on her throat and her bottom lip was quivering. 'I want you to leave me alone,' she said firmly.

'OK,' Nora said, getting up. 'I'll respect that, of course. But if you change your mind, I'd really like you to call me,' she said, rummaging around for that bundle of business cards she thought she had chucked into her handbag. Now they were lost under old newspapers, receipts, hairbands, pens and sesame seeds from a long-eaten bagel. Finally she gave up, found an old envelope from a bank statement, tore off a corner and scribbled down her mobile number.

Anni appeared to relax at the sight of Nora's chaotic battle with her handbag.

'My shift ends at three. You'll find me by the bus stop, if you like. But I won't go on the telly. And I don't want my name made public,' she said at length.

Nora thanked her, scrunched up the napkin, binned it and left Anni to the carrots and the imminent lunch.

She drove to the centre of Viborg, parked outside a supermarket and started looking for a hotdog stall. Whenever she was in Denmark, she always took the opportunity to enjoy a hotdog.

Overall, the British reputation for cooking the world's worst food was undeserved, in Nora's opinion. At least when in London. There you could get the world's best sushi, curry and Thai. But they had no idea how to do a proper hotdog. In Britain sausages were served as 'bangers and mash': Cumberland sausages messed about with sage and served with bland mash and brown gravy straight from a tin.

Nora shuddered at the thought while the hotdog vendor opened a bottle of Cocio chocolate milk and asked if she wanted her hotdog with 'everything'.

Ten minutes later, sated and contented, she had managed to scrape off most of the mustard she had spilt down her T-shirt and avoid getting a parking ticket. She reset her parking disc to the current time, fetched her laptop from the boot and went hunting for a café with Wi-Fi to pass the time until Anni's shift ended.

Anni was standing by the bus stop, shivering. Even without the filthy chef's jacket and the plastic cap over her hair, she looked lost and pathetic. She glanced around quickly before jumping into the passenger seat next to Nora.

'You can drive me home. But I don't want you coming inside. I don't want my boyfriend to know.'

'But what's there to know? Surely it's not your fault you once stayed at a care home where two girls went missing,' Nora said.

'As far as he knows, my only connection with Mikkelsgården is that I work there. He thinks I'm normal. I told him my parents died in a car crash. Turn right here,' Anni said and pointed.

They drove in silence while Nora wondered how to put Anni at ease. Finally she opted for an open question.

'What can you remember from the trip? From the ferry,' she asked, glancing sideways at Anni in order to detect even the slightest hint of panic. Or lying.

Anni rubbed her forehead and agonised. 'It was supposed to have been a great adventure. We all got new passports. I was so excited about going to London. I had seen pictures of Big Ben. Oxford Street. Punk rockers in King's Cross. But it never happened. In fact, I've never been to London, and now I probably never will,' she said, her voice sounding bitter.

'Was there anything unusual about Lisbeth or Lulu that day? Or about any of the others?' Nora fished.

'Everything was unusual. None of us had ever been abroad before. It was amazing. Right until it happened.'

'The girls going missing, you mean?'

'Take the third exit at the roundabout and then straight through the next two junctions.'

Anni took her time before answering the question.

'Something happened before Lisbeth and Lulu went missing. Or at least before we discovered they were gone. Something happened to me.'

Nora kept her eyes on the road and let Anni take her time.

'Turn left here. And then it's number thirty-seven,' she said eventually, pointing to a glum 1970s apartment building of yellow brick with dark brown teak windows.

Nora pulled into the car park and stopped. When she turned off the engine, the silence in the car was deafening. They were parked in front of an abandoned playground with a swing and a partly trashed Wendy house covered in badly executed graffiti.

Anni stayed where she was. But out of the corner of her eye, Nora could see Anni's fingers clenching nervously, unclenching and contracting again in a self-soothing rhythm.

'What happened to you, Anni?' she asked quietly.

It was like pushing a button. Anni took a sharp intake of breath, then the tears started to flow. First a single drop on to her clothes, then a quiet stream while her face contorted in anguish.

'I've never told anyone.'

'Told anyone what?'

'He raped me. He raped me,' Anni sobbed.

Nora reached out and clutched Anni's hand.

'He said I should come with him, and I was stupid, so stupid. I just went with him. I thought he was my friend. But he forced me, and … I … bled. But after the girls went missing, no one else mattered.'

Nora stroked her hand in an attempt to calm her down a little, before asking the inevitable question. 'Who raped you?'

'Oluf, Oluf, that bastard.'

'Bjarke held me down. He was going to as well, but he couldn't do it. And then I escaped. I locked myself in the toilet. When I came back, there was so much commotion. Everyone was looking for Lisbeth and Lulu.'

She forced the words out between dry sobs. 'It took ages before I found Kurt. I tried to make him listen. I pulled his arm, but he looked at me with those beer goggles. He didn't want to know. I've never forgotten his words. He said: "Don't waste your breath." I've never forgotten that.'

'But why didn't you say something? Later?' Nora asked.

'Who was going to believe a loser like me? Bjarke said they would beat me up if I told anyone. What could I have done? Told a grown-up what they'd done and then gone on living in the same house as them, never knowing when they would come for me?'

She looked at Nora with a dull gaze. 'I don't want to talk about it any more. Don't come back.'

She released her seat belt, opened the door, got out of the car, and before Nora could react, she had disappeared across the playground and down one of the alleyways between the blocks.

'Anni?' she called out.

But there was no reply.

Pensively she took out her mobile, rang the main switchboard of one of the big tabloid newspapers and asked to speak to Torstein Abel.

Three seconds later she could hear his deep voice in the handset. 'Crime Section. Abel speaking.'

'Nora Sand,' Nora said, holding the phone away from her ear.

His reaction didn't disappoint. 'Bloody hell, Nora! You old witch! I thought you had put down roots in London, and forgotten all about us back home in Denmark,' he said.

Once, lost in the mists of time, Nora had done work experience at a national newspaper alongside Torstein Abel. The tabloid's foremost crime reporter looked like a tough guy, complete with tattoos, biker leather jacket and motorbike. A week after Nora had first met him, he made her watch his favourite movie, *The Godfather*, which he knew inside out and would often quote.

When they reached the scene where a film director finds a bloody present in his bed, Torstein clapped his hands with joy. 'The day I wake up and find a horse's head in my bed, I'll know I've written the scoop of my life,' he said.

That hadn't happened yet, but a couple of times he had come close and now most tabloid readers knew and loved him. To them he was the perfect, hard-boiled reporter – the kind you only ever read about in those American potboilers you buy at airports. The man who was on the scene of the goriest murders, and had the guts to write about immigrant and biker gangs when other journalists chickened out.

However, the fortunate few who were admitted into his den on Frederiksberg would find – to their enormous surprise – a home of tatami mats, books on Zen Buddhism and a kitchen characterised by a lifelong passion for pickling. Nora still had Torstein to thank for the best recipe for pickled marrow she had ever tasted.

They agreed to have lunch in Copenhagen the next day.

'It's not that I don't believe your sincere motives and your eternal friendship, but is this a special occasion?' he asked.

Nora chuckled. 'As always, your journalistic sixth sense is bang on. I want to learn about biker gangs – and who knows more than you?' she flattered him shamelessly.

'OK, sweetheart. Tomorrow, one o'clock at the paper. Call me from reception. You're buying.'

She ended the call, turned the key in the ignition and drove to

Copenhagen. Even before she had reached the outskirts of Viborg, she had found a radio station with classical music so her mind could run free while Albinoni's 'Adagio' filled the small car.

Was it purely a coincidence that Anni was raped the same evening Lulu and Lisbeth disappeared? Had the girls seen something they shouldn't have?

But then how had the Polaroid of the girls found its way into a suitcase in England? Was it yet another coincidence or possibly evidence that a very special kind of predator had been hunting that night on the ferry? A predator who would make Bjarke and Oluf look like a pair of childish amateurs.

And where did Kurt fit into the picture? Was his drunken talk about the girls being alive more than just that? If he really had received a postcard from them, surely he would have kept it. After all, the case had ruined his career and pretty much his life.

There were too many loose ends.

She crossed the Great Belt Bridge long after dinnertime, grabbed a microwaved panini at a motorway service station, and carried on to Copenhagen Airport, where she returned the rental car and treated herself to a taxi to Bagsværd on expenses. She was too exhausted to even contemplate public transport with a laptop and a suitcase in tow, so that battle with the Crayfish would have to be fought later. And there would definitely be a battle, she thought with a wry smile.

Her father was attending one of his history conferences, so she fished out the key from the tool shed gutter, let herself in, staggered up to her bedroom and collapsed on to her bed.

Three minutes later she was asleep and was woken only once around five o'clock by a distant car alarm that appeared unstoppable.

12

The next morning she rolled drowsily out of bed. She made herself a cup of coffee, went out on the terrace and rang Liselotte to ask if she could remember more about the other participants from the London trip.

This time her call was answered immediately. 'It's Malte.'

Nora ransacked her mind. Oh, yes. Liselotte's son.

'Hi. It's Nora. Can I talk to your mum, please?'

He hesitated. 'She's not feeling too good right now. I don't think …'

Then Nora heard Liselotte's voice in the background. 'Who is it?'

There was clattering as if Malte covered the phone with his hand, then a distant mumbling.

'It's that journalist. The one who was here the other day.'

Then three seconds later Liselotte's voice: 'You won't be speaking to my dad again. Ever.'

'Eh … what?'

'He died last night. We don't know where he was going, but he was walking down the road. They found him in a ditch. Police say it was a hit and run. He died instantly.'

'I'm really very sorry to hear that.'

Nora could hear how Liselotte struggled to suppress the tears.

'And do you know what the worst thing is? A whole life, and all he leaves behind – everything he owned in the whole world – fits in a Lidl plastic bag. Christ, what a waste!'

'I'm so very sorry. I won't keep you any longer.'

'Thank you,' Liselotte said harshly and rang off.

Nora rang the duty officer at Ringkøbing police station.

'You're calling from *Globalt*? It's not often we hear from you,' the officer said with a Jutland drawl.

Once Nora had explained the reason for her call, he flicked through the incident report.

'Yes, it says so here. A sixty-eight-year-old man was found three kilometres south of Søndervig in a ditch. Hit and run. A witness called us at 20.43 last night. She said she had seen what she thought might be a dark blue or black Jeep, a 4x4, or similar, hit the man. No distinguishing features on the car or the number plate. An ambulance was dispatched, but the man was already dead when it arrived. I don't want you quoting me, but there's evidence that the dead man might have been under the influence of alcohol. We found an almost empty bottle of schnapps nearby.'

He flicked through the report.

'Right, I guess that's it. Oh, hang on … Well, I don't know if you'd be interested in this, but we found no skid marks at the scene.'

Nora thanked him, put down her mobile, and sat for a long time staring at her father's apple trees without seeing anything at all.

Then she pulled herself together and got ready to meet Torstein at his office.

The security guard glanced up, but showed no interest when Nora arrived through a swing door at the reception for the newspaper where Torstein worked. Ever since the Danish security services had found a bag at Copenhagen Central Railway Station containing a leaflet about Islam and a map of Copenhagen with the newspaper's address circled in red, the reception was staffed during opening hours by middle-aged security guards with blue sweaters and walkie-talkies. Nora still didn't know if it was a teenage prank or an amateurish plan to bomb the newspaper, but she had a hunch that the most action the security guards ever saw was bleary-eyed journalists who had forgotten their mandatory ID cards and the obligatory conspiracy theorists who stopped by a few times a week hoping to expose radioactivity in the harbour, government corruption or to submit piles of handwritten documents detailing secret oil drilling on Greenland. She helped herself to a complimentary copy of the newspaper from the counter and could see that readers wouldn't be troubled by political news today. A sprained ankle had forced a well-known TV presenter to pull out of *Strictly Come Dancing*, and the tragedy was printed in a large font – there could be no doubt that Nora was visiting a nation in mourning. She flicked through the newspaper and was confronted on page three with the story about the presenter's dance partner's heroic attempts to stay positive.

Against her better judgement, she was sucked into the story about the young dancer who, from a distance, might bear a vague resemblance to Andreas. He had the same corn-yellow hair, the same upright posture.

Again her thoughts jumped back to the past. They had been sitting in Hanne's garden that night after the leavers' ball, because according to some ridiculous student superstition, everyone was supposed to stay awake all night. She could no longer remember why. Only that they had sat on separate swings on a rusty old frame under a lilac. She could still remember the sweet scent of lilac blossom in the twilight, the dew in the soft grass and Andreas's face turned towards hers. She had known it a split second before he said it.

She jumped when she felt a heavy hand on her shoulder.

'What's this I see, Miss Sand? I didn't have you down as a *Strictly* groupie,' Torstein said, glancing sideways at the article still lying open in front of Nora.

She composed herself. 'Oh, totally. What a tragedy. Why didn't you get to cover that scoop?'

Torstein looked down. 'I can't be trusted with such complex material. I'm afraid I'm stuck with crime until I learn my trade,' he said with a sardonic smile, before flinging out his hand towards to door. 'Shall we?'

They walked to Nyhavn where with routine ease Torstein ordered

Christiansø herring on rye bread and a shot of schnapps for himself, which he proceeded to knock back in one go the moment the waitress brought it. Then he leaned back contentedly and looked at Nora. 'Bikers, you say. May I ask why?'

'It's a story that might have links to Denmark.'

'Drugs?'

'No, I don't think so. Actually, I'm only interested in one person. His name is Bjarke Helgaard. Do you know him?'

The waitress brought Torstein's herring and Nora's prawn open sandwich. Torstein ordered another schnapps. 'A bird never flew with one wing,' he said, by way of explanation.

'Bjarke Helgaard.' Torstein tasted the name in between bites of herring.

Nora nodded, her mouth full of prawns.

'Bjarke. Now he's an oddball,' Torstein said, bringing her back to the present. 'Massive beefcake. Clearly on steroids. Used to frequent Box Copenhagen Gym some years ago where he was talent-spotted by the Needle.'

'The Needle, the leader of Dare Devils?'

Though she had lived away from Denmark for the last five years, even Nora had heard of the tall, skinny man with the piercing eyes and his terrifying power over parts of Copenhagen's nightlife.

'The one and only,' Torstein declared gravely. 'Bjarke joined a gang of his enforcers, the thinking being that due to his size, he would rarely have to take his fists out of his pockets. All Bjarke had to do was turn up, grunt a bit and flex his muscles, whereupon people would suddenly find the money they swore they didn't have. Things tended to sort themselves out when Bjarke was sent to deliver a message or collect a debt.'

Nora caught the waitress's eye and quickly ordered coffee, before Torstein realised he needed yet another schnapps to tell his story.

'Bjarke slowly rose up the ranks. My sources tell me he has a good handle on the Needle. He instinctively knows when to step up and when to step back without getting stung. He's no fool.'

The coffee arrived and Torstein looked longingly at a bottle of Linie Akvavit schnapps making its way to a table of Swedish business people.

'Do you remember the Brandy case?'

Nora trawled through her memories. 'She was that young mum who was killed some years ago in a gang shooting on Nørrebro, wasn't she?'

'Yes. Dreadful business. Brandy was killed instantly. As was John Iversen, leader of the local chapter of Blue Bulls. It seems Brandy's only mistake was going to the kiosk to buy cigarettes at the same time as John Iversen. You know what they say: *smoking kills*,' Torstein commented dryly.

'Did Bjarke have anything to do with that?'

'Yes and no. But let me finish my story. At that time, Blue Bulls were at war with Dare Devils, and it was very, very tempting to think that the Needle had given the order to get rid of Iversen. It was – I can reveal to this closed circle – the first and possibly the only lead the police ever investigated.'

Torstein took a sip of his coffee and picked up a sugar sachet from a bowl on the table.

'Right, this was where Bjarke truly came into his own. Discovered his vocation, if you like. He went to the media and told everyone that Dare Devils had absolutely nothing to do with the incident. The media loved him. He said exactly what everybody expected him to say, but he was succinct, to the point and articulate. A media star was born.'

Something clicked in Nora's mind. 'There was something about a baby in a pram, wasn't there?'

'Yes, and this was where Bjarke proved his genius. He gave a long, tear-jerking speech about little Johnny, Brandy's son, who had lost his mother, and how the lads in Bjarke's – incidentally peace-loving and entirely innocent motorcycle club – had held a collection for the poor little lad in a crash helmet. So that little Johnny would have a chance and a future after all, as Bjarke phrased it. The money probably came from drugs or prostitution, but most people swallowed it raw. God help us. What a media circus,' Torstein snorted.

'Our rival paper ran the headline "The biker gang member with a heart of gold". Ever since then Bjarke has been a regular fixture in news broadcasts and a talking head whenever there's trouble on Nørrebro. He has become an expert and he is straight out of central casting. He looks like a thug, but when he opens his mouth, he's capable of coherent and relatively sensible statements. Rumour has it Arte might even hire him for the lecture circuit.'

'But he's violent?'

Torstein shrugged. 'He does have a few convictions for assault, but they're more than five years old now. Bjarke has risen up the ranks and no longer needs to get his hands dirty.'

Nora lowered her voice and looked at Torstein: 'Now don't go telling anyone what I'm about to ask you. Promise? If you tell anyone else, I put a source at great risk.'

Torstein put his hand on his heart. 'Scout's honour.'

'You were never a Boy Scout.'

'All right then, on my mother's grave.'

'Your mother is alive and well and living in Torshavn.'

'Oh, just tell me. What is it? Is it drugs after all? Is it the Albanian connection?'

Nora chewed her lip and decided to take a chance. 'No. It's not the Albanians or drugs. But do you think from what you know of Bjarke that he might have taken part in the rape of a young woman?'

'Ha!' Torstein's laughter made the waitress turn around with a frown. 'That's one question I'm absolutely sure I can answer with a no.'

Nora furrowed her brow. 'And what makes you so sure? Do you know him better than you've let on?'

Torstein grinned cheekily. 'Bjarke is confirmed, utterly and irreversibly, gay.'

Nora's jaw dropped, she had never suspected that.

Torstein elaborated. 'He lives with the Needle. Our little Bjarke isn't into women. The only women in his life are the kind that are tattooed on his considerable biceps. Or the ones the Needle makes his money from.'

'Wow, who would have guessed. Is it possible to get near him, Bjarke, I mean?'

'Oh, yes. He has his own website. Just email him, he usually rings back quickly. Don't forget, he makes his living from the media, and if he keeps appearing on TV, there are no limits to what he can achieve. A book contract, possibly an invitation to *Celebrity Big Brother* or *Strictly*. Who knows?'

After a short pause he added: 'That bit about him being gay – I wouldn't broadcast that, if I were you. Bjarke thinks it's a big secret, and no one wants to be the first person to burst his bubble. It could prove hazardous to their health.'

Nora gestured for the bill and started putting on her jacket.

'Were the murders of Brandy and Iversen ever solved?'

'Yes. It turned out that Iversen was the one who was in the wrong place at the wrong time. The killer was Brandy's pimp, who thought she had ripped him off by giving it away for free during her maternity leave, and he decided to make an example of her. Iversen just happened to get in the way when that little shit fired his pistol.'

Together they walked back to his office.

'When are you moving home? I miss my pickling partner,' Torstein complained.

'When London moves to Denmark, I'll be there in a jiffy,' she promised.

'Hmm. Anyway, don't be a stranger, we'll go to my allotment next time,' he promised and kissed her hand gallantly before he waved goodbye and slipped past the Securitas guard who discovered too late that Torstein wasn't wearing the mandatory ID card around his neck.

'Oi, you! Come back,' the guard called out.

X

Nora found the website, emailed Bjarke from her iPhone, and got a call from an unknown number twenty minutes later.

'Bjarke Helgaard. You emailed me.'

His voice sounded so butch and commanding that Nora briefly wondered if Torstein had tricked her into hacking off a big, beefy biker who didn't share his sense of humour and relaxed attitude to homosexuality.

Nora introduced herself.

'So why does *Globalt* want to talk to me?' Bjarke demanded to know.

Nora decided it would be a mistake to try to get anything out of him over the phone. A meeting would be better. Preferably in a public place, just to be on the safe side.

'It's a bit complicated. But perhaps we could meet?' she said, sounding hopeful.

'Hmm. I've googled you, Nora Sand, and I don't get why a journalist whose two most recent articles were about a man from Rwanda and a political scandal in the UK, would want to talk to a regular Dane from Nørrebro?'

Bjarke Helgaard was a man you would be very foolish to underestimate.

'I promise you it won't take long and it'll make sense eventually. Please could we meet, just for half an hour?'

'You're lucky that I like a good mystery. And that I have a window in my busy schedule. Flora's Coffee Bar in half an hour,' he said and hung up without waiting for her reply.

She caught the bus to Blågårdsgade and walked the last stretch. She ordered a latte with an extra shot of espresso, and sat down at a table with a full view of the room. Ten minutes later Bjarke strolled in. He looked bigger and broader in real life than on the pictures in the paper. It was as if the photographs couldn't quite accommodate the width of his shoulders.

His blue eyes scrutinised her in a thorough but not hostile manner, before he sat down at the table with a cup of filter coffee.

'So how may I be of assistance? A conflict in the Middle East or starving children in India?' he quipped.

Nora shook her head and decided to just go for it. 'No. We're going further back … Do you recall the summer of '85? Lisbeth and Lulu?'

If the question surprised him, he was remarkably adept at controlling his facial expression. 'Lisbeth and Lulu?' he echoed in a calm voice. 'I haven't thought about them for years. Why do you want to know about them now?'

Nora cleared her throat. 'Information relating to their case has become available, which –'

'What kind of information?' he interrupted her, now suddenly very interested.

Nora took time to savour her coffee.

'There might be a link to a British killer. That's all I can tell you right now.'

Bjarke's voice remained deathly calm, but Nora could see a vein starting to throb in his neck. His knuckles whitened as they gripped the coffee cup even more tightly.

'Who is the bastard?'

'I don't know if there really is a connection. So far it's just a hunch. So I need your version of what happened that night on the ferry.'

The giant in the leather jacket didn't appear to have heard her. 'Who is the bastard?' he repeated in a low voice.

'He's in prison. So you can't get to him.'

Bjarke shook his head and looked at her again. 'There's always a way. Always,' he said bluntly.

Then he raised his forefinger, and Nora caught a glimpse of the man who had fought his way up to become the Needle's second-in-command.

'If I tell you anything, then in return you'll tell me what happened to my girls. Is that clear?'

Nora looked him straight in the eye to signal that she wouldn't allow herself to be intimidated. 'If – and I stress if – I find out anything, I'll let you know, but not until I'm ready. I have your email address.'

Bjarke seemed to debate this for a moment, then he leaned back in his chair and flung out his arms. 'Fair enough. What do you want to know?'

'Tell me about your relationship with Lisbeth and Lulu. And what it was like at Vestergården?'

'I thought you wanted to know what happened that night on the ferry?'

'We'll get to that. But I need to understand more about how things were back then,' Nora explained.

'Lulu was like a sister to me. All right, she wasn't the sharpest knife in the drawer. But you could trust her. She kept her mouth shut, no matter what they did to her,' Bjarke said, and his eyes grew distant.

'One night me and Sonny robbed the cinema in Ringkøbing. Nothing that made us rich. A few hundred kroner in the till after a Saturday night. But Sonny helped himself to the biggest bag of sweets you've ever seen from the pick and mix. He had never been to the cinema before and was hell-bent on seeing one of those stupid Stallone films they were showing. We tried getting the projector to work, but the bloody thing started smoking. So we skedaddled and nicked a moped to get us home. Lulu was in the hallway when we came back. She saw us run to our rooms,' he told Nora, then shook his coffee cup as if to make the last mouthful last longer.

'Another one?' Nora looked at him quizzically. He nodded briefly, and she went up to the counter for another round before he continued.

'It took about twenty minutes from the moment the fire brigade was summoned to the cinema before the local cops showed up at Vestergården. It was just how it was. No matter what happened in Ringkøbing, they would blame us. Sometimes it was justified, other times not. But you could be damn sure that Kurt would throw a wobbly. Not just with the police, but also with us, if we stepped out of line. He'd already given me three warnings. If I was caught again, I would be chucked out, and that meant I wouldn't be going with them to London. Back then it was the only thing I cared about,' he said with a wistful smile.

'Lulu saved our arses. I don't know why. We'd never done anything for her. You just didn't at Vestergården. But when the cops turned up and started putting the squeeze on us and picked apart our story that we'd been home all evening getting our beauty sleep, Lulu got involved. She could look the picture of innocence with those big blue eyes. I remember she wore a red nightdress with big bunnies. And she went right up to them, looked them straight in the eye and told them how she had been pacing up and door the corridor for the last hour because she had a tummy ache and couldn't sleep, and nobody had walked past her.'

Bjarke shook his head. 'They totally knew that Sonny and I did it. But after Lulu's account there was nothing they could do, so they had to leave. Kurt had his suspicions, of course, and he scowled at the pair of us for the next few weeks. Especially after he found a stolen moped in a ditch not far from Vestergården. And, of course, we never did go to London,' he said with another melancholy smile.

'What happened that night – what do you remember?' Nora interjected.

'The irony was,' he said, ignoring her question. 'The irony was that after that night me and Sonny both swore to be her protectors. Have her back. There were some guys at the youth club who liked bullying little girls. Sonny and I had a word with them, and from then on they left Lulu alone. We even got Erik to give up his ridiculous porn magazines and all his other crap.'

'Erik?' Nora asked with raised eyebrows.

'That's right. His dad fucked him up. Yes, in that way. And I guess he thought no one would find out as long as he read porn magazines and talked about tits all day. Kurt confiscated them, but somehow

Erik always get new ones. He loved going up to the girls with the magazines and shoving them in their faces. Lisbeth would just laugh and take the piss out of him. Jeanette ignored him. But he really upset both Lulu and that little one ... Now what was her name?'

'Anni?' Nora ventured, holding her breath.

Bjarke nodded. The name of the girl he had allegedly helped rape didn't seem to make much of an impression.

'Yes, that was her name, I think. Small and a bit fat. Ugly.' He heaved a sigh, as if dismissing her as insignificant. 'I think you can safely say that Sonny and I failed badly in our attempt to take care of Lulu that night on the ferry. Just one night, and she was gone forever.'

'But what happened? Do you remember the last time you saw the girls?'

'We'd been trying to buy booze in the duty-free shop. We didn't get any, of course. We all looked like teenagers, and they asked for ID immediately. Then we wanted Lisbeth to give it a go because she looked much older when she wore make-up. But we couldn't find her anywhere. So we sent Lulu off to look for her.'

Bjarke paused for a long time.

'She never came back,' he then said.

One night's chaos and regrets boiled down to a single sentence.

'Did the rest of you stay together?'

'Nah. I don't really remember. I mean, at that point none of us suspected that anything bad had happened. I guess we thought that ... Well, I don't know what we thought. That they had found some older guys who had booze, perhaps. It wasn't a great feeling, and I personally didn't want to look like a fool. So I let them get on with it.'

Nora nodded. 'Can you remember anything else?'

'At one point I thought I caught a glimpse of Lisbeth at the disco, but I'm not sure. I only got as far as the doorway. They wouldn't let me in. Then Oluf, Sonny and me bumped into this Norwegian guy who was over eighteen, and in return for a few strong beers, he bought us a bottle of vodka.'

Bjarke pulled a face at the memory. 'From then on, it gets a bit blurred, as far as I'm concerned.'

'And what about Oluf? Oluf and Anni, do you remember anything about them?' Nora asked more sharply than she had intended to.

He looked at her with surprise. 'No. Not really. Should I?'

Nora made no reply. 'Where's Sonny today and do you know what happened to Oluf?'

'Sonny is doing time in Herstedvester. A totally amateurish bank robbery. Trying to pay off a gambling debt. I believe he'll be out in six or seven years, if he lives that long, that is. From what I hear, he still hasn't paid off his debt and the interest is starting to hurt.'

'And what about Oluf?' she asked again, trying to catch Bjarke's eye.

But he was no longer paying attention to her. He was looking through the open window at two imposing foreign-looking men in black leather jackets who were passing by.

He drained his coffee cup, got up abruptly and reverted seamlessly to the butch tone of voice.

'Thanks for the coffee, lady. I need to go now. Call me with any news, will you?' he said, and put down – in all seriousness – a business card with Dare Devils' red trident logo and the title Chief Press Officer written in flaming letters above a mobile number.

Then he left, making sure that the two in the leather jackets didn't notice him.

Nora leaned out of the window and saw the two men turn the corner by Assistens Cemetery. She briefly wondered whether she could possibly press Bjarke for more information by threatening to give him away to them.

She was wavering in the doorway when her mobile rang.

It was Andreas. She sat down at the table again and planted her feet firmly on the floor. Grounded herself.

'Hey. I just wanted to hear how you were?'

'Great,' she said, pressing the handle of the teaspoon hard into the palm of her hand in the hope that physical pain would distract her from this ridiculous feeling of joy.

'Oh, am I interrupting something? You sound tense?'

'No, no. Everything is fine,' she said and focused on the menu where she could read all about Java beans versus Ethiopian coffee, but the words burst like soap bubbles before they reached her brain.

'Right, I don't want to disturb you if you're busy,' he said, a tad miffed. 'I'm just calling to find out if we're still meeting the day after tomorrow?'

Nora nodded before remembering that he couldn't see her. 'Yes. I'll pick you up around eleven. Please text me your address,' she said.

They rang off, and Nora spontaneously slammed the palm of her hand against her forehead. It was just Andreas. An old friend. How did it get to this point where she could no longer carry on a normal telephone conversation?

'Shit, shit, shit,' she said slowly, as one of the baristas passed her table.

'I really hope that wasn't your bank manager,' he said with a smile.

'I wish. It was a man who's off limits,' she said.

13

The off-limits man was waiting with a bag slung over his shoulder outside his rented flat when she drove around the corner, having battled her way through London's Saturday morning traffic in a microscopic, bright green rented Ford.

'You might have to keep that on your lap. Once I put my handbag in the boot, it was full,' she joked, trying very hard not to notice that he was wearing a white shirt. With buttons.

Andreas adjusted the passenger seat and stretched out his legs – to the extent that was possible. Nora pointed to the back where her, by now, somewhat dog-eared copy of *Murders of the Century* was lying on top of her notebook.

'Page fifty-three,' she said and as Andreas reached for it his arm brushed her shoulder. Rays seemed to emanate from him and she could almost sense an aura of heat around his body.

For the next half an hour the only sound in the car was that of BBC Radio 4, while Nora navigated them out of London and joined the motorway. Andreas was immersed in the book. She glanced sideways to gauge his reaction, but his face was inscrutable.

Finally he looked in the back to read the notes, thorough as always, before slamming it shut.

'So, how about it? What do you think?'

'It's one nasty story,' he commented dryly.

'Yes, of course it is,' she said. 'But do you think Bill Hix might have murdered Lulu and Lisbeth? Could that be why they were never seen again?'

Andreas's brow furrowed. 'It's hard to say. But, as far as I'm aware, he has never before or afterwards abducted two victims at the same time. It would require confidence, control and brute force. Did he have that?'

Nora mulled it over. 'Lulu and Lisbeth disappeared in 1985, and Hix was caught in 1992, seven years later. At that point he had, going by the contents of his cabinet of horrors, killed at least fifteen people. However, if you don't want to alert the police that you're a serial killer, you can't kill every single month. So we have to presume that he spread the killings over a longer period. Perhaps he already had a murder or three on his conscience in 1985. Might that have been enough to convince him to escalate?'

'It might,' Andreas agreed.

They sat for a while in silence, before he turned to her. 'So what are we really doing in Brine?'

'Going for a swim. And finding out where that suitcase came from. I have a hunch it's the key to everything.'

If he was disappointed at her answer, he didn't let on. Instead he started fiddling with the radio until he found a station playing evergreens.

'Perfect. I love this one,' he said when the opening notes of Frank Sinatra's version of 'Come Fly With Me' poured out of the speakers.

'Let's float down to Peeeeruuu,' he screeched enthusiastically and Nora clung to the steering wheel in order not to veer off the road from laughter.

'Come on. Join in. You know you want to!' he invited her and eventually she had to surrender.

'In llama land, there's a one-man band and he'll toot his flute for you ...'

Then followed Shirley Bassey and her diamonds, Marilyn Monroe and her daddy complex, and Nora gave a superb performance with her take on the amorous 'Da-da-da-da-da-da-daddy'.

And before they knew it, they were in Brine. Nora's vocal chords felt raw and her stomach muscles ached from laughing.

'The B&B address is on a piece of paper in my notebook. I printed it out from the web. There's also a map.'

Andreas found it. 'Yes. Dolphin Guesthouse. Two single rooms. It's on the left.'

They drove up to a whitewashed building with a tiled roof and crooked walls framed by blue wisteria and large hydrangeas. In the reception a man in his twenties stuck out his hand and introduced himself as Wesley. He was tanned and looked like someone who spent the least possible time on dry land in the summer season. Nora guessed that the surfboard leaning up against the garage was his.

'Welcome. Breakfast is from eight to nine thirty,' he said, gesturing towards the conservatory.

'We only have one single, so one of you gets a double. The only question is which one of you will it be?' he said, looking from one to the other.

Nora gave a light shrug, and said to Andreas in Danish. 'It doesn't matter. Go on, you have it.'

'I wouldn't dream of it,' he replied.

'Sorry, I don't understand what you're saying,' Wesley said, again looking from one to the other.

'I'll take the single bedroom. Just give me the key,' she said, reverting to English more abruptly than she had intended. And added: 'Thank you.'

Wesley raised his eyebrows without saying anything, as only a true Brit can, and handed her the key. The key ring was a small wooden ship with a big number three painted on the sail.

Nora grabbed her case, ignored Andreas's protests and marched down the narrow passage to a small room with a single bed and a battered chest of drawers.

The view across the car park bordered on panoramic and there was shaggy, moss-green carpet on the bathroom floor. The obligatory tea tray balanced on a wobbly bedside table with curved legs. Just as the Americans would defend their right to bear arms and drive their cars anywhere, including when visiting their next-door neighbours, the Brits would die for the right to a nice cuppa.

Next to the tea cup was a cellophane-wrapped biscuit, which

started to look seriously tempting when Nora remembered how long ago it was since she had wolfed down a slice of toast with marmalade and a cup of coffee and called it breakfast.

Two minutes later there was a knock on her door, and Andreas edged his way in. His very presence made the room shrink. Nora sat down on the bed while he took the only armchair in the room, a plump, upholstered floral monstrosity that looked as if it had survived a couple of wars.

'This is very … green,' Andreas said with a grin.

She lashed out at him.

'By way of consolation may I buy you lunch? I think that the green horror on the bathroom floor requires some form of compensation. We ought to cut out samples and send them to a lab. It represents a chance of discovering hitherto unknown lifeforms.'

Nora couldn't help smiling.

When they stepped outside, the weather had changed as if finally the sun had had enough of its own capriciousness and had decided to hang around for the rest of the day.

The light was golden as they walked down Seaview Street. To her enormous disappointment, the bric-a-brac shop was shut. She walked right up to the window and pressed her nose against the glass to peer inside before she noticed a small sign at the bottom pane in the door announcing that the shop was closed until further notice. She could tell from the curled-up edges that it had been there for a while.

The shop looked dusty and abandoned. A hodgepodge of tat and treasures. A couple of extravagant crystal chandeliers hung from the ceiling alongside brown, glazed ceramic lamps that had never been an aesthetic delight, not even against a background of 1970s Hessian wallpaper. On the floor was an old pram surrounded by stacks of books and toy cars.

Nora quickly scanned the room for more suitcases, but saw none. She considered popping in to see the Russian woman in the Daisy Dairy Café, but changed her mind when she saw the queue of happy summer visitors waiting to taste their organic ice cream.

Andreas dragged her down towards the beach where they found a pub with an open courtyard and a barbecue, which was still serving food though it was way past lunchtime.

They ate grilled sardines with gooseberry compote washed down with cold cider. Andreas finished first and sat watching her pensively, while she struggled to get the last tiny bones out of the white fish.

'Yes?' she said eventually when she couldn't take it any longer. 'What is it?'

'Nothing,' he said enigmatically.

'Are you sure?'

He hesitated, giving her enough time to close her eyes and wonder if he were about to say something terrible. Something unbearably awful.

'I was just wondering … Why did you really bring me here?'

She drank her cider and slowly put down the glass. 'I guess I thought it would be nice,' she said hesitantly. 'Because we're friends. And because you're a police officer and might contribute something that hadn't crossed my mind.'

Thus she slammed the dangerous, secret door shut with a bang.

She started fiddling with the label on the cider bottle. The bottle was covered with condensation and she concentrated on ripping it off in strips with her thumbnail. When one strip came off, she would roll it between her fingers until it turned into a wet ball, before repeating the process.

Andreas kept looking at her. 'Nora Sand,' he said softly.

She opened her mouth to reply, but was overcome by a feeling of rage, which took her completely by surprise. Like a freak wave wrecking a sandcastle just as you thought the tide had gone out. Anger that he had turned up out of the blue after all these years and caused mayhem in her life.

The waitress unknowingly deflected the anticipated reaction. 'Looks like you could do with another round,' she said with feigned jollity.

The wave stopped abruptly, and when Andreas finally turned his attention to the waitress to ask for the bill, Nora could breathe again. She got up and strolled casually to the pub's lavatory.

She turned on the cold tap and used an old trick she had read about in a novel from the Deep South. Back then, young women in crinoline petticoats and whalebone corsets would faint on a regular basis because the slightest emotion made them hyperventilate in their tight clothes. But ice-cold water on the wrist, right where the pulse is closest to the surface of the skin, forces the body to take it easy. Slow down. Be cool.

Nora rested her forehead against the cold mirror, reached out her hands and proved that some advice is timeless and equally effective on overheated, Danish journalists.

When she came back outside, Andreas had paid and she had regained her poise.

'So ice cream or a swim first?' she said in her best Girl Scout voice.

Andreas blinked again, but played along with the mood. 'I'm afraid I have to draw your attention to current health and safety regulations: always wait thirty minutes after eating before you swim,' he said gravely.

Half an hour later, they were standing at the water's edge, eyeing each other up. It was a tradition that whoever jumped in second was a loser. Only one action was more contemptible: trying to get away with a false start.

The sun made the surface of the water explode in thousands of stars, and the moment she hit the water, she felt good again. Everything went back to normal.

Her skin tightened in the cold water and she surfaced for air. Andreas swam in front of her, and she dived under again and pinched his toes. Another one of their old games.

They swam for a while along the shore, Andreas taking long, strong strokes. Nora struggled to keep up, and she promised herself that from now on there would be no more skipping the pool due to work pressure.

Eventually they returned to the shore and when they reached

shallow water, Nora stood on the seabed watching his body undulate in the sea. He looked like a big dolphin.

They dried themselves, walked back up to the town and queued with the other tourists in front of the Daisy Dairy Café. A local girl was serving, and she had all the time in the world.

It took Nora and Andreas half an hour to reach the counter, and while Andreas counted out the money, Nora asked about the Russian woman who had answered the phone earlier. The girl nodded towards the pub across the street. 'Katya doesn't like working when it's hot. There's a good chance she'll be in the pub. She has long, red hair. You can't miss her.'

Nora thanked her, took her ice cream, and she and Andreas returned to the sunshine. They made themselves comfortable on one of the many benches facing the sea and let themselves be caught up in the life of the little bay. A speedboat with a water skier carved through the afternoon calm, a yacht was mooring in the marina, and a dinghy with an outboard motor and fishing rods sticking out in every direction was heading home after a day on the sea.

Andreas's lips had turned dark red from his raspberry ripple.

'You look like a vampire,' Nora burst out, carefully taking a bite of her own chocolate ice cream.

Before she knew it, he was leaning close to her, baring his teeth, and only partly in jest.

Then she felt his tongue on the top of her hand. The touch was so fleeting that she almost thought it hadn't happened. 'You dropped a bit,' was all he said.

Suddenly she was incapable of swallowing another bite. She looked at her hand, surprised that no physical mark had been left on it. It was burning and trembling.

She chucked the rest of her ice cream and got up resolutely. 'Come on, let's go looking for Katya, the mystery redhead.'

Andreas looked away. 'I have a few things I need to sort out,' he said. 'Why don't we meet around eight and go out for dinner?'

Nora gave a light shrug. 'All right then, suit yourself.'

For a moment she regretted inviting him. Then she brushed it aside and made her way to The Oysterman.

The old pub had done nothing to meet middle-class Londoners' expectations of an idyllic life on the coast. There wasn't a single whitewashed wall or a pirate flag in sight. This was a pub for the locals.

There were rows of flashing slot machines along the walls, the tartan carpet was sticky from beer, and Nora could smell that the sign saying 'Smoking Strictly Prohibited' was for decorative purposes only.

All the walls displayed tributes to Elvis's heyday and the men who had made their living making poor-quality mirrors in his memory since the golden era of Las Vegas.

Katya was playing cribbage with two men when Nora entered. Her laughter was shrill, and Nora couldn't decide which of the men would be the lucky one tonight. Possibly both of them.

When one of the men got up to fetch another round from the bar, Nora spied her chance to make contact.

The other man, who was now on his own with the Russian beauty, looked up irritably at the intruder who was ruining his best chance. When he spotted Nora, however, he changed his mind and flashed a smile that revealed that if there was a dentist in Brine, this man wasn't one of his patients.

'What's your poison, gorgeous?' he slurred.

Nora proffered him a friendly but reserved smile. 'No, thanks, I don't need anything. I just wanted a word with Katya.'

'You speak to me, OK,' Katya said in a happy, drunken voice.

Nora recognised her voice from the telephone and came straight to the point. 'I'm looking for Mr Smithfield, your neighbour,' she said.

'You also look for Smithfield. What has he done? Last week, a woman come. Then man come, I think police, and now you come. Mr Smithfield, he be very tired when he come home,' Katya declared.

'He's not at home at the moment?' Nora said.

'No, no, no. He's in India.'

The second man returned to the table. 'You joining in? Five quid a game. Or you can leave,' he said bluntly, as he lined up three foaming pints on the table.

As Nora left, Katya called out after her: 'Ask Polly!'

'Where's Polly?'

'Polly in the bar.'

Nora walked through a saloon door and found a forty-something woman busy putting glasses into a dishwasher.

'Hello,' Nora said, and was rewarded with a not unfriendly nod.

'What can I do for you?' Polly asked and as she straightened up, her pink T-shirt eliminated any doubt as to who might have been in charge of decorating the pub.

'The King is Alive!' it said in rhinestones across her impressive bust.

Nora decided that a bit of diplomacy wouldn't go amiss, and pointed to the image below the statement. 'Isn't that picture from Blue Hawaii?'

'Yes,' Polly said happily. 'Not many people recognise it.'

'My grandmother adored Elvis,' Nora went on. 'I must have seen that movie fifteen times. At least,' she added, and tactfully avoided mentioning how much she had loathed it after only the third viewing, and how throughout her childhood she had pleaded with her grandmother if they could, please, please, watch something better, like the good old-fashioned Danish films.

'It sure was one of his greatest,' Polly stated with a broad grin and wiped the counter. 'Right, what can I get a fellow Elvis fan?' she asked happily.

'Actually I'm looking for Mr Smithfield,' Nora said.

Polly opted for a wait-and-see strategy. 'What do you want with him?'

'Nothing bad. Only I bought a suitcase from him a few weeks ago, and I found something inside it that I'm not sure he intended to sell.'

Polly weighed up the situation. 'You're not the only one who wants to talk to Uncle Harry. He has become very popular this past week.'

'Aha?'

'First there was this really nasty woman asking for him. She pretended they were friends. But if they'd really been friends, then she would have known that Uncle Harry goes to the ashram for a couple of weeks this time every year – as he has done for the past ten years,' Polly said, shaking her head at the woman. 'Two days later a man turned up. I remember his name because it was the same as Princess Diana before she got married. Spencer. But he said he wasn't related to her.'

Nora nodded.

'But anyway, if you want to get hold of Uncle Harry, drop in tomorrow morning, I think he'll be back then. He always stops by to recharge with a couple of pints after all that detoxing,' Polly promised.

'Thank you,' Nora said, making her way towards the exit. 'By the way – the woman who was looking for your uncle? Did she say why?'

Polly rolled her eyes. 'Yes, something about some old stuff that had been put up for sale by accident. And something about an old lady and a nursing home. She was very upset.'

'Did she have a name?'

'I'm sure she did, but she didn't tell me. Like I said, she was really rude, so it wasn't like we were having a conversation, if you get my drift. The only thing I remember is that she had big ugly eyes. She looked like one of those dolls … Now what are they called … Bratz or something?'

Nora nodded by way of a thank you and left Polly as Elvis started on 'Blue Suede Shoes'.

X

Andreas was nowhere to be seen, so Nora wandered back to her room. She opened the window to reduce the stench of pine air freshener, which was fighting a heroic battle against the room's natural aroma of damp and old carpet.

She sat down by the open window and switched on her laptop. Her mobile signal came and went, and it took more than half an hour with countless interruptions to check the news and her most important emails.

While she waited for a stronger signal, she made notes.

Afterwards she lay down on her bed where she had a view of the stained ceiling. She closed her eyes in order to concentrate better. Just for a moment.

She was woken up by the beeping of her mobile. 'Sand? Did you doze off?' Andreas teased her.

'Mmm.'

'So you can't handle a quick swim without fainting from exhaustion?'

'Give me five minutes, please,' she pleaded.

'I'm outside. In the lovely sunshine.'

She ran to the bathroom and splashed her face with water. The pillow had left an imprint on her cheek.

In her travel bag she found a slightly crumpled, blue summer dress with white butterflies and put it on while she tried combing her hair and brushing her teeth at the same time.

'Meow.'

The sound was coming from somewhere under her bed.

'No, kitty – now is not a good time,' she said, lifting up the edge of the bedspread. The cat must have crept inside while she was asleep, but she didn't want to go out and leave the window open in case her laptop got stolen.

'Come on, kitty, go catch some mice. Here, come on,' she tried tempting it.

She saw its eyes like two yellow reflectors under the darkness of the bed, but the cat refused to budge.

She put on her sandals, finished off with a bit of lip gloss and checked she had no sleep in her eyes or had smudged her mascara.

'OK, kitty. This is your last chance. You leave now, or you're staying here until I come back. What will it be?'

No response.

Nora closed the window, swung her handbag over her shoulder, squirted a tiny drop of perfume on one wrist and rubbed it against her neck. She jumped as she remembered his tongue on her hand.

'Pull yourself together, woman!' she said out loud, and at the same time she heard Andreas's voice from the passage.

'Do you have a man in your room? I didn't think that's allowed in a single bedroom.'

She dropped the room key into her handbag, and went outside to join him.

He was wearing a white shirt; of course, he was. She tried visualising him with a beer gut and a Liverpool supporter's nylon shirt. It didn't do the trick.

He took her arm as if it were the most natural thing in the world, and she felt herself stiffen. As did he, and immediately let her go.

'I've booked a table up there,' he said, pointing towards the town's oldest seaside hotel at the top of a hill with a view of the town and the bay.

Their table was in the second row on the roof terrace, and Andreas ordered gin and tonics for both of them. They were surrounded by people in sailing clothes, most of whom had never set foot on a deck, talking idly about what they were going to do for the rest of their holiday and the price of lobsters in the harbour yesterday.

The waiter brought white wine in a cooler, and as if by magic a giant seafood platter appeared on the table between them. She tried to defuse the situation before it grew too awkward.

'I thought you were more of a meat-and-two-veg kind of guy,' she laughed.

Andreas looked at her before reaching for a tiger prawn. 'You think all sorts of things, Nora Sand,' was all he said, and started peeling the prawn without taking his eyes off her.

Nora changed the subject. 'So, what have you been doing this afternoon, apart from working on your tan?'

'Discovered some information that might be of interest to you. Do you know a man called Spencer? Jeff Spencer?' Andreas asked.

'No, but I keep hearing his name. First in Dover and now I've just learned that he has been to Brine. Who is he? Do you know?'

'I called a friend at the Yard. He told me about him. Spencer is very interested in your photos. Very, very interested. And he's a highly respected man.'

'Right, so how can I get hold of him? And why doesn't he just call me, if he's that interested?'

Andreas's face grew serious. 'I don't think you quite understand. Do you know what Jeff Spencer investigates?'

'No. Is he some kind of cold case investigator? A retired policeman doing this as a hobby? Tell me what you know. I can see that you know something.'

'Jeff Spencer heads Scotland Yard's Profile Unit. He never appears in the media; he is fiercely protective of his anonymity in order to work undisturbed. But I haven't given too much away if I tell you that he's Britain's foremost expert on serial killers.'

Nora stared at him, a bit of lobster dangling from the corner of her mouth. Andreas reached across and carefully wiped it away.

'That's why he doesn't call,' he said quietly.

'But he thinks that the girls in the photos in my suitcase are dead?'

Andreas shrugged. 'That's all I can tell you, but I think that someone will contact you very soon. In the meantime, I've promised to take good care of you.'

She rolled her eyes. 'You're joking, aren't you?'

He shook his head. 'There's something else you need to know. After we went our separate ways, I took a walk around Brine and looked behind Mr Smithfield's shop. Someone broke into it recently. Given the state of the place, it's hard to say if anything was taken until we've had a chance to speak to Mr Smithfield. And even then it's the nature of these things that it'll be almost impossible to make a thorough inventory, unless he has photo documentation, stock takes, or an incredibly good memory. But I can tell you that the back door was forced recently. The damage was quite fresh, so I would say less than a week ago.'

Nora sipped her white wine. 'I have an idea who might have done it. A customer who couldn't wait,' she said and told him about her conversation with Polly and the barmaid's encounter with the rude woman who definitely didn't like Elvis.

'Now it could be someone with no connection to the case at all. It's one possibility we have to consider,' Andreas said.

'But you must admit it's unlikely to be a complete coincidence that it's happening now, surely?' Nora argued.

Andreas nodded pensively and gestured for more wine. The sun had started its journey into the sea, leaving behind a flame-red trail across the sky. They sat for a while without speaking and gazed at the horizon as the air cooled and the stars came out.

The waiter arrived discreetly, removed the white wine bottle with a clatter of ice cubes and distributed the last bit equally between their glasses. 'Coffee, dessert, more wine?' he asked.

Andreas looked at her quizzically. She shook her head. She'd had enough food for one day and the wine was starting to undermine her self-control. All she wanted was to go back to her room and hit the sack before she did something she might regret.

On their way along the beach back to Dolphin Guesthouse, they stopped and sat on the jetty. Nora took off her sandals and swung her feet over the water. She leaned back a little and gazed up at the sky.

'Do you know what I miss most in London?' she asked into the air.

Andreas sat down heavily next to her and kicked off his shoes. 'The sea?'

'Yes, that too. But most of all, I miss the darkness. It never gets properly dark in London, so you can't see the stars. Light pollution.'

'But the stars are still there,' Andreas said.

'Yes, but if you can't see them, what's the point?'

'And if you never swim in the sea, does it matter whether or not it's there?' he said with a roguish grin and pushed her over the edge.

Nora discovered in the nick of time what he was up to. She grabbed his arm so he too was pulled into the water.

The tide was out and the waves reached only as far as Nora's chest. She was the first to get on her feet and she splashed water at Andreas while he tried to find his footing.

'Is that what you call taking care of me?' she shouted and swam outside his reach.

When they were back ashore, Nora's dress stuck to her body like a wet rag. Drenched to the skin, they started heading back.

When they reached the streetlights, she saw how his wet shirt clung to his shoulders and chest. It required willpower to walk away from him once they reached the guesthouse.

'Good night!' she called out over her shoulder and let herself into her room.

'Meow,' she heard.

The cat from this afternoon was lying on her bed. With a litter of seven pitch-black kittens.

14

It took five minutes to rouse Wesley who was so fast asleep he didn't even notice that Nora was soaked through.

Eventually she managed to explain the problem to him and having viewed the room, he flung out his hand, somewhat apologetically, and said: 'I'm afraid we have no other rooms available, Miss Sand. I hope you can share the double room with your friend until I get rid of the cats and clean everything up. Would you mind? I'm really sorry, but I can't bring myself to move her and the kittens until tomorrow morning. Would that be all right with you?'

No! It's very much not all right! she wanted to scream at him. But it was no use.

She knocked on the door to Andreas's room. He emerged from the shower with a towel wrapped around his waist. 'Yes?'

'Emergency,' she said, offering no further explanation.

He raised his eyebrows.

'Follow me,' she demanded.

'Give me two minutes,' he said, carefully closing the door in front of her.

Shortly afterwards he appeared in the passage wearing a pair of shorts. She pointed silently to her room. Andreas opened the door and was met with a hiss from an exhausted and very protective mother cat that was thoroughly fed up with the constant interruptions.

Resolutely, he grabbed Nora's case and laptop under much protest from the new mother, and closed the door behind him.

'I guess it's just you and me, kiddo,' he said in his best Bogart accent and ushered her into his room, which was not only three times the size of Nora's, but also redecorated this side of the Thatcher era.

'You and me and PC Perfect,' she mumbled.

'What did you say?'

'Nothing. I'm going to have a shower,' she said, and took out her nightdress from her case.

'I'll make you some tea!' he called out through the bathroom door while the water cascaded over her body and warmed her up again.

When she returned to the bedroom, prim in her nightdress, a cup of tea was waiting on the bedside table on what would now be her side of the four-poster bed.

She had a quick look around. Although it was large, there wasn't room for a makeshift bed on the floor. There was a desk, a small, two-seater sofa and a blanket box.

Andreas was lying with his arm over his eyes, pretending to be asleep. She found the African oil book in her bag, edged herself into the bed, sat upright like Miss Marple with her knitting and opened it at a random chapter.

'The battle for the Niger delta's oil resources,' she read to herself, and carefully sipped her tea. Her hands were shaking slightly and she accidentally spilled a few drops down herself. They burned her naked skin.

She gave up on the tea and wiggled a little deeper into the bed, still gripping the book firmly.

His hair had already dried, and he smelt faintly of sun-warmed straw and salt water.

She had reached page eight before she realised that she hadn't taken in a single word.

His breathing revealed that he was not asleep.

With a sigh Nora put down the book on the bedside table and turned off the lamp. The moonlight shone on his collarbone and it required a considerable effort not to let her finger trail its curve. She clenched her fists.

'Good night,' she said.

'Good night,' he said.

And there they lay.

Nora could feel electricity on her skin and sense his closeness. Yet again her thoughts returned to that night after the leavers' ball in Hanne's garden. Why had she panicked when he told her? Because he had wrecked their friendship by secretly having feelings for her, perhaps?

Back then it had felt like a betrayal. But she was no longer an eighteen-year-old girl – maybe it was time to grow up.

'Andreas?' she said tentatively.

He was asleep.

The next morning she woke up in the crook of his arm. They were completely tangled up in one another, and she couldn't remember how that had happened. Her long hair was trapped under his shoulder and one of his thighs locked her leg in position. At that very moment while she hovered between sleeping and being awake, Nora had a feeling of them being an obvious fit. As if everything had led up to this point.

Persistent buzzing had woken her up, and she searched sleepily for the source. It was Andreas's mobile, which was on the bedside table next to him. Slowly she reached across him, taking care not to disturb him, thinking it was an alarm that needed turning off. But it was a text message. She didn't want to see it. She didn't mean to, but before she had time to close her eyes and put down the phone, the letters seared into her.

Missing you, hon. Bx

She slipped out of the four-poster bed. Out of Andreas, out of the white sheets, put on her swimsuit and went down to the sea.

When she had been swimming for several minutes, she saw him on the jetty. He was looking for her. She dived under the water. When she came up for air, he was gone.

Suddenly his head appeared right next to hers. He was slightly out of breath. 'If that's not cheating, then I don't know what is,' he said.

Nora studied his face. Perhaps he didn't know that they had slept in each other's arms most of the night. Perhaps he hadn't seen the message from PC Perfect.

'Come on,' he said, starting his long, strong crawl.

She followed him. As they sliced through the water, she slowly found a rhythm and last night's thoughts disappeared with each stroke.

They walked back to Dolphin Guesthouse in silence and ate breakfast with their heads buried in the newspapers. Nora read Section Two of the *Guardian* with enormous interest, and would from time to time glance furtively at Andreas, who was wolfing down muesli as if their sharing a bed was completely normal.

'My uncle called this morning,' he said, pouring coffee for her from a cafetière on the table.

'And?'

'He has, with a little help from Karl, got forensics to look more closely at the fingerprints from your picture. They're expecting a result next week.'

'Super,' she said without much enthusiasm and put down her newspaper. Surely he must have seen the message from PC Perfect by now. 'I, however, am in dire need of an internet café. The signal here is quite simply too poor, and I may have to do a little bit of work,' she said.

He shrugged. She knew him well enough to know that he was annoyed, but didn't want it to show.

They packed their bags and walked downstairs to Wesley in the reception, who checked them out. With a hint of a smirk, Nora thought.

'I'm sorry for the inconvenience, Miss Sand. We won't charge you for the room, obviously. Thank you for your patience,' he said politely.

Andreas came with her into town, and settled down with an espresso and *Murders of the Century* at a Parisian-style café, while Nora entered a shop with a low ceiling in the ugliest building in the town, a pink concrete block with a notice in the window advertising internet for five pounds an hour.

She managed to grab the second last computer. The other three were already occupied by a bunch of spotty-faced, prepubescent lads busy playing each other at Counter-Strike. It was only ten in the morning, but each of them already had a large Coke, and a family-sized packet of prawn cocktail crisps was doing the rounds.

Nora assumed they came from the mobile homes rented out to families every summer. The boys were already bored rigid on the first day of their holiday at being separated from their mates back home.

A sign above the gum-chewing lad who took her fiver announced that the consumption of food and beverages was not permitted, but the rule didn't seem to be strictly enforced.

First she checked if the world was still in one piece. The BBC indirectly confirmed this as their lead story was the fatal outcome to a famous comedian's drugs and alcohol binge, and sad though the event was, it was unlikely to pluck the heart strings of *Globalt's* readers.

She checked a couple of other news sites just to be on the safe side, but it soon became clear that the silly season, as the British press had so aptly named it, had well and truly arrived. *The Times* had tested the seawater quality along British coasts, the *Daily Mail* thought they had discovered new and vital evidence in the case they described as 'the murder of Princess Diana'.

At closer inspection it turned out to be a paparazzi photographer who so far had not been interviewed by the media, and had only now come forward. As far as Nora could gather, he had absolutely nothing to add to the tragic accident that had killed the princess in a Paris tunnel. However, you didn't need great analytical skills to work out why the story had ended up on the front page. A picture of Diana could bump up the circulation by as much as twenty per cent on a slow day, and who didn't need that in the silly season?

Nora logged on to her email account. There were forty-three new messages. Thirty-one could go straight to the bin. Then there was an email from Pete.

Where in the world are you, sweetheart? Going to Cambodia on Thursday for The Times. *Dinner before then? Give me a bell. Your mobile is out of range.*

She typed a quick reply: *Deal. How about the Thai place on Wardour Street, Tuesday at 8? Great news about Cambodia. Will you be going with Colin or Tess?*

Four emails from the Crayfish.

The first two were regular round-robin emails sent to every reporter: *Don't forget to submit your expenses on time. The Excel ninjas have been after me again*, one demanded. This was a reference to the magazine's long-suffering accounts department.

The third was the usual weekly plan of what would appear on the front page of the next issue of *Globalt*: Floods in China. Who is responsible? Isabelle tries to find some answers. Jens has been to Kabul and seen women in education. We have bought a freelance story from a Norwegian journalist who has investigated oil pollution in the Niger delta, and I'm working on an analysis of Russia's new energy policy and how it will affect the West. In the centrefold and on a couple of pages afterwards there will be an excellent photo report from a Roma camp in Romania by our new photojournalist intern, Yacub, and then a translation of an excellent feature article from *Frankfurter Allgemeine* about the euro.

As always Nora felt a tiny stab of guilt when her name didn't feature in the weekly plan. But it was only a stab and she had learned to live with it over the years. Some weeks were busier than others; it was just the way it was.

Hi, Nora. Tried your mobile a few times, but no coverage. I'm presuming this is work-related. Call me when you've got something. I'm expecting you to write for next week's issue or the week after that. If not, then call me anyway, the Crayfish wrote in his last email.

She left it unanswered. There were a few more things she needed to investigate before she could be sure she really had a scoop.

There was also an email from Trine who wanted to know about her 'schoolgirl crush' as she called it. Nora chuckled to herself, then wrote a brief reply: *No comment.*

Finally, there was an email from a D. Metcalfe. The name rang a bell. She checked the email address again – *d.metcalfe@crossassociates. com* – and opened it.

Dear Miss Sand,

On behalf of Mr Christian Cross, I am delighted to inform you that his esteemed client, Mr William Hickley, is prepared to meet with you in Wolf Hall Prison on the first Thursday this month at 2.30 p.m. In order to facilitate this, you will be required to sign a number of documents, as well as obtain written permission, which you will need to take to Mr Hickley's current residence. I must therefore ask you to contact our office no later than this Thursday in order to organise these matters.

Yours sincerely,
Doris Metcalfe (Mrs)
Secretary to Christian Cross, Cross Associates.

Nora couldn't believe her luck. Christian Cross had lowered her expectations completely, but something must have convinced William Hickley to meet with her. She wondered if he was expecting a fee. The Crayfish would never agree to that and Nora, too, refused to hand over money to a man to talk about the women he had murdered.

She made a note of Doris Metcalfe's number on a scrap of paper in her handbag. Then she tried calling her, but as there was only one bar on the mobile signal, the call didn't go through.

At that moment her screen went blank. Her time was up. She packed away her things and joined Andreas who was reading quietly in the sun. He looked up from the book when she positioned herself in front of him and blocked out the sun.

'Coffee?' he asked gently, and watched her with an expression that sent her straight back into last night's secret cave and the scent of straw in that bloody four-poster bed.

'Latte, please,' she said, and settled down on the chair opposite him.

He fetched it while she tried Doris Metcalfe again. Still no signal.

While they drank their coffee, she told him about her breakthrough. Then they went over to The Oysterman where Elvis was busy expressing his unreserved praise of Las Vegas.

A slightly overweight man with a reddish beard and a half-empty glass of draught beer in front of him was at the bar. Polly smiled when she saw Nora, and immediately pointed to the bearded man, who was wearing a lilac sweatshirt with the words 'Ollie's Ashram' on the back.

'Uncle Harry. She's here – the woman who wanted to talk to you.'

The moment he turned around, Nora recognised the man who had sold her the suitcase.

'I remember you,' he said, narrowing his eyes. 'Two weeks ago. An old leather suitcase with metal fittings. Thirty quid.'

Nora nodded. 'Impressive memory.'

The man on the barstool bowed slightly and extended his hand for a formal greeting. 'Harry Smithfield. At your service. Listen, why don't you and your boyfriend sit down and have a pint with me? I'm celebrating the end of my annual yoga retreat.'

'He's not my boyfriend,' Nora said before Andreas had time to react. 'But I'm happy to buy you a pint.'

'Hmm,' Uncle Harry said, eyeing Andreas suspiciously.

'He's a good friend,' Nora explained.

Uncle Harry found his smile again. 'All right then, three Chesil, Polly. Large ones, please.'

Polly poured the pints, which she then passed across the counter, and Nora took a symbolic sip, although she thought it was a bit early in the day for alcohol.

Uncle Harry took a sizeable gulp and the foam settled like a blond curtain on his beard. 'I guess you're wondering why I drink beer after my yoga retreat?'

Nora shook her head, but Uncle Harry had already launched into his speech.

'Everything in this life is about balance, you see. Yin and yang. Black and white. Soft and hard. Sweet and sour. Poisoning and detoxing,' he explained, and took another gulp of beer to illustrate his point.

'I've come about the suitcase you sold me. Can you remember how you got it?'

'Yes, but it was one of a kind, if that's what you're asking. There are no more.'

'No, that's all right. However, inside it I found some pictures, which I imagine the original owner might want back. You wouldn't happen to have an address, would you?'

Uncle Harry shook his head. 'Sorry, no. I bought it at a car boot sale over in Bolton, along with a great pile of other tat.'

Nora had time to feel despondent, before Andreas got involved in the conversation. 'Do you remember who sold it to you?'

'Sure I do. It was One-Eyed Joe.'

'And where do you think we might find him?' Andreas asked in his calm voice.

'I'd think he still goes to the weekly car boot sale in Upper Mullet. You can't miss it. It's right in the centre of town. But they'll be closed in less than an hour.'

They left Harry with two barely touched pints and his warning that it really wasn't a very good start to the day to be in such a hurry.

The microscopic green car started immediately and the satnav announced that it would take fourteen minutes to drive to the neighbouring town on the narrow, winding coastal road. What the satnav had failed to take into account was that everyone who lived away from the coast migrated there in the summer heat, while everyone who lived on the coast would head inland to avoid the townies. And that anyone with a tractor considered it their civic duty to take it for a spin every Sunday.

When they finally reached the car boot sale, the stream of customers had tailed off and several of the stalls were packing up. The church's cake sale looked like it had been a big hit. Two elderly women were busy putting something that looked like a Victoria sponge into a cardboard box, while a middle-aged man looked on with approval.

The stalls next to it specialised in china dolls, which a small, bent-over lady was busy wrapping gently in pink tissue paper.

'We're looking for One-Eyed Joe,' Nora said, and the woman pointed silently to the far corner of the square where a man was busy loading furniture and household items into a battered, orange pick-up truck.

He sized up Andreas with a single, grim look: 'Cop.' It was a statement.

Nora intervened before the mood soured. 'We're here on private business. Nothing official.'

The man relaxed somewhat, but carried on working.

'Harry Smithfield,' Nora began.

'Yes, what about him?'

'You sold him some goods about a month ago.'

'And?'

'Including a suitcase?'

'Maybe I did, maybe I didn't,' the man said in a solemn voice and turned his back to them to put a box on to the bed of the pick-up.

'How did you get the suitcase?'

'Don't remember.'

His answer was uttered too quickly to sound convincing. Andreas rolled his eyes. 'Listen, we don't care how you normally get your goods. In fact, we're not even British. We just happen to be interested in this particular suitcase. So please, how did you get it?'

The man shrugged and looked straight at Nora, until he was sure that he had her undivided attention. 'What's in it for me?'

Nora picked up an incredibly hideous cut-glass sugar bowl. A handwritten price tag on the side announced that One-Eyed Joe believed a gullible tourist would pay seven pounds for the treasure.

She weighed it in her hand. 'How about a tenner?'

Joe picked up her cue. 'Can't sell it to you for less than thirty, I'm afraid. It's been in the family for generations.'

They settled on twenty in the end and when money had changed hands, Joe wrapped the sugar bowl in an old copy of the *Daily Telegraph*, and leaned towards Nora. His breath reeked of stale tobacco.

'There's a care home over in Farthington. Bloody ugly, great big box on the outskirts of the town. I drive past it every week and check their skip. The old folks always think they will fit in more than they really can when they move in. The rooms are small and the carers ruthless. Too much stuff gathers dust, so they make sure to clear out. The skip is behind the building, in the car park. That's where I found the suitcase and some other stuff. Like this beautiful painting,' he said, pointing to a picture depicting an ominous, dark forest in a winter landscape with a low-hanging sun.

Andreas was clearly cross as they walked back to the car. 'Tell me I didn't just see you hand money to some lowlife of a habitual criminal in return for information?'

'Certainly not. I was only buying you a present. A permanent reminder of this wonderful trip,' she said, shoving the wrapped sugar bowl at him.

Then she got into the driver's seat and turned the key before he had time to reply. He got in, a little taken aback, the sugar bowl in his hands. 'Where are we going now?'

'To the care home.'

15

Farthington lay a little deeper in the countryside. The care home was right on the edge of the town, and not even the cursive, cast-iron sign entwined with roses declaring that this was the private care home Cedar Residence could lighten up the bleak architecture that served as a reminder than everyone can grow old and frail, and end up in a home where the only care they get is the care they pay for.

The car park was almost full when Nora turned into it. Sunday was the busiest day of the week for visitors.

'What's our plan now?' Andreas wanted to know.

Nora thought about it, then she said: 'They say honesty is the best policy, but that's not necessarily true when you're dealing with self-important, British penpushers.'

She stepped out of the car and smoothed her clothes. 'I'm guessing it must be William Hickley's mother who ended up here. After all, he's in prison, and I can't imagine where else the suitcase might have come from.'

Andreas slammed shut the car door. 'So now we pay Mrs Hickley a visit, is that what you're saying?'

'Yes. You got it in one. Congratulations – you've won an antique sugar bowl.'

The first thing that struck them was the smell of old age, the same in care homes across the world. Even after the smoking ban, the place still reeked of cheroots, mouldy furniture and stale urine under a very thin veneer of detergent. From the visitors' lounge they could hear the sound of clattering teacups, and in the TV lounge further down, BBC's weekly *Eastenders* omnibus was blaring.

They were only three steps inside the door when a woman with steel-framed glasses, short dyed hair and a lilac uniform stopped them.

'I'm sorry. Visiting hours are almost over. We finish at four thirty, that's in fifteen minutes. It's hardly worth disturbing anyone for such a short time,' she declared.

'But we've come a really long way,' Nora tried.

'Yes, you may well have. But there's no need to excite the elderly so near their bedtime. It can have very unfortunate effects on their medication,' she insisted.

'I'm sure Aunt Vanessa can manage. We're all she has.'

'Aunt Vanessa?' the woman said and raised an eyebrow. 'And does Aunt Vanessa have a surname, if I may ask?'

'Hickley,' Andreas replied.

A triumphant smile played on the woman's lips. 'Your information must be wrong. There's no Vanessa Hickley here at Cedar Residence. Perhaps you're not quite so close to your "aunt" as you claim.'

'I don't understand,' Nora said. 'Might she be registered under a different name?'

The contempt in the carer's face was obvious. 'Do you seriously think that I can or would want to give out confidential information about our residents? You claim that your aunt Vanessa Hickley lives here. We have no one by that name. You have two choices: leave right now or wait for me to call the police and expose you for the thieves that you are.'

Twenty seconds later they were back in the car in the car park.

'That went well,' Andreas observed dryly.

X

They drove back to London in almost total silence. Andreas snoozed in the back while Nora's thoughts drifted between the traffic and Jazz FM. She wanted to shake him awake and demand an explanation for how they had ended up in each other's arms last night. But somehow she couldn't cope with his answer. Or what would follow.

It was growing dark inside the car when they joined the M25 and ended up in a long queue of other Londoners heading back to the capital on a Sunday night.

The radio played 'I love you, Porgy' and without Nora noticing it, her voice found Billie Holiday's as she sang about the complexities of love.

A drowsy Andreas sat up in the back and stroked her cheek lightly. 'Hey,' he said softly.

'Andreas. Please, just stop it,' she began, turning to face him.

All further thoughts were interrupted by the loud beeping of a horn. The driver behind them felt she was straying too far into his lane. Nora straightened up the car and indicated that she would be leaving at the next exit, which had a sign for petrol and a McDonald's. She was worn out by her thoughts, by driving, by not having had any lunch, and being with Andreas without *being with* Andreas.

'Stop what?' he said, when they had filled up the car and were sitting with their burgers in the shadow of Ronald McDonald and his motorway disciples.

'Forget it.'

'No. What were you going to say?'

'Only that I'm tired. Would you drive the rest of the way? Please?' she lied.

Andreas nodded. 'OK. I'll do my best though I warn you that I'm not wild about driving on the wrong side of the road.'

Back in the car Andreas made himself comfortable in the driver's seat. Nora sat in the darkness, looking alternately out of the window and at his silhouette in the dashboard glow.

They were both silent until they returned the car and said goodbye outside the rental firm.

'See you later,' was all she said, before hailing a cab. She felt tired to her very soul.

As she looked out of the cab's window, he was still standing where she had left him. When he spotted her, he raised his hand in a quick wave, then turned on his heel.

Nora fished her iPhone out of her pocket. She had twenty-eight missed calls and thirteen messages on her voicemail. Two of them were from Pete. Three were heavy breathers or someone with chest problems who hadn't had the guts to leave a message. Two were work calls from the Crayfish and a single one from her mother telling her she was back from Florence.

The rest were from Jeff Spencer of the Metropolitan Police. He left a mobile number with his fifth message.

Nora checked her watch. It was thirty-five minutes past ten. The chances of him still answering his phone were probably close to zero, but then again, he had asked her to call him as soon as she got his message.

He picked up before the first ringtone had ended. 'Spencer.'

His voice was deep and dark. She imagined that he would have a beautiful baritone singing voice. She introduced herself.

'Miss Sand. I'm delighted to hear from you. I've spent most of my weekend trying to get in touch with you,' he said with a hint of reproach in his voice.

'I had no coverage,' she mumbled.

'Please would you come to Scotland Yard tomorrow morning at nine o'clock?' he asked, without further ado.

'What's this about?'

He hesitated, and she could hear the noise of many people in the background. 'I'm at a party. However, I'm sure you can guess what it's about when I tell you that I've studied a certain suitcase you handed in with great interest.'

'OK. I'll be there tomorrow morning.'

'Good. Just ask for me at reception. Goodbye,' he said and rang off.

Nora sat for a while holding her mobile before she let it slide into her handbag and resumed staring out of the cab window. There wasn't a single star in the sky.

16

Her alarm clock rang a microsecond before the Crayfish called her on her mobile, and in her rush to turn off the ringing, she dropped the phone on the floor.

'What are you doing, woman?' he demanded to know when she finally retrieved him from the floor.

'Nothing. Minor technical issues,' she said, fighting to free herself from the duvet.

'Is that right? Anyway, what do you have for me for this week?'

Nora told him about the weekend's dead ends and how she was on her way to Scotland Yard's Profile Unit. 'And,' she added triumphantly, 'I've been granted permission to visit Bill Hix on Thursday.'

'Wow,' the Crayfish said in a tone of voice that bordered on impressed. 'How did you swing that?'

'Er. I don't really know,' she admitted.

'But that's no use to me this week. What have you got for me right now?'

Nora scratched the back of her head. 'Boss. I'm actually really busy with –'

'How about the Falkland Islands? It's a long time since we've heard anything about them, isn't it? The *New York Times* had an interesting feature in their weekend supplement.'

'Please can it wait? I have to leave for Scotland Yard in half an hour.'

The Crayfish grunted reluctantly. 'All right, call me this afternoon. I want to know where the story is going.'

'Yes, yes,' Nora promised, hung up and jumped in the shower.

The skirt/jacket combo made another appearance, and she just had time to pick up a coffee from her local Starbucks before she flopped down on the last seat on the tube with two days' harvest from her letter box under her arm.

As the tube train made its way towards the city centre, she quickly sorted through her post.

Invitations to a gallery opening and a reception at the Irish Embassy. She stuffed them into the front pocket of her handbag, knowing full well she would probably forget all about them.

At one time, when Nora had been summoned to her first press briefing at Scotland Yard, her head had been filled with romantic detective stories about pipe-smoking detective inspectors with impressive moustaches who solved crime riddles by pure deduction, while sitting behind polished desks in awe-inspiring buildings.

The reality was that Scotland Yard had long since left the original Scotland Yard near Whitehall and Trafalgar Square and moved into a rather anonymous, post-war building on Broadway. The front of the building might just as easily have been that of a Dutch investment bank, if it hadn't been for the concrete blocks to deter car bombs, and the rotating triangular New Scotland Yard sign, which was the favourite background for any BBC journalist when they breathlessly reported that there were no new developments in some crime story or other.

The only connection to countless British crime novels was the fact that the building housed the pioneering British crime database, which some bright spark had christened Home Office Large Major Enquiry System, commonly known as HOLMES. Nora had even heard that the course to teach budding crime experts to search for information using it had been named Elementary.

She was in the reception at five minutes past nine. She had been on time originally, but had spent longer going through security checks than she had expected because a man she had taken to be a Polish police inspector on an exchange had forgotten to empty his trouser pockets. First his keys. Then loose change. Then a pocket knife, which he handed remorsefully to the officers.

A sign near the metal detector, which could match those found in airports, announced that the current threat level was severe.

'What does severe really mean?' she asked the female officer who patted her down.

'We're not allowed to say. It would undermine the system,' the officer replied.

'But then why put up a sign in the first place, if it's that secret?'

The officer shrugged and gestured towards the reception where a young woman was speaking on the telephone behind an armoured-glass window. When she spotted Nora, she pointed to a book, which lay open on the counter, and a pen attached to a metal disc with a small chain.

Nora wrote down her name. Under company, she wrote *Globalt,* and then the date and time. The woman signalled to Nora to hand her the book and entered, with the phone now wedged between her chin and shoulder, her name on a computer. Then she pointed to a wall-mounted camera.

'Smile,' she mimed.

Nora looked straight into the camera. Shortly afterwards a printer buzzed behind the receptionist, and Nora found herself holding a shiny new laminated card.

The receptionist eventually gave up trying to contact whoever she had been looking for, hung up with sigh and spoke to Nora.

'You need to keep the card visible at all times, and it's only valid today. The card is the property of the Metropolitan Police and you must return it when you leave the building,' she reeled off.

Nora nodded.

'And who are you visiting?' the receptionist rounded off.

'Spencer. Mr Jeff Spencer.'

'OK. Spencer? *The* Jeff Spencer?' she asked. She sounded impressed and rang him immediately.

Nora heard several 'yes, sir, yes, sir' fired off in quick succession. Two minutes later a young, red-haired man in uniform came down to meet her.

He introduced himself, ushered her towards the elevator and pressed the button for the fifth floor. They continued down a long corridor with matching doors on both sides. Nora tried reading the names in passing, but the signs only bore number and letter combinations such as Q45 and VA5.

On a yellow cord around his neck the man wore an ID card, which he lifted to swipe through a door lock at the end of the corridor. Finally they arrived at a messy front office where Nora thought she could smell fresh coffee. On the desk was a half-open box from Dunkin' Donuts and Nora counted three doughnuts, which tempted her with their sticky sugar and red jam.

The door opened, and a rotund, white-haired woman wearing a tunic-style garment came towards them.

'Oh, good, you've fetched Miss Sand. Excellent. Jeff's in the meeting room with the others.'

Then she turned to Nora. 'Doughnut?'

'No, thanks. I'm trying to quit.'

They entered the meeting room and Jeff Spencer rose to his full height, which was almost two metres, when he saw Nora in the doorway. She could tell immediately that this was serious.

And yet she couldn't help smiling as she remembered Polly from The Oysterman who had asked Mr Spencer about his possible kinship to Princess Diana. The man's skin was the colour of milky coffee and his hair an Afro rarely seen in the British aristocracy. He was in shirtsleeves, but his suit jacket was hanging over a chair, and on the wall behind him were the pictures of the twelve girls from the suitcase.

Two tables had been pushed together into an L-shape, and Spencer was flanked by a blond woman in her twenties, who introduced herself as Irene, and a man called Stuart Millhouse, who looked to be in his early thirties. Spencer gestured to Nora to take a seat and poured her coffee from a cafetière.

'We're a bit peculiar up here,' he apologised. 'We don't drink as much tea as most other Brits,' he explained, while Millhouse's grin suggested there were plenty more reasons why the rest of Scotland Yard thought the inhabitants of the fifth floor were eccentric.

Nora focused on the pictures on the wall behind him. They were copies, blown up to triple size. That in itself wasn't frightening. What made the hairs on Nora's arms stand up was that under pretty much every picture, there was a name. And underneath the name, the laconic message: Missing.

A blond girl with a bob and dimples had been identified as Inge Husted from Stavanger, Norway. A dark-haired beauty with corkscrew curls had been identified as Louise Laan from Rotterdam, the Netherlands. Gertrud Neuberg from Munich, Germany, was hanging between two girls from Bruges, Belgium and Halmstad, Sweden.

Nora gulped.

'Are they the victims of Bill Hix? Victims who weren't identified back then? Are they the girls whose tongues were found in the cabinet of horrors?' The questions flew out of her, and she was already pulling out her notebook and pen from her bag.

'Miss Sand,' Spencer said with exquisite manners and an accent she would guess had its foundation at Eton and later finished off at either Cambridge or Oxford. 'May I remind you that you're at a police station, and politely point out that things here work a little differently than in your world. Here we're the ones asking the questions,' he said.

Irene started to giggle, but quickly controlled herself.

'The suitcase. Tell me all about it,' Spencer said, throwing up his hands. 'I want to know everything.'

He wasn't joking.

Nora told them how she and Pete had happened to stop off in Brine after an interview. He asked about the interview. When had they left Mr Benn? When did they arrive in Brine? Had they stopped off on the way for any other reason? What was the registration number of Pete's car? Nora didn't know, and even before she got to the part about the bric-a-brac shop, she was exhausted from his many questions.

She told them about Brine, about her collection of suitcases at home, how the brown suitcase in the window had caught her eye, and how she had bought it from Mr Smithfield. Did she have receipt, Spencer wanted to know.

Nora shook her head. But then how could they be sure that the suitcase really did come from Mr Smithfield's shop? She could have found it anywhere; it might even be her own.

'Well, I guess you'll have to ask Mr Smithfield about that,' she snapped irritably.

'We would like to,' Spencer said. 'But the man seems to have taken himself off to some yoga ashram, which doesn't permit mobile phones or indeed any contact with the outside world that doesn't include the use of chakras.'

Nora made a mental note of this information. So there was something Mr Spencer didn't know. He was starting to get on her nerves, and out of sheer spite she decided that if he wouldn't let her tell her story in her own time, she wouldn't volunteer any information. Of course, if he asked her directly if she had had a beer with Uncle Harry, she would tell him. And she might even be willing to divulge that she had traced the suitcase to a nursing home in Farthington. But if he carried on like this, the chances of her sharing her research with him were vanishingly small.

He made careful notes of her answers in a black moleskin notebook. They had now reached the point in her account where Nora had found the pictures in her flat.

'And what did you do when you discovered pictures of young women who most likely were the victims of a violent crime?' Spencer asked with raised eyebrows.

'I had no reason to think that a crime had been committed. They were just pictures someone had left behind. So I made a cup of coffee.'

'Aha. You made a cup of coffee?'

Nora was aware that her irritation was getting the better of her. 'Hey, how about we just rewind a bit. I had no – absolutely no – idea of anything untoward. I mean, just look at the pictures,' she said, gesturing towards the wall. 'Do any of these pictures scream crime to you?'

For the first time Stuart Millhouse opened his mouth. 'Perhaps the fact that the girls are missing and very much missed by their relatives and families – and have been for years,' he pointed out.

'But I couldn't know that!'

'No, Miss Sand couldn't know that,' Spencer said, pouring oil on troubled waters.

'So perhaps Miss Sand would like to share with us what first roused her suspicion?'

Nora told them about the photograph that appeared to have been taken on board the England ferry, and how she had discovered the Danish TV documentary with the Karl Stark interview, and about her friend, Andreas, who was a Danish police officer.

Spencer noted down their names and asked Nora to spell them twice to be absolutely sure.

'And where's that picture now?'

Nora explained that it was currently being investigated in Denmark.

'So that means we're missing a photo?' Spencer said, clearly annoyed.

Nora showed him her copy and was told to email it to the Profile Unit. Millhouse disappeared and came back two minutes later with a printout, which he put up next to the other pictures.

'And what's your relationship to Andreas Jansson, if you don't mind me asking?'

'Personal,' Nora hissed.

'How can we get hold of Mr Jansson?'

'Try the second floor.'

'I beg your pardon?'

'No, I mean it. He's on some sort of anti-terror course on behalf of Danish police.'

'Very well. So tell me how you ended up visiting my old friend James McCormey?'

Nora told them about the book she had bought in the airport, the similarity between the poses in the pictures and the account of the case against William Hickley, also known as Bill Hix. She told them how she had found his name on the suitcase.

'And not even at that point does it cross your mind to contact the police directly and hand over this incredibly important piece of evidence to an expert?'

Nora shook her head. 'Mr Spencer,' she said wearily. 'I know you work for the government, but have you ever found yourself in a situation where you had to contact the police through official channels? Say your bike or wallet was nicked?'

Spencer proffered a measured nod. 'Once.'

'Right. Then perhaps I can ask you what you think would have happened if I'd called police and said that I had a suitcase full of pictures and absolutely no idea if a crime had been committed? That is, if I had been put through to a real person, rather than just pressing my way through a telephone system that ended up suggesting I report my concern online?'

'Touché,' said Millhouse, who seemed to regard himself as a commentator on the conversation, as if he were at a Wimbledon semi-final.

His remark appeared to make Jeff Spencer realise – at long last, in Nora's opinion – that they might be on the same side after all.

'OK. I accept that you found the suitcase as you've described. For some reason James trusts you. And I trust James.'

Spencer leaned back in his chair with his arms folded across his chest and something that resembled a smile on his lips. 'You found the suitcase and you found the pictures. And somehow you had the presence of mind to contact the police. And not only that, you also tracked down the one person in the police force most likely to listen to you once you mentioned the name Bill Hix,' Spencer said, holding a rhetorical pause.

'So my question is this: What's your theory about the girls? Who are they, and what happened to them?'

Nora looked up at the wall with the pictures and the many names, and then down at Spencer again. 'Well, surely that's obvious, isn't it? The pictures were found in a suitcase that used to belong to Bill Hix. Anyone with the slightest knowledge of the cabinet of horrors and that vile man would immediately conclude that they must be the girls who were never identified or found. Perhaps some of those girls whose tongues are still pickled in a jar at the Institute of Forensic Medicine? Isn't it just a matter of carrying out some DNA tests?'

Spencer watched her gravely. 'Yes, you would think so, wouldn't you?'

Nora waited for him to continue.

Spencer pointed to one of the pictures on the wall behind him. It showed a girl of about seventeen years old wearing cheap jewellery and more mascara and lipstick than her young face could carry off. She was standing against the obligatory white wall, smiling nervously to the photographer with her arms folded under her breast to make her chest measurement a little more impressive. There could be no mistaking the image on her T-shirt. Madonna's iconic features advertised the singer's *The Girlie Show Tour*. Underneath the picture was a name: Zoë Bellman, Manchester. She looked no more or less unhappy than any of the other girls.

Nora got up and studied the picture closely.

After a moment's silence Spencer appeared to adopt a more amicable approach and said: 'Can you see what's wrong?'

She was on the verge of seeing it. It was on the tip of her tongue, ready to be uttered. There was something about –

'To be fair, it was Irene who spotted it. Just between us, she's a bit of a Madonna freak. Our problem is as follows: Madonna's *Girlie Show Tour* took place in 1993. William Hickley was jailed in 1992.'

Nora sat still while the information sank in.

'Let me make sure I've got this right. It means Hix couldn't have taken the pictures?'

Spencer shook his head. 'No, he couldn't. We've identified most of the girls. We know that they're missing and that they went missing *after* Bill Hix was apprehended. But it gets even weirder – because on your suitcase we found a tiny, barely detectable thumbprint, which undoubtedly belongs to William Hickley. Do you see the problem?'

Spencer nodded to Millhouse to indicate that he could take over.

'Bill Hix knows something. He must know who took the pictures,' Millhouse began by asserting.

'But Hix is a man who lives to lie, deceive and misdirect. All attempts – and let me add that there have been many – to make him reveal anything that could help the investigation, have failed. Therapists, psychologists and psychiatrists – he toys with them. And when he gets bored, he crushes them and all their hopes. We're stuck.'

Nora started to get an unpleasant feeling of where this was heading.

'Last week you met with Christian Cross to get permission to visit Bill Hix in prison.'

It wasn't a question. Millhouse told Nora they were fully aware of what had been said during the meeting.

'We've spoken to Christian Cross and as far as we can gather, for the first time in years, Hix has expressed an interest in meeting someone other than his family,' Millhouse said, clearing his throat.

'Usually Hix refuses to speak to outsiders. However, it just so happens that Christian Cross owes this office a favour, so he has been kind enough to strongly encourage his client to talk to you, and Mr Hickley has chosen to listen to his esteemed solicitor. So far, so good.'

Nora had flashbacks to the movie scene where Clarice Starling is sent down a long, dark basement corridor with the criminally insane in cells on either side until she reaches a folding chair in front of Hannibal Lecter, who converses politely with her behind armoured glass while reminiscing about eating a census-taker's liver with a good Chianti and fava beans.

'I'm sorry, did I just walk on to the set of *Silence of the Lambs* part four?'

She looked imploringly at Spencer who couldn't help smiling, although he made a concerted effort not to. 'Just let the man speak,' he reassured her.

Nora folded her arms across her chest and looked hard at Millhouse.

'The meeting will take place in a room that is under surveillance. He'll be restrained. You'll have a unique opportunity to interview him. A scoop. All we're asking in return is that you slip in a few questions on our behalf.'

'I can't just share my research with the police. It goes against all principles of a free press.'

'No, and we totally appreciate that,' Spencer interjected. 'But you could view it as a form of cooperation. A swap. We have information that might benefit your story. You might be able to get information that would help our investigation. Think about it.'

For a microsecond Nora wished she was still a smoker. What she needed now was to stand with a cigarette in her hand, weighing up the pros and cons, while gazing at the London skyline.

Spencer pushed her. 'Listen. We've already shared information with you by letting you into this room and telling you about the girls and their names. Before you stepped across the threshold, you didn't even know if there was a story. If the girls were alive or dead –'

'True, but then again, you wouldn't have a new lead without my suitcase,' Nora retorted.

'It's evidence now and because of that we've made some progress.'

'But if it's not Hix, then who on earth is it?' Nora asked with a frown.

Spencer took a deep breath. 'That's what we're hoping Hix might know.'

Nora shook her head. 'Why now? I just don't understand it. I mean, how can so many young women disappear without anyone noticing, without anyone joining the dots? It doesn't seem possible.'

'Oh, it does when you think about it,' Millhouse replied. 'We're talking about twelve girls here, plus your two from the ferry, but if we set aside the picture from Denmark, let's say twelve. They come from the UK, but also Germany, Norway, Sweden, the Netherlands, Belgium and Italy. The ones we've been able to identify disappeared over several years. In dribs and drabs. Girls travel abroad and drop off the radar all the time. They meet men. They fall in love and move in with them, and perhaps they forget to phone home. Perhaps they fall through the cracks in the system; they get fired from their au pair jobs for refusing to have sex with daddy. Anything can happen to girls in those situations. Some experiment with drugs, some end up at King's Cross along with the other junkie prostitutes. In which case they're unlikely to call their family to update them about their career trajectory in the capital. Their faces are like snowflakes in a snowstorm,' Millhouse said with an unexpected hint of poetry.

'Yes, but surely their families are still looking for them?'

'We're dealing with seven or eight different embassies here. Perhaps some of them did politely contact the UK police to ask them to keep an eye out in case a missing Malin Bergqvist, who came over to seek her fortune in the West End's theatre land, turns up at a hospital, or for signs of life from a Gertrud Neuberg, who never showed up for her intensive English language course in Hampstead. Perhaps the British police even went to the trouble of actually checking out the reports, made a few enquiries here and there. But the chances of anyone joining the dots were miniscule. None of the girls has ever been found. There's not much to work with and until you found the suitcase, there was no reason to think there even was a case.'

'But surely the girls must have something in common, apart from that?' Nora insisted.

'Yes. Bill Hix. They have him in common,' Spencer said.

Nora shuddered. 'So what you're saying is there's a copycat out there. Someone who stole Bill Hix's suitcase?'

Spencer nodded. 'A copycat or an accomplice. We don't know which. But we believe that William Hickley does. And you may be our best chance of getting him to talk about it. We know it's a long shot, but we have to try. If for no other reason than for the sake of these girls and their families. There are still parents looking for their missing daughters and an explanation for what happened to them,' he said.

Millhouse opened the file and took out a picture of an elderly couple standing with their suitcases in front of what looked like a departure terminal at Heathrow Airport. The grief was chiselled into every line in their faces.

'This is Hannelore and Helmuth Neuberg from Munich. Every year they use their summer holiday to travel to London to look for their daughter. They have done so ever since she disappeared seventeen years ago. They still believe that their beloved Gertrud is alive, but somehow unable to communicate with them. Or, that's to say – I'm starting to think that Helmuth may have reached the stage where he knows that the most he can hope for is one day to get Gertrud's earthly remains home and buried in the family plot. It's not something he has ever said out loud, but it's my impression when I meet with them every year and I tell them that, no, unfortunately we haven't been able to find Gertrud since their last visit. We haven't even been able to give them an explanation as to what happened to her, let alone a body.'

Millhouse produced another picture from the file. 'This is Siri Galtung. She has spent fifteen years looking for Inge. Do you want me to go on?'

Nora shook her head. 'But how do I handle him? I've no experience of talking to murderers, and if countless psychologists have already tried, I struggle to see what I would be able to do that hasn't already been tried by them?'

Irene cleared her throat and spoke up. 'We've discussed it. Extensively. Whether you should play the part of his domineering mother and try to make him submit to you and confess. If we should change his medication before the meeting. Or if you should play the obsessive serial killer groupie. But the truth is that he would probably see through it in the three seconds it'll take you to park your backside on the seat opposite him. Our best bet is that you're yourself. Plain and simple. He has expressed an interest in meeting a Danish journalist and agreed to an interview. So that's what will happen. If you're going to get anything from it, you'll succeed by being authentic. If not, well, at least you tried.'

Spencer clarified: 'In other words, don't do very much you wouldn't otherwise have done. The only difference is that you now know something you didn't know before you came here today. And, well, that you share any new information with us.'

Nora could have sworn that he winked at her.

'OK. But then I also want an interview with you for my final article,' Nora said.

'I never give interviews. You have to use Millhouse or Irene.'

'Seriously? What a shame. I'm sure that James will be just a little upset when he hears how easily you let the only new lead in the Hix investigation slip through your fingers. Because you never give interviews.'

'OK. You can interview me, but don't mention my name,' Spencer said reluctantly.

'So how do I refer to you?'

'As a senior analyst from Scotland Yard's Profile Unit.'

Nora stuck out her hand. 'Done. We have a deal.'

'You drive a hard bargain, Miss Sand,' Spencer said wearily and held out the pastry box to her. 'How about a doughnut to seal our deal?'

'Hard bargainers don't eat stuff like that,' she said with a smile.

It didn't occur to her until she was back in the street that it might not be clear who had struck the best deal.

After all, what kind of moron enters a room with three profiling experts and thinks she can walk away with the psychological advantage?

She was briefly tempted to text Andreas, seeing as she was at Scotland Yard anyway. Perhaps she could pump him for information about Spencer – for example, if he was a man of his word. It was her gut feeling that he was. In the end, she let her mobile stay in her pocket. She didn't have the energy for any more drama today.

At that very moment her iPhone vibrated. It was a text message from Svend Jansson. *Call me* was all it said. Nora found his number and pressed redial.

'Jansson,' she heard almost immediately.

'It's Nora.'

She could tell that he was in a room full of people. 'Hang on. I'm in the canteen,' he said. She could hear him move away from the noise of clattering cutlery and chatter. Then she heard a door open and a slightly out of breath Jansson: 'OK. I'm in my office. I promised to let you know when I got the results of the fingerprints from the picture, remember.'

'Yes?'

'It's a very strange result, and I don't really know what use you can make of it. Or what use I can make of it. There were five different prints on the picture. Two of them we can eliminate. They are yours and Andreas's. A further complication is that the database we use for comparison only covers people registered in Danish police archives. It means that if the fingerprint is from a foreign source, we don't have a snowball's chance in hell of finding it. For that we would have to go through Europol or Interpol, and that's a whole new process which requires several applications and authorisations. It can take months, and I can't imagine that my boss will be willing to bother the big boys at the Lyon headquarters, unless we have something more solid.'

'Yes, OK, Svend. But that doesn't change anything, does it? We've known that from the start.'

'Sure. I just think it's important that you understand the limitations.'

'And now I do,' Nora said, struggling to suppress her curiosity.

'Good. We couldn't identify two prints on the picture, but the fifth paid off and alarm bells started ringing.'

'Aha?'

'It belongs to a certain Oluf Mikkelsen.'

'*The* Oluf Mikkelsen?'

'Yes, *the* Oluf Mikkelsen, former resident at Vestergården and participant of the fatal trip to London.'

'But that makes no sense?'

'Nope. Not right now it doesn't. But his fingerprints were in our system not only because of a series of break-ins in Ringkøbing he committed while he was in care at Vestergården, but also as a result of a later conviction for assault in Copenhagen. It's him. There can be no doubt.'

'And where is he now?'

She could hear Svend Jansson chuckle to himself. 'How did I know you were going to ask me that?' he said, and Nora could hear him hit a few keys on his keyboard.

'Now here's another strange thing. Oluf Mikkelsen appears to have moved to Greve for a while. We have some information about him on our system. Minor stuff, really. Antisocial behaviour, pickpocketing, insurance fraud. Petty crimes, to be honest. The records go on until the start of 1991, after which all traces of him disappear. He doesn't claim any benefits, he doesn't pay tax, he doesn't see a doctor. He drops off the face of the earth. But no one reports him missing. It's very odd.'

'Do you have his last known address?'

'You know perfectly well I'm not allowed to give that information to civilians,' Svend Jansson said sternly.

'But I have to have something to go on?'

'I couldn't even tell you that Oluf Mikkelsen left Greve, or that he was a keen amateur boxer, if it wasn't because I'm convinced that you can google this information yourself in five seconds.'

'Thank you so much, Svend.'

'Don't mention it. I'm sure that Annika sends her love. She's overjoyed that you might become a part of the family.'

Nora blushed right up to the roots of her hair.

'Eh, I'll call you if I find out anything more about Lulu and Lisbeth,' she said quickly, and rang off before Jansson had time to ask probing questions.

17

She shopped in Whole Foods on her way home where she lingered over a fruit and vegetable section that banished all thoughts of serial killers. The shelves were laden with fat white asparagus, cherries bursting with juice, deep violet blueberries and soft feathery peaches, still smelling of flowers and Italian sunshine.

Nora was reminded of the time she interviewed a famous female chef in London as part of a feature on high-achieving women. When they had finished the obligatory questions about how hard it was for a woman to break into a male-dominated world, and how big the sacrifices on the domestic front were, out of sheer curiosity Nora asked the chef about the best meal she had ever had.

The woman's eyes had taken on a dreamy expression as she told her about a lunch she had eaten at the age of fourteen with her father on the roof terrace of a restaurant on Capri.

'I don't remember the starter or the main course,' she said to Nora's surprise. 'But when we got to the dessert, the waiter brought two peaches on a plate and a knife. It was as simple as that. They were just picked and warmed by the sun. I can still recall the sensation of my knife slicing through the skin to the golden, juicy, sweet flesh. It was heavenly. It was perfection.'

Nora had never forgotten that, and she now selected a couple of peaches and placed them carefully in her basket, followed by a bunch of rocket and the best Parma ham from the deli. Sliced very thinly. At the cheese counter she tasted her way to the softest, creamiest buffalo mozzarella. Then she weighed a few handfuls of fat, salted Spanish Marcona almonds, popped a bottle of prosecco into the basket along with a loaf of ciabatta so freshly baked that she could feel the heat through the brown paper bag.

That was dinner taken care of when the time came. All that was left on her list now was a serial killer and a bit of research.

She turned on her computer the moment she stepped through the door and let it warm up while she put the food away. She rested the peaches on her windowsill where they could take in the last few hours of sunlight.

Her flat was humid and she drank water straight from the bottle in the fridge before settling down to work.

The last thing she wanted to do was read more about Bill Hix and his dreadful deeds, but it was crucial if she were to be properly prepared for her visit to Wolf Hall Prison in three days.

Her window was ajar and she could hear the sound of London traffic in the background. Frustrated drivers beeping their horns at each other, Filipina maids picking up schoolchildren, teenage girls with mobiles pressed to their ear and builders catcalling beautiful women from the rolled-down windows of their white vans.

There were days when the noise distracted and frustrated her, and she envied *Globalt's* Italy correspondent, who had rented accommodation in an old monastery on a Tuscany hilltop, from where in exalted calm and peace, he could write about brutal Mafia murders and intrigues in the Berlusconi government.

But today when her laptop took her into a sick universe, Nora was grateful for the sound of normality coming through the window as a low but steady pulse. A link to a world where the sun was still shining and where girls who dreamed of becoming models slept safely in their beds and didn't hang around King's Cross waiting to be picked up by a smug banker in a Mercedes looking for a cheap thrill. A world where young girls' tongues didn't end up pickled in a jar in a warehouse.

After Nora had ploughed her way through the first five websites, she had a fairly good idea about Bill Hix and his dark deeds. There wasn't much that hadn't already been covered by *Murders of the Century*. Most of the sites were merely an extension of what she already knew, and many sites decidedly wallowed in the details of the individual murders.

Nora tried staying objective. She made notes and prepared a time-line to get an overview, but she had a feeling of wading through a stinking cesspit. The blood-dripping graphics that glorified violence made her feel nauseous, as did the ecstatic and admiring comments that so-called fans of Bill Hix had left on allegedly factual sites.

She wondered what drove Hix. Vanity? Arrogance, conceit, a God complex with the right to choose who would live and who would die? Or was he a scared little boy at the mercy of his desires? She quickly dismissed the last thought. He hadn't been caught for years. That proved he was cold-blooded and calculating. Only a flat tyre, an unpredictable event, had brought him down in the end.

He had run rings round James McCormey. Played on his concern for the victims' relatives. Used it to torment everyone. He enjoyed the game. He loved being the centre of everyone's attention. She had to let him think that he had the upper hand. But not make it too obvious. It had to be a challenge or he would lose interest immediately.

Finally she couldn't take it any longer and turned on the news by way of a brain break. Anything, please.

They were in the middle of a weather forecast so she channel-hopped and came across a documentary on biker gangs. Suddenly she had a light-bulb moment. She dug into her bag, pulled out the invitation from the Irish Embassy before she found the Dare Devils business card in a front pocket.

'Helgaard,' he said when he answered his mobile. She could hear background noise from a bar.

'Nora Sand.'

'Speak,' he ordered her.

'You never told me what happened to Oluf.'

'Because I don't know. We drifted apart. For a time I used to see him at Box Copenhagen Gym. He was good. Had the killer instinct you need to make it inside the ring. He was merciless. If you hesi-tated, Oluf would just punch you twice as hard. For him it wasn't enough to floor his opponent, he had to hurt him too. A fight where his opponent ended up in casualty was a good fight, as far as Oluf was concerned. There was talk about him boxing abroad. But I don't know if anything ever came of it.'

'Can you think of anyone who might know?' Nora asked.

Bjarne Helgaard mulled it over. In the silence Nora could hear something that might be a super league match on the television.

'He was with some woman. Betina or … No, that wasn't it. Benita, I think her name was. Her mum had a jewellery shop in Lyngby. Oluf was a real shit – he actually suggested that we do her shop over. He had tricked his girlfriend into revealing the security code.'

'Thank you.'

'Before you run along, I want an update on what's happening to my girls. Have you caught the bastard who did it?'

'Not yet,' Nora said.

'But you'll tell me when you know, won't you? Sometimes justice can be swifter than you think,' he said pompously.

'Yes, and sometimes justice needs to think twice,' she said and rang off.

A search on www.krak.dk offered her two jewellers in Lyngby: Strand & Sons and True as Gold. Nora thought the latter sounded more likely and did indeed strike gold with a shop assistant who introduced herself on the phone as Natasha, and with no sense of discretion told her that Benita had just nipped out to the chemist, but would be back in ten minutes.

Nora rang back twenty minutes later. This time it was Benita Svaneholm herself who answered the phone.

Nora introduced herself and explained that she was trying to research a cold case as part of an investigative report, but deliberately used vague phrases on the assumption that few people would be cooperative on learning that their ex might be mixed up in a murder case.

'Is this about his boxing?' Benita Svaneholm asked, and Nora replied that it might be linked to his career as a boxer and asked casually about her relationship with Oluf.

'Well, it was a long time ago,' Benita said. 'But I thought we would go the distance. We met at Bakken Amusement Park in the summer of 1990. He was tall and good-looking. Ripped. All the girls fancied him. We were together for six months, and I was starting to hope that we might get engaged,' she said and emitted a small sigh at the memory.

'But he had bigger fish to fry, poor Oluf. His boxing. He had been picked to join some amateur team going to Liverpool, I think it was, to fight some Brits. It was all really exciting, and Oluf was sure that if he did well over there, he would be able to go pro.'

'And then what happened?' Nora had time to interject before Benita started talking again.

'I don't know. Perhaps he really was talent-spotted as he'd hoped. He never came back to Denmark. After three weeks without a word from him, I called Box Copenhagen Gym. No one knew anything. I spoke to a secretary who thought that Oluf might have stayed in London, but he didn't sound as if he knew Oluf personally, and I had a feeling he was only saying it to get rid of me because I'd been calling them every evening for a week,' Benita said.

'Did you try anyone else?' Nora asked.

'No, I didn't have the surnames of the guys he used to box with, so I didn't know who else to call. I had never met his family, so I couldn't contact them either. Finally I had to accept that me and Oluf were over. That I'd been building castles in the air, or however the saying goes. I know that it's been too long now, but I'm still hoping that one day I'll read about "professional boxer Oluf Mik-kelsen" in the papers. But so far nothing,' Benita said.

'Do you remember the name of the boxing club secretary?'

'Yes, I do, because it was funny. His name was Rudolf, and Oluf told me that the guy had a massive red nose after all the fighting, so they had nicknamed him Red-nosed Rudolf.'

It took Nora less than thirty seconds to find the number for Box Copenhagen Gym on the internet.

'Willy speaking,' said a man with a Copenhagen accent.

Nora told him that she was looking for Rudolf.

'Rudolf? He retired years ago.'

Nora's optimism began to evaporate.

'But the old fool can't stay away,' the man said, holding the handset away from his mouth as he yelled across the room.

'Rudooolf. There's a lady who wants to talk to you.'

Soon afterwards the handset crackled. 'Rudolf speaking.' The voice sounded crisp and old.

Nora introduced herself again and explained that she was trying to find out if he knew what had happened to Oluf Mikkelsen.

'Noooo. I don't think so. I don't remember him,' Rudolf said very slowly. He sounded apologetic.

Nora tried to prompt his memory. 'He went on a trip with some other amateur boxers in 1991. To Liverpool or maybe London, and there's a possibility he didn't travel back with them.'

At this the voice became much more lucid. 'Oh, yes, bloody hell! Now I remember him. We used to call him Oluf the Buffalo. Welterweight. Always fought in yellow. Three knockouts in five fights. Very, very promising. He'd started training a bit late, not much support on the home front, as far as I recall, but the lad had a left hook to make a grown man cry.'

'Yes, that's him,' Nora said to encourage him. 'Do you know what happened to him in England?'

Rudolf's voice grew faint again, as if someone had turned his volume down. 'No. Not really. It was very odd. He was with us for the first part of the trip. We were in Liverpool and were due to go on to London. We'd had three really good nights. He won two of his fights straight out. The third one his opponent won on points, but it was daylight robbery. The judges voting for a local boy ...'

He paused as if to recall past triumphs, injustices and defeats.

'Right then, on the fourth morning as we were getting on the coach, we couldn't find Oluf anywhere. We checked his room and found his suitcase, but he was gone as were his wallet and his passport. At first we thought he'd gone on a bender. Truth be told, he was no angel. We thought he might be sleeping it off in a police cell or lying in the gutter after being mugged. I was really hacked off, and it caused a lot of problems for our schedule with the other clubs.'

'Yes, I can imagine,' Nora said sympathetically.

'Well, in the end we had to drive off without him. I left the address of our next stop at the hotel, but he never came back. I called the hotel a few days later and he hadn't even bothered to pick up his luggage. I also tried the police, but they had never heard of him. At that point I'd had enough and thought that he had made his bed and could lie on it. When we came home, his girlfriend rang us day and night. I wondered if he had got her up the duff, to be honest with you, and that he might have decided it was more responsibility than he could cope with. If the trip to England had offered him an easy way out. Yes, I guess that's what I thought. We never saw him again. And he was a really good welterweight.'

Nora thanked him and rang off.

Another dead end. Or perhaps not. Oluf Mikkelsen had travelled to the UK. What had happened to him there? Was he still alive? And if he was, why had he never contacted anyone back home in Denmark? Had he simply cut all ties?

Nora gave up looking for the answer and went to pour herself a glass of chilled prosecco to clear her mind. She carefully eased out the cork and avoided spilling a single drop while thinking how decadent it was to have a whole bottle of prosecco all to herself. She sat down and visualised how she would shortly take out the big blue ceramic plate from Istanbul, make a salad starting with the Parma ham at the bottom. How she would tear the mozzarella into fat strips and scatter them across the rocket, and how the warm ripe peaches would taste against the cool soft cheese. That is, if she could be bothered to get up again.

The hiss of her entryphone interrupted her food fantasy.

'It's me,' Andreas said when she picked up the handset.

'Andreas, I'm working,' she said dismissively.

'No, you're not. I'm coming up.'

She buzzed him in with a sigh. All right, so they would have to have the talk about PC Perfect and boundaries now, and how it might be time to say goodbye to a friendship that was clearly too volatile to be resurrected on anything other than Facebook.

Andreas's words in Hanne's garden had let the genie out of the bottle, and no matter how much they had both pretended it had been put back in, it loomed large whenever they met. Like a fat little turban-clad figure from the *Tales from the Arabian Nights*, but sadly not one that would grant you three wishes.

When he reached her second-floor flat, she had already built up a considerable amount of outrage and was ready to clear the air.

'Andreas,' she said firmly, before she had opened the door fully.

He marched right past her. 'My uncle called. When were you going to tell me that he had found Oluf Mikkelsen's fingerprints on the Polaroid?' Andreas said angrily.

Nora inhaled, but didn't have time to answer him before he continued.

'And here was I thinking we were a team. But it turns out we're not. This was Nora Sand on a solo mission all along, so thanks for your help and bye-bye, Andreas.'

Nora had never seen him so angry. The expression in his brown eyes was furious and the muscles in his neck were taut. He paced up and down the small room, looking like somebody who needed a lot more space.

'But, please, listen –'

'No, please listen to me!' he thundered.

Nora felt as if she had swallowed a puffer fish and her guts would be skewered from its spikes if she were to breathe.

'It's always about you and your work. Anyone you meet can come along for the ride until you're done with them, then you chew them up and spit them out, without –'

That was enough. Nora could feel the puffer fish and she simply had to spit out the spikes.

'That's just so unfair,' she said and took a deep breath. 'Firstly, you were at work –'

'Yes, but my mobile was turned on –'

'Secondly, let me tell you who's on a solo mission here. It was *you*, not me who decided back then not to stay in touch. Screw you, Andreas! You were my best friend and you decided with an over-whelming majority of one single vote, your own, to remove yourself completely from my life. And now you've come back and you expect me to trust you from day one?' she retorted, horrified at the words that were spewing from her mouth.

'So your pride was hurt or something. But let me tell you that I was hurt, too! One minute we had a friendship I really cared about, and the next – it was all over. Why? Why, Andreas? You just pissed off!'

She could see that he was white from rage. He walked right up to her and stood with his face very close to hers. He was either about to slap her or kiss her, Nora thought. His face neared hers a fraction, and she began to feel the anger draining from her body like poison, and the blood rushing to her lips. Then he regained his composure. He turned on his heel, stormed out of the door and slammed it shut.

She flopped on to the nearest chair, accidentally knocking her half-full glass of prosecco all over her skirt. Shit, shit, shit.

She changed into a pair of shorts, sat on the windowsill and drank the rest of the prosecco straight from the bottle, while she watched the light across London change from golden daylight to light purple twilight and finally steel-grey night. Hours later she noticed the two plump peaches on the windowsill and ate them. They had lost their appeal.

18

The next morning she needed a cup of Nescafé to resurrect her. The milk, however, was off so she was forced to tip the first cup into the sink and start over. The coffee tasted strong and bitter without the milk. It matched her mood.

She found Enzo's number on her mobile and he picked up immediately when she called. 'I need an hour of your time. Are you free now?' she said.

They agreed to meet at the entrance to the park in Primrose Hill in half an hour.

The small park, which had given its name to the area between Belsize Park and Chalk Farm, was one of Nora's favourite London parks. It bordered London Zoo on one side, the other was lined with Victorian houses inhabited by a typical London mix of rich Russians, actors and writers and anyone who had had the good fortune to move in before celebrities such as Jude Law, Gwen Stefani and Kate Moss made this small enclave of London into one of the city's most desirable neighbourhoods.

Nora still cringed at the memory of the time she had been boxing with Enzo and they had both been so busy pretending not to notice the actor Alan Rickman watching them on a nearby path that Enzo had dropped his guard for a split second, and Nora had accidentally found an opening for her jab and given her trainer a black eye, which he wore as penance for two weeks.

She walked towards the big oak tree under which they usually trained, and spotted him the second he raised his hand to greet her.

The short compact Italian had brought along his worn leather pads, but before Nora was allowed even a circle kick, he studied her closely. Then he pointed firmly to the hill.

'*Carissima*. We can kickbox, but not while you're angry. You're angry today, eh? I can tell from your shoulders. First, you run. Three times up and three times down,' he said in an accent that suggested it was two months rather than two decades since he had left his beloved Florence to seek his fortune in London.

It almost didn't matter how stressed she was, there was something strangely calming in the satisfying slam of a circle kick hitting cleanly and a left hook landing precisely where it should.

Enzo had repeatedly tried to persuade her to take part in a fight, but Nora wasn't interested in hitting people. Except today.

She sprinted the last stretch down the hill and drank half the contents of her water bottle before Enzo helped her wrap protective bands around her knuckles and slipped her hands inside the blue leather gloves which were starting to split.

They took up position underneath the oak tree and for the next forty minutes the only sound was that of Enzo's brief orders and the incessant staccato of leather hitting leather.

'Hooks. Give me one hundred.'

'Sidekicks. Ten with each leg.'

Nora could feel the anger leave her body as the sweat gathered along her hairline, trickled down her back or into her eyes. They practised parrying, combinations of punches and kicks in a flowing stream of arms and legs exploding against one another.

For the last ten minutes, her heels weren't allowed to touch the ground.

'I want to see you on your toes. On your toes!' Enzo roared over and over.

Enzo's precise instructions made her gather all her strength in her legs, take off and focus everything on the tiny black dot on the red pad. Her heel needed to hit that particular spot cleanly when she took off from the ground.

To finish her off, he made her do push-ups and then stretches before the hour-long session was over.

Afterwards they went, as was their habit, to one of the few cafés in London that, in Enzo's opinion, could produce a decent espresso, according to Italian standards, and sat down at a round table outside.

Enzo gazed lovingly at the small cup of black liquid. Then he looked closely at Nora.

'Hey, *carissima*. I don't know who he is or what he has done, that man. But I'm glad that I'm not him,' he said, and pushed his sunglasses down over his eyes.

Nora finished her coffee, walked home to the flat and showered.

It was time to meet a certain lawyer.

She promised herself to take her jacket and skirt to the dry cleaners later, and instead put on a relatively clean navy skirt and her absolute last clean shirt, before catching the tube to Cross Associates.

The Cross office hadn't changed. The same edition of *The Economist* was still displayed on the table. Nora nodded politely, sat down on the sofa, and looked for the article she hadn't finished the last time. She had only just found the right page when she was summoned by Mr Cross.

If Christian Cross had been reserved the last time, he had now switched to that unique form of icy politeness the Brits mastered better than any other nation on earth.

'You have friends in high places, Miss Sand. Good for you. You never know when you might need them,' he said archly.

Nora waited.

He placed three pieces of paper on his desk. 'You need to sign here, here and here,' he said, pointing with a heavy gold-plated fountain pen, which Nora recognised as Waterman's most expensive model and which she had frequently coveted at the airport.

Nora took the documents and read them slowly while sensing Christian Cross's impatience travel through the air like white noise.

'Pure formality,' he said to speed up the process.

'Even so I prefer to know what I'm signing. You, being a lawyer, would surely understand that better than anyone,' Nora retorted.

The first document for signature was from Wolf Hall Prison. A very formal document where Nora signed to confirm that she had no criminal record and that she would comply with prison regulations for what she could bring during a visit, which was practically nothing. Nora didn't object and signed at the bottom.

The second piece of paper stated that Christian Cross Associates had facilitated contact with William Hickley at Nora's own request, and that she assumed full responsibility for the meeting and any consequences it might have. With her signature she also waived the right to hold Christian Cross Associates or its employees liable for any financial, physical, mental or other harm, which might arise from the meeting. Nora wondered what other forms of harm there could be, then she signed.

At length she reached the third and final piece of paper. It stated that anything that was said or any information arising from the meeting between Nora Sand and William Hickley was to be treated as confidential. If the conversation or parts thereof were to be made public, this was purely the decision of William Hickley. He, and he alone, would own the copyright to his own words. A copyright that would be managed and administered by Christian Cross Associates, no less.

Nora gave him the killer look. 'Nice try. But you can forget it. This is my interview and I decide what happens to it. Mr Hickley speaks to me on my terms or not at all.'

Christian Cross merely shrugged. It had been worth a try.

'Well, then I believe that concludes our business, Miss Sand. As I said, he can see you on Thursday afternoon. At two thirty. Don't forget to arrive in plenty of time. Security checks are ... how can I put it ... enthusiastic. You'll have one hour with Mr Hickley.'

Christian Cross sat down heavily behind his desk and was already checking his diary when Nora got up.

He looked up. 'Miss Sand, I would appreciate it if you would be kind enough to treat what I'm about to tell you as confidential. My point being that when this conversation is over, it never happened. If you ever refer to it in public or in writing, you can be quite sure that I'll deny everything. Do you understand?'

Nora nodded and sat down again. Bloody lawyers.

'We once had a young lawyer here at this office, Janet. Her surname doesn't matter. She was one of the brightest in her year at Oxford. Stellar career and future ahead of her. Engaged to a lawyer from the Ministry of Defence. Some years ago I had to take leave for reasons that are irrelevant to my story. The upshot was that I assigned Hickley to her as her client. Not because I expected anything to happen, it was mainly for practical purposes. The forwarding of letters and so on.'

He paused and pulled down his cuffs as if to steel himself for the next part.

'Hickley must have noticed that his letters were now signed by someone else. He demanded to meet his new lawyer, so Janet drove to visit him in Wolf Hall. At that point I was abroad, so she didn't inform me. Then again, I doubt that I would have stopped her had she done so. He was just one of many clients.'

Nora nodded to encourage him to continue.

'We don't know what happened between the two of them. We don't know what was said. There were no witnesses. It is in the nature of these things that all inmates have the right to meet with their lawyer privately. And even if Janet made notes about their conversation or if Mr Hickley gave her specific instructions, no such notes were ever found. Neither here at the office or in Janet's home.'

He took a deep breath. 'After her third visit – a Thursday afternoon – Janet had a car accident. We don't know where she was going. Her family could provide no explanation as to why she had left Wolf Hall and driven down a minor country road in Buckinghamshire. The car had gone straight into a tree. It was a write-off. Janet was in a coma for three days, but never regained consciousness.'

'Did you ever consider getting rid of Hickley as a client?'

Cross looked out of the window. 'On what grounds? We couldn't prove anything. Perhaps there was nothing to prove. But I thought you ought to know. On your way out, please would you ask my secretary to join me?'

Moments later Nora was squinting against the sunshine and trying earnestly to imagine what it would be like to be face to face with Bill Hix – the man who had an unknown number of women's lives on his conscience.

However, every time she tried to visualise herself meeting him in the role of interviewer, the picture turned into a blank screen. Would she be frightened? Would he be a pathetic old man in chains or a predator that could strike without warning, if given the slightest chance?

She walked past St James's Park and thought with a pang of Andreas and the way he had looked at her during their picnic lunch. Calling him to say hi and pretending that everything was OK should be easy. Only it wasn't. And it wouldn't help matters.

She took the tube home and spent the rest of her afternoon deleting the subject Andreas from her internal hard drive by researching amateur boxing contests that took place in Liverpool years ago. She deep-searched PDF files and old archives, but the search engines could find no Oluf the Buffalo.

Just as she was, very appropriately, about to throw in the towel, her iPhone danced marimba rhythms in her handbag. A tune that could mean only one thing.

'Hi, Mum,' she said, trying to sound carefree and relaxed.

'You're stressed, aren't you,' her mother said. 'I can tell from your voice.'

Nora rolled her eyes. 'Everything is fine. It's the summer. The silly season, you know.'

When she spoke to her mother, she would often end up speaking a strange mix of English and Danish. In her childhood home they had spoken Danish to each other, obviously, but since they had both moved to London, English words, phrases or idioms would often slip in here and there.

'How was Florence?'

'A-ma-zing, I tell you,' her mother declared. 'I simply have to live in Italy. I was never made for this dull, Nordic, Anglo-Saxon lethargy. I'm Latin at heart.'

'Yes, of course you are,' Nora agreed. She knew from experience that it was easier to tell her mother whatever she wanted to hear.

'But that wouldn't work for Patrick. He has to look after his apples,' her mother said.

'Yes, and you have your Cromwell. They don't have him in Florence,' Nora pointed out sensibly.

'I know, but even so ... they have the Medici family. And those sunsets, that passion. They truly understand what it means to be an artist in that part of the world,' her mother insisted.

'I'm sure they do.'

'Well, anyway, why don't you pop by Patrick's orchard one weekend soon? And don't work too hard. You'll never find a man that way,' Elizabeth said, and continued in the same vein for a considerable period of time.

There were days when Nora felt her mother's sense of tact could make Shrek look like a diplomatic and skilled courtier, but eventually she gave up and promised to visit soon.

As an adult Nora had fought her way to a working relationship with her mother. However, she had reached that point only after years of shutting down completely the memory of the woman standing on the drive one morning, ready to abandon her family in a taxi. And the fear of abandonment still lingered right under the surface like a crocodile in a stagnant river. Ready to strike, if Nora ever dropped her guard.

When they finally rang off, it was almost time to go to Soho to meet Pete.

She just had time to gather a large bag of dirty laundry to take to the Indian dry cleaner around the corner, a place quaintly named Mr

Percy's Butler. Strictly speaking, not everything needed dry cleaning, however, if you dropped off a bag at Mr and Mrs Patel's, you could pick it up two days later, filled with clean, folded clothes, smelling faintly of cardamom and chai. There were some weeks when that was worth every penny.

'You work too hard, my girl,' Mrs Patel said, who was today sporting a lime-green sari, which flattered her brown skin. 'I can tell from your chakras that something has upset you. Your love chakra glows red and irritated. You really must take the time to meditate,' she added in an accent that sang of Mumbai.

Nora took a deep breath. 'Dearest darling, Mrs Patel. I've just had my mother on the phone. A twenty-minute lecture is more than I can handle. But it's kind of you to care.'

'Ah,' Mrs Patel said knowingly. 'It'll be ready the day after tomorrow after four p.m.'

'Thank you.'

'May peace find you before then,' Mrs Patel said softly when Nora had almost closed the door.

19

Pete was already queuing outside the Thai restaurant, which was so popular that in contrast to most other Soho restaurants tables could not be booked. Diners had to join a lengthy queue outside where they could stare through the windows at other guests enjoying their meal until a table became available. The food was so amazing that it was worth the wait.

He took one look at her and launched into his best Madame Arcati impression. Like a fortune teller at a fair, he covered his eyes with his hands, pretending to be in so deep a trance that any visual impression would disturb his unique connection to the spiritual world and the messages channelled through his not-so-humble persona.

'OK. It's bad. Let me guess. Your mother? A man? Your work? … No, I've got it. You'll meet a tall dark stranger who'll change your life forever. Am I right about just one of those things?'

'All of them,' she said laconically.

'Right then, we'd better start at the beginning. Trust me to go to Cambodia in the middle of your life crisis.'

Nora couldn't suppress a wry smile. 'Ignore me. Tell me about Cambodia. What's happening out there that's so interesting to *The Times*? Who are you going with, and how did it come about?'

Not long afterwards they were shown to a table shared with ten other guests, and the conversation trailed off as they ordered Guava Collins cocktails, fried tiger prawns, noodles with smoked chicken, Chinese broccoli and chicken wings with tamarind.

Pete told her how George, an Australian reporter with *The Times*, had long been working with a charity to uncover the kidnapping and trafficking of children, who were subsequently sold as slaves in Cambodia's extensive sex industry. After months of research, he had finally progressed so far with his investigation that the Cambodian police had allowed him to attend a raid on a brothel suspected of offering children as young as six to their clients, mostly white, Western tourists. The local photographer he normally worked with had felt forced to turn down the job. He had a wife and children, and simply couldn't risk his family's safety by going up against the powerful mafia that controlled the brothels. Pete had been thoroughly briefed about possible consequences, including the risk of death threats, once it became known that he was in Cambodia in order to photograph sex slaves. If he succeeded in capturing child prostitution on camera, he would be a marked man until he was safely out of Cambodia with the pictures.

In other words, it was Pete's dream assignment.

'I hate, hate, hate the thought of what goes on in those dreadful places. But if I can expose it, help put a stop to it, it'll all have been worth it,' he said gravely.

'When are you leaving?'

'Thursday morning from Heathrow.'

'OK – call me if you need to talk. George isn't known for being chatty,' Nora said.

Pete flashed a droll grin. 'That's the understatement of the century. Typical Australian. Understatement promotes understanding. Silence cements it.'

They skipped dessert and went for a walk around the streets of Soho. It had been a warm day and the tarmac was still giving off heat. Tourists poured out of the theatres looking for food and more entertainment around Shaftesbury Avenue and Leicester Square.

'All right,' Pete said eventually. 'There's not a lot we can do about your mum, but what's this about a man? And is he the tall dark stranger?'

Nora squirmed.

'Out with it, darling. I've seen you have the runs in Delhi, leeches on your thigh in Zambia, and I let you have my second last clean pair of boxers in Macedonia. I'm pretty sure there's a contract somewhere stating you can have no secrets from me.'

'Did I ever tell you about Andreas?'

Pete thought about it for a moment. 'From Denmark? A guy you used to know and go swimming with? Yes, you did mention him once, but I got the impression that he was dead to you, so I chose not to pry.'

'He's not. He's in London.'

'And?'

Nora gave him a brief summary of the whole sorry tale. About their friendship, which had been terminated without warning. About how she had only recently realised that Andreas had wanted something more than friendship, not just at the end of sixth form, but pretty much from the start.

'But that was years ago, Nora. You're both adults now, so what's the problem?' said Pete, the voice of reason.

'But there's more,' she objected and went on to tell him about their failed trip to Brine and how they had somehow ended up sleeping in each other's arms. About PC Perfect. And about what she had already decided to call 'the great confrontation of last night'.

'It sounded promising, right up until PC Perfect entered the scene.'

Nora shrugged. 'I don't know. It's too complicated in my opinion.'

'Really?' Pete said in that irritating way of his. 'I'm not trying to lecture you, but I've never regarded you as someone who is attracted to simple men. And the more I think about it, I've never seen you walk away from a challenge either. I'm just saying.'

Nora shook her head. 'This isn't a challenge. We're talking about Andreas, my ex-friend.'

'Rubbish. This is about common sense. You know absolutely nothing about PC Perfect.'

'All right, fair point, Pete. But they're still together. He told me so himself. It means I can't count on him. It's that simple.'

'Oh, I thought you just said it was complicated?'

She lashed out at him, and he evaded her easily. 'You know exactly what I mean.'

'All I know is the way you feel about him, is the way I felt about Caroline. I thought tying myself down would be a drag. It would complicate everything. And now she lives in bloody Armadale outside Melbourne with a surgeon, and she's expecting their first child,' Pete said with a slight jolt in his voice.

It was rare for Pete to mention Caroline as anything other than a throwaway remark. The great love of his life that never fully blossomed was still an open wound, which in true Australian style was mostly silenced to death. Nora went quiet.

'When did you hear that?' she said eventually in a low voice.

Pete kicked the kerb. 'Last night. On bloody Facebook. God, I hate Facebook,' he said.

Following that announcement, there was really only one thing to do. They found a still-open Oddbins that, to Nora's delight, stocked Bowmore Legend. They needed nothing more.

They walked down to the Thames with the bottle and, in the shadow of Cleopatra's Needle with Big Ben and the Houses of Parliament on their starboard side, they took turns drinking from it while watching the illuminated river boats, where tourists sat with their cardboard wine and rubber chicken dinner thinking they were seeing the real London with their guide.

When it was almost two o'clock in the morning, Pete's considerable repertoire of sea shanties was nearly exhausted and he had reached the defiant stage.

'I'm better off without her. She's probably gotten fat and boring as hell. It would never have worked,' he said, before throwing up over the railings that were stopping him from falling into the river.

Nora hailed a cab and assured the taxi driver that Pete would not throw up on the journey to Belsize Park. She kept her word, but only just. Pete regurgitated the other half of his Thai dinner the moment he stepped on to the pavement, just as Nora was paying.

Pete tried to regain control of himself. 'Right, then, sssseee you tomorrow,' he slurred before walking straight into next door's front garden.

'Pete, Godammit. You can't go home in that state. You're coming with me and I'm putting you in the recovery position.'

'No, no, no, no, all I need is an itsy-bitsy bus,' he slurred, before launching into a particularly grating version of the 1950s hit 'Oh, Carol' where he, without any sense of rhythm, renamed the love interest 'Carol-iiine'.

Her neighbour flung open a window. 'Do you think you could shut up, so we can all get some sleep!'

Nora had to go into her neighbour's front garden to retrieve Pete. She grabbed him firmly by the arm and steered him to her front door. Pete clung to her like a drowning man in a storm, and Nora fumbled for her keys in her handbag, so she didn't spot him immediately.

Andreas was sitting on the doorstep, looking like a thundercloud. When they came closer, he stood up.

'What are you doing here?' Nora blurted out without thinking.

'Nothing. Nothing at all, clearly,' he said with a contemptuous glance at Pete who had lost all sense of decorum several hours ago.

'Hey, mate – are you Andreas? He's really cute, Nora.'

'Shut up, Pete, just shut up!' she hissed, then managed to park him on the doorstep recently vacated by Andreas.

She turned and called out to Andreas, who had started to leave. She could see his back in the white shirt as he slowly walked away from her. She called his name again.

But he didn't turn around.

✗

The next morning Nora woke up to the aroma of freshly brewed coffee. Pete had showered, dug out her coffee grinder from the cupboard, found the beans and been to the shops for croissants and orange juice.

'Strewth, Sand,' he said, feigning jollity. 'I've grown too old to carry off a bender with dignity.'

Nora nodded her head gingerly to make sure she could stand up without her brain falling out. She could, but only just. Pete had nicked her Oxford University sweatshirt from her wardrobe. The sleeves were straining.

'I had to have something to wear,' he said apologetically, pointing to last night's outfit that looked like it had collided with a herd of cattle fleeing a wildfire.

Nora staggered to the kitchen sink and drank cold water straight from the tap. It tasted of chlorine and she grimaced.

'So did you hear this from Caroline?'

Pete shook his head. 'Oh no, we're no longer in touch. I don't think the surgeon would approve. He's not known for his open-mindedness and tolerance. It was her cousin, Miranda, who told me when we were chatting on Facebook. The worst thing was she just dropped it into the conversation as if I already knew.'

'Ouch.'

'I don't know. Perhaps I thought the surgeon was just a phase. That she missed Australia and all she needed was to go home and be reminded of what it's like. But she stayed, believe it or not. And now there's a baby on the way.' He shook his head. 'A baby. That's the end of that, isn't it?'

Nora poured coffee for both of them. 'Do we have any milk?'

Pete produced a milk bottle with a cheeky smile. 'Courtesy of your neighbour. He shouldn't have shouted at me last night.'

'Really, Pete, that's not on.'

'Ah, the police will never catch me. I'm going to Phnom Penh tomorrow.'

She reached across him, tore off a bit of croissant and popped it into her mouth.

'But apart from that, once you're done in Cambodia, perhaps you could nip home via Melbourne and just double-check the news about Caroline. It might even be worth meeting with her. You're pretty much in her neck of the woods, and I'm sure that George wouldn't mind –'

'George! Fuck! What time is it?'

'A quarter past ten.'

'Fuck, fuck, fuck. I'm meeting him in Docklands at eleven o'clock.'

Pete grabbed his bag, knocked back half of his coffee and ran out of the door. He took three steps, then turned around, came back, and gave her a quick hug.

'Bye, Sand. See you when I see you.'

She winked at him. 'Yeah, when you run out of money. And call me when you're back at Heathrow.'

He blew her a kiss and raced down the stairs. Nora shut the door after him and took out her mobile. No missed calls, no messages on her voicemail. What had Andreas wanted last night?

She sat for a while with the mobile in her hand, wondering if she should call him. Explain. But she decided against it.

Screw him. He could think whatever he wanted to. He was the one with a girlfriend. He was the one in a relationship. Not her.

20

She turned on her laptop and showered before going out for papers and more milk.

Tomorrow was H-Day. H for Hix. But she sensed that today should be kept free from murders. And Andreas.

She scanned the newspapers and the online news before she called the Crayfish and convinced him that it was a matter of pressing urgency that she write an article about the Irish construction boom. She started researching it immediately and tried getting interview appointments in place. But no matter how many dull reports she ploughed her way through on housing statistics, variable interest rates and predictions of foreclosures south of Cork, Hix kept looming on the fringes of her mind like a black shadow.

She thought about Spencer and his instruction to be herself. Be herself while she asked questions on behalf of the police, so Hix wouldn't figure out who was behind them.

She dearly wished that Andreas could have come with her on the journey to Wolf Hall Prison. Wait outside for her. He didn't have to say anything, just be there. With his calming presence.

But it was not to be. Then again, she had managed fine without him for years. Survived conflicts, malaria, and even being robbed in Nairobi, without having Andreas by her side. So why would tomorrow be any different?

Right then her mobile rang. She experienced a microsecond of hope, but it was only Spencer.

'Just calling to check if you're ready for tomorrow?'

'Well, I don't know. Can you ever prepare yourself for meeting a killer?'

'Remember, he can't hurt you. He can't touch you. He's restrained, and he'll spend the rest of his life in jail.'

'I thought I heard his lawyer say something about an appeal to the parole board?'

'Don't worry, Miss Sand. He doesn't stand a chance. We think he has killed many more young women than those we already know about. He hasn't cooperated with our investigation. He has nothing to trade with. Life means life unless the Home Secretary decides otherwise, and the odds on that are just as big as the chances of finding a politician who doesn't give a damn about negative publicity.'

'Right. I'll have to take your word for it.'

'Don't start by asking him about the girls who went missing *after* he went to jail. We want him to think that you know something he doesn't, if you get my drift. Unless he has to work for it, Hix doesn't care about anything. And he doesn't care about other people's feelings either, he finds them dull. Pain and tears interest him only as an intellectual phenomenon. Something he can trigger in other people to a greater or lesser extent. Appealing to his so-called conscience will get you nowhere. I think that was James's biggest mistake with Hix. He kept thinking he could uncover some kind of humanity. Believe me, Miss Sand, I've known Hix for years, and if that humanity exists, I've yet to catch a glimpse of it. My theory is that he cut out the tongues of his victims to make them shut up. He couldn't be bothered to listen to them plead for their lives. That might be worth bearing in mind,' Spencer warned her.

Nora gulped. 'Well, when you put it like that it's impossible to think of anything else.'

'My point is, he wants to be the one doing the talking, never forget that. He's not interested in listening to other people. That was all I wanted to tell you.'

'Hmm. I guess I should say thank you.'

'Why don't you start with two Danish girls? As far as I could gather from Mr Cross, they were what piqued his interest.'

'Yes, and that was the reason I originally wanted to talk to him.'

'There's just one more thing, Miss Sand. I know you probably think I'm being intrusive, but believe me – that's not my intention. What are you planning on wearing tomorrow?'

'Planning? I don't plan my outfits. Especially not when visiting a prison,' Nora said.

Her throat felt dry. She went to the fridge to get the carton of orange juice that Pete had left behind. With her mobile wedged between her chin and shoulder, she reached for a glass in the cupboard.

'But you should be. There's no point in leaving it to chance,' Spencer said.

'Mmm,' she said, sneaking in a sip of juice. 'Right then, the honest answer is that I was thinking a pair of jeans and a white shirt. With buttons. A pair of sandals. Nothing special.'

'That would be a mistake.'

'You're entitled to your opinion, Mr Spencer. But I don't regard tomorrow's interview as a dating opportunity. It's work. Filthy, shitty work, to be completely honest, and if you really want to know what I would like to wear after reading about Bill Hix and his crimes, my choice would be an old-fashioned diving suit with a copper helmet on my head, like you see in *Tintin*. But this isn't *Tintin*.'

'No, it isn't. It's so very much isn't,' Spencer agreed.

She heaved a deep sigh and caved in. 'All right. I'm not saying I'll follow your instructions down to the last detail, but I'm listening. What should I wear tomorrow?'

'Dress like a modest woman. With the emphasis on woman. A dress or a skirt would be fine, but it must go below the knee. Make-up is acceptable as long as it's discreet. Imagine how his mother would have dressed. You don't have to be her, but perhaps evoke a few memories. Put up your hair. Pearls and a cardigan would be great. As far as we know, the only woman he has ever shown any kind of respect is his mother.'

'Hmm. I guess that does make sense,' she conceded.

'I'm not making any promises, but it's worth a try,' Spencer said.

'It's worth a try,' she agreed.

'We'll send a car to pick you up when you've finished at the prison. It's best that we talk while it's all still fresh in your mind. You're aware that you won't be allowed to bring your mobile or Dictaphone into the prison, aren't you?'

Nora began to think that she might grow to like Spencer on closer acquaintance. For a brief moment she considered sharing the information about Oluf Mikkelsen with him.

Then the moment passed, and they rang off. Once again Nora felt that the one person in all the world she wanted to talk to more than any other was the one person she couldn't call. Not ever.

X

The next morning she woke up with a jolt.

The last time she had checked the clock it had said three forty-five, and this was the fourth time she woke up in a cold sweat of fear. Every time she was on the verge of nodding off, she felt herself fall backwards into a deep nameless darkness and she would wake up again in sheer terror.

She staggered to the bathroom while she tried to work out why visiting Bill Hix was turning into such a problem.

It wouldn't be the first or the last time she spoke to a killer. The Rwandan schoolteacher she had interviewed on the south coast probably had many more lives on his conscience than a busy British serial killer would ever manage.

Nor did she presume that Hix outdid 'Mr Benn' when it came to the torture of helpless victims. Her thoughts slipped back to her interview with Mr Benn and the monotonous voice in which, without any sign of emotion, he told her how he and his gang of guerrillas had given women, children and old people the choice between long or short sleeves, when he passed by with his machete to chop off their arms.

And before the schoolteacher, there had been Serbian soldiers,

Kosovo-Albanian rebel fighters and visits to mass graves telling their own story of how far the human soul can travel into the darkness of evil without perishing. Many of those killings were committed ostensibly for political reasons, but often by soldiers who were set on personal gain, or who simply acted out of pure, senseless brutality.

It wasn't the violence as such that had kept her awake that night. Rather it was the thought that Bill Hix had enjoyed every moment of it while his victims had lived in fear for their lives. The thought that every single abduction and every subsequent murder had been planned down to the last detail, and that even today, after so many years, he was willing to let the victims' families live in ignorance of what happened, where the girls' last resting place was and why they had died.

There was no reason other than his own personal pleasure.

Perhaps it was the absence of other reasons that scared her the most. Even in the darkest times in the Balkans or during inhuman conflicts in Africa, Nora had somehow been able to navigate her way to an understanding, if not of the violence, then at least of the cause of it. Explanations frequently rooted in poverty, unscrupulous leaders, greed or external factors. She could unpick her way back from effect to cause via the many links that had led to torched villages, rapes, murders and destruction. There were reasons to be found.

However, when she looked into Bill Hix's soul there was only darkness. A gaping hole like the one he had left in the mouths of his victims. And now it appeared that there were more girls who had been robbed of their lives, more parents suffering the slowest and most agonising death a parent can experience. To lose a child and never know what happened to it.

She shuddered and turned up the cold tap to distract herself. Afterwards she dried her hair and tried getting a grip on herself.

It was up to her to tread so skilfully that Hix would slip up and reveal his connection to Lisbeth, Lulu and the other twelve girls, or if he had had an accomplice. The responsibility weighed on her chest like a black lump, and Nora recognised that it was this lump that had stopped her from sleeping.

She took a tweed midi skirt from a hanger, bought in a winter sale when she had been going through a short Virginia Woolf phase. However, the right Bloomsbury mood had never arisen and she hadn't worn the skirt until today. She smoothed yesterday's shirt and put on a grey marl cardigan.

Nora completed her look by putting her hair in a bun, and snarled at her own reflection in the mirror. She looked like a model in an ad for support stockings. To brighten things up a bit, she applied a little make-up, and rummaged around her Indian jewellery box until she found a necklace with three antique keys she had once bought from a street vendor in Amalfi. Very fitting for a prison.

As an afterthought she went to her computer, found the picture file with the photo of Lulu and Lisbeth that Magnus had scanned for her, and pressed print.

As usual, her printer played up and produced three boarding passes and a long article about multicultural schools, before the photograph of the two girls finally appeared in the tray. The quality wasn't brilliant, but you could easily see them and where the photo had been taken.

Nora pensively folded it into a small square and tucked it inside her bra.

Finally there was nothing more to do. She put her Dictaphone, notepad and pens into her bag. It was time to meet the monster face to face.

21

Prisons have a very special smell, the individual components of which are hard to identify. There was sweat, desperation, industrial soap, chlorine, chemicals, urine and boiled cabbage in the mix, but also something that was trickier to make out, Nora thought, as a grumpy prison guard checked her papers.

Without a word he waved her through and pointed to a dilapidated redbrick building marked 'Administration'.

Nora heard the gate behind her slam shut with a bang, and couldn't help smiling as she was reminded of the old Danish heist comedies where Egon Olsen invariably ended up in Vridsløselille Prison after yet another brilliant plan that simply couldn't go wrong. But the smile was wiped off her face when she glanced up at the high walls topped with Dannert wire. This was serious. No one ever escaped from Wolf Hall.

Some kind soul had tried to cheer up the office with a bouquet of fake pink roses, but their efforts had had pretty much the opposite effect. Right now Nora couldn't think of anything more depressing than the neon-lit room, which was the first stop for relatives, friends and families who had the misfortune to know someone in prison.

An angular woman with a blond perm and a pinched fox-like face got up from her desk and went to the counter as Nora entered. The woman took a quick look at her.

'Prison visit service? You usually come on Wednesdays,' she said in a sullen voice.

Nora shook her head. 'No, my name is Sand. I'm here to speak to Mr Hix – eh, sorry, I mean Mr Hickley,' she said, producing her paperwork again.

The woman frowned and sat down behind her computer with a sigh, which more than hinted that Nora couldn't be more of a nuisance if she spent the rest of her life trying.

She typed on the keyboard with two fingers and hit the keys so hard that every single click made a loud noise.

'Hmm. Miss Sand. Yes, I've found you,' she sneered and glared at a colleague who appeared to be on the phone to his mother or girlfriend while drinking Pepsi Max.

The woman got up reluctantly for the second time while Nora passed the documents though a small slot in the thick glass window enclosing the counter. Nora was thus able to read from the woman's name badge that she was being served by M. Foggsey. Nora wondered if anyone had ever dared call the surly jobsworth 'foxy' to her face. She guessed not.

Mrs Foggsey took the papers with another sigh and passed a dog-eared, marbled notebook with stiff, lined paper out to Nora. 'You sign in here. And I'll need to see some ID.'

This was one of the occasions where a press card would most likely only make the situation worse, so Nora took out her driver's licence from her purse.

Foxy completed a form using carbon paper, which produced three copies of Nora's personal details. One white, one yellow and one blue.

'What do you need that for?'

'Procedure,' was all Mrs Foxy said.

'But I would like to know what use you make of the information, and where it ends up.'

Foxy shrugged. 'The archive would be my guess. I think a copy goes to the Home Office.'

'Does that mean I can submit a Freedom of Information request to find out, say, who has visited William Hickley during the time he has been in prison?'

'In theory, yes. But in reality I think you'd get a resounding no. Such information is private and confidential.'

Nora was about to sigh when the Pepsi Max guy rang off and got involved in the conversation: 'Besides, there would be nothing to see. No one comes to see that freak Hix. Only that detective with the weird eyes, and he hasn't been here for years. Then there's his mum and his sour-faced sister.'

Foxy shot him a withering look. 'Jameson, you're speaking out of turn.'

She turned to Nora again. 'Are you carrying any sharp objects?'

Nora shook her head.

'You can leave your bag in the lockers over there,' she explained and pointed to a poster with educational drawings and large red crosses over various items indicating what you could and could not bring into a prison. It looked like a very sad and far too adult version of Pictionary.

Visitors were not even allowed to bring teddy bears, and Nora couldn't help thinking that it was exceptionally heartless that young children, who came to visit their father in prison, wouldn't be allowed to bring in a soft toy.

Foxy had read her mind. 'You would be amazed if you knew how often people try to hide drugs in soft toys. Eventually it was easier to put a stop to it. One less place to search,' she said.

With a sigh, Nora realised that her Dictaphone would have to stay in her handbag, exactly as Spencer had predicted. The same applied to her pencils and pens, which made her notepad somewhat super-fluous. Her mobile, obviously, wasn't welcome either.

Nora found an empty locker, deposited her bag and entered a four-digit code.

Foxy ushered her through a metal detector, which reacted to her necklace, so Nora had to hand it over at the counter and complete another form. She was given a receipt, which she stuffed into a pocket in her skirt, and went through the scanner again. This time without any beeping.

'All we need now is to pat you down,' Foxy said with feigned jolliness and checked what felt like every single cranny of Nora's body without discovering the folded picture she had hidden in her bra.

At long last it was over and Nora walked through a door on the other side of the scanner, which took her to a car park where a prison van was waiting for her.

The driver – who looked like Vladimir Putin's poor relation – flashed her a grin.

'Jump in the back, sweetheart. No room in the front for civilians, I'm afraid.'

Nora sat down on one of the bolted-down plastic seats and tried to ignore the stench of sweat and urine.

The drive lasted only a few minutes before the van pulled up in front of a drab grey building. The driver nodded in the direction of something that looked like an iron-clad door. 'Your stop. This is as far as we go, darling,' he said, winking at Nora in a way that made her flesh crawl.

She went through the door and found herself in a pastel green hall at the start of a long corridor. A prison officer was ready to receive her. He had piggy eyes and a smirk, which more than suggested that he enjoyed his job. For all the wrong reasons, Nora thought.

He stuck out his hand. Nora shook it and felt a lump of clammy flesh between her fingers.

'My name is Jimmy Archer,' he said, and ran his eyes up and down her body. It required considerable strength to ignore him.

'Are you from the legal team?' he said, making conversation as he walked her down the long empty corridor. Nora could hear how the clicking of her heels against the worn linoleum echoed against the bare walls.

She mumbled something that could be taken as an affirmation or a denial, depending on what the prison officer preferred.

'We tend not to chain him up any more. Old age seems to have mellowed him. But we've restrained him today, just to be on the safe side,' he reassured her.

Nora followed him.

'We don't see many women in here. Under normal circumstances,' Jimmy Archer chatted on.

At the end of the long corridor, he took out a bunch of keys, unlocked and opened a door with a theatrical gesture, as if holding open the door for a woman in a restaurant.

She had been expecting a kind of counter like the ones she had seen in American movies. Armoured glass separating the inmate and the visitor who had to watch each other like fish in separate aquariums and speak on old-fashioned telephones in order to communicate.

Instead there was a battered steel table and two chairs. Everything was bolted to the worn linoleum floor.

Bill Hix was already sitting on one of the chairs. His forearms were chained to the armrests, but that wasn't the first thing she noticed. What really caught her attention were his piercing eyes, which scrutinised her from under his long fringe. His black eyes resembled two shiny buttons on a soft toy, but when he winked at her with one eye, slowly and deliberately, and flashed a smile, the hairs stood up right under her bun.

'Nice,' he said in a voice that was deeper than she had been expecting. It sounded rusty, as if he didn't speak very much, and had forgotten to clear his throat.

Nora tried making her face as blank as possible and gave Hickley a measured nod before she sat down opposite him. She desperately missed her pad and pencil. Something to occupy her eyes and hands so she could escape his stare and avoid the intimacy of the table where his face was so close that she could easily reach out and touch him.

The prison officer drew an imaginary line across the table and looked at Nora. 'If you keep on this side, he can't touch you. Do you understand?'

Nora nodded mutely.

He gestured to the door with his thumb. 'I'll be sitting right outside. Any trouble with our friend Bill here, you just call me,' he said before leaving the room with a last, lingering look at Nora.

Hickley didn't even deign to acknowledge him, but kept his eyes pinned on Nora. She forced herself to look back at him.

'Right, Mr Hickley. Do you know why I'm here?'

He ignored her question.

'You have a fine bone structure. Very fine. The high cheekbones work well. It's just a question of photographing you in the right light,' he said with a face like a horse trader at a market.

Nora pretended to also ignore his words.

'Mr Hickley, I don't know if you have had an opportunity to discuss with your lawyer what –'

'Have you ever been a model?'

'Mr Hickley. I'm a journalist, and –'

'Bill.'

'What?'

'Call me Bill. I won't talk to anyone who insists on calling me by my surname. This conversation is over, if you don't.'

With superhuman self-control, Nora swallowed her reply and reminded herself that she wasn't just here for herself, but also for the parents of at least fourteen girls and possibly many more. People with big holes in their hearts who needed an answer.

'Very well, Bill. I'm here to talk about the girls you killed.'

He shook his head.

'No. No. No. And you were just doing so well, Miss Nora. You said Bill. I was happy. I was prepared to trust you, and then you raise that tiresome subject, about which I know nothing, of course.'

'I find that hard to believe, Mr Hi … Bill.'

He gave a light shrug and smirked at her. 'Let's talk about something else.'

Nora cleared her throat. The adrenaline in her body surged and ebbed. Fear and rage combined in an explosive mix, which made her want to shake the truth out of the arrogant bastard sitting there mocking her, mocking the girls he had killed.

'Sure, Bill. Let's talk about something else. How about we talk about your travels? Do you like travelling?'

He flung out his arms to the extent that he could. 'The opportunities are somewhat limited, of course. But, yes, I travelled extensively with my mother as a child. Tenerife. Costa del Sol. Rhodes.'

'Have you ever been to Denmark?'

He pretended to search for the answer. He tilted his head, acting as if he were combing through his memories. Nora had seen Bollywood extras deliver more convincing performances.

'Yes. I think I have a couple of times,' he said when he couldn't drag it out any longer.

'You went by boat?'

'Yes. Why?'

'Do you remember when you took the ferry to Denmark?'

'No. Not really. Why, is it important?' he said with feigned indifference.

Nora noticed that he was starting to squirm on his seat and his chains rattled.

'This conversation is starting to bore me, to be frank,' he sulked.

'Lulu. Lisbeth.' She took the plunge.

Hickley just looked at her, but he grew deathly quiet. He sat very still, as if playing a game of sleeping lions. As if he were scared that a rash movement might give him away.

Nora let him stew.

Eventually he exhaled and shrugged. 'I met loads of girls back then. Don't forget, I was scouting for models, the girls were throwing themselves at me,' he said with scorn in his voice. 'But I can't claim that those names mean anything to me. Not in the least. Not at all.'

He was protesting too much. It sounded like a triple denial so she wouldn't detect his lie. He knew exactly who she was talking about. Nora was just as sure of that as she was that Hix wouldn't tell her one syllable more than he himself had planned.

Nora decided to change tack. 'Do you get any visitors in prison?'

He sent her an arch look. 'You mean apart from my lawyer and silly journalists on fishing expeditions?'

Nora let the silence unfold between them as she held on to the thought that very soon she would be out in the open air again. Free to go wherever she wanted to go. Hix would rot in this place.

'Apart from them, yes,' she said at last.

'That's none of your business. Anything else?' he said, making as if to get up. An exercise, which was pointless, given that he was still restrained.

Slowly and deliberately Nora slipped her hand inside her white shirt and fished out the paper. She half-unfolded it, so that it was clear that there was something on it, but not what.

She had Hix's undivided attention.

'You like pictures, don't you?'

He gulped and nodded.

'Does anyone ever visit you in prison?'

He gave a light shrug. 'My mother.'

'And your sister?'

He nodded.

'No one else?'

'No.'

'Pen pals?'

'What's on the picture?'

Nora unfolded it and held it up to him.

Hix reached for it instinctively, and his handcuffs rattled before he stopped himself.

'First you tell me who writes to you in prison. Who is playing Bill Hix on your behalf?'

'I've no idea what you're talking about.'

He didn't look at her. His eyes followed the unfolded piece of paper.

Nora made to leave. 'Right, what a shame, Mr Hickley.'

'Bill,' he interjected with a furious expression in his eyes.

'Like I said, it's a shame, but I don't really think there's anything interesting to write about here.'

She watched as incredulity spread across his face like spilled coffee on a piece of paper.

'You … You …'

'I'm clearly wasting my time,' she said.

'But you haven't even asked me about –' he stuttered in a voice so whiny, it almost became falsetto. He sounded like a spoiled brat.

Nora watched as he slowly recovered his composure like a man who has walked to the very edge of a cliff as a joke.

'Nice try, Miss Sand,' he said, and there was approval in his voice, which had dropped a few octaves again. His gaze was flinty, and he nodded slowly and with admiration.

'Yes. You clearly have wasted your time. But nice try. You're one of the better ones,' he said, glancing down at his hands still chained to the armrests. 'As you can see, my current position sadly prevents me from giving you the applause you deserve. You'll have to imagine that.'

With those words he turned his head and called for the prison officer. The visit was over. Nora could feel her frustration like red flushes on her cheeks.

Right before the door opened to reveal Jimmy Archer, Hix looked her straight in the eye and hissed: 'I'll get you, you bitch. I always get what I want.'

Nora could feel panic pulsating right under her skin. There was no way he could touch her, but she felt like she was standing with her nose pressed right up against the glass in a reptile house, watching a rattlesnake ready to strike. Hypnotised by fear, the brain knows that the snake can't strike through the glass. But it forgets to pass on the message to the body.

It took all her concentration to get up calmly. To act as if she didn't care. Her movements became stiff and controlled. Her eyes grew distant and she shut everything out. She heard no sounds.

It wasn't until she was back in the corridor that Nora realised that she had forgotten to breathe since leaving Hix. Sod it. She had blown her chance. She had sat opposite him, possibly with the key to everything – so close to unpicking the lock. And then she had lost it all by gambling with too-high stakes.

The image of Hannelore and Helmuth Neuberg from Munich

followed her all the way on her walk of shame back down the grey linoleum corridor. Two ageing parents with a hole in their life the size of a missing daughter.

Jimmy Archer stuffed a card in her hand just before she got into the prison van, which had been waiting for her outside the building. She took a seat and stared at the card in disbelief as the door was shut and the driver drove her back to the administration block. It was a business card with Jimmy Archer's mobile number. The kind you can print yourself from a machine at a railway station. It had a small Playboy Bunny logo in one corner.

On the back Jimmy Archer had written in a childish hand: 'Call me. I'll buy you dinner, gorgeous x.'

Nora scrunched up the card and stuffed it in her jacket pocket.

When she returned to the reception, Foxy was on the phone, while her colleague was playing a very advanced form of Tetris on his computer. He paused his game at the sight of her and found the visitors' log.

'Good visit?' he asked without interest.

Nora shrugged, signed the log and her necklace was returned. She retrieved her bag from the locker and had reached the car park when her mobile rang.

It was Spencer, telling her the car was on its way and would be there in five minutes.

'It was a decent try. Don't be too hard on yourself –'

'But he didn't say anything –'

'And that picture of the girls. Good thinking. You almost tripped him up.'

Nora shook her head as she tried to grasp the implication of what he had just said.

'What? How would you know? Only Hix and I were in the room.'

'Hix and you and the hidden camera right above the notice board. I was in the room next door. We had to be there for your safety. Don't forget that Hix is a killer. And seeing his body language was useful.'

'Why didn't you tell me? I thought I was in there all alone.'

'That was the whole point. If you had known, it wouldn't have been natural.'

She blurted out the words without thinking. Out of frustration at her failure. Although she knew it wasn't a reasonable expectation of herself, she had still hoped that she could make a difference.

'Fuck you!'

Then she pressed Spencer out of her mobile and called a cab to take her to the station. He called her back twice while she waited for the cab to arrive. But she didn't pick up.

22

Back in London, while the taxi crawled slowly through the traffic, she stared at buildings and people in the streets rushing off to meetings about things that would mean nothing to people who had lost a daughter. Meetings about money, property and inanimate objects that ultimately didn't matter.

She tried to clear her mind and let it work unencumbered while she vaguely registered that the driver had tuned his radio to BBC Radio 4, where a woman with an Indian accent was engaged in a passionate discussion with the presenter. 'But it says so in the book. It says so in the book,' she kept insisting.

The presenter tried his best to pour oil on troubled waters. 'Mrs Singh. I don't think we're going to get anywhere, and we have other listeners waiting to give their opinion on what it's like for children in stepfamilies. But thank you for calling,' he said, and got her effortlessly off the line before listing the number for listeners to call.

Something stirred at the edge of Nora's mind. Something about a book. Something written in a book.

Her thoughts travelled back as she tried to reconstruct events at the reception. She had signed the visitors' log. A form in triplicate, which Foxy had left somewhere in the office. Nora replayed the movie in slow motion in her mind's eye as she took her pad out of her bag and made notes while her memories were still fresh.

She visualised Foxy's colleague, who had given too much away by telling her that Hix was visited only by his mother and sister. Something about the scene grated.

Her train of thought was interrupted when the cab driver slammed on the brakes to avoid hitting a young man listening to an iPod. The man's head was covered by a hoodie and he had crossed the road without looking. The driver rolled down his window and shouted at the top of his lungs: 'Watch where you're going, you moron!'

The only one on the street who didn't react was the iPod guy who continued to sway to music only he could hear.

The taxi drove along Regent's Park with the radio still on. 'But what about the government's family policy – has it failed?' the presenter wondered out loud on the radio.

Family. Book. The two words collided in her brain and suddenly Nora realised what was wrong. She could barely wait to get home to check if she had remembered correctly. When the taxi pulled up outside her flat, she raced up the stairs without waiting for change or even a receipt to send to the Crayfish.

She found *Murders of the Century* on the floor. It had fallen from her bedside table and was lying half-hidden under a grubby T-shirt. She quickly looked up the chapter on young William Hickley and his mother.

Her memory was right: Something didn't add up. The writer could be wrong, of course. Not done their research. It wouldn't be the first time.

She found McCormey's number, called Dover police and introduced herself. To her surprise, she was put through to McCormey immediately.

'Miss Sand. I think for you to call Spencer would be a really good idea. I know he's very keen to get hold of you,' he said, without introducing himself.

'Hmm,' Nora grunted in what she hoped could be interpreted as a non-committal response.

'I'm just telling you. Spencer is a man who usually gets what he wants. And he's not happy right now.'

'Neither am I,' Nora retorted brazenly.

A short laugh escaped McCormey. 'No, Spencer seems to have that effect on most people. But trust me – the work he's doing is very, very important. More important than him and his manners. Seriously, call him. Now.'

'All right, all right, I will. But I'm not calling for advice on how to bond with Spencer. I was hoping you could help me with something. I'm trying to construct a profile of Hix. What he was like before he went to prison, that kind of thing, to get the full picture.'

'Aha?'

'And it got me thinking: during your investigation did you ever come across any family members, brothers or sisters or close friends possibly, whom I could contact to learn a bit more about what he was like as a child?'

A lengthy pause followed.

'Eh, hello?' Nora said to make sure that he hadn't hung up.

'Miss Sand. I'm not allowed to share information of that nature with the press, or indeed anyone else. I can't tell you the name of a suspect's siblings. Even if that person was an only child, without any family or friends, I wouldn't be able to tell you. Do you understand?'

'Completely. Thank you,' Nora said.

'Was that all?'

'There's just one more thing,' she said, with fond memories of episodes of *Columbo*, which she had seen as a child, where the detective in his crumpled trench coat would always turn around in the doorway with one last and fatal question.

'I know you can't tell me anything, and this is a shot in the dark because I'm trying to follow a lead from Denmark. But have you ever come across a Danish man by the name Oluf Mikkelsen?'

McCormey seemed to think about it.

'I can't comment on individual investigations, of course. But I can tell you this much, that during my entire career as a police officer I've never come across that name. And I have a memory like an elephant,' he then said.

23

The moment Nora had rung off, her voicemail beeped. Spencer had left four messages. She heaved a sigh and rang him back.

'Miss Sand. You're returning my call,' he quipped.

'Yes, so it seems,' she replied.

A lengthy pause followed and Nora was in no hurry to fill it. Spencer was at fault here, not her.

'Listen. I'm not someone who normally makes apologies,' he began.

'But?'

'But nothing. That's just the way it is,' he said bluntly, and yet Nora couldn't help smiling down the phone. He reminded her of her brother David. A man on a mission.

'I would like – we would like,' he corrected himself, 'to meet with you in here tomorrow morning at ten. We have important matters to discuss.'

'Hmm. Not sure I can do tomorrow,' she said.

'Miss Sand. I'm asking you in the most tactful way I can. I'm not asking for myself, but on behalf of many other people. You need to come here for their sake,' he said, pulling no punches.

Nora knew only too well that she had no real choice, if she were to have any hope of shaking off the images of Mr and Mrs Neuberg and the many missing girls.

When she had ended the call, she went back to her computer and found the pictures she had scanned from the newspaper coverage of Lulu's and Lisbeth's disappearance. She clicked until she found a group photo from Vestergården and enlarged it as much as she could, before zooming in on Oluf Mikkelsen.

The fact that he was one of three people out of a group of eight to go missing without a trace in the UK was unlikely to be a coincidence. If he had gone missing, that is. However, his fingerprint on the picture of Lisbeth and Lulu surely indicated some sort of connection.

Nora vaguely remembered a feature she had written a few years ago about British police launching a database for missing people, and a few Google clicks later, she had found it.

The National Missing Persons Register had been set up with a view to solving the mystery of the approximately twelve hundred unidentified bodies that at any given day lie forgotten in mortuaries across the UK. The earthly remains of people with no relatives to claim them and hold a funeral. Dead bodies with no names, life stories or the slightest evidence that someone once loved them.

Many of them were people who had succumbed to life in London and chosen to end it on the underground railway track, while others had drifted ashore along the coast, been found in burned-out houses or on park benches, their veins full of drugs. All they had in common was that they had left this life unnoticed by anyone, and that they had no names.

At the National Missing Persons Register all such findings were documented, photographed and collated from every police force in the country. With a heavy heart Nora clicked on the homepage, bracing herself for pictures of frozen masks of what was once a living human being.

However, the homepage listed only a telephone number and an address you could visit if you had what they described as a 'legitimate' interest in getting access to the register's archives. It was in Walthamstow and it closed in exactly half an hour.

It was fair enough that they didn't post pictures of dead people on the internet. There were already plenty of terrible things you could view by clicking, she thought.

She called the number and made an appointment for the following day, just after lunch.

24

Spencer was ready for her the moment she was sent up from reception, and he showed her into a meeting room where Irene and Millhouse were waiting with broad smiles and freshly sharpened pencils. At the centre of the table was a fruit bowl with delicious grapes, bananas and plums.

'Miss Sand. How nice of you to join us,' he said without a hint of irony.

Nora perched on the edge of her seat, reached for a banana, peeled it and wolfed it down in three bites. Breakfast.

'Coffee?' Millhouse offered, and she nodded, her mouth still full of banana.

He poured her a cup from the cafetière, while Spencer connected his laptop to an overhead projector and searched for what looked like a picture folder. Nora took a carton of whole milk and adjusted her coffee from black to light brown.

'You did well yesterday,' Irene said and winked at her.

'I don't think I made any difference,' Nora said. 'Because he didn't tell us anything we didn't already know, did he?'

Spencer cleared his throat. 'Oh, he did. Perhaps not intentionally, but this is where we come into the picture. Where *you* come into the picture,' he replied.

Nora took her first restorative sip and acknowledged yet again that not only was the coffee in Spencer's office at the higher end of what she had ever been served in a public institution, it was in a galaxy of its own compared to any coffee she had ever had anywhere in the UK.

She gawped at Millhouse. 'What is this?'

He grinned from ear to ear. 'Jamaican Blue Mountain. My father has a coffee shop in Soho. During my first week here at the Yard, I nearly went mental over the rubbish teabags and industrial mixes they had here, so I agreed with Spencer that I would take charge of the coffee,' he explained.

Nora swirled the hot liquid around her mouth, tasting softness and a slightly burned aroma. Her animosity was washed away and she looked at Spencer with fresh eyes.

'OK, how can I help you?' she said, pulling out her notebook from her bag.

'You can start by putting that notebook away,' Spencer said acidly.

'You never give up, do you?'

He shook his head with a hint of a smile and pressed a key on his computer. The grainy film of her meeting with Hickley appeared on the screen, and Nora couldn't help shuddering at the sight of those eyes again. The camera was almost pointing straight at Hickley, and Nora concluded that it must have been wall-mounted diagonally behind her left shoulder. The volume was turned down and in one corner a timecode was running, displaying large white numbers.

'I'll let Irene start. She's a body language expert. In fact, she wrote her PhD based on TV recordings of Jeffrey Dahmer,' Spencer said, referring to the notorious American serial killer who managed to murder seventeen boys and men before he was finally caught.

Irene leaned forward in readiness to review a recording she had presumably already gone over with a fine-tooth comb since yester-day, Nora imagined.

'Please forward to four minutes and twenty seconds,' she said.

Spencer did as she had asked.

'Watch him now,' Irene said, walking up to the white screen where the picture from Spencer's computer had been projected. She pointed with a green marker pen. 'Here he's in total control of himself. He's leaning back. His gaze is steady, bordering on triumphant. Pay attention to his hands. They're relaxed.'

Nora nodded. After all, she had been there herself.

'Right, now try fast-forwarding about ten minutes.'

Spencer moved the mouse back and forth a bit, and stopped the recording near the end.

The change was noticeable and more obvious because there was no sound to distract them. Hickley was rocking restlessly back and forth on his seat. His hands clenching and unclenching. His eyes kept looking up sideways as people do when trying to access long-stored memories.

'What are we talking about at that point?' Nora blurted out.

Irene turned to Spencer. 'Can we have the volume on, please?'

'… been to Denmark?'

Nora's voice boomed across the room.

'You've touched a nerve there,' Spencer said softly. 'There's something about Denmark. Something he'll go a long way to hide.'

Nora nodded. 'I had the same feeling myself when I was in there. But when you watch the recording, it becomes really obvious.'

Spencer smiled broadly. 'I knew you'd understand.'

'Hey, that still doesn't mean it was all right of you to let me think I was going in there alone,' Nora said, sounding more peevish than she had intended.

Millhouse poured her more coffee in an attempt to smooth her ruffled feathers. 'What's important now is that we decide a strategy for our next move,' he said.

Nora drank her coffee pensively. 'I think I've blown my one chance. I don't think he'll slip up again. He lost control for a moment, but will he allow himself to do so again? Surely he'll be even more guarded if I turn up a second time, won't he?' she said to no one in particular.

Spencer picked up on that. 'We have to try again, and I must stress once more that you got further with him than anyone else.'

'OK. Then let's just ignore for now that I have to go back and face an insane killer, and let's presume that I'm happy to do so in order to help solve the case. Seriously, what can I do to get him to talk? McCormey spent – how long was it – over ten years and never got anything out of him.'

Millhouse leaned forward. 'But this is where you're different, Nora,' he said sincerely. 'He's interested in you. He wants your approval.'

Nora's jaw dropped. 'What do you base that on?'

'On the fact that he tried very hard to impress you and build up a kind of rapport with you. He wanted you to call him Bill. With every other visitor, except family, he insists on being addressed as Mr Hix.'

Millhouse pulled a pile of papers stapled together out of the file. Nora could see it was a printout of their entire conversation. Millhouse had highlighted several passages in yellow.

'You got a lot of things right. You weren't submissive. You didn't plead with him to answer your questions. And your decision to walk out bordered on genius,' he said with admiration.

Nora stared blankly at him. 'I just couldn't stand being in the room with him any longer,' she said.

Spencer pulled a face that could almost be taken to indicate regret. But only just, she thought.

'You'll have to get over that. You'll be seeing a lot more of Hix,' he said. 'We're trying to get a permanent permit in place. It'll take a few days and then you can visit him whenever you want to.'

Nora shuddered at the thought. 'But –'

Spencer interrupted her: 'It's Saturday tomorrow, so the earliest I can have something ready is Wednesday. That's probably just as well. If you turn up any sooner, he'll only get suspicious. And I need to talk to Cross, so he can prepare Hix. Get him in the right frame of mind, so to speak,' he said.

'And you think Cross will agree to it? Isn't his first duty to his client?' Nora asked.

'Like I said, he owes me a favour. A big one,' Spencer said, without elaborating any further.

Millhouse interjected: 'And we have an extra ace up our sleeve. We can tempt him with the prospect of being transferred from a Category A prison. On … how can I put it … more relaxed terms.'

Spencer took over again. 'We have the weekend to work out a

plan of action. I have some colleagues at Quantico and one in New Zealand whom I would like to consult. They have experience of how one goes about something like this.'

Nora chose her words with care. 'I want to help as much as I can. However, I still have my day job …'

Spencer nodded. 'I appreciate that. And I think that even at this stage I can promise you that we're talking about a limited number of visits. But this might be our only chance to crack the case. I know that McCormey has great faith in you. You must have made a very favourable impression on him. For a journalist that's rare,' he said.

Nora drank the rest of her coffee. Although it had grown cold, it left no trace of bitterness on her tongue.

'Be ready for a briefing on Tuesday and possibly a meeting later next week. Deal?' Spencer asked, and his eyes were grave.

She nodded and made to get up. 'Right, then –'

'And one last thing, Miss Sand. There was a reason why I told you to put back your notebook. Everything that happens in this room is confidential.'

'But then how will I be able to –'

'Confidential, until we agree otherwise.'

Nora sighed. All right, if that was how he wanted to play it. However, it also meant she was under no obligation to share information with him.

She said goodbye, walked to Green Park tube station and caught the Victoria line to Walthamstow.

25

She managed to walk past the Missing Persons Register twice before she finally spotted the small office in a basement under a pink hairdressing salon offering half-price Brazilian waxing.

Nora checked her watch. She was twenty minutes early and she toyed briefly with the idea of a spot of lunch at a pub called The Crown two doors down, but lost her appetite the moment she popped her head inside. It reeked of old chip oil and sour beer. Roxette's greatest hits poured effortlessly from the speakers, indicating that the new millennium had yet to reach this far-flung corner of Walthamstow.

Instead she decided to find out if it was acceptable to be a little early for her appointment. She walked the four steps down to the basement office, which looked like it might have been a bicycle repair shop in the old days.

A guy in his mid-twenties was behind the counter, sporting an obliging smile and a bright orange T-shirt announcing with a big yellow smiley that he was 'Born to Party'. Opened in front of him was a dog-eared copy of *Moby Dick*.

'The hairdresser's is upstairs,' he said.

'Yes, it's hard to miss,' Nora quipped.

'Ah, you're here to look at the archives,' he said, surprised, and tried frantically to hide his book under a pile of brochures, then noticed the look on Nora's face and gave a shrug. 'Third year. American Literature. I need to make some money while I study, and we hardly get any visitors.'

'Do you know how it ends? The butler did it,' Nora said, deadpan.

'I'm Dave,' he said as his face split in a grin. 'And you must be

Sand. Mike did put you in the diary yesterday. It's not often we get a visitor who isn't from the police.'

'That explains the T-shirt. Maybe it's not the first piece of information relatives need when they step through this door,' Nora observed.

Dave looked down at himself and reddened slightly. 'The computer is in there,' he said, showing her into an austere room with gurgling water pipes running under the ceiling, white walls and two battered desks facing each other, each with a computer on top.

He bent down and turned one of them on. It warmed up with a groan while he leaned across the table and switched on the screen, which looked as if it had been built sometime between a Commodore 64 and an early Apple.

'It's like walking into an episode of *Star Trek* with all this high-tech equipment.'

Dave rewarded her with a dry grin: 'Let me put it this way: there's not a lot of money to be made from missing or unidentified people. This isn't where the Home Office wants to spend its budget. There are no votes in it,' he said and took a deep breath; he was just getting started.

'We're actually a registered charity, but you try a street collection for dead people. And I'm talking about people who may well have committed suicide out of loneliness because no one cared about them while they were still alive. Now that they're dead, people care even less ... You try shaking a bucket right next to some idiot in a kangaroo costume collecting for cats or Great Ormond Street Hospital ... People walk on before you've even opened your mouth –'

The computer beeped and Dave broke off to enter a password so quickly that Nora only had time to catch the number 66 and an X. He pointed to a decrepit printer blinking with one red eye.

'If you need to print anything out, please use the printer. You can come to me for paper. I'm afraid we have to charge you fifty pence per sheet. But the good news is that we have a limit of five pounds, so if you need more than ten sheets, the rest are free. Sorry about that, it's to cover expenses,' he said.

Nora pulled out a five-pound note from her purse immediately. 'For the coffee tin.'

Dave went back to the reception and returned with a handwritten receipt and a glass of water. For a while he stood looking over her shoulder, until he realised that his presence was superfluous.

'I'll go back to Captain Ahab then,' he said.

Nora took out the picture of Oluf Mikkelsen and clicked to access the list of unidentified deceased. It contained one thousand one hundred and forty-five people, whom the British police had never managed to identify.

At first she removed all the women. That left eight hundred and thirty-two. Then she clicked the box to select white people – or as forensic scientists the world over preferred to call them: Caucasians. That eliminated another three hundred and fifty.

Then she clicked on the search field for dates. If Oluf Mikkelsen had disappeared several years ago, there was no need to look for him in the last five.

When she had removed men under twenty and over fifty from the equation, the group of possible candidates had reduced considerably.

If Oluf Mikkelsen – and it was a big if – had died in the UK and his body had been found, but never identified, he would probably be in this group.

Finally there was nothing left but to review the remaining men one by one. Case number after case number. She clicked her way through pictures of lifeless faces whose pale features, staring, blind or closed eyes and sometimes contorted expressions had permanently said goodbye to life.

Listed next to each picture was the kind of basic information you would find in a passport: hair colour, eye colour, estimated height and weight. And then the extras passport officers would be grateful never to see: cause of death, location found and distinguishing features.

After approximately forty-five minutes' intense work, she was delighted with her decision not to have lunch at the pub. She had viewed a stomach-churning parade of faces. Some bloated from having been submerged in water for days, others smashed to a pulp after falls from bridges or buildings or the sudden encounter with an underground train. She had selected three as potential candidates and eliminated everyone else.

Finally she reached a category of incomplete bodies, but in four instances the police had done what they could, given their few leads, and paid a specialist sculptor to reconstruct the face with modelling clay based on cranial dimensions.

Nora flicked through them quickly, but stopped at a wax head of a man vaguely similar to Oluf. His nose might be a little too straight, but how would a sculptor know that Oluf Mikkelsen had been a boxer and broken his nose for the first time before he turned fifteen?

The hair colour was dark brown, which matched what she could see in the picture from Vestergården. It was impossible to determine his eye colour in the enlargement.

She read on. Distinguishing features: a tattoo on the right bicep. A bull, possibly of Spanish origin. A twenty-eight-centimetre scar on his left leg.

On impulse she pulled out her mobile and checked the signal. She had two bars, so it would just about work.

He answered after three rings with a surly: 'Humph?'

'Hi, it's Nora Sand.'

'I know it's you, Nora Sand. I don't get calls from anyone else from a number beginning 0044.' Bjarke sounded pissed off. 'Have you got more information for me?'

Nora had to admit that she didn't.

'So why are you wasting my time?' he wanted to know, and Nora could hear that someone was playing pool in the background, so not a good time to chat.

'I'll make it quick. Oluf.'

'Oluf?'

'Mikkelsen. Did he have any distinguishing features?'

'You've lost me. What the hell does Oluf have to do with anything? Was he mixed up in it, that little shit – I'm going to bloody well –'

'No, I don't think so. Or rather, I don't know if there is a link, but I need to look into it. Process of elimination, you know,' Nora said to placate him. She didn't have the energy to explain everything to an already irritable biker-gang member who was showing off to his pool friends.

'Features?' Bjarke echoed.

'Yes, tattoos, that kind of things. Scars?'

'Funny you should mention it, Sand. He does, as it happens,' Bjarke said.

'Really, what are they?' Nora said, a little too keen.

'Hang on, little lady. We have a small problem here. The thing is I asked *you* for information, but I'm not getting any. Instead, *you* keep ringing me, asking what I can give you. Do you see the problem?'

Nora could feel her irritation come out as red flushes on her cheeks. 'Oh, give over, Bjarke. I've already promised you that I'll tell you once I know for sure. But I haven't got anything yet. I need peace and quiet so I can work.'

'Humph,' she heard him grunt, before what sounded like him putting down the phone and shouting out across the room. 'Hey, can we get some beers over here.'

Nora rolled her eyes.

'What did you say again?' he said, pretending to have forgotten her question.

'I asked if he had a tattoo of a bull?'

'You're close. It was a bison. But now that you mention it, I'm not really sure Tattoo-Flemming at the prison would have known the difference. It did look more like a bull. But few people would have had the balls to say so to Oluf's face.'

'Thank you,' Nora said, and her heart was pounding as she ended the call.

The dead man could be Oluf Mikkelsen and she might be the one who finally found him after all these years. All right, so no one had been looking for him. But there was a chance that the mystery of what had happened to him might prove to be the key to what happened to Lulu and Lisbeth.

She went out to Dave, who was lost in whaling troubles off the coast of Canada, and gestured vaguely in the direction of a pile of paper.

'Take whatever you need. You've already paid,' he said.

The register held four pages of information on the man who might be Oluf Mikkelsen, and Nora sent them all to the printer. There wasn't a lot to go on. The cause of death was possibly drowning, but the coroner's inquest had concluded with a vague phrase saying it was still inconclusive how the man in question had met his death.

However, it did suggest that the body had been found approximately two weeks after someone – according to Rudolf from the boxing club in Denmark – had last seen Oluf Mikkelsen. And the description was that of a muscular man 'in good health, well-nourished with healthy organs'. His height was 1.75 metres, his weight estimated at around seventy-two kilos, which sounded appropriate for a welterweight..

The body had been found by a fisherman, Arthur Thompson, when it got caught up in the propeller on his boat. Which explained why Oluf Mikkelsen had no face.

That is, if the man really was Oluf Mikkelsen.

At the bottom of the last page she found the information she really needed: 'Investigating officer: Dale Moss, Waybridge Police.'

She shut down the computer happily, waved goodbye to Dave, and caught the tube back home to Belsize Park.

There was still a little sunshine left, and mentally Nora was already in Rosie's coffee bar sipping iced coffee. Her plan was to dump her laptop and heavy bag in her flat and pick up a couple of newspapers before sitting down at one of the wobbly tables Rosie had optimistically set out on the pavement. In the hallway she discovered a small pile of post and picked it up. More than half was for Mrs Fleming in the ground-floor flat, but there were a couple of window envelopes addressed to Miss Sand and one of those stiff grey envelopes photographers use for sending pictures so they won't bend. From Pete? Nora frowned and turned over the envelope. There was no sender. She tore off the tape and slipped her fingers inside to retrieve the contents.

It took a split second for her to decode the faded picture. The black eye sockets, the gaping mouth like a big hole with blood seeping out. It was Jean Eastman. The victim who was found in Hix's boot when he was caught.

Nora turned over the picture.

THIS IS WHAT HAPPENS TO LITTLE GIRLS WHO SEE TOO MUCH AND TALK TOO MUCH, it said in jagged capital letters.

Her heart reacted like a sparrow that has accidentally flown inside a house. It flits around in panic, bashing into walls and window panes; no matter how many doors and windows you open to create a safe exit, it carries on its self-destructive flight.

Then she realised that there were no stamps on the letter. It meant that it must have been delivered by hand. Someone not only knew where she lived, but had also been to her address.

Her hands trembled as she found Spencer's number on her mobile. Her call went straight to voicemail. She gulped, swallowed her pride and called Andreas.

'Yes?' he sounded a little fraught.

'Andreas. Someone has sent me a letter. Someone who knows where I live.'

'Eh?'

She repeated it, though she could hear there was a lot of noise in the background.

'I can't hear you … what did you say?'

Nora could hear her own voice hit falsetto, but couldn't do anything about it. Her panic was lurking just under the surface. Did she dare go outside again? Go up to her flat?

'Andreas, I think Hix knows where I live, and –'

At that moment she heard the familiar announcement jingle used in airports the world over.

'Nora, I'm struggling to hear you. I have to board my plane now. I'm on my way to Denmark. We'll have to do this later.'

'Do this later? What do you mean we'll –'

The connection was lost.

She tried Spencer three times in a row. To no avail.

Typical! He would sulk if she didn't pick up the microsecond he rang, yet when she really needed him, he was unavailable.

She opened the front door and peered nervously left and right. No suspicious activity. Completely normal people on their way to meetings, afternoon coffee or going to Sainsbury's for tomato sauce and kitchen towels.

She tried a logical approach. Her address was public knowledge. Her picture and contact details were on *Globalt's* homepage – it was essential for a correspondent, something she had never questioned before.

But who could have sent the letter? Hix's accomplice? Or a copycat?

Nora had no wish to find out. She raced up the stairs, entered her flat and found her old sports bag. In less than ten minute she had packed the essentials. She slung her laptop bag over her other shoulder, locked the door, went downstairs, hailed the first cab she saw and asked to be taken to Waterloo Station. She would have to ring her mother from the train.

X

The train journey to Honiton took three hours. Nora stared out at a landscape of meadows, woods and small, white cottages huddled together. She tried to talk some sense into herself. No one knew that her mother's boyfriend was an apple grower in Devon. Hix would never find her there. The further the train took her away from London, the safer she would be. An hour later Elizabeth finally picked up the phone.

'Mum, I'm coming down to Patrick's for a few days … I had to get away from London,' Nora began.

There was a pause.

'You are? Oh, all right then,' her mother said coolly.

'Mum, I really had to get away,' Nora insisted.

'Just a minute,' her mother said.

Nora could hear clattering and mumbled conversation, which she presumed must be with Patrick.

'Very well. You can have the guest cottage. You're not giving us much warning, are you?'

'But, Mum –'

'Just so you know it, we won't be here. It's Angela Dartford's sixtieth birthday, so we'll be away most of the weekend. But Patrick says that he can leave out a key for you.'

'But, Mum –'

'When are you coming?'

Nora checked her watch. 'In about two hours?'

'So soon?' The irritation in Elizabeth's voice simmered under a thin veneer of politeness.

Nora said nothing.

'Hmm. We've organised a dinner party tonight. Can't you just take a taxi from the station? Picking you up right when our guests are due to arrive will be tricky for us. I'll be in the middle of cooking three courses, and I need Patrick around to mix the cocktails,' she said.

'Yes, Mum. Of course I can,' Nora said and rang off.

At least she would be safe tonight, but spending the weekend in the arms of her loving family clearly wasn't an option. There were no loving arms when it came to Elizabeth, and Nora wondered why it seemed that she had to learn this lesson over and over every time she went against her better judgement and asked her mother for help.

She still couldn't get through to Spencer. Out of sheer desperation she tried leaving a message at Scotland Yard's reception, but in accordance with protocol, they vehemently denied knowing anything about Spencer's existence.

She had stuffed the envelope into her laptop bag, where the grey edges stuck out and reminded her of its terrible contents like a ticking bomb. Her thoughts buzzed around her head like wasps in a bottle. They kept bumping into the question of who had delivered the gruesome close-up of what was once the smiling young woman in a florist's with eyes that could flirt and a tongue that could speak.

Nora forced herself to think about Oluf and the mystery of how he might have ended up in the sea. But to no avail. It was as if the stiff edges of the envelope kept poking the outskirts of her mind.

The moment the train pulled up in front of the low redbrick station building in Honiton, it started to rain. Nora hurried out to the cab rank in time to see the lights of the only taxi disappear on the horizon. She reconciled herself to waiting and took the opportunity to ring the Crayfish. He was at home and she could tell from his voice that he was busy, purely from the way he introduced himself.

'What is it, Sand? And can we make it quick? Family get-together.'

'I've received a threatening letter. Either from Hix or an accomplice, I think.'

'You think? Go on.'

Nora told him.

'And you're sure it's not someone from Scotland Yard who has sent you the picture as part of your research?'

Nora rolled her eyes. 'Yes. Why would they do that?'

'Because it's something you have to eliminate before we can take this seriously. You need to check it out, and then we'll discuss it on Monday. If it's a genuine threat, you'll have the magazine's unconditional support, of course. That's our standard procedure. No one threatens *Globalt's* reporters with anything. OK?' the Crayfish said, sounding rushed.

'Yes,' Nora said in despair and rang off. The Crayfish had a habit of going on autopilot when he was stressed.

Twilight was starting to settle over Honiton, and she wondered whether it was worth calling her mother and asking her for the number of a local taxi company that could pick her up from the station, when a black Toyota with a taxi sign on the roof pulled up in front of her.

Nora opened the door and got in the back with her bags on her lap. The smell of pine air freshener and leather was overwhelming. The driver didn't turn around. Nora gave him the address of Patrick's orchard, and he drove off without saying anything, leaving the station and turning right.

She tried making conversation about the weather to cover up her nerves, but the driver answered her reluctantly with monosyllabic grunts, and soon the car was quiet. Not even the radio was on. There was only the faint rumble of the engine and the small, hard slam of raindrops hitting the windscreen. And then the monotone squeal of windscreen wipers that had seen better days.

Nora had only visited Patrick a few times. She thought the drive from the station took about fifteen minutes, and tried reconstructing the route from memory. It was down a road where there was a pub with a horse – or was it a unicorn – on the sign. And after that there was a big black barn and a side road.

When they had been driving for what felt like forever, Nora was relieved to see the pub sign through the now steamed-up windows. Nearly there. From here it was only another five minutes' drive, she thought. The next moment they passed The Unicorn & Maiden.

'Hey? Don't we turn off here?'

The driver made no reply.

Nora tried again, a little louder this time: 'I think we were supposed to have turned back there!'

The man stayed silent, but she thought he stepped harder on the accelerator because the car gained speed. Cold sweat erupted while she tried keeping what was left of her nerve intact.

'Hello? Did you not understand the address?' she tried.

The driver shrugged and accelerated even more.

Nora quickly considered her options. The car was going too fast for her to jump out now, but she knew that at some point it would have to slow down on the narrow country road. She discreetly pressed her bags close to her body and tensed her muscles, preparing herself for flight.

When the car slowed down at a sharp bend, she grabbed the door handle firmly, ready to jump out. The handle clicked impotently. The child lock was on.

She caught the driver's eye in the rear-view mirror. Her attempt to escape seemed to amuse him. 'Relax. We're nearly there,' he said.

His voice was strangely distorted, he sounded as if he might be on drugs. Nora wondered if she should pull the handbrake to try to stop the car.

At that moment her mobile rang. It was Spencer. 'Miss Sand, where's the fire?'

Her words stumbled, refusing to arrange themselves in a proper sentence. She didn't dare tell him about the picture while she was in a car with a madman who was taking her God knows where.

'Track my mobile. It's important!'

Spencer sounded calm and professional. 'You need to give me more information before we can –'

'Do it now! It's a matter of life and death,' she had time to say before the black Toyota pulled up outside Patrick's house.

The driver turned around and looked at her.

'That'll be fifteen quid. Sorry for not being more chatty,' he said, pointing to his cheek, which was swollen. 'Root canal surgery this afternoon.'

'Miss Sand, what's happening?' Spencer shouted on the phone.

'Nothing. Forget it. Sorry,' she said and hung up.

Nora found twenty pounds and gave it to the driver. He got out of the car and opened the door for her, and soon afterwards she knocked on the front door of the house.

Her mother opened the door, while the two King Charles spaniels, Whisky and Soda, barked with excitement around her legs. Her hair was artfully styled, her make-up impeccable, and Nora suddenly felt scruffy and unkempt.

'Oh. There you are. We're just about to sit down for dinner. Why don't you get yourself a sandwich in the kitchen when things have settled down a bit?'

Nora nodded.

Her mother kissed her formally on both cheeks and Nora stood passively on the steps, letting her do it.

'Good. Got to run. The key to the guest cottage is in the green flowerpot next to the door. Patrick has already turned on the heating.'

In the background Nora could hear male laughter and a couple of chirping female voices. She forced a smile and shuffled across the well-kept yard to the cottage.

Almost as an afterthought her mother called out: 'Eh – is everything OK?'

'Yes,' Nora said mechanically, with no conviction in her voice.

'Right, then we might as well chat over breakfast tomorrow morning, mightn't we? Good night for whenever you go to bed,' her mother said, and closed the door so hard that the ring in the mouth of the antique lion doorknocker banged against the heavy oak a couple of times.

Nora shrugged, picked herself up and entered the cottage. It was clean and dry and there was a scent of lavender. There was no Hix, and there was Wi-Fi. That was all she needed right now.

She took a shower and walked back across the yard and into the kitchen where she made herself a couple of cheese sandwiches which she smothered in Patrick's home-made apple chutney. She put them on to a plate, stuffed a couple of apples from the fruit bowl into her pocket, and went back to the cottage to work.

She realised that in all the confusion, she had completely forgotten to tell Spencer about the picture, so she tried calling him again. No luck. She sent him a short text with the message: 'Have been threatened. Possibly by Hix. Call me.'

Then she opened her laptop and tried organising her notes from her visit to the Register for Missing Persons.

Two hours later she woke up on the bed, fully clothed and with the laptop still resting on her lap. She shut it, brushed her teeth, undressed, and fell back into a dreamless sleep.

X

Around eight o'clock the next morning when she tiptoed into the kitchen to make herself the first cup of coffee, only Whisky and Soda were up and about. Upstairs was quiet, and from the living room came the stale stench of sour wine, abandoned brandy glasses and the cigars Patrick tended to produce on festive occasions. Nora made herself toast with marmalade, looked in vain for coffee, and ended up brewing herself a strong cup of Earl Grey with milk and plenty of sugar.

Then she went back to the cottage and sat down at the small antique bureau that had to make do as her desk, and reviewed once more her notes from yesterday.

It didn't take her long to google the number of Waybridge police, the home base of Dale Moss, who had investigated the case she thought might concern Oluf.

A woman answered the phone after a few rings.

'Dale Moss?' she said. 'He hasn't worked here for over ten years. What's this about?'

'An old case,' Nora said.

'Would you like to be put through to his successor?'

Nora said yes, and soon afterwards she heard a commanding, female voice.

'DC Summers speaking.'

The woman listened patiently to Nora's account of how she had pursued a lead about a missing Danish man. A man who had never been reported missing admittedly, but it might be possible to solve this mystery now. A chance to replace a question mark with a full stop.

'And how exactly do you think that I can help you, Miss Sand?'

'I thought that perhaps I could stop by and have a look at the file –'

Summers interrupted her immediately. 'We're not allowed to hand them over. I'm sorry. No matter how much I'd like to, they're not accessible to the public. Unless, of course, you submit a Freedom of Information Request – or you can produce written permission from the man you're referring to. Though that sounds highly unlikely,' she said dryly.

Nora sighed.

'But I can possibly go one better,' Summers went on.

'How?' Nora asked expectantly.

'I can arrange a meeting with Dale Moss. He can tell you everything he remembers about the case. He might even be interested in what you have to say. Can you get here by Sunday lunchtime?'

Nora said yes.

'Every Sunday he has lunch at a small pub called The Three Mermaids as he has done for the last fifteen years, and you can set your watch by the time he arrives. A quarter past one. And he stays for at least an hour.'

'But how can I be sure he'll even be willing to talk to me?'

'I'll ask him to do me a special favour, he won't mind.'

'Really?' Nora said, thinking it was a very long drive only to sit in a pub and stare at a retired police officer who refused to utter one word about an old case.

Summers let out a short laugh. 'Yes, I'm pretty sure he'll do it if I ask him. He's my dad, and I usually have Sunday lunch with him, unless I'm on duty. I'll pull up the file and have a quick look at it. Then I can assist, in case of any … memory issues.'

Nora looked up a car rental firm in Exeter and booked a hire car that same morning. There was no point in sitting here staring at Patrick's apple trees all on her own.

When she went over to the main house with her mug, there was still no one around. She found the number of a taxi firm on the noticeboard and booked a car immediately. Then she wrote a quick note on the back of an open envelope from a pile on the windowsill.

'Thanks for your hospitality. Enjoy the party. Hugs.'

Fifteen minutes later a different driver pulled up outside, thank God. The dogs barked half-heartedly when Nora locked the door to the cottage and returned the key.

From the taxi she phoned the Crayfish. She should probably clear the visit with him, and he might already be at the office. For once he wasn't. Yet still he picked up his phone, panting into the handset.

'I'm making my way up Valby Bakke,' he announced proudly.

'You're speaking to me on your bike?' Nora was taken aback.

'Yes. The kids gave me a hands-free set for my mobile phone for my birthday, so now I can take calls on my mountain bike,' he explained.

Nora updated him on the situation.

'How much will it cost us?' he wanted to know.

'A few thousand kroner, three or four with everything.'

'And you're sure it's worth it? Does it have legs?'

Nora hesitated. 'Well, my gut instinct says yes. I think it's Oluf, and I think there is a connection. But that's as much as I have right now.'

The Crayfish had stopped panting. Perhaps he had pulled over or stopped at a red light.

'Hmm. OK, go for it. But call me tonight.'

'OK.'

'And, Sand?'

'Yes?'

Whatever he wanted to say was drowned by violent hooting.

'Yes, all right, I'll move. Relax, why don't you!' the Crayfish shouted angrily. She could hear him mutter curses under his breath, before addressing her again. 'Sand, are you still there?'

'Anything else?'

'Yes. Watch your back. And get me a few lines for the magazine soon, won't you? You can't keep running around taking one seaside holiday after another. Ah, that's Washington calling. Talk to you later.'

And with a beep the Crayfish was gone. Somewhere on a hill in Copenhagen.

26

At the car rental counter at Exeter Airport, she was handed the keys to a small, ugly, yellow car.

The customer service assistant shrugged in her grass-green polyester uniform. 'We didn't get much notice,' she said, while Nora signed the eight places indicated with small crosses by the assistant.

When she got into the car and tried to find Waybridge on the map of her mobile, a text message arrived. Unknown number. Spencer, most likely.

Her thumb hovered for a microsecond over the message, before she pressed to open it.

'I'll get you, you bitch. I always get what I want.'

Nora felt as if all the blood had drained from her body. Those were the very same words Hix had said to her. The exact same.

Her hands were trembling when she called Spencer. Voicemail. She left a short message. Completely irrationally she looked over her shoulder and central-locked every door in the car.

He's not here, she tried telling her pounding heart. Of course he wasn't. He was rotting in his cell in Wolf Hall. Of course he was. Even so ... She jumped when her mobile rang. It was Spencer calling her back.

'Make it quick. I'm in the middle of something,' he said brusquely.

Nora told him about the text message. His initial reaction was scepticism.

'Surely anyone can get your number just by looking at *Globalt's* homepage? That's how I found it,' he said dismissively.

'But it's the exact same words,' she objected. 'And that's not all –'

Spencer's voice sounded completely indifferent as he cut her off.

'Miss Sand. You seemed very agitated when we spoke yesterday. And for no reason, as it turned out.'

'Yes, but there's more. Someone left a picture of Jean Eastman at my home address. With a warning written on the back.'

'Anyone could have done that. Those pictures are in the public domain. They can be downloaded from some of the nastier websites,' Spencer argued.

Nora tried entering the debate on his terms. 'Sure, but is it also public knowledge that I'm working on this case?'

Spencer thought about it for a moment, and took a quick decision. 'OK. Don't ask me how because I'll never tell you, but I'll get Millhouse to look into it. All right? He'll call you when he knows something. And let me make one thing clear: Don't expect me to return any more of your calls this weekend. I have to devote all my time to this investigation,' he rounded off.

'But we're working on the same case,' Nora protested.

He had already hung up.

Nora forwarded the threatening text message to Spencer and left the airport. Her hands were still shaking when she changed gear, but she consoled herself with the knowledge that as long as she was on the road, no one could know where she was. Including Hix.

And yet how was it possible that a man seemingly under such scrutiny was allowed to send a text message? If he could get hold of her mobile number as easy as that, it wouldn't have presented much of a challenge for him to find her address.

Then another message arrived. She didn't recognise the number and had to brace herself before she opened it.

'Millhouse here. Spencer asked me check out the text message you got. The number belongs to a Jimmy F. Archer. No criminal record, but three unpaid parking fines. Mean anything to you?'

Nora didn't know whether to laugh or cry.

She pulled over and pressed 'call'. Millhouse answered his phone immediately. Nora didn't even wait for him to introduce himself. 'Tell me, just what the hell is going on with the British prison system?

Jimmy Archer is the moron who is supposed to be guarding Hix! The creep asked me out. Don't you run any security checks on your staff these days?' she ranted on. A part of her did know that no one was less to blame than Millhouse, but he happened to be at the other end of the phone right now.

'Nora. I understand that what happened to you is upsetting. But perhaps it's just a spurned man who saw a way of getting his own back,' Millhouse said to reassure her.

Nora concluded that this was the kind of brush-off officers were taught during the first thirty minutes of Scotland Yard's hostage negotiation course: show understanding and sympathy. Build trust. Open every sentence with the pointless phrase: I understand …

She was not being fobbed off with that.

'Millhouse. I want you to listen to me: he used the exact same words. Exactly the same words as Hix. But Archer wasn't in the room when Hix spoke them, so how could he have known what Hix said to me? Word for word?'

Millhouse was silent as he pondered it. 'There could be all sorts of explanations. Perhaps Hix trusts him.'

'Bullshit.'

'All right. Perhaps not. But he could have been eavesdropping.'

Nora thought about it. 'OK. I'll buy that. But I need to know without a shadow of a doubt that Hix is still in prison. Is that something you can check for me?'

'Fair point. I'll call you back,' Millhouse said.

A torturous hour went by.

She was startled when her mobile rang. Millhouse's voice was professional and reassuring. 'I made a call to the duty officer at Wolf Hall. He could tell from his computer that Hix, along with all other inmates on his wing, has been in his cell since five minutes past ten last night. The system is automated, and unless something happens, they don't see any of the prisoners until a headcount and a shift change at twelve thirty today. It's the weekend,' Millhouse said.

'But what about Archer?' she asked.

'I examined the data from the text message, and it looks as if it was sent from Wolf Hall, so everything points to Archer being our bad guy. I spoke to the duty manager about it, and he has promised to have a word with Archer when he turns up for his shift this afternoon. Whether or not you wish to report him, his conduct is highly inappropriate. However, his last shift ended at eleven p.m. last night, so there's not much they can do for now.'

Nora heaved a sigh. 'All right then.'

After the call she sat in the car, staring across the fields. That was when it struck her: how could Archer send her a text message from Wolf Hall this morning if he wasn't at work? Something didn't add up.

She called Millhouse back. He didn't pick up. So she tried Spencer yet again. It went straight to voicemail. This time she didn't leave a message.

27

Back in the car, she re-joined the road and turned on the radio. She didn't want to listen to jazz, it would remind her too much of Andreas, nor could she be bothered with the news or talk radio, with angry listeners calling in to complain about streetlights being turned off too early, or the shortage of parking spaces in central Stratford. Instead, she found a station that played saccharine love songs interspersed with listeners' messages to one another. *Luuuurve Radio* as the presenter called it in a tone that must have been what Barry White sounded like before his voice broke.

'This is a song for Tim from Emma. I miss you every minute and can't wait until you get home from work tonight,' the presenter smirked on behalf of Tim before, to Nora's surprise, he played an early song by The Cure. This was preferable to the sickly soundscape of Celine Dion, which was what she had feared. She considered contacting Summers as soon as she reached Waybridge, but decided Summers wouldn't be in a position to tell her much about the investigation her father and former colleague had handled years ago. Besides, they had already made arrangements to meet tomorrow.

Perhaps she should track down the fisherman who had found the body that might be Oluf. Try to uncover how a Danish amateur boxer had ended up in a fisherman's net off the English south coast, and find out if the fisherman might have seen something that wasn't included in the very brief report attached to the picture of the alleged Oluf. Now what was his name again? Thompson? Finding him on Yellow Pages would be no easy task, but if she drove down to Waybridge harbour, someone might know who he was and where he was.

After all, hauling a dead man out of the sea along with your catch didn't happen every day.

Had Oluf been involved in the disappearance of Lisbeth and Lulu? And why had he himself died? Was it about revenge? And who was taking revenge, and for what?

Nora explored various scenarios in her mind. She found it hard to imagine a lad, who after all had only been sixteen or seventeen years old back then, as a cold-blooded killer, as someone who could make not only one but two young and relatively strong women disappear into thin air, leaving absolutely no trace at all. From what she had read about serial killers recently, killing was like any other craft. The more you practised, the better you got, and the more daring your techniques.

It would have taken an older and much more experienced man than a teenage Oluf to carry out the double murder. Then again, if Anni was to be believed, he had managed to rape her that night without it looking as if it had affected the rest of his life very much at all.

Had Lulu and Lisbeth seen something they shouldn't? Again, that didn't make sense either. Because if this was about not being caught for the rape, then why not get rid of Anni as well? Or did he know that she would keep her mouth shut, or that no one would believe her even if she did speak up. However, if there were three witnesses whose stories supported each other, then Oluf was in trouble. He risked going to prison, and given the petty crimes and everything else already hanging over his head, that could be for a considerable period of time.

The radio was now playing Lady Gaga singing about her 'Poker Face' in honour of Jack, for whom Janet from Aylesbury was still holding a torch. Janet just wanted him to know that. Along with thousands of other listeners. Nora cringed on poor Jack's behalf and thought that if he really was listening to *Luuuurve Radio* right now, he only had himself to blame. And if he wasn't, then no harm was done. She chuckled to herself and couldn't help singing along to the catchy chorus. The music cheered her up. Everything would be all right. She had got hold of the right end of the thread, and all she had to do was pull and untangle it until she could roll it into a tidy ball of yarn and write a coherent story. Someone would probably find a mobile in Hix's cell, confiscate it, and that would be the end of that, she tried telling herself.

The car chewed up the miles, and Nora settled into her own rhythm, winding her way in and out between the other cars. Then without warning, a blast from the past.

After Kevin had said sorry to Tina for something Nora could only guess at with John Lennon's 'Jealous Guy', the next song hit her like a punch to the stomach. The moment she heard the confused radio signals interrupted by the crisp guitar that conjured up melancholy so effortlessly, she was taken back in time.

'Wish You Were Here,' Pink Floyd sang, and Nora was no longer on the road miles from the next exit.

She was wearing her best dress, the dark blue one with the pink flowers, to her first sixth form party and she was tipsy from drinking rum and Coke at Trine's house earlier. The dance floor was crowded with teenagers trying to look cool, while U2 set socio-political issues to music.

A tall gangly guy from her year, whose name might be Jan, caught Nora's attention. He was so obviously trying to pull Trine and used dancing as his means of seduction. Even Nora in her early stages of inebriation could see that the project was doomed to fail. Partly because Jan was so atrocious a dancer that if you took the music out of the equation and simply observed his movements, most people's first response would be to call for medical assistance, and also because the attractive Trine with the big blue eyes and the long blond hair was way out of his league.

Nora was watching them idly, making bets with herself about when the horrible truth would dawn on the poor lad.

Jan twisted backwards in a particularly daring move that might have looked more natural had there been a broom handle and a limbo involved. Nora couldn't help but laugh.

Suddenly her view was blocked by a tall broad-shouldered guy. At first she tried craning her neck to follow the performance on the dance floor, but he was too big. 'Oi, I'm trying to watch this.'

He moved to stand alongside her and followed her gaze. 'Ah. Jan. He's in my class. He doesn't stand a chance. It's never gonna happen!' he shouted to her over the music.

'No. Of course not!' Nora shouted back. 'The only question is will it take one or two songs before he realises.'

The mountain shrugged his broad shoulders and thought about it for five seconds. 'Next song, I say. What's at stake?'

'A beer?' Nora suggested.

'Breakfast?' he outbid her.

They just had time to shake hands on it, before Pink Floyd poured out of the speakers with 'Wish You Were Here', and most couples on the floor came together in a close embrace to the slow song. Halfway through it, Trine appeared in front of Nora.

'Right, listen, darling – I've decided to go home with Kristoffer. Are you OK with that?' she slurred.

Nora just had time to nod before Trine disappeared with a guitar-playing and supercool boy from the year above, who was the object of desire for most of the girls in their year. Jan was still on the dance floor with his eyes closed, swaying to the music. He hadn't even noticed Trine taking off.

The mountain turned around with raised eyebrows. 'Looks like breakfast is on you,' he commented dryly, and added after a small pause: 'Andreas.'

'Nora,' she said.

'Let's get out of here,' he said, taking her arm.

When they left the darkened sports hall, dawn was just breaking. She checked him out while they unlocked the bikes.

He was actually quite good-looking. Brown eyes, hair the colour of corn. Good lips and those broad shoulders. Oh, God, don't let him be one of those self-obsessed morons who love posing in front of the mirror while they lift weights, she prayed.

They cycled to a bakery known for selling bread rolls round the back to people on their way home after a night out, and knocked on the door. One of the bakery assistants opened it and, in return for cash, handed them a couple of buttered bread rolls and two bottles of Cocio chocolate milk. They would have to imagine the coffee.

'So where will we consume this feast?' asked Nora, who was starting to sober up.

'Follow me,' he said.

They cycled through the town and down to the beach. As far as Nora was concerned, this was perfect. There was nothing more she wanted right now than to gaze at the sea, while she ate her breakfast as the sun rose for yet another warm August day.

They found a hollow in the dunes with a great view and made themselves comfortable with their bread rolls. Andreas talked about other sunrises, and before Nora knew it, they were discussing Hemingway, triathlons, Pink Floyd and the Trans-Siberian railway. And how Nora had been scared of purple monsters when she was little, whether Bob Dylan was overrated, and Andreas's father, who had been a police officer before he was killed in a motorbike accident.

A few hours later, their conversation started to trail off. It was time to go home, only Andreas wasn't ready for it.

'Come on – time for a morning swim,' he said in a voice that would accept no contradiction.

It was still a few hours after sunrise and there was no one else on the beach. They had jumped into the waves and thus established a tradition that would last until the end of their school days. Exams, parties, break-ups and other feeble excuses didn't count. The morning swim was sacred.

So why hadn't they taken the next step that morning? Had it been on the verge of happening, had there been a moment when he looked into her eyes a little too long. Had she herself wanted to reach for him?

She tried to recall exactly how she had felt that morning. Remembered the sensation of seawater against her body, the sand between her toes. The salt on her skin. Standing alone on a deserted beach with a man she didn't yet know, but who had beautiful eyes.

When they got out of the water, Nora started shivering and she quickly put on her blue dress over her soaked underwear.

'I need to get home, have a hot shower and put on some dry clothes or I'll catch cold,' she had said. And he had let her leave.

When she pushed her bike over the first row of dunes and glanced back, he was still watching her. But by then it was already too late.

Nora didn't surface from her reverie until a big burgundy sign announced that she was one mile from a service station with a Costa Coffee. She moved to the inside lane, pulled into the service station, parked, and got out of the car. She needed a break, and she needed lunch.

She brought her laptop inside and tried to get Wi-Fi while she munched her way through a stale club sandwich washed down with a small bottle of sparkling mineral water that alone set her back two pounds.

While she ate, she looked up the rest of the route to Waybridge. And felt an icy shiver down her spine.

She already had a vague idea that Waybridge was in the same part of the UK as Brine, but the roadmap showed her it was less than five kilometres from the small coastal town where she had bought the suitcase.

She then logged on to www.britishnewspaperarchive.co.uk and searched for articles about the discovery of a man who might be Oluf. There was frustratingly little and nothing she didn't already know.

There was a brief mention in some local papers, and the *Waybridge Courier* had taken the trouble to interview the fisherman, who stated that he was in 'deep shock' at what the journalist called 'his macabre catch'. Next to the article, which was just as lurid as it was sparse on detail, was a black-and-white photograph of a sombre man wearing overalls and a black beanie in front of a fishing boat. The caption announced it was Arthur Thompson and his trawler *Norma*.

Norma. She wrote down the name on her notepad. At least it was a start. Then she searched for Arthur Thompson in Waybridge. There were fourteen Thompsons within the postcode, but no one with the initial A. Then again, that would have been too easy.

She was full and threw the last third of the revolting sandwich in the bin. She briefly considered stocking up on Liquorice Allsorts, but got a Coke from the kiosk instead.

One and a half hours later she turned off towards Waybridge and pulled into a layby to stretch her legs and assess her situation. She had a view of endlessly rolling hills dotted with big gnarled oak trees. It was one of the things she loved about the English countryside: the way proud old trees weren't sacrificed just to make it easier for the tractor to plough.

Whenever she passed one of those fairy tale trees, she was always tempted to stop, walk up to it and lie on her back with her head close to the trunk so she could look up at the foliage, catch a glimpse of blue sky and wonder about nothing in particular.

But not today. She entered the address of the harbour office on the satnav without getting her hopes up. The chances of finding fresh information at the harbour were slim, but it was something to do while waiting for the lunch meeting with Summers and her retired father tomorrow.

28

She parked a short distance from the harbour behind a fish and chip shop, which advertised fresh fish with a picture of a cheery captain wearing a stripy jumper and a pipe dangling from the corner of his mouth, clearly from a time before the smoking ban reached the UK. Nora glanced through the window. The place looked nice and clean, and she decided on the spot that she would have dinner there when the time came. Surely the occasional fish and chips couldn't do any harm, especially after that appalling lunch.

It took her only minutes to walk down to the harbour basin, but even from this short distance, Nora could tell that her visit was likely to be in vain. Only two trawlers were moored, and neither of them was called *Norma*. Instead, the harbour area was busy with tourists eating ice cream, buying postcards and fighting off the seagulls so they could eat their chips in peace. An elderly couple were sitting on a bench, and while Nora watched them the man put his arm around his wife's shoulder and kissed her cheek with such affection that Nora's tummy ached as though she had swallowed ice cream too quickly.

She made her way to one of the two trawlers. At that very moment her mobile rang. She fumbled for it in her pocket without checking the display before she answered it.

'Sand speaking.'

'It's me.' Andreas's voice sounded strange. As if he had a cold. Or had been crying.

'OK?' she said with forced neutrality.

'Where are you?' he asked.

'Somewhere along the coast, not far from Brine. A small town called Waybridge.'

'Why did you go on your own? There might be a killer at large, and you running around playing Miss Marple without backup is quite simply too dangerous,' he said, sounding agitated.

'But, Andreas,' she protested piously. 'You were so very welcome to join me this weekend, but now what was it again? Something about you going home to Denmark to your girlfriend?'

'She wants to get married,' he interrupted her.

Nora thought she must have misheard. 'What?'

'She wants to get married,' he repeated. His voice was strangely weak and flat.

The pause between them was deep and black like the Mariana Trench.

She could hear him inhale, as if he was about to say something. Something she very much didn't want to hear. 'But I –'

'Congratulations to you both. How lovely,' she cut him off in a voice she didn't recognise as her own.

'Nora, Goddammit.'

'Well, that's great news. But I have to run,' she managed to say, and pressed him away from the screen.

She wanted nothing more than to hurl her mobile straight into the sea, but instead she dumped it in her pocket a fraction of a second before she buckled up and sacrificed the dismal club sandwich to the sea gods.

A cheeky red-haired teenager shouted out after her, 'Someone can't hold their drink!' but was met with a look so venomous that he shut up immediately.

She found a McDonald's two streets from the harbour-front and went to the loo to inspect the damage. Her mascara was streaked down her cheeks, her skin was pale, and her eyes looked bloodshot. Shit. She had only gone and done a Pete: met someone who could be the One, only to stand by while they married someone else. When that person was wrong for them.

At the very moment Andreas was permanently out of her reach, she knew that he was the only man for her.

She turned on the cold tap until icy water cascaded out, and stuck her head under the spray. That helped. She tried gathering her thoughts about Andreas into small parcels and putting them away carefully in the bottom drawer of her brain, in a place she didn't look very often. She dabbed her face with lavatory paper and tried drying her hair as best she could under one of the hand dryers.

In the front pocket of her bag she found a crumbled packet of chewing gum with a few pieces remaining. She popped them into her mouth, and a deep breath later she was back out in the street, heading for the harbour and the two fishing boats.

On the deck of one a middle-aged man was busy examining a bright orange net for holes. He raised his head when he sensed Nora looking at him. 'No pictures. I'm not a bloody tourist attraction,' he sneered.

Nora shook her head. 'No, no. I'm looking for a trawler called *Norma*. Thompson.'

He gave her a suspicious stare. 'Are you from the Marine Management Organisation?'

'No.'

'No, you don't look it,' he conceded.

Nora waited. Stood her ground. He pretended not to notice her and went back to his nets. Some minutes passed. She stuffed her hands into her pockets. Her mobile vibrated like crazy. She ignored it.

At length he gave in reluctantly. 'Most trawlers come in before the tide changes. If you're down here about five, *Norma* might be coming in,' he said, spitting a gob of saliva into the water.

'Thank you,' Nora said.

He said nothing, but got started on another pile of nets.

She found a café with a view of the bay, took a seat on the first floor and ordered a pot of Earl Grey tea. Initially after her move to the UK, she had laughed at the British belief that every problem could be sorted with a nice cup of tea, but now she was a convert. Hot tea with milk and sugar could soothe even the greatest calamity.

Of course, you couldn't magic away all the problems in the world by chucking some dried leaves into hot water and pouring it into floral china mugs. But it made them a little easier to bear.

Her mobile kept bouncing insistently like a small, furious man in a Czech cartoon. She took it out of her pocket against her better judgement. It was Andreas, and it was the seventh time he had called since she had hung up on him.

She put the phone on silent.

The tea was hot and she added lots of sugar before filling the cup to the brim with milk. It spread a temporary calm inside her. A kind of truce with the world that made it possible for her to focus on being in Waybridge and watch the harbour and the fishing boats.

She gave up thirty seconds later and called Trine. She would know what to do. More than anything, what Nora wanted to do right now was find the nearest hotel and curl up in a foetal position on the bed, but it wasn't terribly convenient when she was on an assignment. If there was an alternative, Trine would know it. Her call was answered after four rings, when she was starting to have second thoughts and had almost hung up.

She could hear happy voices and a dog barking in the background.

'Hello, Nora, darling,' Trine said. She sounded rushed.

'Hello.'

'Listen, Johannes and the kids have just come back from Sweden. Please could we talk tonight?' she asked. And then, after a short pause: 'Are you OK?'

'Yes. Everything is fine. Have a nice time,' Nora said quietly, and rang off.

She raised the cup to her lips and swallowed the rest of her tea in one big gulp, before she realised that it was still hot and she had scalded the roof of her mouth. She wanted to cry.

Nora gazed across the harbour in the hope of finding something to distract her from thoughts of Andreas and his rural copper picking china patterns for their wedding list.

Late afternoon was approaching and the trawlers returned to the harbour for the night. Nora counted four on the horizon and two that had docked while she had been busy feeling sorry for herself. She pulled herself together, put on her coat and walked the short stretch down to the harbour.

The man from earlier was on the deck smoking, and when Nora caught his eye, he nodded imperceptibly to his left where a man in his early thirties was mooring a small trawler. His hair was blond and curly, almost spiky, and his facial expression permanently frozen somewhere between sceptical and suspicious.

She walked right up to the trawler. The big white letters spelling out *Norma* were peeling off and by the looks of it, the trawler itself had given up long ago, but its owner had decided to wring a few last trips out of the wreck before the inevitable breaker's yard.

The man looked up at Nora. 'Can I help you?' he said in a tone of voice that pretty much suggested it was the last thing he wanted to do.

Nora wondered for a split second how best to approach the situation. 'I'm looking for Arthur Thompson.'

'Why?'

She hesitated. 'It's in connection with a project. Do you know where I can find him?'

The man straightened up and, for the first time, looked directly at her. 'A project about what?'

'I'm investigating historical events, something that happened in Waybridge years ago,' she said, balancing on a thin line between truth and misrepresentation.

The man was unimpressed. He leaned against the wheelhouse, searched his pockets for a packet of Marlboro, lit a cigarette and blew out the first plume of smoke in a long column. 'A project about what?'

'It might be easier if I speak to Mr Thompson. Then perhaps I can explain what it's about. Do you know where he is or where I can find him?'

The man said that he might know.

'Any money in it?'

Nora shook her head. 'I'm afraid not.'

The man shrugged. 'Then why would I help you?'

'Why not?'

To her astonishment he broke into a grin, which took even him by surprise. 'Good answer. My dad is a right chatterbox. And he loves nothing more than going on about the old days. Are you a historian? If so, you've stumbled across a goldmine. Funny, he can't remember what happened last week, but if you ask him about when he was a kid or a young lad, his memory is as sharp as a pin.'

Nora returned his smile. 'Where can I find your dad?'

Thompson Jr checked his watch. 'You won't manage it today. He lives at Cedar Residence over in Farthington, and I know they put the old folks to bed around seven p.m.,' he said. 'But I believe visiting hours are from ten tomorrow morning, so you'll be able to talk to him then.'

'Cedar Residence?' Nora was taken aback.

The last time she had been there, she had managed to get herself thrown out, but now she had a valid reason to go back and possibly find out if William Hickley's mother lived there and where the suitcase with the pictures might have come from.

'Thank you so much,' Nora said, then she remembered that they hadn't been introduced. 'By the way, I'm Nora Sand.'

'Sounds almost like Norma. Tell my dad Dennis sends his best, and that we'll be round tomorrow to pick him up for lunch. He's bound to forget it right away, but at least he has been told,' he said, flicking the butt of his cigarette into the harbour basin.

Nora turned around and walked back to the car. She stuck her hand in her pocket and took out her mobile. Two missed calls. One from a British number she didn't recognise and one from the Crayfish. No one else had called her.

So Andreas had already given up. Just like the last time.

She entered the cheery captain's fish and chips, and ordered a small portion of cod with fat, golden chips, and a bright green dollop of mushy peas.

The first few years Nora had lived in the UK, she had failed to understand the British love of this simple dish. Why would anyone get so excited over something that was ultimately a fish fillet with potatoes? If you absolutely had to have fast food, then why not an American hotdog, a Mexican tortilla or a juicy cheeseburger?

However, one day on a job in Dover, the local chippy had been the one place that was open for lunch, and she had been forced to capitulate. She was hooked from the first bite. White, flaky fish hidden under crisp, golden batter, the sweet taste of mushy peas and feather-light chips sprinkled with vinegar and dipped in sharp tartar sauce with chopped capers was as inspired as it was obvious, once you had tried it.

Nora sat down at a table with her chips, which were served in a red plastic basket, and a piece of cod that tasted as if it had been pulled from the sea that same morning.

She tried forcing herself to enjoy the meal, really taste it, but soon her hand was going back and forth on autopilot and she munched and swallowed while staring into the distance. Andreas and PC Perfect. Perhaps she only had herself to blame. Maybe she shouldn't have let him disappear out of her life back then. But would it have made any difference?

She pulled herself together and decided to think about something else. All she was doing was picking at a scab. She shook her head in despair at herself and was knocking back her Coke Light when her mobile vibrated in her pocket again. She took the call, grateful for any distraction. It was Spencer.

'Miss Sand,' he said with something Nora thought sounded like relief in his voice.

'Yes?' she said coolly.

'Where are you?'

'In a small seaside town in the south of England. Why?'

'I would like you to return to London and report to me at Scotland Yard.'

'I can't just drop everything and come running to you. It's a Saturday and I happen to be on a job, just so you know it –'

Spencer cut her off: 'Hix escaped from Wolf Hall last night. Is that a good enough reason?'

Nora pushed aside the remains of her meal. The nausea came back and she struggled to suppress it as her panic surged.

'The chances of him wanting to find you, or being able to, are probably miniscule. But we can't be too careful. He's on the run and likely to be desperate.'

'Why wasn't I told sooner?'

'The prison only discovered that he was missing an hour ago. Officers are looking for him all over the country, and I've tried calling you ever since we were told.'

'Mobile coverage here is appalling. What happened?'

'We don't know the details, but when the guards opened the door to his cell this morning, Jimmy Archer was lying on the bed in his underwear, sobbing his heart out. Hix was long gone in Archer's uniform and with his ID ... and, as you've already worked out, his mobile.'

'How could it happen?' Nora heard her own voice turn into a squeak.

'Now that's something Multicorp, the American company that runs Wolf Hall, will have to explain to the Justice Secretary. Fortunately, it's not my problem,' Spencer said, sounding steely. 'If you can't get to us, then contact the local police where you are. I'd never forgive myself if something were to happen to you. We don't know if your visit somehow prompted Hix to escape,' he added.

Nora gulped.

'I want you to understand what we're dealing with here,' he continued, 'and so I've spoken to Amy Brooks in New Zealand. It was her investigation that uncovered Malcolm and Ralph Bennett,' he explained.

Nora vaguely recalled a particularly gruesome case involving two brothers at a remote farm in northern Australia. The Bennett brothers had tricked backpackers into visiting the family farm where they raped them, robbed them, and afterwards marinated and grilled them on a specially constructed, oversized barbecue in their backyard. Cold sweat gathered on her forehead.

'OK?'

'She has looked at Hickley's case file, and I also sent her descriptions of some of the missing girls. Brooks is certain: Hix isn't working alone. He has a fan, an accomplice, someone who either tries to emulate him or is under his direct order. This accomplice is either repeating events leading up to the time Hix was arrested, finishing his work, or – possibly even worse – trying to outdo his so-called achievements.'

'But –' Nora tried to object.

'Please let me finish. Brooks also discussed the case with a couple of her colleagues at the FBI in Quantico. They share her view. Even Tom Johnson has had a look at the file.'

Nora noticed how Spencer uttered the name Tom Johnson in the same tone of voice as Pete when he said Lionel Messi. She could only assume that anyone who mattered in criminal psychology would know who Tom Johnson was.

'There's a broad consensus that Hix must be in contact with this person. It's the only conclusion that makes any sense. Everything suggests that this person helped him escape, and whether this person is a friend or an enemy, it's likely to be the first place Hix will go. So I'm not all that worried that Hix might be coming after you. He doesn't know where you are, and he has bigger problems right now in that he's wanted across the UK,' Spencer argued.

Nora told herself to listen to Spencer's logic, but when she reached for her can of Coke, her hand was shaking.

'Personally I think we need to check out his visitors. I'm guessing that one of them – possibly without knowing it – smuggled letters back and forth between Hix and his disciple. Perhaps the pictures in the suitcase were meant to have been smuggled into him in prison,' Spencer ventured.

'But they search you very thoroughly before you're even let into a prison,' Nora objected.

'Miss Sand. I'm sure you're aware that a number of British prisoners have a drug problem?'

Nora confirmed it.

'How do you think the drugs get in? There's a weak link in any system. Always. It's a fact, and it's those very weaknesses that, in a strange way, cause a prison to operate like a coherent organism. But that's a subject for another day.'

'But,' Nora objected again, 'I thought only his family ever visited? His mother … and his sister. By the way, are you sure he even has a sister?'

For once Spencer sounded taken aback. 'Someone is already checking up on his visitors, but as long as an inmate gives consent in writing that he's willing to receive visits from someone, and that this person has no criminal record, the authorities don't usually get involved in the inmate's family situation.'

'I don't think he has a sister,' Nora stated.

'We'll have to see. It'll take a while to get to the bottom of this.'

'Hmm. What about his mother?'

'We'll send somebody to his mother's last known address to check on her. She hasn't been terribly cooperative in the past, but perhaps we can put pressure on her and make her tell us who visits him, and about his circle of acquaintances in general. That is, if she knows,' Spencer said.

'What about Archer? Could he be the accomplice?' Nora suggested.

'I don't think so. In my opinion he's too stupid to appeal to Hix in any way. But Millhouse is interviewing him as we speak.'

After a short pause she could hear how his voice became even more grave. 'Miss Sand. I'm aware that you're a reporter and you're free to act as you wish. I'm also aware that you have the right to investigate anything you like within the law. I completely respect that you have professional principles –'

'I'm sensing a but –' Nora dared to interject.

'But,' Spencer ploughed on regardless, 'what I want to stress is that Hix, and possibly his partner, have demonstrated that they're unpredictable and have no scruples. They're ready to strike again. Something drove Hix to risk everything and escape from prison. I would feel better knowing you have protection. What about the Danish officer you were working with?'

'Sadly he's not available this weekend,' she said grimly.

Spencer sighed. 'All right. But avoid isolated locations and call the local police and explain the situation to them. I'll get back to you if I hear any news of Hix,' he promised.

Back in the car she made sure to lock the doors. She could feel paranoia nibble at the fringes of her mind. But surely it was only her mind playing tricks on her. Hix couldn't possibly know where she was. How could he work out that she was in a car park behind a fish and chip shop? Besides, he probably had enough on his plate, hiding from the police who were looking for him high and low. If she stayed in public areas with plenty of people around, she would be safe.

Just to be sure, Nora took out her mobile and called Summers' direct line. It rang seven times before she gave up and started the car. She would try her again later.

29

On leaving the harbour she spotted a sign advertising cheap rooms and Sunday lunch, and pulled into the car park of the Seahorse Hotel, which looked more than usually run-down. The paint on the window frames was peeling, and the door stuck, but to Nora's relief they did have a vacant room.

The receptionist could be any age between fifty and seventy. Her silver hair was put up in a bun, and her face deeply lined by decades of salty winds.

'You're lucky,' she said. 'We don't usually have any vacancies during the season, but we had a Belgian couple who were arguing so loudly that several of the other guests complained. I was actually on the verge of having a word with them myself. However, just this morning they too seemed to have had enough and they left two days earlier than expected! You're not from Belgium by any chance, are you?'

Nora confirmed that she wasn't, and added that neither did she have a male companion to have loud rows with.

'That's excellent,' the woman said, reading the Visa card Nora had left on the counter. 'Miss Sand. My name is Mrs Morris. May I take the liberty of asking you what brings you to Waybridge alone? Business?'

'In a way,' Nora said evasively. Many people bridled if you told them up front that you were a reporter. Others had a misguided belief from the London tabloids that every single utterance was worth its weight in gold, and demanded money for an ordinary interview.

Mrs Morris looked at her expectantly.

'I write a bit about –' she managed to say before she was interrupted.

'Oh! A writer. How wonderful. Mr Morris will be so happy to hear that we have a writer staying at the hotel. He was a poet himself in his younger years, before he became a postmaster,' she said.

'I'm afraid I don't write fiction,' Nora said, in accordance with the truth, but Mrs Morris didn't seem to notice.

'You just call me Edna,' she chirped as she practically danced out into a back room. 'Let me just put the kettle on and make us a cup of tea. How exciting. A writer among us.'

Nora gave up trying to correct the misunderstanding.

'So what do you write about?' Edna shouted over what sounded like a rumbling electric kettle.

'Crime,' Nora said.

'Oh, then you've come to the right place,' she said as she returned with a tray of clattering cups, saucers, and a chipped sugar bowl. 'Everyone thinks British provincial towns are sleepy, but it's pure *Midsomer Murders* here,' she said with a conspiratorial wink.

'Is that right,' Nora said in a neutral voice. And that was all it took before her new friend launched into an account of local history that would make guides in the London Dungeons' Cabinet of Horror pale with envy under their greasepaint.

First there was the story about a pirate ship that drifted ashore in 1654 with a dead crew and a captain who had gone berserk with his sword, and had stood alone and blood-soaked on the bridge, screaming curses at the beach.

Then there was the story of the plague ravaging Waybridge, and the local clergyman who decided that the only way to avoid the infection and appease God was to burn down the church. With the congregation inside.

As her tea grew cold and Nora got restless and started glancing at her watch, Edna worked her way to the current century.

'Yes. And then of course there was the Hix case. That was gruesome,' her hostess sighed.

Nora pricked up her ears. Edna raised the teapot and shook it.

'Oh, dear. We seem to have run out of tea. I'd better make another pot if we're to have that story. It's a long one. Perhaps we should wait until Mr Morris comes back from the whist club?'

Nora was tempted to shake her. 'I think I've had enough tea for one evening. But the story about Hix sounds exciting. Wasn't he the one who killed young women … now where was it?'

And that was all it took to get Edna to sit down, lower her voice and whisper the gory details, which Nora already knew from her research.

Nora let her tell her story about the discovery Jean Eastman's body in the boot of Hix's car, Hix's escape and ultimate imprisonment, as well as the attempt to uncover where the tongues in the jar came from.

'Mr Morris said that they searched Underwood for months. They dug holes and they brought in sniffer dogs, so no one could go shooting there all autumn. But they never ever found any remains of those girls,' Edna said with a shudder.

'What about his family?' Nora asked eagerly.

Edna offered up a resigned shrug. 'It's a shameful story. I never could stand his mother. She was several years above me when I started school. Us little ones were scared of Vanessa.'

'It can't have been very pleasant for her to see her only son accused of such dreadful crimes,' Nora interjected.

'Hah!' Edna snorted contemptuously. 'She never admitted that there was the slightest thing wrong with her darling William. Oh no. The police had made a mistake. A miscarriage of justice. She has been blind to the evil staring her straight in the face her whole life and will defend him until the bitter end,' she said, slamming her palm on to the table to emphasise her words. 'He was a bad lad.'

Nora looked encouragingly at her hostess over the rim of her teacup.

'I didn't know him when he was a boy, but my neighbour, Mrs Ponds, taught at the school where he went, and she said that even when he was a little lad in shorts, you could tell he was pure evil. She caught him several times wringing the necks of pigeons behind the school. And once when his class held one of those bring-your-pet-to-school days, a little girl came back from break and found her rabbit dead in its cage. They said he'd done it.' Edna shook her head.

'What happened to Vanessa Hickley?' Nora asked, holding her breath.

'She moved to Spain, I believe.'

Nora could feel her new lead crumble in her hands, before Edna interrupted herself. 'Yes, Costa Brava. My cousin James saw her down there some years later. She was working in a nail salon and called herself Vanessa Holmes.'

'OK?'

'It didn't last, of course. I hear she lost all her money, and so she came back home. She had nowhere else to go except the old family home in Farthington.

Nora nearly knocked her teacup off the table. 'Are you telling me that Bill Hickley's mother is back living in Farthington?'

'Yes. She lives in that big, dark grey house on the hill. The one with the green shutters. You can't miss it. It's the most run-down house for miles. The children are scared of her. They think she's some kind of witch, and they dare each other to climb the wall to her orchard and go apple-scrumping in the autumn. In the old days, she would chase after them with a stick, and she would hit them if she got the chance. But it's been years since she could last run after a child. She's in a wheelchair now and her carer pushes her around. They breed dogs. I think that's how she makes a living. There's a terrible racket from the dogs up there.'

'So she's not in a care home?'

Edna shook her head again. 'Not as far as I know. The time might well have come for her to go to Cedar Residence. She's the right age, but somehow she can afford a live-in carer, so if she's got someone, I don't really see why she would want to …' she wondered out loud.

Nora interrupted her train of thought. 'What about Hix's sister – doesn't she look after their mother?'

'Sister? William never had any brothers or sisters,' Edna stated firmly.
'Are you sure?'

'William's father hanged himself when the boy was four years old.
Vanessa never married again, nor did she have any more children. I
swear on a stack of bibles. She had a completely unhealthy obsession
with William.'

Nora nodded. She wondered if she should call Foxy and her Tet-
ris-playing colleague on Monday and get a better description of the
woman who was allowed to visit Hix with family privileges. Was she
the go-between for Hix and his groupie? She could always try, but
whether she would get a useful answer was another matter.

It might be better to get Spencer to do it. Should she call him with
an update? She decided it could wait until the morning and started
the lengthy process of saying goodnight to Edna, who was talking
as if she had been stranded alone on a desert island for thirty years.

Finally Nora had to resort to yawning discreetly.

'Ah. And here I am keeping you up. I think I had better show you
to your room.'

Edna unhooked a large, golden key from a board behind the
reception counter and ushered Nora down a long corridor with a
dark red carpet and copper etchings on the wall. Nora feared the
worst, but when her hostess opened the door, she saw an enchanting
and bright room with a sea view and the window ajar, and she could
smell sea salt and wild roses.

Edna closed the door behind her. Nora located the remote control
for the TV and selected the first news channel she could find. Not
because she really wanted to see the latest prices from the New York
Stock Exchange or hear a breathless reporter talk about Beijing smog.
It was more the familiar soundscape that assured her she wasn't completely alone in the world in a strange hotel room.

She went to the bathroom, which was everything she had hoped it
would be. Chequerboard tiles and a big, old-fashioned lion foot tub.

The tap squeaked and groaned, but eventually hot water poured
out in a steamy cascade. She adjusted it with some cold. On her

bed she found two soft white towels and absent-mindedly started to undress as the bath tub slowly filled.

As a child, she had rarely been allowed a bath. Hardly ever in fact. Christian Sand was of the opinion that a bath was wasteful, and that humanity in general was better off with morning swims and cold showers. It was still a deep-seated belief in her that a bath was a luxurious indulgence you must make use of whenever you found yourself in a hotel room with a bath tub.

First she dipped her toe and let the hot water almost scald it before, little by little, she lowered herself into the water until she lay with her feet on the tap, ready to add more hot water as soon as her body had adjusted to the temperature. The water enveloped her, and she let her head slip under the surface while she held her breath and tried to imagine that she was in the sea, snorkelling around a coral reef.

She sensed rather than heard the sound. The noise of her mobile penetrated the water and made her sit up with a jolt.

As she tried edging her way out of the tub, she slipped and banged her elbow against the rim. The pain almost made her fall back into the water. She grabbed one of the towels on her way out to dry her hands while she struggled to remember where she had left her mobile. Her jacket pocket!

Just as she reached it, it rang for the last time. She checked the display. All it said was unknown number. It could be the Crayfish calling from home. He had been given an ex-directory number after a couple of unfortunate incidents with readers of strong views, who didn't understand why *Globalt* wouldn't publish their letters or support their particular pet cause – or who simply believed it was acceptable to turn up at the Crayfish's home to discuss in detail the extent to which he had got his analysis of Israel's foreign policy completely wrong.

Irritated, she chucked the mobile on to the bed and was heading back to the bathroom when a small beep indicated a text message had arrived. 'You have one new voicemail message,' it said.

She entered the pin code and heard first a deep intake of breath, then Andreas's voice: 'Nora, Goddamn you! I'm not letting you do this. Not again.'

Pause. 'Nora. If you're near your phone, please pick up.'

Another pause. 'OK. You're not going to pick up your phone.'

He sounded weird. Sad. And then suddenly: 'Oh, fuck it, Sand. I'm not going to have a conversation with your voicemail. Get your shit together and call me! You should have let me finish when we last spoke. I'm calling from my Uncle Svend's. For some reason I can't get through on my own mobile. Just pick up the phone. How old are you? Fifteen?'

She chucked the phone on to the bed again, went to the bathroom and submerged herself in the water. It had grown cold by now and no matter how much more hot water she added, she just couldn't get the temperature right.

In the end she gave up, washed her hair, wrapped herself in one towel, twisted the other around her hair and curled up on the bed.

What did he mean when he said that he wouldn't let her 'do this again'?

She turned up the volume on the television and channel-hopped to find another news channel, but it soon became clear that the Sea-horse Hotel hadn't spent its budget on a sophisticated TV package. BBC2 was repeating a garden programme, while BBC1 was halfway through a studio discussion about the NHS. She finally found a news bulletin on ITV, but the moment she selected it, they switched to the sports update.

She was starting to feel tired and had almost nodded off when her mobile rang again.

It was Trine who had managed to get her kids to bed and sent Johannes off to the petrol station to buy wine. Nora told her the heart-breaking news about PC Perfect and the imminent marriage. 'Then again, white was never really my colour.'

'Nora, for God's sake. You're upset! So give in to it.'

'What do you mean?'

'Exactly what I'm saying. You're really upset. Allow yourself to feel it. Don't do what you did last time.'

'Don't you start that last time business as well. What's your point?'

'Don't you remember how you went into complete lockdown after Hanne's party?'

'I went into lockdown? No way, it was Andreas who –'

'Nora. You wouldn't even talk to him.'

'The way I remember it –'

'You went Interrailing two days later without even saying goodbye to him. Then you came back with that guy from Florence, Tommasino or whatever his name was. And you were really pissed off that Andreas wasn't at the station waving a flag when you rocked up weeks later with an Italian boyfriend in tow, when you hadn't sent him as much as a postcard.'

Nora blushed when she realised that Trine was right. It wasn't Andreas who had cut her off.

'Nora, you have to learn from this and move on. Andreas is gone – but the next time try being a little more –'

She could feel herself tuning out. Like a kid pressing its eyes shut and stuffing its fingers in their ears, chanting nah nah nah nah nah. This conversation was the last thing she needed. She said goodbye to Trine and wondered if she had the energy to get dressed and go looking for a corner shop selling cheap wine. But eventually she just pulled the blanket over her head, closed her eyes, and the next moment she was fast asleep.

30

Breakfast was served in a basement where the only natural light came from a couple of narrow windows just below the ceiling. Nora gave the buffet with the wrinkled grilled sausages, watery mushrooms and rubbery scrambled eggs a wide berth, and asked for poached eggs instead. They were served on toast with margarine, which she tried scraping off, before taking a sip of what claimed to be orange juice, but which had only the colour in common with the fruit.

She had helped herself to a copy of *The Sunday Times* from a selection of newspapers at reception and she flicked absent-mindedly through it. She came across an interview with an author and, out of habit, tore out the page and put it in her pocket. It might be an idea to ask her arts editor if she would be interested in a similar feature. The business pages announced new banking mergers, and the weather forecast promised rain later that evening. None of the papers had mentioned Hix's escape from prison.

She returned to her room and charged her mobile, while she turned on her computer to check her emails.

There was a single email from the Crayfish asking her to call him Monday morning before the editorial meeting. To be on the safe side she also checked her Hotmail account, but found only junk mail, invitations to press briefings and a message from David, attaching a file with three photographs of lush, pink peonies in bloom. She replied with a smiley. She didn't have the energy to write a proper reply, something he of all people would understand.

Her signal showed a single, unstable bar. Nora presumed this worked both ways, and was pleased that at least she wouldn't be bothered by calls from the Crayfish, Andreas, or an over-anxious Spencer.

It took her only minutes to pack. She had never been one for putting her clothes on hangers or in drawers when staying in hotels. You never knew when you might have to make a quick exit. All she had to do was put her toothbrush in her toiletries bag, chuck it into the sports bag with her clothes and zip it up before she went back to reception, ready to settle her bill.

'So, where next?' Edna said with a wink. 'Any murders that need solving before lunch?'

Nora shook her head. 'I'm afraid not. My job isn't as glamorous as it sounds. This morning I'm paying a visit to a care home, and then I'm having lunch with an OAP at The Three Mermaids.'

Edna launched into a lengthy explanation of how the pub's owner had squandered most of his fortune and the pub's reputation due to his unfortunate urge to gamble on horses. 'Then again, he's half-Irish,' she said in a tone of voice that more than hinted it explained everything.

However, he had found true love in the form of Bessie, who came all the way from Yorkshire and during a short and incredibly passionate summer holiday, she had taken on, not only the broken half-Irishman, but also the pub's kitchen and worked to make it one of the best places in the area to eat.

'Try their Yorkshire pudding. You'll remember it for the rest of your life, no matter what you eat afterwards,' Edna encouraged her.

Nora promised, picked up her bag, and walked outside to the yellow rental car. The moment she turned the key in the ignition, the radio blasted her at full volume. She had forgotten to turn it off last night, and now Adele's crisp, pain-marbled voice cut through the small car with assurances that she would definitely find a man just as good as the one she had lost to someone else. 'Someone Like You.'

She turned it off resolutely and entered 'Cedar Residence' into the satnav. It was a ten-minute drive. Enough time to switch stations and she ended up listening to an enthusiastic report from a local rugby match.

She parked outside a Ladbrokes betting shop in the high street.

Nora saw no need to alert the dragon from last time before she even stepped inside the building. If she arrived on foot, she would look like a local and she might be able to slip unnoticed through the main entrance.

While she was pondering her next move, her mobile rang. She took it out of her pocket and heaved a sigh. Spencer.

'Miss Sand. I'm very close to swearing. You really must learn to answer your phone,' he said, by way of an angry introduction.

Before Nora had time to respond, he went on: 'I must ask you to go straight to Waybridge police station and ask DC Summers for protection. She has been briefed. I can't imagine what you're doing right now, running around as if nothing had happened. It's completely inappropriate.'

'Yes, but I've already tried her ... And I don't believe there's any danger that –'

'Listen. I'm astonished, to put it mildly, that you didn't see the news this morning, and conclude that you ought to get yourself to a place of safety ASAP. It's possible that Hix has already killed again. A woman's body was found near Dorchester. We haven't released any details yet, but there's a lot to suggest that it might be Hix. Waybridge is much too close for it to be safe for you to run around on your own.'

'Yes, but I thought he was wanted across the UK? He's probably trying to leave the country as we speak. And how on earth would he know where I am?' Nora asked when she had composed herself a little.

'Miss Sand. Are you willing to run that risk? I'm not. We don't know where he is. And until we do, you need protection. It's not up for debate.'

Nora considered his point for a moment. 'OK. I see what you mean. I'll make my way to Waybridge police station,' she then promised him.

'Good. I'll expect to hear from Summers that you're safely with her in the next thirty minutes. Goodbye,' he said.

'There's just one little thing I need to do first,' she mumbled.

But Spencer had already hung up.

After a five-minute walk, she reached the gloomy building that had been given a name more suited to a mansion in the American Deep South with columns at the front and a view of the swamp. A more appropriate name would be: Last Stop. Final Destination or The Scrapheap.

The main entrance was locked and a code was needed to enter. Nora muttered curses under her breath, then after a quick think pressed one-two-three-four. She heard a small click. It was common in places like this, where staff, visitors and relatives needed to come and go quickly. A code so simple that everyone could remember it was probably of little use, except to assure people that management did indeed care about the safety of the elderly residents.

Nora slipped inside. The reception was unmanned, but she could hear noises from a back room, which indicated that the staff were having their morning tea break. She could hear the clatter of cups and teaspoons, and there was a faint smell of cigarettes being smoked through an open window.

She marched purposefully past the counter. It was one of the first lessons she had learned about entering places where people normally threw journalists out before you had time to say 'I'm from –' The trick was always to look as if you had business there, and that that business was a duty to be carried out as quickly as possible.

She turned right down a long, dark and narrow corridor with numbered doors on either side. The thought of having to check possibly forty rooms, spread across several corridors before she found Mr Thompson, filled her with dismay.

Near the end of the corridor, she could see an open door and hear mumbling and clattering cutlery. She swiftly made her way there and crossed her fingers that she wouldn't bump into the dragon from last time.

An elderly woman was sitting alone in front of the window, pushing a spoon back and forth in a bowl of porridge. The bowl was almost empty, and Nora could see immediately that the woman was blind. The voices were coming from an old-fashioned tape recorder, where someone was reading aloud *Pride and Prejudice* and was in the middle of Elizabeth Bennett's travails with her younger sister's escapades.

'George? Is that you?' the woman said, sensing instantly that there was someone in the doorway.

Nora cleared her throat. 'No. It's not George. Do you know where I can –'

'But where is George? He promised to visit me today. I know he did, because today is Wednesday,' the woman said. She sounded upset.

'Maybe George is on his way?' Nora ventured in an attempt to calm her down before she became agitated. And indeed her suggestion made the woman sink into a kind of inner calm. 'I'm looking for Mr Thompson.'

The woman shrugged. 'Oh. He's always in the vegetable garden. Always. You would think he was a gardener. But he's a good man. Sometimes he brings flowers for me to smell,' the woman explained.

'Thank you,' Nora had time to say before the woman was consumed by despair once more.

'I want George. I want him to come *now*!'

Nora retreated and looked around for a carer. There was no one in sight. She left the woman to her fate, and continued towards the very end of the corridor where a set of French doors with a double lock led to a formally laid-out garden. The geometric rose beds were flanked by lavender bushes.

The lawn looked perfect for croquet, but there was little activity in the garden. Along a pergola were benches and tables waiting for Sunday visitors.

Nora went further out into the garden and finally reached a gap in the hedge, which led to a piece of open land the size of a football pitch. It was divided into small allotments partitioned by picket fences and looked like a smaller version of municipal allotments. At the far end Nora could make out two elderly men who were busy weeding with hoes, and a third who was pushing a wheelbarrow laden with weeds.

A fat woman with black hair scraped back from her face and an unfiltered cigarette dangling from the corner of her mouth was sitting nearby. She was on her mobile to someone she addressed as 'Darryl darling', while she kept an occasional eye on the three men.

As Nora came closer, she could see that one of the men was weeding a carrot bed, while the other had gone to a freestanding tap to fill an old zinc watering can. When the man looked up, she recognised Mr Thompson from the picture in the newspaper. Nora waved, and Mr Thompson waved back with an expression of guilt that this might be yet another face his memory had erased in recent years in the cruellest manner imaginable.

The woman glared partly with hostility and partly with curiosity at Nora and covered the mouthpiece of the mobile without interrupting her conversation.

'Yes? Can I help you?'

Nora gestured to Mr Thompson. 'I have a message for Mr Thompson. From his family,' Nora said, more or less in accordance with the truth.

The woman briefly looked as if she was going to stop Nora, but then 'Darryl darling' appeared to say something that demanded her attention, and she let Nora pass with a grimace.

'No, no, darling. You know you're the only one for me,' she said coyly.

Nora walked over to Mr Thompson, who was holding a full watering can. He smiled shyly when Nora reached him. 'Hello, Miss,' he said kindly.

'Sand,' Nora introduced herself. 'Your son asked me to say hello and tell you that he will be here later today to pick you up for Sunday lunch,' she said before he had time to ask any questions.

'Aha. Dennis,' he said absent-mindedly, and made his way towards a lettuce bed behind the carrots.

Nora followed him. 'Do you have a moment to speak to me?'

He looked at her with surprise. 'What about? Dennis?'

She shook her head and guided him to a ramshackle bench leaning against a black painted tool shed. Mr Thompson perched on the edge of the bench with a nervous glance at the woman who was still talking away on her mobile.

'I can only sit down for a little while. They don't like us taking too many breaks,' he explained.

Nora nodded and got straight to the point. 'Mr Thompson. It's about your boat. About a discovery you made on a fishing trip.'

Mr Thompson shook his head; he looked confused. 'But Dennis has the boat now. I'm sorry, but if you're from the Marine Management Organisation, you need to speak to him,' he said.

Nora tried fixing his attention.

'So you're not here about Dennis, after all?' he said anxiously.

'It was that day, Mr Thompson, when the body of a young man got caught up in your net. Do remember that day?'

Nora could see immediately that this was a memory that hadn't yet left the old fisherman's brain. He shuddered although he was sitting in the sunshine, and she saw him press his lips together.

'Yes. It was a horrible, horrible day.'

'What happened, Mr Thompson – please can you tell me what happened that day?'

He raised his head and looked into the distance. 'Albert and I had landed some cod and the plan was that on the way home we put out the net one extra time. I wish we never had.' He gulped. 'We tried … we tried to look at his face to see if he was someone we knew …'

The corners of his mouth turned down in disgust or regret. It was hard for Nora to decide. 'But his face had got caught in the propeller.'

Nora let the sentence hang in the air between them.

'Did you notice if he had any tattoos?'

Mr Thompson closed his eyes to concentrate harder. 'A big bison on his upper arm. I remember I kept staring at it in order not to look at his face. It had been shredded. And the fish had got his eyes.'

He turned to Nora again and grabbed her upper arm. 'They had got his eyes!'

Then he shook his head and looked straight at her. 'I'm sorry, Miss. I'm very forgetful these days. Do I know you? Why are you here?'

Nora didn't have time to open her mouth before the woman with the mobile loomed large in front of her. She had been forced to interrupt her conversation with 'Darryl darling', something that hadn't improved her mood.

'Who are you and what do you think you're you doing here?' she demanded to know.

'Well, I'm here to –'

'ID, please,' the woman insisted.

Nora dug her heels in. 'Mr Thompson is an adult. I don't have to show ID to speak to him about a private matter,' she said firmly.

'You're on private property,' the woman retorted.

'Yes, but I'm visiting one of your guests. At his request. Isn't that right, Mr Thompson?' she asked, appealing to him in the hope that his support would end the argument.

But Mr Thompson had already got up. 'I'll go check on the carrots,' he announced and padded down to the corner of the vegetable garden without looking back.

The carer refused to be placated.

Nora decided to leave too. 'Right, I've given Mr Thompson my message, so there's no need for me –' she said.

She got up so abruptly that her purse fell out of her handbag and her British press card landed picture side up with the black letters on the bright yellow background announcing that Nora Sand was a member of the British press, and that anyone who doubted the validity of this information could call Scotland Yard and have it confirmed.

'You're staying here,' the woman snarled and pushed her back on the bench. 'I need to speak to my manager about this. No one has given a journalist permission to sniff around here. That much I do know.'

Nora's anger surged and settled in icy outrage at the woman's demonstration of power. She knew that in about three microseconds, she could have the woman lying flat on the grass in such agony that it would block out thoughts of Darryl for a long time.

But Enzo had taught her better than that. Right from the start he had made it clear that he only initiated his students into the noble art of kickboxing on the condition that they would never use it anywhere but in the boxing ring.

'When there are signs of battle, what does a true warrior do?' he would ask over and over, and by now all his students knew the answer so well that they would reply in unison: 'Use their brains and get out.'

Nora took a deep breath and focused on the woman once more. 'Do you know something? I came here to speak to Mr Thompson on a private matter,' she said, holding a rhetorical pause. 'But your behaviour makes me think you have something to hide. And that your boss would just love it if you were to provoke me into investigating what that might be.'

Nora saw doubt appear in the woman's eyes. The carer's usual bullying technique, highly effective with frail and semi-senile elderly people and their anxious relatives, had no effect on Nora.

The carer had two options: let the reporter leave or carry out her threat to involve the boss.

Nora watched the inner struggle play out in the carer like a hesitant reader mouthing words to themselves. Finally the desire to escape censure and the fear of being held accountable won; it was above her pay grade.

'I'll have to check with Mrs Rosen,' the woman said and spun around on her heel. Three steps later she turned and pinned her harshly made-up eyes on Nora. 'Stay here,' she ordered her sternly.

Nora shrugged. She had all the time in the world. Even with his weak memory, Mr Thompson had confirmed, to the extent that he could, that Oluf was the man whose corpse he had salvaged. The chances of it being someone else with a bison tattoo were non-existent, in Nora's opinion. The only question was what had he been doing off the coast of Brine?

And was there a link to Hix? And what about Lisbeth and Lulu? Had Oluf come looking for them here? It made no sense. He had come to the UK to box. That much was clear, and there was nothing to indicate that the girls' disappearance had upset him to the extent that he had devoted the rest of his life to finding out what had happened to them.

If anyone still cared about the girls, it was ironically the man who was supposed to be the toughest guy of the group: Bjarke. But he seemed genuine in his wish to get to the truth.

Hopefully her meeting with DC Summers and her father, Dale Moss, would pay off and provide her with an explanation for what Oluf had been doing so far away from his planned boxing tour. And perhaps they could suggest an answer as to why his life had ended in the bay.

Nora's thoughts were interrupted by the sound of crunching gravel. The carer was marching down the garden path at a speed that suggested it was an urgent matter.

'Mrs Rosen will see you now,' she said, looking as if she had just informed Nora that she had been granted a rare audience with the Queen.

'I'll escort you to her office,' she sniffled. And added in a tone of voice that was probably meant to be ominous: 'I hope you can come up with a really good explanation. Or we may have to call the police.'

Nora eyed her coolly. 'As far as I'm concerned we can call DC Summers right now. I've nothing to hide,' she said.

The woman made no reply, but opened a side door into the main building, which led to a small hall. A brass plate with cursive letters on a heavy, dark-varnished door announced that this was the office of Mrs Rosen, the warden of Cedar Residence.

The carer knocked timidly, as if she were a servant from another era, and it crossed Nora's mind that if she showed the elderly residents the same respect, their stay at Cedar Residence could be improved several times over.

'Enter.'

The voice was firm, and Nora just had time to visualise a terrifying matron with broad shoulders, fat ankles and dressed in an impeccable suit, before the door swung open to reveal the exact opposite.

Mrs Rosen was beautiful and gentle to look at. She was wearing a dusky pink dress that fell softly over her body and her blond hair was put up in a loose bun. More than anything she looked like she was advertising detergent or Werther's Original toffees – a fantasy housewife who had just put an apple pie on the windowsill to cool.

Her handshake was firm and warm, and her blue eyes studied Nora through a pair of gold-framed spectacles, which were designed to exude authority and calm at the same time.

'Right, would you like to sit down? Miss …?'

'Sand,' Nora said.

'Miss Sand,' Mrs Rosen echoed, and gestured to two carved wooden chairs in front of a walnut desk, clearly put there to handle conversations with anxious relatives.

Nora perched on the edge of one chair and looked expectantly at Mrs Rosen. She had made up her mind to let the warden start the conversation.

Mrs Rosen sat down behind her desk, folded her hands in front of her and observed Nora for a moment. 'Well, Miss Sand. You seem to have upset not only our residents, but also Mrs Fletcher,' she started.

Nora looked steadily back at her without saying anything.

'I gather that you're a journalist. Would you mind telling me what exactly you're doing here?'

Nora shrugged. 'I'm here to visit Mr Thompson. That's all.'

Mrs Rosen looked almost sad. 'And would you mind telling me why you needed to speak to Mr Thompson?' she continued in a tone of voice that more than suggested she didn't believe Nora.

'Yes, I would mind, as it happens. As far as I'm aware, Mr Thompson is entitled to a private life, whether or not he's in a care home. Or perhaps I'm wrong?'

Nora saw the rage flash across Mrs Rosen's face as swiftly as if someone had pulled the emergency brake on a train. But then she reined in her emotions and composed her facial features. The rage sank below her chin where it sat tight and throbbing in her neck, Nora noticed.

'Of course Mr Thompson is entitled to a private life, of course he is,' Mrs Rosen said in a placating voice. 'Only I have a hunch that there is – how can I put it – some other reason for your presence here …'

Nora said nothing. Instead her eyes scanned the bookcase behind Mrs Rosen. Everything had been done to make the office seem like an extension of a private home in order to divert attention from the fact that it was an institution, a business, which every month collected astronomical amounts from families that couldn't cope with looking after their elderly, decrepit, incontinent or senile parents, and it eased their conscience somewhat if they bought their way out of the problem in the private sector.

The books in the bookcase would reassure anyone that quality of life and care were the priorities here. There were books with recipes for jam and chutney, books on walking in the Scottish Highlands, places of interest in Shropshire; she even spotted a copy of the New Testament on the bottom shelf.

Mrs Rosen shifted nervously on her chair. 'Miss Sand. What I'm trying to understand is why you think it's appropriate to turn up without an appointment, and what you're doing here in the first place?'

Nora turned her attention back to her again. 'Mrs Rosen. I owe you no explanation for why I'm here, except the one I've already given you, which also happens to be the truth. I came to visit Mr Thompson. That's all,' she said archly. 'I'm a journalist, that's correct, but I don't work for a British newspaper. I work for a Danish weekly magazine called *Globalt*. You've probably never heard of it, and I've no plans to uncover appalling conditions in the British care system, if that's what you're worried about,' she continued. 'Although I'm starting to think that I ought to, or tip off a British colleague, because everyone here acts as if they've something to hide.'

Mrs Rosen coughed. 'Danish?' she said.

'Yes,' Nora said. 'So you can relax. Whatever's going on here, if your staff steal from petty cash, put the old folks to bed at four in the afternoon or starve them, it's not my business. I'm here in connection with an old criminal investigation, which has links to Denmark. It has nothing to do with you or your care home, but Mr Thompson might have some information. That was all,' she said.

'What kind of … information?' Mrs Rosen asked.

'That's confidential,' Nora said.

After a pause, which was so protracted that she became aware of a clock ticking in the room next door and chatter from a radio that might be on in the kitchen, Mrs Rosen took a deep breath and produced a rather forced smile.

'Miss Sand. I believe that we got off on the wrong foot. I would like to help you in any way I can,' she said.

Nora looked at her in surprise.

'Let's start over. I'll make us some tea, and then you can tell me what you've found out so far,' she said and caught Nora's look of disbelief. 'I mean, whatever you feel comfortable disclosing to me. Perhaps I can be of use,' she said and got up. 'Please excuse me. I'll just go to the kitchen to fetch the tea.'

While she was gone, Nora checked her mobile.

No one had called her. There wasn't even a text message from Andreas, only a small window announcing that her battery was down to less than thirty per cent. She slipped her mobile back into her trouser pocket.

Clattering teacups announced Mrs Rosen's arrival before she entered the room, balancing a tray with a rose-patterned teapot, two cups, a sugar bowl and a milk jug and a small plate of chocolate biscuits.

As she bent over to pour the tea, Nora detected a faint scent like that of clothes that had been stored in a cupboard with lavender bags to deter mould and moths. It was as if someone had tried to cover up the stench of death, old people and disease with perfume – yet she could still smell what lay beneath.

Nora took her teacup. Suddenly she felt overcome by hunger and exhaustion, and she couldn't wait to return to London, climb into bed and pull the duvet over her head. She selected a sugar lump and gave it plenty of time to dissolve before adding milk.

Mrs Rosen watched her with a stiff smile. 'Right. So tell me everything. What's this case about?'

Nora took a big gulp. The tea was perfect, hot and sweet, exactly what she needed. 'Mrs Rosen, how long have you lived in this town?'

The warden shrugged. 'Years. Why do you ask?'

Nora wondered whether to ask Mrs Rosen if she knew anything about Bill Hix and his connection to the area. Suddenly it seemed like an insurmountable task. Far too complicated. In fact, right now Nora didn't know if she could even summon up the energy to get up and walk to her car. She was bushed. Dog-tired. Of Andreas. Of this bloody case. Of Mrs Rosen, whose face was starting to blur at the edges. Whose eyes were growing bigger and bigger. Then they expanded and contracted in a manner that simultaneously fascinated and terrified Nora more than she could express.

'I'm sorry. I suddenly feel very tired. You don't happen to have …' Nora began, but halfway through her sentence, she could no longer remember what she wanted to say.

'Yes, you're tired,' Mrs Rosen said, and she didn't sound entirely unkind.

It was the bookcase. Something about the bookcase was very wrong.

'I just need …' Nora said, and heard how her voice slowed down like an old audiotape just before it tangles up.

Then everything turned black.

31

When she woke up, she didn't know how much time had passed. For one brief, panicky moment she thought that she had gone blind. Her eyes were wide open, but she could see nothing in the pitch-black darkness.

She returned to her body in violent jolts. Nora's throat hurt, she had a gag in her mouth, and her hands were tied in front of her body. She could smell earth and mulch, a hint of mouldy clothes and rust.

Slowly she began to make out contours. Some things were less black than others, dark grey against grey.

Her feet were tied together, and she had been left on the ground in what she took to be the tool shed outside which she had been chatting to Mr Thompson earlier.

It was cold. She could feel the chill from the beaten-earth floor, and she guessed that it was night time. She turned on to her side and wiggled until she reached a sitting position, while her calf muscles screamed as cramp set in. She ignored the pain and tried tentatively to stand up. She was yanked back by a rattling iron chain, one end of which was attached to the back of her belt while the other appeared to be fixed to an oversized garden tractor, as far as she could work out.

How the hell had this happened to her? One moment she was drinking tea with a nice care-home warden, the next she was trussed up in a tool shed like a lamb for the slaughter.

Mrs Rosen? Nora tried to recall their meeting. Everything swirled together in a confusing mosaic. The angry terrier that was Mrs Fletcher, the trip to Mrs Rosen's office. Tea being poured from a rose-patterned teapot, Mrs Rosen's strained smile, the radio going in the kitchen, the bookcase.

There was something about that bookcase. Nora knew it – if only she could remember what it was. She closed her eyes again and tried to appeal to the photographic part of her memory.

First she visualised the top shelf. Two books on jam and chutney. One book about hiking trails in Wales. A china owl figurine. Five leather-bound novels with gold print, probably bought by the yard from a second-hand bookshop to give the office the right cultured air.

Second shelf: a dog-eared version of *Scotland on Foot*, its spine badly cracked from years of use. A picture book of Shropshire landscapes. A garland of dried flowers that had seen better days.

Frustrated, Nora kicked out at the garden tractor in the darkness and rolled on to her side again. That didn't get her anywhere, and now she was lying pretty much on show, waiting for some psycho to step out of the darkness and attack her.

She strained and tore at the chain in sheer rage. The garden tractor shifted a few centimetres when she managed to raise two of its wheels from the ground, before they thumped back down with a sigh. Her rage came out as something that would have resembled the roar of a wounded animal, only the gag in her mouth muffled all sound.

If she stretched the chain as far as it would go, she could just about reach the wooden wall. First she tried bumping her shoulders against the wall to attract attention, but it made no noise at all. In sheer desperation she tried banging her head against the wall, but the noise was limited and the pain severe.

She could feel the tears well up and with them a deep fear she simply couldn't afford to indulge. The most important thing was not thinking about all the things that *might* happen. Who or what might be behind the door when it was opened. If it was ever opened. Those were futile thoughts. Right now it was about finding a way out.

Nora recalled the many times she had found herself in a tight spot. How she had been in the middle of a war zone and her satellite phone had cut out three minutes before the deadline. How once she had been caught behind a roadblock between Macedonia and Kosovo with three mercenaries, who were trigger-happy and high on cocaine. How her laptop had once deleted five hours of work on an express train to Manchester, and how she had recreated the article in twenty-five minutes, because that was all the time she had.

Nora Sand solves problems. And she does it cool, calm and collected. Afterwards she might have a total meltdown. That is, if she has any energy left.

That could be her epitaph one day. But today was not that day.

Third shelf. More books by the yard. A snow globe paperweight with a plastic model of *Il Duomo*, the cathedral in Florence financed and built by the Medici family, who presumably had never imagined that their life's work would one day be encapsulated in a plastic globe with artificial snow. A pile of yellowing paper sticking out from a file. The New Testament. The New Testament.

It was at that very moment when Nora realised what was so very, very wrong – that the door opened.

The light from a torch searched the room until the beam landed on Nora's face, forcing her to close her eyes. Then she heard Mrs Rosen's voice again. This time it was stripped of false politeness and sympathy.

'Oh, Miss Sand. You're awake at last. Sleeping on the job is a very bad idea,' she said sarcastically.

Nora tried staring back at her, but could see nothing except her outline behind the beam of the flashlight. It wasn't until Mrs Rosen was very close to her that Nora noticed the filled syringe. She tried protesting, promising anything as long as Mrs Rosen didn't inject whatever it was at the other end of that needle into her. But the words didn't get past the gag covering her mouth.

'There, there …' Mrs Rosen spoke to her like an adult trying to soothe a restless child.

Nora tried wriggling out of her reach.

'Miss Sand. I'm going to inject you whatever you do. I've had to keep you here for practical reasons. But now I need to move you, hence the injection. It's up to you whether or not it'll hurt. If you lie still, all you'll feel is a tiny little scratch.'

Her voice was calm. Her sentences short and concise. Nora realised that to Mrs Rosen, capturing and drugging a journalist wasn't something that caused her any kind of agitation, raised her blood pressure or indeed her voice. She might as well have been telling her how to tie her shoelaces or reminding her to buy porridge oats. And that scared Nora more than anything.

She forced herself to lie still and wait for the right moment. Her muscles tensed and suddenly it happened very quickly. Mrs Rosen was on top of her. Nora kicked out, squirmed and felt the sharp scratch from the needle where her shoulder joined her neck. Then everything turned black again.

32

When she regained consciousness, she was tied to a chair in a room that had to be a basement. The gag over her mouth was gone, but the walls looked so thick that no one would hear her scream anyway. Near the ceiling she could see small windows that let in grey daylight. She could smell damp concrete, stored apples and oil. In a corner a chest freezer was humming away. Its glowing, green lamp announced that everything was normal, but nothing was normal. She was trapped in some madwoman's basement, and as she slowly came round, the image of the book came back to her. Few people in the UK had a copy of the New Testament. Most British homes with a Bible used the King James authorised version. The spine of this book had been in Danish.

If Nora's hands had been free, she would have slapped her forehead. Every clue had led her to this place. What an idiot she had been. How blind.

The chill crept up around her legs, her bladder was full to bursting, and her mouth was dry. She could feel her mobile digging into her hip and decided that today's best news was that that bitch Mrs Rosen hadn't had the presence of mind to search her. Nora was only one phone call away from help. One call and a whole universe, she thought, and glanced at her cold, pale hands tied firmly to the armrests.

As long as her mobile was alive, there was hope.

She cleared her throat and tried talking into the room. 'Hello?' There was no response. 'Hello, is anyone there?'

Still no response. Nora thought her voice sounded small and desperate. She took a deep breath and forced herself to calm down.

'Mrs Rosen. Hello?' she called out.

Silence.

She listened out for the tiniest sound that would reveal that she was in a building with life other than the humming chest freezer. She thought she heard a dog bark in the distance.

Then it came. Faint at first, like creaking. Then louder. Someone was walking around upstairs. Nora could hear footsteps. There was a human being nearby.

She called out again. The footsteps stopped. Someone had heard her.

'Hello? Help!' she tried again, louder this time.

The footsteps came closer. Nora heard a door being opened behind her and felt cool air.

'Shut up,' the voice ordered her.

'Please may I have some water?'

If she could get some water, she might be allowed to free her hands to drink it. And that would give her a chance.

'I'm just asking for some water. That's all,' she tried again.

The door was slammed shut. Silence. Treacherous sobs forced their way up Nora's throat.

Was she supposed to just sit here until she died of thirst? Or would something even worse happen to her? She couldn't allow herself to wonder what Mrs Rosen might want to do to her. She just had to make sure that it never got that far.

She heard footfall on the steps and the door opened again. This time she sensed that someone was standing behind her.

'Close your eyes,' a female voice said.

'Who are you?' Nora said in a voice that was shaking more than she would have liked.

'Shut up and close your eyes.' The command was hard and sharp like a whiplash.

Nora did as she was told. The next moment a plastic cup was pressed against her lips. She drank greedily. Some of the water trickled down her chin, and she choked, spluttered and coughed. But then she found a rhythm with the hand and drained the cup.

'Can I have some more?' she said in an attempt to buy time.

The voice didn't reply. Instead she heard the door being closed again and someone walking away.

'Please?' she called out into the empty space, and hated herself for it. Shortly afterwards the door was opened once more.

'Close your eyes.'

Nora closed them, almost. Leaving a tiny crack, she saw the outline of a white plastic cup held in a hand at the end of a green sweater.

The woman let her drink in silence.

'I need the loo,' Nora said.

The woman said nothing.

'I mean, I *really* need the loo,' Nora insisted. 'Please?'

The ritual repeated itself. Silence, cold air, the door being slammed and someone leaving. This time Nora was sure that she had heard a dog bark.

She was alone again. For how long she didn't know. She tried calculating the minutes by counting to sixty over and over, like her father had taught her on countless car journeys to archaeological sites, but soon gave up. It didn't really matter what time it was. Her instinct told her that she had been drugged for about twelve hours.

She had pins and needles in her fingers due to lack of circulation, and tried moving her arms back and forth under the brown parcel tape keeping her fixed to the armrests. It shifted every time, but only millimetres. After what felt like half an hour's hard work, Nora hadn't achieved much apart from a sweaty brow and loosening her restraints a useless half-centimetre.

She started rocking back and forth on the chair. Perhaps she could damage it enough to wrench off one armrest? She looked around desperately for something – anything – that might help her. There was a spade next to the chest freezer. If she could get it into tension under the armrest, she might be able to …

Inch by inch Nora rocked the chair towards the spade. It was hard going, and she was scared of moving quickly in case she made too much noise. Finally it was within reach.

The challenge now was to flip the spade towards the chair so she could place it under the armrest, push it up with her thigh and use it as a kind of lever that could twist off the armrest. She edged the chair closer with great care and nudged the spade. It started sliding towards the chest freezer, hit the lid with a clonk, and settled there like an unstable Mikado stick. Shit! She tried getting closer to it, but the chair was in her way.

She wanted to scream in rage at herself.

The door opened again. This time it was Mrs Rosen. Trying to pretend she wasn't in the middle of an escape attempt was pointless. A furious Nora glared at her blue eyes.

This seemed to amuse Mrs Rosen. 'Oh dear, oh dear, oh dear, Miss Sand. You don't give up easily, do you?'

Nora gave her a hard stare. 'I know who you are,' she said in Danish.

Mrs Rosen made no reply, but Nora saw her face twitch in a way that revealed she had heard and understood the sentence.

Nora repeated: 'I know who you are.'

Mrs Rosen shrugged and replied in perfect English: 'You do? I very much doubt it.'

She nodded towards the chest freezer. 'Why were you trying to get into the freezer? Your wish can come true much sooner than you imagine,' she said calmly. 'Do you really want to know what's inside the freezer? You wouldn't be the first. Or indeed the last, for that matter. But you do get to decide if you want to be the most awkward. You'll only make it worse for yourself.'

Nora's body throbbed as if to tell her that her earlier panic had never gone away, but merely hung around nearby.

'The loo. I need the loo,' she squawked.

Mrs Rosen looked uninterested.

'Listen,' Nora said, 'I really need the loo. If you don't let me use it, I'll pee right here. On the chair. On the floor. I don't know what you plan to do with me, but I imagine leaving DNA evidence isn't a very good idea.'

Mrs Rosen appeared to consider that point for a moment. 'If I –' she had time to say.

Then Nora's mobile started ringing.

Nora closed her eyes, as if that could make the sound go away, but Mrs Rosen had already located it and she thrust her hand brutally into Nora's trouser pocket to retrieve the mobile.

'I have to take that call,' Nora bluffed.

Mrs Rosen checked the mobile to see who was calling. The number was withheld. Out of the corner of her eye, Nora could see she had fifty-two missed calls.

'It's the magazine. If I don't answer it, they'll get worried and move heaven and earth to find me.'

Mrs Rosen made a quick decision and put it on speaker. 'Hello. Who is this?' she said in a measured voice.

'Yes, hello. It's Gareth from Vodafone. I'm calling to tell you about a great new offer for our customers –'

Mrs Rosen hung up without saying a word and rolled her eyes. Then she turned off the mobile and dropped it into her own pocket.

Nora played her last card, betting everything that her guess was right. That she had finally got hold of one end of the truth.

'Lisbeth. Is this really what became of you?'

Mrs Rosen's mouth turned into a narrow line.

'Listen, Lisbeth – it's no use. You can't hide your true identity for the rest of your life. Keeping me here won't solve any problems. All my notes are on my laptop. Sooner or later someone will find them.'

For the first time Mrs Rosen switched to Danish.

'Oh. You mean the Mac in the turquoise bag in the boot of that small, yellow rental car you parked in front of Ladbrokes in the high street? I'm afraid the car was involved in an accident. The driver appears to have driven too close to the crash barrier and gone over the cliffs near Brine. This can happen if you're a little tipsy or depressed.'

'Is that what happened to Oluf?'

Lisbeth watched Nora in silence.

'Is that what you have in mind for me?'

Lisbeth shook her head. 'No. You'll be a present. He likes his girls fresh.'

She let the sentence linger in the air for a moment.

'And you're welcome, of course, to take a look inside the freezer. If you have the guts, that is.'

Then she spun on her heel and slammed the door.

Nora screamed for help until her voice grew hoarse and her throat was raw. Then she fell into a restless sleep.

33

Sometime later the door opened again. It was the woman in the green sweater. This time Nora wasn't told to close her eyes. By now her bladder was in agony.

Once again the woman held the cup to Nora's lips and she drank obediently. Then the woman opened a packet of Digestive biscuits, took one and let Nora eat it one bite at a time.

'She says you need feeding for the next two days. I'm not sure what to give you,' the woman said. Her voice had grown timid and small. 'It's the first time we've had anyone here for a long time.'

Nora forced herself to stay calm. It's just an interview, she told herself. It's just an article that needs writing and I'm gathering information. I've interviewed war criminals, killers and dictators. This is just another job.

'Would you happen to have a banana or some other fruit?'

The woman shrugged. 'I could go upstairs and have a look.'

Nora attempted her most reassuring smile. 'That would be really nice, Lulu.'

The woman jumped. 'You know my name?'

'Yes, I do. There are still people in Denmark looking for you. After all these years.'

'Who?'

Nora tried to buy time. 'So, can I have that banana?'

Lulu got up from the floor and went outside. This time she left the door open. Nora could hear loud barking and something that might be traffic from a main road some distance away.

A little later she returned with two bananas and a red plastic bucket. Her body language reminded Nora of a cowed dog. She slinked along the walls and kept her gaze fixed on the ground, never looking straight at Nora.

'She says that if you need the loo, you have to go in this,' Lulu mumbled so quietly that Nora almost missed it.

Nora tried to catch her eye to establish some sort of contact. 'Can I have that banana now?' she asked softly.

Lulu gave a light shrug, put down the bucket on the floor and started peeling one of the bananas. She offered it to Nora, who took a bite.

'What's going to happen to me? Will I end up like Oluf?'

Again Lulu jumped. For the first time she looked straight at Nora. 'Oluf went back to Denmark,' she said in a trembling voice that revealed how nervous she was.

'You know what Lisbeth is like. What makes you think he was allowed to leave?' Nora asked calmly.

'But she said …'

Nora shook her head as if talking to a child. 'Lulu. You're not like Lisbeth. I know that. Tell me what happened. Tell me what happened to Oluf,' she said with as much authority in her voice as she could muster.

'Nothing happened to Oluf,' Lulu said in a quivering voice. 'I have to go now.'

She hurried away, leaving Nora behind in the basement. With the humming chest freezer and its evil, green eye.

Nora saw her only chance disappear and found her pleading voice. 'I'm sure you're right. Please would you … Please would you help me have a pee? I'm really desperate.'

Lulu hesitated near the door, then she turned and came back. She eyed Nora suspiciously.

'I really need a pee – please would you loosen my restraints? Just so I can sit on the bucket,' Nora begged.

Lulu shook her head and pressed her lips together.

'Did you know that your dad is still looking for you?'

Lulu snorted so emphatically that Nora realised her mistake at once. Instead she tried again to appeal to Lulu's common sense.

'Look at me. I can't pee into that bucket unless you untie me. Please. I'm about to wet myself. And you know that Lisbeth wouldn't want that.'

Lulu glanced nervously at the door, hesitated, but then produced a blunt pair of kitchen scissors from her back pocket.

'I'll free one hand and your legs. Any sign of trouble and I'll set the dogs on you,' she warned her.

Nora nodded gravely. 'I won't try anything. I promise.'

She felt cold metal against the skin on her arm, then pain as the blood returned to the veins that had been almost completely cut off by the tight tape.

She clenched and unclenched her hand tentatively. It very nearly refused to obey her and her knuckles felt sore and stiff. Nora gritted her teeth in response to the pain, and looked up apologetically at Lulu, while trying to appear as harmless as possible.

'I'm being very, very still. But I can't undo my trousers with just one hand.'

Lulu chewed her lip. 'OK, but then –'

'Lulu! What the hell do you think you're doing?'

Lisbeth was standing in the doorway, her voice sliced through the room.

'I was only –' Lulu began, turning towards the voice. In that split second Nora seized the chance to kick her.

If she had learned anything from kickboxing, it was that whoever hesitates bites the dust. There was no room for thinking. Only action.

The scissors clattered to the floor. At virtually the same moment as her foot made contact with Lulu's hand, Nora bent down, quick as lightning, grabbed them with her aching fingers and pressed them against Lulu's throat.

'Take another step and I'll cut her,' she snarled at Lisbeth.

Lulu stood paralysed like a deer that had strayed on to a motorway at night.

Lisbeth wavered for a few seconds, then she laughed scornfully.

'Go on. Stab away.'

Nora looked quickly up at her. 'I mean it.'

Lisbeth's voice was just as steady as when she pretended to be Mrs Rosen. 'So do I. In fact, you two idiots deserve each another. So why don't you take the time to get to know one another. It'll be the last thing either of you will ever do. Have fun,' she said.

Then she turned on her heel, slammed the door and turned the key in the lock. Twice.

34

With her eyes fixed on Lulu, watching for the slightest sign of a counter-attack, Nora very carefully lowered the scissors.

Lulu slumped even further. Then she burst into tears.

Nora cut her other hand free, crouched on the bucket and was finally able to relieve her bladder, while Lulu sobbed compulsively. Nora let her cry for a few minutes, before putting her arm around her shoulder.

'Lulu. It doesn't have to be this way.'

'Yes, it does,' she choked.

'You can be free. I can help you.'

'No. You can't help me.'

'Yes. We can help each other.'

'You don't know what we've done. You don't know what we've done.' Lulu clasped her hand over her mouth and shook her head, as if she could physically keep the terrible words inside her head.

Nora gently helped her up on to the chair and handed her the other banana. 'Eat this and try to calm down. We'll be all right,' she said with more conviction than she really possessed.

Lulu did as she was told. Nora had a hunch that she had done so ever since she first met Lisbeth. Possibly even before that. Probably her whole life.

'Lulu. Lisbeth doesn't care about you. She's willing to sacrifice you. Why are you protecting her? Oluf is dead. And the police know about it. I've already told them what I know. They can be here any minute. And if you help me now, I'll help you later. The police are definitely on their way,' Nora lied.

Lulu only slumped even further, falling through the years, turning into a timid teenager having to confess a misdemeanour to the head teacher. Her dark hair had thinned and there were streaks of grey, she had bags under her eyes and wrinkles that dragged her mouth downwards in a sad and beaten expression. But it was Lulu, sweet little Lulu, as her drug addict dad had called her. Lulu from Vestergården.

Nora tried to catch her eye. 'What happened to Oluf? How did you meet him?'

'It happened some years after ... after we had come here. No one knew us. Lisbeth and me and Bill were ... It was just a night out. We had never been out all three of us, and Bill really wanted to watch the boxing. A colleague got him tickets. So we drove up to Liverpool. It was meant to be a fun evening.'

'But that wasn't how it turned out?'

'No, it wasn't,' Lulu replied. 'When we got there, everything was all right at first. We had really good seats, right up close. The boxers were just hitting each other, and I wasn't interested in that. But I liked watching everything else. The women in their glamorous dresses. The men shouting the whole time.'

She heaved a sigh. 'It happened after the third fight. I hadn't noticed anything, but Lisbeth spotted him immediately. Oluf was in the ring. Oluf from back home. I wanted to leave before he saw us, but Lisbeth just laughed and said no. We could talk to Oluf afterwards, and she would make sure that he kept his mouth shut for the rest of his life. Because she had seen him do something on the ferry that night when we ... That night we sailed to England.

'I never heard what they said. But afterwards Bill told me to wait by the car. I did as I was told. You always did around Bill.'

She narrowed her eyes, and Nora wondered whether it was to bring back a clearer memory from that night or an attempt to suppress it.

'Half an hour later, they came out to the car. Oluf was drunk. I don't know how he got drunk so quickly. Perhaps they had put something in his beer. Bill was sober because he was driving, and Lisbeth was only pretending to be tipsy. She got in the back with Oluf.'

Lulu's voice had grown small and scared. 'She kept quizzing him about the investigation back home in Denmark. Had they looked for us for a long time? Did the police have any leads? Had any witnesses come forward?'

She gulped before she continued. 'Oluf was really drunk. Bill lost his rag every time Oluf switched to Danish, and kept shouting towards the back: "In English! In English!" But Lisbeth just laughed. Bill was getting more and more angry. I tried making myself invisible and looked out the window without saying anything, but it was no good. He couldn't reach Lisbeth, so he started hitting me instead.'

'And then what happened?' Nora interjected.

'When we were nearly home, Oluf started kissing Lisbeth, and Bill could see them in the rear-view mirror. He was seething with rage. I don't think I've ever seen him so mad. It was very, very scary. When we pulled into the yard, he stopped the car without saying a word. He and I sat in silence, while we heard Lisbeth giggle in between the slobbering.'

Again Lulu closed her eyes. This time it took a while before she opened them and resumed her story.

'Not much else to tell really. Bill told me to go to bed. Told me to wait for him. I was terrified. He was usually so together, so calm. Even when we ... Well. I mean, he was always calm. Measured. But that night, he was red hot with rage. I went to check on Mrs Hickley. She was asleep, so I went to bed. I might have heard Lisbeth scream once during the night. I remember waking up with a jolt without quite knowing why.'

Lulu's voice was monotonous, as if she needed to reel off her account in order to get it over with: 'Bill didn't come to me that night, so I figured he was with Lisbeth. The next morning they came down for breakfast as if nothing had happened. But Oluf wasn't with them. Later I asked Lisbeth about him, but she just pulled a face and asked if I was jealous because Oluf didn't want me. When I asked her again later, she said that Oluf had gone back to Denmark, and that he had promised to keep his mouth shut about having seen us. I thought she must be right because we never heard anything.'

'They threw him in the harbour. He was eaten by the fish,' Nora said harshly.

Lulu clasped her hand over her mouth. And, at that moment, she looked like the petite fifteen-year-old who had gone missing from a ferry. Her eyes were round and trusting and she had a puzzled expression as if she was constantly asking a question she already knew would be answered with a hard slap across the face.

'No!'

Nora nodded. 'I've seen a picture of his body. There's no doubt. He was found off the coast of Brine.'

'No,' Lulu repeated automatically.

The silence spread across the basement, while Lulu stared into space like a zombie. Nora checked out the room. Apart from the spade and the chest freezer, which she could now see had a padlock, there was a dark brown cupboard, also locked. She shuddered, then crawled up on to the freezer to see if she could reach the small windows near the ceiling.

They were made from thick, frosted glass, which made it impossible to see what was on the other side. Even if she managed to break the window, the frame itself would be too small to allow either her or Lulu to crawl through it and get help. And the risk that Lisbeth would discover what she was up to before she managed to bash the spade through the glass was high.

'Where are we, Lulu? Where is this place?'

There was no reply.

The only way out was through the door. But how?

Nora checked to see if it was possible to force the door, but the blade of the spade was too thick to be eased in between the door and the frame. She decided to open the cupboard to see if that contained anything useful.

Nora attacked the lock on the cupboard with a well-aimed kick. She felt the pain start in the ball of her foot and shoot up her knee.

It was completely different from kicking a living opponent with a yielding body wrapped in padded protection. The lock didn't budge. The wardrobe stayed where it was.

Nora tried again to rouse her fellow prisoner. 'Lulu. Are we in the countryside? Are we in the city? Where is Lisbeth? Talk to me.'

Lulu had withdrawn into herself. She sat in silence shaking her head.

Nora tried kicking the lock again. This time she used her other leg and made sure to hit it with her heel, like Enzo had taught her. It didn't hurt quite as much and one door seemed to give slightly.

The light in the room was growing dimmer. The grey squares of light from the windows had changed slowly from mother-of-pearl to dark grey. Lulu watched her passively.

The cupboard got another kick. One hinge eased enough to allow her to force the blade of the spade underneath it and wriggle it lose. Nora fetched the spade. Lulu sat as if she had long since left behind her body in the basement like an empty shell.

Nora tried getting through to her again; she walked right up to her and looked straight into her eyes. 'Lulu, tell me where we are?'

'But we're at home,' she said, baffled, as if she had woken up from a dream.

'Where is home?'

'We moved in here when the terrible thing happened. When the police took Bill. Back then the house belonged to his grandfather, but we never met the police officers because we moved in here before they came to Vanessa's house, to Mrs Hickley's. Vanessa's father had died a long time ago and his house was empty. Apart from the dogs.'

Nora continued to battle with the lock, while glancing across to Lulu. Finally she put down the spade and focused her full attention on Lulu.

'Tell me about Bill. How did you meet him?' she asked her in the softest voice she could muster. Her hand was throbbing, and she had a constant pain in one ankle, which she tried to ignore while Lulu took a deep breath and started talking.

'We met him on the ferry. He said his name was Ian and that he was a photographer. He wanted to take pictures of us. Lisbeth wanted to go to London to become a supermodel. He said he knew George Michael and might be able to get us featured in a music video, like the ones they show on MTV. We fell for it hook, line and sinker. Lisbeth wanted him all to herself. She tried to get me to go back to the others. I don't know how many times I've lain awake at night wishing I had. But Bill wouldn't hear talk of it. He said we suited one another. That he wanted to take pictures of us together.'

Lulu searched her pockets and found what seemed to be her last cigarette. She carried on rummaging and was rewarded with a white, promotional lighter. Soon the tip of the cigarette lit up in a bright orange glow.

'He took pictures of us on the deck. His camera looked really professional, and he said all the things a photographer would say. That we looked great, but that the light was bad. It was far too bright on the deck, he said …' she trailed off and stared at the tip of her cigarette.

'We went with him down to his cabin. I remember thinking that nothing bad could happen as long as there were two of us.' Her smile was bitter.

'I can still remember the number of his cabin. 317. I don't know why. There was a bottle of rum and some Coke. He mixed the drinks and he talked about collarbones. Saying how they brought out your facial features. That the only way he could really show your beauty was if you were willing to show your collarbone. But that it was up to us, of course, if we wanted to meet George Michael.'

'So that's how he got you to undress?' Nora asked.

'Lisbeth took off her top first. So I had to follow suit. What an idiot I was! Ha!' she said with a small, hard laugh.

'First I covered my breasts with my hands, but then we started competing for his attention. He gave us more rum, but he must have put something in it. The last thing I remember was Lisbeth laughing.' The cigarette had almost burned down, and Lulu's hands were shaking.

'It doesn't sound like it was your fault, Lulu,' Nora said quietly.

'But you haven't heard the whole story,' Lulu interrupted her. 'When I woke up again it was dark, my body was sore and my head hurt. I felt like throwing up, but I couldn't. I had been gagged ... I tried to scream, but I couldn't. I was naked and shivering from cold. My legs were cramping, but I couldn't stretch them out. I was in a tiny room. At first I thought it was a coffin, and I screamed and I screamed, but hardly a sound came out. When I calmed down, I realised that I was in the boot of a moving car. We must have got off the ferry. I was terrified. I was convinced that he had killed Lisbeth, and that I would be next.'

They sat for a while, silent in the darkness, listening out for any signs that Lisbeth was on her way, then Lulu continued: 'I don't know how long we drove. One hour. Maybe four. I lost track of time. I was sobbing, but no one heard me. Eventually I felt the car slow down. We joined a bumpy road. Then we stopped, and I heard a car door slam. I was sure I was going to die. I was so scared that I wet myself.'

Lulu's face was a frozen mask.

'At first I couldn't see anything. Someone was pointing a torch at my face. But then I heard them. Lisbeth and Bill. They were laughing at me. Bill called me a bitch. He still does. I didn't understand what was so funny. They could see that I was awake, but they talked about me as if I wasn't there. Lisbeth said that I could make myself useful. She may have saved my life.'

The hooting of an owl broke the silence of the night, and Nora jumped. Lulu was far away and oblivious of the noise.

'We went inside the house. Bill herded us down to the basement. We didn't meet his mum until later. I didn't want to be there. I was crying and begging them to let me go. First Bill locked me inside a small, stinking room with no windows. They left me there for some days, I think. There was a tap, so I had water to drink. But no food. I found a sheet I could wrap around myself.'

She was trembling as if her body could still remember the cold and the terror.

'Lisbeth came down on her own. At first I thought she had come to set me free. I pleaded with her. Talked about Bjarke, about life back at Vestergården. I said we could go to London and look for the others. Anything to make her take my side. But her voice was hard. She showed me pictures they had taken of me while I was unconscious. In one of them, Bill was having sex with me, in another Lisbeth was pushing a bottle into me. I recognised her hands in that picture, those bitten nails could only be hers. Lisbeth said that if I didn't do as I was told, the pictures would be sent to my dad.'

A tear trickled from the corner of her eye, and she wiped it away.

'My dad. I would do anything to prevent that. Eventually I said I would. I had no choice. Lisbeth was in the house as Bill's girlfriend, and I was their servant. His mother just accepted the situation. She never asked where we had come from or who we were. We didn't leave the house for months. Lisbeth dyed her hair red and cut it short. They started arguing almost immediately. Sometimes, after the really big rows, Bill would come down to me in the basement at night. I let him do what he wanted. He was no worse than my dad.'

Lulu shook her head and carried on with her story: 'I cried a lot at the start. Lisbeth promised me that I'd be allowed to leave after six months. I just had to do them one small favour, then they would give me the negatives of the pictures and let me go. Eventually I said I'd do it though I knew it was wrong.'

'What did you have to do, Lulu?'

'I don't remember her name. I think it might have been ... Angela ... something like that. We found her on Brighton Pier. Bill spotted her,' Lulu said, and sat still for a while.

'And what happened?' Nora said at length.

Lulu heaved a deep sigh. 'Angela – or whatever her name was – came out from a fortune teller's tent in floods of tears. She had just had a Tarot reading. We followed her. She was heading into town, and me and Bill walked up to her together. He thought that if there was another woman there, the girl wouldn't worry about coming with him. He was right. We talked her into going with us to Bill's studio to have her photo taken. I told her she was as pretty as Bill said she was. Of course she came with us. Young women are easily taken in by flattery, and I was there to reassure her that she was perfectly safe. Lisbeth was waiting in the studio. I did know that something bad was going to happen to her. After all, it had happened to me, but I thought it was someone else's turn. I wanted out. I'd no idea that they would ... that they would ...'

'Would do what?' Nora said.

'They gave her a glass of water with something in it. I don't know what. The girl had dropped her guard because Lisbeth and I were there. It never crossed her mind that something bad could happen to her.'

'But you knew?'

'I thought they might take pictures of her, like they had done with me. I couldn't stop them. They were going to do it anyway, with or without my help, and I thought rather her than me. I hoped that after I'd helped them, they would let me go. And I thought, well, at least she was drugged.'

Nora tried running through the names of the many missing girls in her mind, but couldn't recall an Angela.

'What happened next?'

Lulu took a deep breath and let it out in small puffs.

'What happened next?' Nora insisted.

'She passed out before she had managed to pose for even one picture. They tied her to a chair. And then they did it.'

Silence.

'What did they do, Lulu?' Nora asked, trying to make her voice as neutral as possible.

'They cut out her tongue! With a scalpel. They opened her mouth and Bill cut away at it, only the last bit wouldn't come out, so he started pulling it. He ripped the tongue out of her mouth and stuffed it into his own mouth. I was screaming and screaming. I tried to run, but Lisbeth grabbed me. Forced me to watch. Bill was laughing.

I think that Lisbeth was scared too, but she still held me back. I couldn't get out. I couldn't get out. I couldn't get out.'

She repeated this sentence like a dismissal prayer, which ended in a dry sob.

'There was so much blood. Much more than you'd think. It just kept pouring out. She died in the studio. I think she bled out. When she had stopped moving, Bill gouged out her eyes. I was told to clean up. Bill and Lisbeth took the girl and they were gone for hours. There was linoleum on the floor. I washed it over and over with bleach. I cried as I knelt on the floor. I was so scared. Finally Lisbeth came back to get me. She took away all the cleaning cloths, and when we got home, we burned them on a bonfire in the garden. Afterwards I asked what they'd done with the girl. But Lisbeth didn't want to talk about it. It was weeks before Bill started coming down to the basement again.'

'Why didn't you run away?' Nora said.

'Lisbeth said I was an accessory to murder. And where would I have gone? She said she would make it look as if I had done it. As if it was all my fault. That people would have seen me talking to the girl on Brighton Pier. I had cleaned up after the killing and my fingerprints would be everywhere. So I stayed and there were more girls. Lots more.'

'How many?'

'I don't know. Lots.'

'More than ten? Twenty?'

Silence descended upon them again. Lulu stared at the floor.

'What did they do with them – the girls?'

'Bill always kept their tongues. But the rest of them ...' she glanced nervously at Nora.

'The rest of them ... was cut up and fed to the dogs.'

Nora could feel herself break out in a cold sweat. 'The dogs?'

'Yes. In little bits, so as not to leave any evidence. Vanessa's hunting dogs. They'll eat anything. We have a kennel here. There are always at least ten hungry dogs.'

Nora's disgust must have been plain to see because Lulu looked straight at her and said: 'You'll end up like the others. Lisbeth helps Bill. When you least expect it, she'll cut out your tongue and give it to Bill. She always brings him a tongue when she visits him in prison. She puts it in a sandwich. They check her packed lunch, but they never lift up the bread to see what's underneath.'

Lulu started giggling like a little girl.

'Once, when Lisbeth was visiting Bill, she told me they had asked her what was in the sandwich. And she said tongue.'

Nora shook her head.

'Lulu, will you help me? Do you want to leave this place?'

'And go where?'

Nora abandoned her efforts and returned to the cupboard. She bashed the hinge with renewed strength. Whacked the spade against the doors over and over, and was eventually rewarded with the sound of splintering wood when one door gave up holding on to the hinge. She pulled at the remaining wood and felt it give.

When the cupboard turned out to be nearly empty, she wanted to burst into tears. No toolbox. Nothing that could serve as a weapon. Only a pile of old cloths and two bottles of cleaning fluid. Nora picked one of them up. Bleach. The other was a small, blue plastic bottle. White spirit. An idea began to take shape.

Lulu sat passively with her hands in her lap.

'Give me your lighter,' Nora ordered her.

Lulu looked up lethargically.

'Give me your lighter.'

Lulu fumbled in her pocket, found the lighter and handed it to Nora indifferently.

Nora shook the bottle of white spirit. There was just about enough. Now it was a question of timing.

'Lulu. Listen. Where do you think Lisbeth is? Is she still upstairs?'

Lulu shrugged.

Nora gritted her teeth and was sorely tempted to shake her. The girl who had disappeared from the England ferry was long gone. The girl whose gentle nature Bjarke still remembered was nothing but an empty shell.

She cut the cloths into strips with the scissors. Her hands still hurt when she used the scissors. Then she soaked the strips in white spirit and stuffed them into the bottle. A sharp smell hit her nostrils. It reminded her of winter mornings when she would potter down to the living room in Bagsværd and light a fire in the wood burner.

Then she picked up the spade again, aimed it at one of the two small windows and hit it hard. A crack appeared in the glass. It spread and turned into a star until finally she managed to whack a hole for fresh air.

Nora could hear hysterical dog-barking very close and feel cold air whistling in. She took a deep breath and screamed at the top of her lungs: 'Lisbeth! Come down here right now or I'll burn down the house!'

No response.

'Let me out or we'll burn it! The fire brigade will turn up! How are you going to explain to them that you've got me locked up in your basement?!'

Suddenly she noticed that the barking had changed. As if someone was trying to settle the dogs. She took out the lighter and walked closer to the door with her home-made Molotov cocktail at the ready.

When she heard footsteps above, she flicked the lighter. At that very moment she saw Lulu get up.

'Stop! You can't –' Lulu called out.

The door opened.

Nora lit the flame and as soon as it had caught, she hurled the bottle at Lisbeth. She heard it smash into the wall and saw the orange flare out of the corner of her eye as she pushed Lisbeth aside and raced up the steps. She was free at last and found herself in a back garden enclosed by a high wall. A big, dark grey house was blocking her path to freedom.

The barking grew louder and she saw the dogs. Her knees almost buckled when one snarling cur got hold of her trouser leg. She shook it off with much difficulty and ran towards the house. She could hear Lisbeth shouting behind her.

Nora twisted her ankle as she stumbled up the steps to the back door. She hobbled the last stretch and managed to push open the door while she kicked out at the two barking dogs still at her heels.

Then she slammed shut the door behind her and locked it.

She walked through a small hallway and found herself in a filthy kitchen. The sink was full of dirty plates, the tap was dripping, and the curtains were closed. She went back out into the hall and onwards into the house, looking for a telephone, and found a dining room with cumbersome, dark furniture. From there Nora could see into a crammed living room, which lay in twilight. She limped on her sore ankle and looked over her shoulder. She could hear the dogs scratching the back door and barking in frustration at their prey that had got away.

She quickly scanned the living room. On the small side table by the window was an old-fashioned telephone with a dial. Nora said a silent prayer as she tottered towards it.

'Who are you? And where's Liz?'

The voice was simultaneously fragile and titanium hard. Nora jumped and tried to work out where it had come from.

In the remotest corner of the darkness, slumped in front of a flickering TV with the sound turned down, an old lady was peering at her through a pair of spectacles.

The woman raised her voice. 'Who are you and what are you doing in my house?'

Nora tried to think of an answer while making her way to the small table with the telephone, desperate to buy time.

'Mrs Hickley ... I'm –'

She got no further before the woman started screaming: 'Help! Help! Thief!'

Nora picked up the handset and dialled 112. There was no ring tone. She shook the handset and followed the cable to see if the telephone was even plugged in.

She sensed the cold air before she saw the door move. Then she looked up and right into a pair of black eyes watching her under a dark fringe.

'I warned you, bitch!' Bill Hix said.

35

Slowly he walked up to her with an icy smile on his lips. In one hand he held a kitchen knife that had been sharpened so many times the blade looked stiletto thin.

Nora didn't dare take her eyes off him.

'Bill, what's going on? Why are you here? Who's that girl? Where is Liz?' Mrs Hickley's confused chatter, however, wasn't rewarded with as much as a single glance from Hix.

Nora scanned the room frantically for a weapon. Anything that would give her a small advantage. Hix smiled indulgently when he saw her eyes dart around the living room.

'Oh, Nora, Nora, Nora,' he chanted. 'You know that the more you resist, the more fun it'll be for me. What a good girl you are,' he said, and pulled the corners of his mouth into a grim imitation of a smile.

There was scrambling at the back door that Nora had locked. Then she heard the jingling of keys and in the distance the hysterical barking of the dogs. The back door was opened, and soon afterwards a furious Lisbeth appeared in the living room. She looked first at Nora, before she discovered Hix.

'Bill! You came!' she cried out.

Hix didn't turn around to look at her. 'You fucking well stay out of this. She's mine,' he merely snarled.

Lisbeth lingered in the doorway, not knowing what to do with herself. Behind her the dogs were going crazy.

'I said get out of here!' Hix screamed and glared viciously at Lisbeth.

In that split second Nora spotted her chance. With lightning speed she lunged forwards and grabbed a brass candlestick from the coffee table, and in an almost fluid movement, as hard as she could, she hit Hix across the hand holding the knife.

Enzo had drilled it into her: For the best possible odds, always disarm your enemy. Faced with an unarmed Hix now distracted by a screaming Lisbeth in the doorway and a confused old woman at the other end of the room, she had a chance.

He dropped the knife, bellowed in agony and instinctively clutched his injured hand. At that moment Nora delivered him a left hook, which sent him straight into a large vase and onwards into a radiator.

The pain, which reached her knuckles two seconds later, was so fierce that she almost closed her eyes, but she didn't give into it. She raced to the hallway only to find Lisbeth blocking the front door.

Nora ran back to the kitchen, slamming the kitchen door behind her and wedging a chair under the handle, while she tried getting a grip on the situation. She tore open the top drawer and found a huge carving fork with long, sharp tines. The knife block on the table was empty, and Nora guessed that the only sharp knife in the house was currently held firmly in Hix's other, uninjured hand.

She could hear him roar out in the passage. 'You fucking bitch! Just you wait. I'll get you!'

Then he was outside the flimsy woodchip door where only a kitchen chair was keeping him out. Her hand was throbbing with pain and the bruising had already caused her knuckles to swell to double size.

She watched the door give. Every time Hix kicked it, it would budge another few millimetres. Nora searched frantically under the sink for a weapon. She found a couple of old plastic bottles with crumbling labels, which looked like they had been there for years. She poured half the contents on to a tea towel she found next to the cooker, and the rest out into a small pool in front of the door. It gave off a strong, chemical smell. Hix had stopped shouting and was working methodically on the door. She could hear his breathing and see the old kitchen chair quiver under the pressure.

She fumbled in her pocket for Lulu's lighter, but realised that she must have lost it when she fled the basement. Panic whizzed around her body like a chainsaw nearing her neural paths.

Then suddenly, next to the radio on a shelf above the kitchen table, she spotted a box of matches. She opened it. Three left. The first match snapped in her hands.

She almost squealed out of sheer terror. She stuck the carving fork into the waistband of her trousers, climbed up on to the kitchen table, ready to make her escape through the window at the last minute, while she clutched the box of matches.

The window refused to budge. It hadn't been opened for years, and decades of moss and ivy had grown across it.

She was out of time. The door hinges were giving up. The angle of the window made it impossible for her to open it, so she lay down on her side on the kitchen table and tried with one last, desperate kick to hit one corner of the window frame. It opened slightly with a wounded squeak. She pushed it and finally managed to open the window. She climbed up on to the windowsill and swung her legs over it as she whispered another silent prayer and struck the second last match. It flared up, and Nora threw it towards the pool by the door just as the chair under the handle gave up with a final last snap, and she saw Hix's black eyes stare into the room.

Then she landed on the grass. She had time to smell the stench of burnt hair, before one dog with bared teeth loomed over her.

Three seconds later dog number two was at her other side in an attack position, awaiting orders from its master, who had now appeared.

Lisbeth had red patches on her face where she had been burned during Nora's escape from the basement. They made her look even more furious.

'Sit!' she ordered the dogs, which were following Nora's slightest movement with bloodshot eyes.

Flames and black smoke poured out of the kitchen window. Lisbeth stared up at it. Then back at Nora. Then back at the window.

'If you move even an inch, they'll rip you to pieces,' Lisbeth said, then she turned and ran back inside the house.

Little by little Nora moved herself up into a sitting position. The two hounds gave her a bloodthirsty look and their snarling terrified her. They were so close she could see saliva drip from their needle-sharp teeth, but they obeyed their orders.

Calmly and without any sudden movements, she eased her unin-jured hand behind her back in order to pull out the carving fork.

'There, there, good boy,' she said in her softest voice. The bigger of the two dogs tilted its head and looked confused. 'Come here, boy,' she tempted it, as she moved closer towards it.

Its growl was deep and ominous. As if to make it quite clear that it was in no way a lapdog, it snapped at her with an angry bark. Nora snatched back her hand. Time for plan B. And be quick about it. It wouldn't be long before Lisbeth – or Hix – came back for her.

She got up while holding the carving fork in front of her like a shield. The bigger dog moved closer, ready to attack, while its smaller fellow yakked hysterically.

Then it went straight for Nora's ankles and tried closing its jaws around her leg, before she managed to pull back her foot and give that bloody dog the worst upper cut it had ever had.

It keeled over on the grass like a tree stump with all four legs in the air. This seemed to blindside its four-legged friend enough to temporarily forget that their mission was to guard and growl at Nora. It whined as it ran to its unconscious friend and sniffed its face anx-iously. It looked bewildered and a tad taken aback at Nora. However, she didn't have time for lengthy explanations. She raced around to the front of the house.

Smoke was pouring out of the front door, and it crossed Nora's mind that it would slow Hix down if he decided to save his ageing mother from the flames.

She hoped that by now someone would have seen the smoke and called the fire brigade. Police cars would arrive along with the fire engines. However, realistically, the nearest fire station was likely to be miles away and staffed by volunteers, who would first have to be contacted. Before help arrived, that psycho Hix would have plenty of time to kill and bury a Danish journalist. Nora felt no urge to hang around to help him realise that particular ambition.

36

She discovered an outbuilding that looked like an old stable, inside which a battered, red pick-up truck and a dark grey BMW were parked. The door to the pick-up was unlocked, but there was no key in the ignition. She wasted precious seconds searching for it under the driver's seat, under the visor, and finally in the glove compartment. No key.

She ran back to the basement.

Lulu was still sitting on the floor, clutching her head, curled up like a child. When she spotted Nora, she looked up at her, her big eyes overflowing with tears.

'She pushed me,' was all she said. As if she were seven years old and could tell tales to a teacher.

Nora glanced nervously up at the house where the flickering flames glowed orange in the twilight. Hix or Lisbeth or one of the dogs could appear at any minute.

'Lulu. You're coming with me now!' she ordered her.

Lulu stood up mechanically. 'Oh, OK.'

'Hurry up!'

Lulu accelerated ever so slightly and they made it to the outbuilding at last.

'Where do they keep the car keys?'

Lulu pointed silently to the left side of the stable door. Nora ran on ahead and started searching for them. She cut herself on a rusty nail and swore.

'Where's that bloody key?!' she screamed in frustration.

Lulu wailed. 'It's always there. It's on the nail …'

Nora looked around frantically. There was only the one nail, but no key. She started pulling down tins from a shelf next to the door. Still no key.

'Lulu. We really need that key. Where else could it be?'

Nora kicked the car out of sheer anger and as she did so, she spotted a glimmer of metal in a pile of rags near the door. She rummaged through the pile with her uninjured hand, and finally her fingertips found a bundle of keys. She snatched it and got into the pick-up truck.

Thankfully it started at her first attempt. Lulu stared at her, but remained frozen.

'Get in, for Christ's sake! NOW!' Nora yelled.

After what felt like an eternity to Nora, Lulu finally did as she was told. Nora put the car in gear and drove like a maniac down the gravel road, out through the forest and away from that cursed house.

'Lulu. I need your help. Where are we?'

Lulu said nothing.

They drove on, while Nora tried desperately to get her bearings. There would have to be a big gap between her and Hix before she dared breathe or stop to find a place from where she could call the police.

Finally they reached a tarmac road.

'We need to go left here,' Lulu piped up at last.

Nora turned the wheel so hard she almost lost control of the car. She managed to straighten it up and followed the winding country lane while praying for no oncoming traffic. It had grown dark by now, and Nora was only too aware that if Hix or Lisbeth followed them, the pick-up's headlights would broadcast their location to high heaven, but she didn't dare turn them off.

They drove on. Nora could feel her adrenaline stabilise just below panic and a fair level above extreme emergency. She could see no road signs or houses.

She turned to Lulu. 'That little road coming up, where does it lead to?'

'Brown's potato farm.'

Nora decided to risk it and turned down the muddy side road.

They soon reached the farm. Nora pulled up behind a barn, so the pick-up couldn't be seen from the tarmac road.

No lights were on and the farm appeared deserted.

'Lulu. Does anyone live here who has a phone we could borrow?'

Lulu shook her head. 'No, I guess they've all gone home by now.'

Nora turned off the engine and the lights, ran up to the barn and tried the door. It was locked. She clutched her head. Several minutes wasted. Minutes where Hix could catch up with her. She made a quick decision.

They were better off staying here for a while, and hoping that Hix would drive straight past without seeing them. They sat very still in the car in the darkness, and Nora could hear faint ticking from the engine as it cooled down. She turned to Lulu.

'OK. We'll just have to wait here and hope for the best.'

Lulu snorted. 'With Bill it's always the worst,' she said emphatically.

And then, the still of the night was broken by the sound of a highly tuned engine. Very much like that of a BMW. The sound got closer and closer.

Inside the pick-up Lulu whimpered: 'I'm scared.'

Nora said nothing, but turned the key in the ignition and put her foot on the clutch, ready to press it with a second's warning.

She didn't have to wait long in the darkness. The next moment she saw the yellow headlights of the BMW. They were getting closer, and their glow through the dark trees behind the barn told Nora that the car must have turned down the side road. Now it was a question of perfect timing, so the BMW didn't block their escape.

Nora bit her lip and waited … and waited … and waited. Then suddenly everything happened at once. The BMW came round the barn and drove up behind them. Nora started the pick-up with a roar and raced back to the tarmac road. She could only just feel solid tarmac under the wheels when the dark grey BMW came right up her tail. The driver had put the headlights on full beam. The reflection in the rear-view mirror hurt her eyes and made it impossible for her to see who was behind the wheel.

'Oh no, oh no. He's coming to get us,' Lulu whimpered.

Although Nora didn't disagree with Lulu's analysis of the situation, she still wished that she would just shut up.

'Where does this road end? Somewhere with other cars? Lots of people? A phone?' she asked desperately.

'It leads to the care home.'

37

Three minutes later the road came to an end in the car park behind Cedar Residence. Nora slammed on the brakes, so the pick-up skidded diagonally and blocked the narrow entrance to the car park. It wouldn't stop Hix, but it might buy them a few extra seconds.

She grabbed Lulu's arm and ran as fast as her sore ankle permitted towards the care home. The door was locked. She entered one-two-three-four, but the expected click never came. Her heart was in her mouth. She tried desperately to come up with other obvious combinations. Four-three-two-one didn't work either. Her fingers flew across the keypad, while she looked nervously over her shoulder. Lulu was whimpering.

'He's coming after us. He's coming to get us.'

'Will you shut up!' Nora hissed.

In sheer frustration she hit the button marked 'one' four times and was rewarded with a dry click from the lock, which opened, and they stumbled into the care home's reception area. She slammed shut the door behind her. She caught a glimpse of Hix crawling over the bonnet of the pick-up truck, and a flash of a knife.

Lulu was sobbing openly now.

'Follow me,' Nora said, yanking her arm. Lulu, however, stood frozen like a pillar of salt.

'No, we had better split up,' she insisted.

Nora didn't have time to argue with her, so she ran as fast as she could down the nearest corridor. She stopped halfway, went through a door and found herself in a large, dark room.

She fumbled her way around, too scared to turn on the light in case it attracted attention. Steel surfaces. Plenty of cupboards. A kitchen. She was aware that it wouldn't take Hix long to find a way into the care home.

She tiptoed further into the kitchen, while searching walls and surfaces for a telephone. Just her luck to have ended up in possibly the only room that wasn't equipped with a telephone. Had she been in any of the offices or one of the residents' rooms, she would now be enjoying a pleasant conversation with the emergency services. Instead *Globalt's* star reporter was staring at a pile of industrial-sized saucepans. Great job, Nora Sand!

She heard a bang that sounded like a door slamming into a wall at full force. OK. Hix had arrived.

Nora stood very still and listened with every nerve in her body on high alert. In her mind she returned to her most recent visit and tried to calculate the easiest route to Lisbeth's office. There was bound to be a telephone there. Nora thought she even remembered seeing one on the desk.

Carefully she opened the door to the corridor a fraction. In the beam of light pouring in from the deserted corridor, she spotted a wall-mounted telephone beside the gigantic fridge in the kitchen. She quickly closed the door again and fumbled her way to the telephone, picked up the receiver and pressed the biggest button in the hope of getting an outside line.

Beep-beep-beep.

'Shit,' she burst out as she realised it wasn't a telephone. What she had done was activate the intercom and just announced via every single speaker in the care home that she was a massive technological dunce. Oh, and she had let Hix know that she was still in the building.

She steeled herself, opened the door, looked left and right, crossed the corridor and ran back to the reception area where she nearly tripped over a wheelchair someone had left out. She tried the door to the reception office because she could see a telephone through the glass in the door, but it was locked. Where was the duty manager?

She heard the sound of someone kicking down a door, followed by a short, high-pitched scream. Then it grew silent. Eerily silent.

Nora swallowed her nausea and tried to work out where the noise could have come from. The silence was rent by something that sounded like a chair being upended and a muffled roar coming from Lisbeth's office.

She ran down another corridor, her heart pounding, and she didn't slow down until she reached the door. It was ajar, and in the light from the corridor, she could see the contours of two people in a close embrace. She caught a flash of Lulu's protruding eyes, heard her wheezing breathing. Nora then realised that Hix was trying to strangle Lulu with the cable of the telephone on which she must have tried to ring for help. Hix had his back to Nora, and she entered the room instinctively. She had to distract him, make him release Lulu. She looked around for a weapon, spotted the paperweight with the Duomo and hurled it at his head. At the critical moment, he shifted unexpectedly to one side and the snow dome merely clipped his ear without doing much damage. Hix roared with rage, but he didn't let go of Lulu.

In a last desperate attempt she grabbed hold of the top of the bookcase and pulled it over the pair of them. Books cascaded on to the floor, and she heard Hix grunt before she ran down the next corridor as fast as she could. By now there was an infernal cacophony of call bells each trying to ring louder than the other, and several lights were turned on.

She knew it was only a matter of time before Hix came after her, so she sprinted down the corridor and into the next. The fourth door she tried was unlocked and she stumbled into the room.

An old lady was lying in a hospital bed, her eyes wide open. Above her, a nightlight cast a golden glow across the room. Nora recognised where she was. The tape recorder that had narrated Jane Austen. The old lady who had sat in her armchair calling out for George in that heart-breaking manner.

Nora quickly surveyed the place. On the bedside table, next to a pewter tankard with flowers, was something that looked like an ancient, black Nokia phone. She tiptoed as softly as she could towards the bed, while trying to keep her panting breathing under control. When she was three paces from the bed, so close that she could almost touch the mobile with her fingertips, the old lady opened her blind eyes.

'Hello? Is anyone there?' she called out.

Nora tried to settle her. 'Shh. I can't explain right now. But, please, please, be quiet.'

'Who's there?' the woman cried out. There was fear in her voice.

'Shh. Please be quiet. It's a matter of life and death,' Nora tried, before reaching for the mobile.

But the woman was quicker. In a practised movement, she snatched the mobile and hid it under her duvet. 'I'm calling George. I'm calling him right now!'

Nora threw all decency to the winds, reached under the duvet and prised the mobile out of the old woman's hands. 'I'm sorry, I'm so, so sorry. I really am. I'll explain later.'

'Help! Help! Thief!' the old woman screamed.

Nora checked the display. It showed two words in a childish font: *Fisher Price*. She was holding a useless toy that had been given to a confused elderly lady who 'called' George several times a day.

It was only a matter of time before the old lady's screams would attract Hix. Nora snatched the pewter tankard and tipped out the water and the flowers. It weighed solid and heavy in her hand. Then she turned off the nightlight and took up position behind the door. On second thought she dragged the woman's Zimmer frame, which was parked beside her bed, and placed it in front of the door to stall Hix when he arrived.

She could hear him coming down the corridor. The old woman kept shouting: 'Help! Help! George! I want George to come now!'

And with a bang the door swung open. Nora was ready with her pewter tankard and aimed it straight at the back of Hix's head. He, however, tripped over the Zimmer frame, and the mug hit only the empty air.

He had fallen flat on the floor and attempted to get up at the same time as he was trying to drag Nora down. She kicked out at him, but overbalanced when he punched her in the knee.

Nora felt Hix's hands around her neck. Saw his piercing, black eyes and arrogant smile very close to her face. The effect bordered on hypnotic. She could feel the onset of dizziness and white spots started dancing in front of her eyes. With considerable effort she managed to force her hands in between his arms and she groped for his eyes in order to poke her thumbs in them, as Enzo had taught her to do 'in an extreme emergency'.

This manoeuvre surprised Hix, who wasn't used to his victims fighting back; they had always been drugged and incapacitated. He relaxed his grip for a second, and that was enough for Nora to wriggle free and scramble to her feet. Her hands searched the floor frantically and found the pewter tankard. As she bent down to pick it up, he lunged at her, and her head collided with the door frame. She, however, let herself roll with him so that he encountered much less resistance than he had expected, and he lost his footing. At that moment she used what felt like her very last strength and hammered the pewter tankard into his temple. Hix passed out as if someone had pressed his off switch.

'And that's a knockout,' Nora whispered to herself, turned on the light, and looked at the tankard in her hand, which was engraved with the words 'To George Ashcroft for honourable service to Cornwall Miners' Association'.

'I owe you one, George,' she whispered.

With adrenaline pumping through her body, she went hunting in the bathroom and took the cord from a dressing gown. She used it to tie Hix's hands behind his back. In the bathroom cabinet she found three rolls of support bandages. She rolled all three around his ankles as quickly as she could manage. She had to work fast. He could wake up at any moment. She raced back to reception, found the abandoned wheelchair waiting at the reception area, and pushed it to the room.

'What's going on? Who is it? Where's George?' the old lady was distraught.

'Mrs Ashcroft?' Nora said in her most reassuring voice.

'Yes, that's me.'

'I can't explain everything right now, but someone will be with you soon to take care of you. I promise.'

The woman appeared to calm down somewhat once she was addressed by her name. Nora rummaged through the woman's wardrobe and stole the belt from a moth-eaten trench coat. She tied the now faintly groaning Hix to the wheelchair. He was close to regaining consciousness.

She pushed him out into the corridor, right down to the end where a door led to the garden. The key was in the door. She unlocked it and pushed him out on the terrace. The cold evening air made Hix stir again. She could see his eyelids quiver.

With her very last strength, she pushed the wheelchair through the pea shingle, out on to the lawn and onwards. He was starting to resist and when he finally opened his mouth, she regretted not having gagged him.

'I'll make sure you suffer so much that you'll beg me to kill you. But I won't let you die. I'll torture you until you no longer know your own name,' he groaned.

Nora tried ignoring him, but her strength was nearly used up. They had arrived. She parked the wheelchair and tried the door. It was unlocked. She pushed Hix inside the darkness of the tool shed and slammed the door shut.

Outside the tool shed she found an abandoned broom, which she wedged under the handle thus locking the door, before her legs buckled underneath her like cooked spaghetti. When she came round a few seconds later, she was propped up against the door and a furious Mrs Fletcher was looming over her, both hands planted firmly on her hips.

'Well, I must say! What's going on here? This time you've gone too far. Who do you think you are? And don't give me any more of your stories. You're staying right here. I've called police, and they're on their way.'

Nora looked up at her with a grateful smile. 'Thank you. I thank you with all my heart.'

She never heard Mrs Fletcher's reply before she slipped back into a soft darkness.

38

She woke up to the sound of clattering china. She tried opening one eye as an experiment. She was lying in white bed linen. In a hospital. On the bedside table was a glass of water and a steel vase empty of flowers. On the wall facing the bed was a television, which was turned off, and a poster of an oversized yellow rose with droplets of moisture on the petals. It was hideous, Nora decided, before closing her eye again. A door rattled in the distance. The side ward was very quiet. She tried sitting up, but felt a searing pain to the back of her head, and raised her hand. She felt a bandage. She touched it carefully and tried to remember what had happened.

Bill Hix. The black, almost hypnotising gaze that had skewered her. The sudden pain to the back of her head. The barking of the dogs.

The door opened and a tanned nurse entered.

'Good morning, Nora. May I call you Nora? I'm Melinda.'

Nora tried nodding, but the slightest movement caused her nausea to surge. 'Where am I?'

'At St John's Hospital. You're concussed. The doctor will be making his round in half an hour. How are you feeling?'

'How did I end up here?'

The nurse flashed her beaming smile. 'You arrived here late last night. You've had a good night's sleep, and now you're under observation for concussion. And just to be on the safe side, we've given you a tetanus shot for the bites.'

'Bites?'

'Yes. Dog bites.'

Nora tried taking it all in, but Melinda interrupted her.

'Are you in pain?'

Having learned her lesson, Nora kept her head still this time and avoided nodding. Instead she answered yes.

Melinda tipped two pills into a small plastic cup and handed it to her. 'Wash them down with water,' she said.

Nora did she was told, and could feel herself slipping back into sleep.

'My mobile,' she managed to say, '… where's my mobile?'

'I don't know. But then again, it's probably not important right now. Besides, you're not permitted to use mobiles in this ward. However, a man has called us several times to find out how you are.'

'Spencer?' Nora asked.

'No, that wasn't his name. Andre … Andreas, something like that? He was very persistent.'

Nora smiled. Then she fell back into the darkness.

She awoke briefly when the doctor did his rounds, but could manage only monosyllabic answers. After a brief consultation the young doctor, whose name Nora didn't catch, announced that she would be staying at the hospital for another twenty-four hours. 'Complete rest,' he ordered her as he moved on.

Nora drifted off again. When she opened her eyes again, she found herself looking into Spencer's face.

'Miss Sand,' he said sternly. 'The next time you go off on one of your adventures, please advise the relevant authorities. It could have gone very, very wrong. For you. For us.'

Nora tried to reply, but managed only a small squawk. She reached for the water glass, and Spencer leaned forwards to help her pick it up.

'What happened?'

Spencer sat for a while rubbing his face. He looked like a man who hadn't slept last night. And possibly not the night before that, either. His shirt was relatively clean, he had probably brought an overnight bag and changed this morning, but otherwise he looked more crumpled than Nora had ever seen him.

'Hix is on his way back to Wolf Hall. A woman called Mrs Rosen is in custody. We found her in the house, along with Hix's mother. His mother is in shock. Mrs Rosen hasn't said anything yet. But she will. We found a dead woman in Mrs Rosen's office at the care home.'

Nora felt a dart of compassion for Lulu. A life that had gone wrong, almost from day one, and now it was over.

'We discovered Bill Hix in a shed trying to free himself from a wheelchair. A mystery which you can hopefully help the forces of law and order solve?' Spencer said with raised eyebrows.

'How did you find me?'

He shook his head. 'Well, you didn't exactly make it easy.'

Nora looked at him quizzically.

'After a few hours when I hadn't had confirmation from Summers that you were OK, I had to do something. To be frank, I was furious that we had to waste resources intended for our investigation on something so trivial.'

'But –' Nora tried to interject.

'I think you should let me do the talking right now,' Spencer announced. 'You'll get plenty of opportunity to explain yourself later.'

There was a knock on the door. Three quick taps.

Spencer looked up. 'Ah, DC Summers. Do come in. She's awake.'

DC Summers turned out to be a tall, angular woman with short, dark hair and grave eyes under a pair of bushy brows that reminded Nora of Frida Kahlo.

'Miss Sand. I thought we were meeting for lunch?' she said with a wry smile.

Nora smiled back. 'I'm sorry. I would have called. But …'

Spencer explained how DC Summers had received a call from two Welsh amateur ornithologists walking along the coast. They had spotted the damaged, yellow rental car and used their binoculars to read the registration plate. Summers was about to trace the registration number and contact the rental firm to find out whose name was on the contract, when she got a call from Spencer about protecting a

Danish journalist, the very same woman Summers was meeting for lunch. While Summers waited for the emergency services, Spencer got his technicians to trace Nora's mobile.

'We tried calling you repeatedly, but without success. At the same time, we were able to establish that your mobile was switched on and that it wasn't in the rental car. When we finally got through and someone other than you answered the mobile, we knew for certain that something had gone wrong.'

'But you never called?'

Spencer smiled acidly. 'We're not total amateurs. I could hear immediately that it wasn't your voice answering the phone. Gareth from Vodafone? That was me.'

'Thank you,' Nora said quietly.

Summers pulled up a chair to the bed and sat down. 'Miss Sand, how much can you remember of what happened up until that moment?'

'All of it, I think.'

Spencer produced an old-fashioned Dictaphone from his pocket and turned it on. Nora looked at him.

'We're in a hospital. Mobiles have to be turned off,' he said with a shrug.

For the next half an hour Nora told them everything she could remember. Spencer filled in the gaps, and Summers went down to the kiosk for cold Cokes when Nora's voice was on the verge of giving up.

Nora tried to focus, but one thought kept going round the back of her mind: Andreas had called.

The last thing she remembered was Melinda's voice, which somewhere from the other side of the earth said: 'Right, that's enough for today …'

39

Spencer had organised a relatively comfortable police car and a young officer to take them back to London. The young officer gripped the steering wheel hard and kept his eye on the speedometer, while Spencer sat in the front passenger seat.

He half-turned and continued his interrogation of Nora, who had been allowed to curl up in the back with a pillow and a blanket. Only two days had passed since she had been tied up in a basement, waiting to have her tongue torn out, and she hadn't had enough time to shake off the memory of the scary room with the terrifying freezer.

The road whizzed past the window. Every time she tried to settle on a fixed point to alleviate the worst of her nausea, it would disappear again at a dizzying speed. She tried focusing on her mobile, which was now lying silent, and charging from what had once been a cigarette lighter.

When she had been discharged from the hospital, Summers had solemnly handed her both her laptop and her mobile. They had found the laptop in Lisbeth's office.

'Mrs Rosen or Lisbeth Mogensen as we now know her, will be remanded in custody. Even if she refuses to talk, there's enough evidence to keep her behind bars forever. And then there's Lulu Brandt's account to you. I don't know if we'll be allowed to use it in court, but it will form the basis for our investigation. Hickley was masterminding everything from his cell, we think,' Summers had explained. That was all she was prepared to say.

Nora kept quizzing her, but Summers knew the law well and pointed out that any information she gave might prejudice a future trial – reeling off the stock phrase, which Nora suspected all police officers had to know in their sleep before they were allowed to issue as much as a parking ticket.

Spencer wasn't any more forthcoming. Not even here in the car was he willing to say much, no matter how hard Nora tried to squeeze him between her fits of nausea.

'What will happen to Vanessa Hickley?' she asked during one of the pauses where her nausea had retreated only to come back twice as strongly.

Spencer shrugged. 'I don't know. Perhaps she'll end up at Cedar Residence. She's old and confused. She thinks that Lisbeth is her daughter and doesn't understand where she is. We believe she threw out the suitcase without knowing the pictures were inside it.'

'But how did it end up in a skip behind Cedar Residence?' Nora asked.

'Miss Sand, for the umpteenth time: I'm asking the questions,' Spencer ordered her with a paper-thin smile.

'But I just want to know if Hannelore and Helmuth will find peace,' she said at last, thinking about the elderly German couple who travelled to London every year to plead with Scotland Yard to keep investigating the fate of their daughter Gertrud.

Bullseye.

Spencer turned back and stared out of the windscreen for some time.

'Yes, I think they'll find peace now. A kind of peace. Our forensic technicians are still busy, but this was where they ended up, the girls. They were here all the time. Vanessa Hickley inherited the house and the dogs from her father when he died, but no one from the original investigation knew that. We've started digging up the kennel. There's much forensic work to be done. It'll take months. But I believe that Hannelore and Helmuth will find as much peace as they can after all these years,' he said eventually.

After a short pause he continued: 'All those trips to Underwood that Hickley arranged to look for the girls,' he said bitterly. 'He must have been laughing at us the whole time. A picnic footed by the taxpayer – and all that grief. All that heartache.'

He pulled himself together and continued in his normal voice: 'I've given James McCormey permission to interview Hickley. I think the man deserves it. He may well contact you at some point,' he said.

'How much of this will I be allowed to write about?' Nora interjected.

'Most of it, I think,' Spencer said. 'You'll have to accept that the story is everywhere. However, you have first-hand knowledge of Hix. It's the crime sensation of the year. We'll stop off at a newsagent on our way back to your flat. However, I strongly advise you not to speak to anyone,' Spencer said dryly.

Nora nodded off again. Exhaustion took over and she had time to disappear into a black abyss before she was jolted awake by the bells of Big Ben. They had finally reached an area with mobile coverage, and the first to realise that was of course the Crayfish.

'Bloody hell, Sand. What's going on? You haven't called me for days. And now suddenly you're at the centre of the biggest crime story since the Yorkshire Ripper.'

The Crayfish was never one to waste time on small talk.

Nora could feel how the journalist in her snapped back into place, concussed or not. She outlined the case and briefly explained her own part.

The Crayfish was uncharacteristically quiet. Or maybe mobile coverage had disappeared again as they drove along the motorway. Nora checked her screen. Four bars.

'Well I never. Concussion, eh?' she heard him say eventually. 'But you're all right now, aren't you?'

'Well, I can still write, if that's what you mean.'

The Crayfish held a tactful pause, which made it clear that that was precisely what he had been worried about. 'Now I'm not saying it's urgent. The deadline isn't until Friday, so ...'

'Mmm,' Nora said.

'Yes, so how about Friday after lunch? And stress your own role in this. That's a unique angle we can offer our readers. Otherwise we'll just be reporting the same news as everybody else.'

She was overcome by a strong urge to open the window and hurl her mobile on to the verge with its soggy pizza boxes and empty beer cans, and never ever come back for it. But then she remembered that she was in a police car, and that it would be a complete waste of time to try to open the window.

As promised Spencer got the silent driver to stop at a petrol station when they reached London. He returned with *The Times,* the *Daily Telegraph,* the *Guardian,* the *Daily Mail,* and the *Sun.* The two tabloids had plastered the murders across their front pages with blurred black-and-white pictures of a demonic-looking Hix.

'The serial killer's groupie!' screamed the *Sun* in huge letters. The *Daily Mail*'s photographer had walked right up to the yellow police cordons and taken a picture of the kennel where forensic technicians in white coveralls were working away, so the paper could serve up the macabre detail to its readers of how the girls had ended their lives with the not terribly sensitive headline 'Missing Girls Eaten by Mad Killer Dogs'.

When the car pulled up at her flat in Belsize Park, a group of photographers had gathered outside the front door. Nora didn't have the energy to deal with them. Why would they want a picture of a shattered journalist getting out of a car? She had never pursued that kind of journalism herself, and had privately always wondered at the way it was portrayed in the movies. Surely photographers couldn't be that frenzied in real life. Now, however, she was on the receiving end of ten cameras herself, and shouting men constantly trying to make eye contact through the lens: 'Nora, over here! Hey, Nora, over here! Is it true that you caught the killer? Nora Sand, did you know the girls?'

Everything merged into an impossible cacophony of noise that forced her to the ground. If Spencer hadn't grabbed her arm, she would have collapsed on the spot. The moment she stumbled, the camera clicking increased.

Spencer took charge. 'That's enough, gentlemen. As you can see Miss Sand is clearly tired. If you want any comments, you'll have to contact her paper.'

The clicking subsided, but only marginally. Nora fumbled in her pocket for her keys and handed them to Spencer. He let them in and helped her up the stairs and into the flat. There was a stuffy smell inside it. She leaned over the sink, turned on the cold tap and drank and drank. The dizziness refused to go away.

Spencer opened a couple of kitchen cupboards and inspected her fridge. 'There's no food. This won't do. You're still not well.'

'Oh, I'll be all right,' Nora squawked feebly. 'I'm not hungry.'

'Then you won't get better,' Spencer said firmly.

Nora pushed a pile of clothes off an armchair and flopped down on it.

'I'll send the driver out for essentials. You have to be able to make yourself a cup of tea or civilisation, as we know it, will end. And bread. And bacon. And bananas. You don't have to face the photographers again, of course. He'll only be ten minutes,' Spencer announced in a tone that brooked no contradiction.

When he had extracted a promise from her to turn up at Scotland Yard in three days' time and closed the door behind him, Nora slipped out of her clothes, plodded to the bathroom and crawled into her old, pale blue Marks & Spencer dressing down. It was as soft as a hug from a teddy bear, and she realised how physically exhausted she still was when she put on the kettle to make some tea and searched randomly for a packet of cheesy biscuits she thought she might have left in a corner of a cupboard somewhere. She abandoned her search when the kettle boiled and started looking for tea instead. She found a scrunched-up chamomile and vanilla teabag, a free sample from a magazine, and dropped it into the nearest mug.

She carried the tea to the armchair, blew on it, then put the mug on the floor so the tea could cool own, and closed her eyes briefly. She awoke with a start when she heard three hard knocks on her door.

Her first thought was Hix, and her heart beat wildly in her chest. But she was safely back in her own home, of course. Then she remembered the photographers. Oh, no. She sat up. Her head ached and her face felt puffy. For the first time since moving in, she wished she had a peephole. Then she realised that it had to be the driver with her shopping. Her stomach rumbled from hunger. She smoothed her hair, composed herself, tied the cord on her dressing down and went to open the door.

40

He said nothing. He just stood there. And she stood stock still, as if someone had turned off all connections between her neural pathways, downed tools and gone home.

'I thought you were getting married?' she said at last.

'I never said that. I said that *she* wanted to get married. For a journalist, you're one crap listener,' he said, taking a step towards her.

Nora remained rooted to the spot.

'But I –'

'Will you shut up for once,' he said.

And then his lips met hers, and it was like falling and being weightless at the same time. Somewhere in a distant corner of her mind, she was aware that she was still standing, but it didn't feel like it. It was as if she had melted into a small pool of butter at his feet.

And then there was the white shirt, which was quickly removed, there was the bed, his arms, his eyes above hers, and the inscrutable smile she had seen a thousand times before, yet never like this.

The next morning they found a loaf of stale bread and a pint of lumpy milk in a bag outside the door. Andreas decided to go out for fresh supplies.

While he was out, Nora looked up BBC News on her mobile. It was the only broadcaster so far to discover the real connection between the two missing Danish girls and Hickley's carnage. They had interviewed McCormey, the investigator who had almost cracked the case, and could now look forward to its resolution. She copied the link and clicked through her list of contacts until she found Bjarke and forwarded the link as a text message saying only: 'Best wishes, Nora'. He replied a minute later.

'Thanks. I'll be in touch.'

She dozed for a while until Andreas appeared in the doorway with a loaf of fresh bread and a completely idiotic smile, which she simply had to kiss away as quickly as possible.

41

Before she began writing the story, she called the jeweller's in Lyngby. Benita Svaneholm answered the phone immediately. Nora told her about Oluf's fate.

'Oh, OK. So I can stop looking for him in the sports section, then,' she said. The bell above the door rang, and Benita hung up.

Three days later when Nora had put the finishing touches to her story and was about to place it into the claws of the Crayfish, a text message arrived. It was a link to Reuters news agency. The telegram was short.

It stated that the UK Home Office would be setting up a special investigative committee to carry out an in-depth enquiry into security in British prisons after an inmate had been found close to death, brutally beaten up in the showers at Wolf Hall Prison. It was, the telegram explained, the notorious serial killer William Hickley, better known as Bill Hix, whose case was under review following the new, macabre discoveries of his crimes.

Nora mulled it over for a moment, then added a single sentence to the conclusion of her story: 'William Hickley is now back in Wolf Hall Prison, where he is expected to spend the rest of his life.'

Then she hit 'send'.

She heard a throat being cleared behind her. 'Are you done?'

'Sort of. I just need to check something. I've got a job to do, you know.'

'I dare you to come over here and say that again,' Andreas said, flinging aside the duvet.

She was totally up for that – only suddenly she couldn't quite remember what she was going to say. Or why.

Acknowledgements

Thank you to Søren and Sune who turned up in London and brought me chai-hitos because they believed in Nora. A special thank you to the lovely and eagle-eyed editors at L&R, who have gone through the book and thus saved me from major howlers and errors. If any still exist, it is certainly not their fault.

Thank you also to my lovely friends, who have read and sometimes kept me company or in general tolerated and encouraged me, as I sat writing in holiday cottages, in cafés, on a mountaintop outside Amalfi and in other people's dining rooms.

Viv. I have a thousand things to thank you for, and punctuation is the least of them.

Thank you also to John Stead, the very kind and knowledgeable fireman who helped me solve a few technical issues on how to start a fire. Your kindness is very much appreciated.

Hazel, the 'reading photographer', thank you for your amazing pictures and friendship.

And finally a special thank you to Alex and Errol for keeping me sane during editing by willingly letting me punch and kick you (or the pads, at least) a couple of times a week. It made all the difference.

Fatal Crossing is work of fiction. Characters, plot and locations such as Wolf Hall and Brine are exclusively the product of the author's imagination.